NIGHTSTRIDER

NIGHTSTRIDER: BOOK 1

SOPHIA SLADE

orbitbooks.net
orbitworks.net

Cover design by Alexia E. Pereira and Lauren Panepinto
Cover illustration by Irina Nordsol Kuzmina

Author photograph by Julie Hanson

Orbit
Hachette Book Group
1290 Avenue of the Americas
New York, NY 10104
orbitbooks.net
orbitworks.net

First Orbit eBook and Print on Demand Edition: September 2024
Originally published in August 2022 by Calida Lux Publishing LLC

Orbit is an imprint of Hachette Book Group.
The Orbit name and logo are registered trademarks of Little, Brown Book Group Limited.

Library of Congress Cataloging-in-Publication Data
Names: Slade, Sophia, author.
Title: Nightstrider / Sophia Slade.
Description: First Orbit eBook and Print on Demand Edition. | New York, NY : Orbit, 2024. | Series: Nightstrider ; book 1
Identifiers: LCCN 2024022805 | ISBN 9780316580458 (trade paperback) | ISBN 9780316580175 (ebook)
Subjects: LCGFT: Fantasy fiction. | Novels.
Classification: LCC PS3619.L349 N54 2024 | DDC 813/.6—dc23/eng/20240521
LC record available at https://lccn.loc.gov/2024022805

ISBNs: 9780316580175 (ebook), 9780316580458 (print on demand)

For my mother, the flame keeper

CONTENT NOTE

Please be advised that *Nightstrider* contains fantasy violence, murder, attempted sexual assault, torture, emotional abuse, blood, misogyny, xenophobia, forced engagement, suicidal ideation, and imperialism.

CHARACTERS

Alaric (*all-ar-ick*)—a rogue nightmare, part of the rebellion

Caine Fallon (*cane fahl-on*)—Prince of Wolfhelm

Ila Enevoldson (*eye-la en-eh-vold-son*)—Queen of Galesborough, a weaver

Mica (*me-ka*)—a luminae, part of the rebellion

Morthil (*more-thil*)—a luminae innkeeper and former member of the rebellion

Nils (*n-ihls*)—guardian and Ila's former lover

Ondine (*on-deen*)—a nightmare, created by Para Warwick; also known as Souldrinker

Para Warwick (*paer-a war-wick*)—a night terror, ruler of the Reverie, and the King of Wolfhelm in the Wake

Saoirse (*sor-sha*)—a dreambreaker

Thomas Hendricks (*tom-as hen-driks*)—captain of the Skysteel Guard, friend to Caine

Wren (*ren*)—a nightmare, created by Para Warwick; also known as Nightstrider

LOCATIONS

Black Root—the village near Caer Sidi in the Reverie

Caer Bheinn (*care bane*)—the ruined castle in the Shadowrise Mountains home to the rebellion

Caer Sidi (*care see-dee*)—the echopoint castle that exists in both the Wake and the Reverie ruled by Warwick in both realms

Galesborough—the isolated northern kingdom in the Wake, home to the Vaettir

Llyr—the weaver temple north of Galesborough

Marrowrun—a city off the coast of the Evendark Sea in the Reverie

the Reverie—the dream realm populated by the living dreams of humans

Sandmere—the southernmost kingdom in the Wake

the Tanglewood—the forest surrounding Caer Sidi, home to many vexes and nightmares

the Wake—the waking world populated by humans

Wolfhelm—the kingdom in the Wake ruled by King Warwick

TERMS

anchor—*noun*, a physical object that a nightmare or luminae is tied to that gives them their immortality

the Boundary—*noun*, the omnipresent barrier between the Wake and the Reverie that keeps them separate; if it were to fall, it would bring about the destruction of both worlds

dasak—*noun*, "idiot" in Vaettirin

dream being—*noun*, a broad term encompassing all species of dreams

dreambreaker—*noun*, a mortal being that is half luminae, half weaver and capable of crossing the Boundary at will

echopoint—*noun*, a place that exists both in the Wake and the Reverie as a near exact mirror

kip—*noun*, the most common species of dream being; mortal

luminae—*noun*, an immortal dream being thought to be pure of heart

manifest—*verb*, the act of becoming conscious as a living dream being in the Reverie

nightmare—*noun*, an immortal nightmare thought to be villainous; colloquially known as 'mares

para—*noun*, an immortal night terror, the rarest and strongest species of dream being

skysteel—*noun*, extremely tough metal present in both the Wake and the Reverie

splinter—*noun*, a half-manifested dream that feeds on the essence of other dream beings in an attempt to fully manifest

the Vaettir—*noun*, the indigenous people of Galesborough

vex—*noun*, a low-level dream being; mortal

weaver—*noun*, a member of the ancient order of human women with the ability to manipulate the threads of reality and traverse the Boundary at will

NIGHTSTRIDER

PROLOGUE

The air was thick with the scent of decay. It seemed to shiver, recoil as King Warwick strode down the dank tunnel. He carried a torch to scatter the dark. The limitations of his human eyes were vexing indeed.

Still, he walked as though he stood seven feet tall, a crown of bone on his head and a blade at his hip.

The king slowed as he approached his destination, a vast circular chamber drowned in shadow. He paused at the yawning entrance. Then, out of the abyss, a single quavering word.

"H-hello?"

Warwick stepped into the sanctum and touched his torch to the channel of oil set into the wall. It ignited, the flames following its path around the circumference of the room. Rivers of script scaled the stone walls, spiraling toward the cavernous ceiling. Thousands of years of history were entombed here, but the king had no interest in history. His sights were set on the future, on his divine right to dominate two worlds, and the path to that future was crumpled on the floor before him.

"Good evening, little weaver," Warwick said.

The girl had barely reached maturity. Her cheeks were still round beneath her bruises. Her robes may have once been white but were now stained with blood and filth. She struggled to raise herself into a sitting position, her shackles clanking dully.

One of her eyes was swollen shut, purple and bulbous. The other was already filling with tears.

Satisfaction knifed through Warwick. He would never tire of that look. The haunted, guttering gaze of a prisoner inches from breaking.

"Are you prepared to tell me where the weavers are hiding the dreambreaker?"

The girl looked down and away, her matted blond hair curtaining her face. Warwick cast his torch aside. It skidded across the floor and hit the wall with a crack, drawing a flinch from his prisoner. He started toward her from the edge of the room at a leisurely pace, allowing her fear to simmer.

"I grow weary, little weaver," Warwick murmured as he arrived before her.

That was a lie. Her spirit was an unprecedented challenge but a welcome one. It had been a year since he had indulged this way. His last interrogation had been in another world, his victim born not of flesh and bone, but of a nightmare.

"I must admit, however, I am intrigued."

Warwick crouched before the girl and brushed a stiff lock of hair from her face. She recoiled from his touch, refusing eye contact. This close, he could see the layers of healing cuts and bruises beneath the fresh wounds.

"You weavers, so obsessed with the separation of the Wake and the Reverie." His lip curled. "Insular fools."

The girl snapped her working eye to his, bloodshot and blazing.

"The Boundary must never fall," she rasped. "Too much contact between the worlds could unravel the fabric of reality."

"Yet weavers walk between worlds at their leisure."

"That's different," she snapped. "Unlike you, we close every door we open."

"Unlike me," Warwick repeated under his breath. "And what am I, little weaver?"

The girl lifted her chin. Her split lip quivered, but when she spoke, her voice was steady.

"You're a mistake, an abomination. The night terror who wormed into the waking world and tried to claim it as his own."

She tried to spit at him, but days without water worked against her.

"So the story goes," Warwick acknowledged. "Indeed, walking between worlds is an uncommon gift. Tell me then, if you're so against anyone but your own kind crossing the Boundary, why are you protecting a child with the same ability?"

"We weren't. We were studying her, and I would rather her go free than let you get your *filthy* hands on her."

Warwick considered her with a tilted head. "Go free?"

Confusion struck the blistering hatred from her face. Then it melted into horror.

"Oh gods," she breathed.

"You lost the child."

"No, we—"

"You fool, you should have known better than to try to contain her. She is more powerful than you can fathom."

Warwick drew the slender skysteel blade at his side. The

black metal gleamed viciously in the ring of fire around them. The girl shrank back, curling in on herself like a starving rabbit. He gripped her by the hair and rose, forcing her to her knees.

"You're of no use to me, then," Warwick said dispassionately.

"No! Wait, please! I have information!"

The king cocked a brow, unmoved.

"Please, p-please," she sobbed, squirming in his iron grip. "I don't know where the dreambreaker is, but I know who she's with." When Warwick did not respond, she continued, the words tumbling out of her like boulders down a mountainside. "One of our own, a traitor, left a year ago. She stole the child and hid her away. We can't touch either of them."

"Why?"

"Because the traitor is Queen Ila Enevoldson of Galesborough."

Bone-deep silence in the sanctum, buffered only by the whispering breath of the flames and the sniveling of the girl at his feet. Warwick stared straight through her. His knuckles whitened around the hilt of his knife.

Then he smiled like the curve of a scythe.

"The Vaettir queen, a rogue weaver." A laugh burst from his chest. Warwick flipped the blade in his hand. The girl swallowed, bruised throat rippling. "Thank you for your cooperation, little weaver. You've been most entertaining."

The girl opened her mouth to scream, but he had already forced her head back and slashed her neck. By the time she hit the flagstones, Warwick was halfway across the sanctum. The delicious sound of her drowning in her own blood followed him, but for once, he did not stop to savor it.

There was much work to be done.

PART ONE

STEEL AND SHADOW

1

Ila

The solitary moon hunched over Galesborough as Ila cantered down the narrow, wooded path. She cracked the reins, urging her mount faster. Branches raked her skin and clothes as they whipped past.

"Raske, Ailo! Raske!"

Ailo whinnied, the sound nearly lost to the storm of riders in their wake. The forest, black and blue in the night, gave way to open land in an instant. Ila caught a glimpse of a star-strewn sky before a gasp was ripped from her.

She yanked the reins. Ailo reared and slammed down again. Pebbles skittered over a sheer cliff, plunging to the rapids below.

Ila swore, her eyes darting between the cliff and the forest. Panic sparked in her chest as the thunder of hooves drew nearer. She pulled her hood over her dyed hair as the Skysteel Guard shot out of the wood and screamed to a halt ten paces away. Their black armor was almost indigo in the moonlight. The crest of House Fallon, a wolf, snarled at her from their breastplates.

The captain whistled through his teeth. His men fanned out, backing Ila toward the edge of the cliff.

"Where is the child?" he shouted over the roar of the rapids. "We know you have her."

Ila reached into her saddlebag and withdrew a box the size of her palm. Morthil had warded the box against all manner of nightmares at her request; it would only open at her command, and the child inside would be safe.

For now.

Blades scraped from scabbards. The captain spoke again, louder this time.

"In the name of King Warwick of Wolfhelm, I order you to take us to the child."

Ila ignored him, curling the silver box to her breast. A single pulse rippled through the metal, reverberating in her bones. A wordless farewell from the soul inside.

"Sol liv hjent warren, Saoirse," Ila breathed.

Light erupted from her every pore, beaming through her heavy furs. The wind rose, threatening to blow back her cowl. The Skysteel Guard cried out in shock and terror, shielding their faces as the sky split open. The radiant white light of the Boundary between the Wake and the Reverie poured over them.

"Stop this, witch!"

Ila released the box with a scream of exertion. A thunderclap echoed as the portal swallowed it and slammed shut. The trees groaned as their trunks were bowed by the resulting shock wave. Uncanny stillness settled over the land. Ila slumped in her saddle.

Her hands were empty.

Saoirse was gone.

"Seize her!"

Ila scrambled off her mount, putting Ailo between her and the Skysteel Guard as they closed in. Her horse snorted and dug at the dirt as if sensing her next move. Ila retreated to the cusp of the cliff with her heart in her mouth.

The captain dismounted and approached on foot, one hand raised as if to calm her. There was no malice in his expression, only focus. He was just another man who believed he was on the right side of history.

Ila threw a glance over her shoulder. Her fur cloak fluttered over the edge of the cliff.

The captain froze.

"No! Stop!"

Ila fell backward, choking on a prayer.

Striking the water felt like hitting stone, yet somehow, she sank. Dye coiled from her hair, swirling in the freezing water like ribbons of blood. Her cloak dragged her toward the bottom of the river. It looked to be alive, furs rippling in the moonlight that lanced through the waves. She blinked sluggishly, sending columns of pinprick bubbles skyward.

It was only when her lungs began to burn that fear seared away her shock. Ila fumbled with the clasp of her cloak and wriggled free but forced herself not to surface.

A single thought blazed in her mind like an iron brand.

The Skysteel Guard must think me dead.

Numbness crept in, swift and lethal. Ila let the current take her.

The river trundled on ruthlessly. When her thoughts began to muddy and her limbs lost feeling, she knew the cold would take her before her enemies did.

Drawing on the last shreds of her strength, she broke the surface and swam against the pull of the river. She dragged herself ashore on her stomach, shuddering and retching in the watery pebbles. As she struggled to her knees and raised her head, she was greeted by a puff of warm, musky air and a velvety snout.

"Ailo," she gasped, reaching for her horse. "How did you find me?"

Ailo whickered, nuzzling her affectionately. Ila grabbed a fistful of his ivory mane and pulled herself up, silt shifting beneath her boots.

"Takja, my friend."

The river had dumped Ila on a beach strewn with tree boughs and other natural debris. A swathe of snowcapped pines farther inland. Through them, Ila glimpsed the first shreds of honeyed daylight.

Hot tears pricked her eyes.

Day was breaking here in the Wake, which meant night would be settling over the Reverie. The two realms had existed in tandem since the dawn of time, separated by the Boundary and the ignorance of the humans in the Wake.

At least, they were supposed to be.

Focus.

Teeth chattering, Ila stripped off her stiff clothes and dressed in fresh ones from her saddlebag. The river had washed the dark dye from her hair to reveal her true white blond. She braided the drenched locks as she scanned the area. They appeared to be alone, but there was only one way to be certain.

Bracing herself against Ailo, Ila called on her weaver sight.

The pulse of the Wake rushed to fill her.

A glorious golden tapestry unfurled, blanketing the trees, the soil, the sky, and the river. Individual lives were embers threaded into the ever-shifting fabric. The land around Ila was quiet, disturbed only by the faint presence of a doe grazing nearby and the birds nestled in the trees. If she extended herself, she could detect the animals sleeping the winter away underground.

Ila blinked away her weaver sight, allowing the mundane shell of the world to bleed back into view.

No sign of the Skysteel Guard. More importantly, no sign of the weavers. She had narrowly evaded the white-clad priestesses the night before, but it was they who instilled persistence in her. They would not rest until they found the dreambreaker and the traitor who stole her.

Ila bit her lip to stifle a sob.

It would be a fortnight before she could gather the strength to open another portal to the Reverie and retrieve Saoirse. She was expected in Wolfhelm in nine days. Once she entered the kingdom, there would be no turning back. No one would be able to open the box without the password, but Saoirse could not survive inside forever.

Think, dasak. Think.

Ailo snorted as Ila spun and began to rummage through her saddlebag. She gathered flint, steel, charcoal, and a scrap of parchment. Kneeling, she spread the paper on her thighs and scrawled a note in her mother tongue.

"Hoste, guide me," Ila prayed as she took the flint and steel in hand. Both bore the silver aura of the Reverie. They stood in stark contrast to the buttery glow of the Wake. "Askar valem, Morthil."

Ila struck the flint. Sparks flew, peppering the parchment and chewing rapid holes in it. Her eyes watered as the flames belched white smoke. The parchment dissolved from the Wake, taking her words with it to the Reverie.

Not even ashes remained.

Hoste, protect us, Ila thought as she stowed her belongings again. The rising golden sun kissed the side of her face as she mounted Ailo. She turned south toward Wolfhelm, toward a different kind of battle.

Protect her.

2

Wren

The air blistered with salt and anticipation. Wren kept her eyes peeled despite the sting, scanning the shores of the Evendark Sea from her clifftop perch as another toxic black wave slammed aground.

The beach had been quiet all night, but if her source was telling the truth, her target would arrive soon. She was banking on his honesty. Only the foolish or very brave lied to nightmares, and only those with a death wish lied to the Hand of the Para.

The faintest rumble grazed her pointed ears. She inhaled through her nose.

There.

Fresh water and fertile earth. The scent of a mortal dream being—a kip. Wren drew her skysteel blades with a ringing hiss and rose. Strands of her dark hair wriggled from their braid, whispering against her skin as she waited with predatory stillness. Far above, the three gemstone Reverie moons peered out from behind towering red and violet nebulas.

Then four kips on horseback burst into view, cantering down the waterline.

Wren stepped off the edge of the cliff.

She relished the fall, eyes closed and lips parted. Two heartbeats came and went before she snapped her wings open. Airwaves rolled beneath her charcoal feathers as she sailed to the ground, landing twenty paces ahead of the riders.

The kips yanked their reins and skidded to a halt. Wren studied them in the light of the moons. All male, their faces obscured by hoods. One rode a horse with a split face ending in two upturned snouts, the by-product of some strange dream.

Three of the kips were armed with swords. The other had a longbow slung across his back.

Fear clung to them.

"Good somnia, gentleman," Wren called over the rush of the sea.

"We're just passing through," one of the kips shouted back. "We're not looking for trouble."

"I've been waiting for you, Finnian." Wren folded her wings flush against her back and gave her blades a twirl. The kips shifted in their saddles. She could hear the rapid patter of their hearts over the roar of the sea. "I am not in the mood for games."

Finnian removed his hood, staring her down with bitter resolve. His fingers twitched toward the hilt of his sword.

Too slow.

Wren let a blade fly, nailing the kip to his left between the eyes. He tumbled from his mount and landed with a crunch on the black sand. His horse screamed and bolted.

Wren twisted out of its path, sending another knife flying at a kip as he drew his sword. It struck him in the neck, and he went down. The archer nocked an arrow, aimed, and fired. He was fast, but not fast enough.

They never were.

Wren dodged the arrow, drawing one of the daggers strapped to her thigh. It struck the archer before he could fire again. He fell with a fractured cry and did not move. Para Warwick had ordered Wren to make their deaths hurt, but days on the road had filled her bones with a persistent ache. She was not keen to draw this out.

Still astride his horse, Finnian stared at the bodies of his comrades. His eyes flashed to hers. Wren raised a brow. He drew his sword. Faint red moonlight glanced off the metal as he dismounted and sank into a fighting stance.

"What's the rebellion after, Finnian?" Wren asked as if nothing had happened.

The kip lifted his chin. Defiant, reckless, and all too mortal. "I told you, we were just passing through."

"Answer honestly and I'll give you a quick death." Wren examined her nails. They were closer to talons, really. Dark as flint and tough as iron. "Or I can bring you back to Caer Sidi and you'll suffer at the hands of Bloodreaper; I don't particularly care."

A brittle laugh from Finnian. "You'd love nothing more than to slit my throat, you fucking 'mare."

"You overestimate your importance." She flicked her braid over her shoulder. It dusted the small of her back. "We've seen a rise in activity from the rebellion lately. Parties riding out in every direction, like they're looking for something. Care to tell me what that is?"

"You know I'm not going to talk, Nightstrider."

Her teeth gnashed together at the sound of that name. She once wore it like a badge of honor, the title her creator, Para Warwick, had bestowed on her the night of her manifestation.

Now she wore it like a noose.

"If you're going to kill me, you may as well get it over with." His words did not match his rioting pulse. "The rebellion lives."

Wren rolled her eyes. She'd had about enough of these sanctimonious rebels. They thought they were freeing the Reverie from the clutches of a tyrant, but they only brought chaos and destruction on themselves and those caught in their path.

"You make your lives infinitely more difficult," she said.

"We won't bow to a leader who kills and enslaves kips and luminae for sport," Finnian spat. "I'll never talk."

"Fine," Wren muttered. "Let's get this over with."

Finnian flew at her with a roar, cranking his sword back to swing. The blade whistled over her head as she ducked. She darted away on the balls of her feet, tapping him on the shoulder when she came up behind him. He whipped around, panting, and lunged again. Wren sidestepped him easily.

She wondered if this was what dancing felt like.

Finnian made another brazen charge at her. He had left his torso unprotected, sloppy in his desperation. Elongating, Wren drove her heel into his sternum.

Crack.

Finnian flew back, body and blade skidding across the beach. He landed on his back with his arms and legs splayed. He did not try to get up or retrieve his sword, which was mere inches away.

Wren prowled toward the rebel, drawing her final blade. His breath rattled through his shattered rib cage. She pressed her boot to his chest. He let out a scream that could shake rain from the sky.

"Tell me what the rebellion is after." She leaned down, applying more pressure through her sole. "Tell me!"

Finnian coughed fiercely, and her stomach sank. He would no doubt bleed to death from the inside before they made it back to Caer Sidi. She had forgotten how fragile kips were—perhaps she was spending too much time around vexes. Mortal though they were, the sundry bad dreams were still tougher than the average kip.

Wren took her boot off his caved-in chest. A wheeze bled from Finnian as she straightened her leather jacket with a tug and raised her knife overhead.

"Last words?" she asked flatly.

Finnian let out an agonized laugh. Her eyes narrowed to slits.

"Something funny?"

"You." He grinned, exposing stained red teeth. "I expected more from the infamous Nightstrider." Finnian dissolved into another hacking fit, spitting up his guts. Her lip curled as gore speckled her boots. "They say you're heartless, but here you are, taking my last words like a fucking monk."

"Not a monk."

Wren plunged her blade into his heart, burying it to the hilt.

Finnian let out a gurgling screech. His blood drowned her hands. She yanked the knife out and wiped it on his tunic. His eyes were glassy and as round as the moons. His heart stilled.

The scalding waters of the Evendark Sea crashed to the shore as Wren rose, sheathing her blade again.

"A nightmare."

☽○☾

The journey back to Caer Sidi took three days. The red, white, and violet moons were already on the rise by the time Wren spotted the castle. From above, it looked like a miniature she could crush between her thumb and forefinger.

Wren angled toward the ground, skimming the inky hands of the Tanglewood. The forest was punctured by the balding sore of Black Root. Even from the air, she could smell it. Smoke and piss and desperation. The mob of dark trees swallowed the landscape again.

Then Caer Sidi burst into full view.

The twelve towers stood like jagged teeth against the skyline, ringed by an impenetrable black wall. Vexes were mounted on the ramparts. A handful resembled creatures from human mythos—stories had a way of creeping into dreams—but most were unique. Some were there for the muscle, hulking beasts with arms like tree trunks and jaws of iron. Others leaned into the uncanny, creatures too tall to be kips, their mouths too wide to be human, and eyes that only blinked when you looked at them. They all pointedly pretended not to notice Wren as she sailed overhead.

She let the wind cradle her, lowering her into the deserted courtyard. Her feet were the first to taint the fresh snow settled there. Nothing moved but the torchlight that seemed to cower from the night.

Night. Thank the gods.

As night rose in the Reverie, day broke in the Wake. Para Warwick would be tending to his duties in that realm from the halls of the other Caer Sidi, the home to his children. Though Wren and many other nightmares were created by Para Warwick, they were not his offspring. They were closer to weapons with skin and teeth than children, each manifesting as a fully realized adult in a separate dream.

Wren sometimes wondered if Para Warwick treated his children as he did his nightmares, and if they were better or worse than he was.

The towering double doors across the courtyard peeled apart with a tired groan. Cold light spilled onto the snow. Wren retracted her wings and approached. Identical guards with the heads of rats saluted her as she crossed the threshold. She paid them no mind. She had never once heard them speak, nor did she care to.

The entry hall was deserted. The soaring walls were lined with portraits of past paras. Faceless apparitions, leathery demons with jaundiced eyes, a woman with slit cheeks and dozens of snakes coiling from her scalp that Wren had always been fond of.

Born of a phenomenon in the Wake known as sleep paralysis wherein the dreamer was suspended in terror between wakefulness and sleep, paras only manifested once every few centuries. They were stronger than luminae, more vicious than nightmares, virtually unkillable and insatiable.

Few could remember a time a para did not lord over the Reverie, making the word *para* synonymous with *king*.

And none was more powerful than Para Warwick.

The doors slammed behind Wren with a reverberating thud. She continued forward, eyes ahead and steps sure. The buzz of rowdy conversation pricked her ears.

Must be another feast, she thought, bristling. What they were celebrating, she did not know. Probably the razing of another rebel camp to the ground.

Wren turned the corner at the end of the hall, moving away from the noise. She passed a handful of soldiers and servants, all of whom paused to offer curtsies, bows, and stiff salutes. She nodded at the soldiers and ignored the servants. Attention from the likes of her would only frighten them.

Eventually, she reached the spiral staircase that led to her chambers. Her pack weighed heavy on her shoulders as she ascended. By the time she reached her door, her legs were burning. She turned the knob and traipsed inside.

"You're late."

Ondine lounged on her stomach on the massive curtained bed, wearing nothing but a cream robe tied at her waist. Her coppery hair spilled down her back. Her hazel eyes were heavy-lidded. Wren tasted the air. Sure enough, the intoxicating scent of her drug of choice, lucidia, permeated the room.

"I'm tired, Ondine," Wren said. She dropped her pack and started to unbuckle her leather armor. "And you're high."

"Barely."

Wren shot her a withering look. Ondine smiled, slipping off the bed and padding over to the winged nightmare. Her full hips shifted beneath her silk robe. Wren swallowed as Ondine began to unbuckle her chest plate, pausing to caress the two-headed wolf stamped into the leather. Wren looked away and caught sight of their reflections in the standing mirror.

The two nightmares could not have been more different. Ondine was all milky curves. Wren was all sharp edges from her cheekbones to her blackened nails.

"Did you figure it out?"

Wren glanced down at Ondine as she removed the chest plate, setting it on the table with a muted *thunk*. She drew Wren into an embrace, ignoring the fact that she reeked from days of travel. Wren placed a hand on the small of her back absentmindedly.

"Wren?"

"What?"

"Did you figure out what the rebels are up to?" Ondine repeated.

"No," Wren answered tersely. "Finnian refused to talk."

Ondine gave a condescending chuckle. "He's got balls, for a kip."

Wren grunted, then stepped back and pulled her tunic over her head.

"*Had* balls," she admitted, tossing it aside. "I hit him too hard. He died before I could get an answer out of him."

She shed her leggings and undergarments and made for the washroom. Ondine followed, her footsteps lithe on the flag-stones. Wren let out a noise of satisfaction when she found a bath had been drawn in the deep porcelain tub. A sweet, airy scent wafted from the water. Dozens of candles had been lit and placed on the stone counter, windowsill, and floor.

"Did you do this?" Wren asked, knowing the answer.

"Maybe," Ondine teased, tossing her gleaming hair over her shoulder. "Well, I had one of the servants do it."

"How considerate."

Ondine smiled, then reached for the sash on her robe, undoing the knot. The garment pooled around her ankles, revealing her full breasts and soft stomach. Wren felt her mouth go dry. Perhaps sleep could wait.

"You poor, dreadful thing," Ondine purred. She walked over to Wren and began to kiss her, first on the neck, then on the lips, lingering so Wren could taste her next words. "You've had such a long night. How can I make it better?"

Something not unlike a smile twitched on Wren's lips as she took Ondine by the hand and led her to the steaming tub. She stepped into it and turned to watch Ondine, mesmerized by her lithe movements, the shivering caress of the water circling her waist.

Wren pulled Ondine to her and kissed her fiercely, a predator snaring its prey. Bathwater sloshed over the edge of the tub and onto the floor. Ondine moaned as Wren drew her bottom lip into her teeth and began to tease her under the waterline.

Whimpers bled from Ondine as she squirmed, unable to string together anything resembling a sentence, much less muster her usual snark. This *was* what Wren had needed. To be in control of something, anything.

Ondine dug her fingernails into her strong back as Wren

plunged her fingers inside her to the hilt, triggering a broken cry.

"There you are," Wren murmured. "Beautiful."

She began to rock her hand back and forth, bringing Ondine to the height of pleasure with precision learned from their many encounters. Mere minutes passed before Ondine seized, panting and shivering as Wren encouraged her through the aftershocks. Wren could have kept going forever, but Ondine flipped her onto her back. Bathwater arched across the chamber, snuffing several candles.

Without catching her breath, the redheaded nightmare pinned Wren against the porcelain with a sloppy kiss, her hand trailing down her toned stomach.

"My turn," she whispered.

Wren let her eyes flutter shut, and for a moment, she was nothing but a girl in the arms of her lover.

Eventually, they fell still in the lukewarm remains of the bath. Ondine lay on top of Wren, breathing hard though her pulse was slow and resolute. Wren had always found it oddly comforting. Her own heartbeat was much faster.

Eventually, Ondine broke the silence.

"What are you going to do about the rebels?"

Wren, who had been tracing the path of Ondine's spine with the pad of her finger, froze. She was not in the mood for talking, much less about this. "What do you mean?"

"This is the third assignment you've returned from empty-handed."

Wren propped her elbow on the edge of the tub, scrutinizing Ondine. Her expression had changed, revealing a glimmer of the killer lurking beneath her lovely features. In some ways, Ondine was the most dangerous sort of nightmare.

She was the kind you never saw coming.

"I'm aware," Wren said, selecting her words with care.

"Para Warwick won't be pleased."

"Neither are you, clearly."

Ondine rose on her knees to straddle Wren, the soaked tips of her hair dripping down the planes of her soft stomach. "You're supposed to be his greatest weapon. His hand. His Nightstrider."

Wren suppressed a flinch. "I told you to stop calling me that."

Ondine tilted her head to the side, a pearl of water collecting at her earlobe. Her ears were round and deceptively kiplike. She could pass as one until her eyes went black from lid to pupil.

"Have I ever asked you not to call me Souldrinker?"

"I never call you that."

"You used to," Ondine snapped. Wren pursed her lips, glancing away from her lover. A tense, prickling moment inched past. Then Ondine sighed, her moon-white shoulders sloping down. "Do you understand how lucky you are to be who you are, Wren? To be the favorite?"

Wren shook her head, still not looking at Ondine. "I'm not the favorite."

Not anymore.

"Please," Ondine scoffed. "You get every good mission, every worthy kill, while the rest of us just sit here waiting for you to come back and act like you don't love every second of it."

"I do," Wren shot back, finally flicking her eyes back to Ondine's. "Maybe I'm just tired of you clinging to me like a fucking leech."

Ondine recoiled as if Wren had slapped her. Her hurt morphed to rage. Without another word, she climbed from the bath and marched from the washroom, swiping up her robe along the way. Wren waited until she heard the door slam to sink deeper into the sweet water.

She had not intended to hurt Ondine, but better to let her think Wren was bored of her than weary of life as the Hand of Para Warwick.

Especially because she was.

3

Caine

"On your feet, Prince Caine."

Caine winced as light streaked across his face, slicing through his dreamless sleep. He sat up too quickly, a curse bubbling up on his lips.

"What time is it?" he garbled.

Last night was a wine-soaked blur. He forced his eyes open, bluish-green and bloodshot as all hells. It looked like a storm had blown through his chambers, scattering clothes, bottles, and half a feast.

"Noon," Thomas replied, parting the gold-threaded drapes the rest of the way to reveal the blizzard raging outside the castle.

Even for Wolfhelm, the weather was grim.

Caine flopped back onto his pillows, slinging his arm across his aching eyes. "What happened?"

"Well, you started in on the wine around eleven and snuck off with Viola around three. Though, *sneaking* is a generous word—she told half the court."

The memories came slinking back like scolded hounds.

Viola, depositing herself in his lap in the middle of the feast, her fingers in his hair, her teeth scraping the skin of his neck. It was no secret they had been dancing around each other for months. It was her last chance to make a move before the wedding.

The wedding. Or, as Caine called it, the reason for his blistering hangover.

The prince sat up. Slowly.

"When will they arrive?" he asked as he began to massage his temples.

"They should be here by sundown," Thomas answered.

Caine let his hands drop, examining the captain with mounting suspicion. Thomas was a few years older than him with broad shoulders and a smile quick to ignite. He was also a notoriously bad liar. The captain shifted from foot to foot, fidgeting with the hilt of the ceremonial rapier at his side.

"Out with it," Caine ordered.

"Out with what?"

"Whatever has you hopping around like a rabbit."

Thomas ran a hand over his coarse curls, looking anywhere but the prince. "Your father wants to see you."

Caine groaned. "Of course he does."

"I can go with you if you'd like."

"You have better things to do." His silence confirmed this, but Thomas still looked worried. The prince smiled despite himself. He was lucky to have the captain as a guardian and friend. "I'll see you tonight at the feast."

"I'll be there when the procession arrives, as will the rest of the Skysteel Guard."

Caine felt his muscles relax a sliver. The thought of the legendary guard at his back soothed his nerves.

"Thank you, Thomas."

The captain took the hint. He bowed and departed swiftly. Caine waited until the door clicked shut to slouch into his pillows again. If it were up to him, he would spend the day in his room, or weather permitting, in the forest beyond the grounds.

Wishes are wasteful, his mother used to say. *Face reality with your wits in hand.*

Not the warmest woman, his mother. He still missed her every day.

Caine rolled out of bed and made for the porcelain washbasin perched on the dresser. He splashed some water on his pale face and neck, scrubbing away the remains of the night. His thoughts hummed as he gathered his clothes from the wardrobe.

He knew almost nothing about her, the girl he was to marry in a week. Her name was Ila Enevoldson. She was three and twenty years old, a year younger than him. She was from Galesborough, a wild kingdom far to the north, and had ascended the throne last winter after losing her family to rust fever.

A tragedy, to be sure, though he had not heard anyone in Wolfhelm say as much.

According to his father, a marriage with the Queen of Galesborough would secure their position in the realm, though it was not just about territory: They would also gain the fearsome Vaettir warriors, said to ride the howling northern winds into battle.

We take the Vaettir, we take the world, his father told him.

"Caine."

The prince nearly dropped the tunic he was holding. "Gods, Theo. You're supposed to be with your tutor."

Theodosia leaned against the doorframe with a smirk. She was dressed in battered riding clothes that did not suit her noble birth. Flecks of snow crowned her long chestnut braids.

"And you're supposed to be with Father, but here we are," she replied snidely. "The longer you put it off, the worse mood he'll be in."

"You should be worrying about yourself." Caine pulled his shirt over his head. "He'll have it out for you if he hears you've been skipping lessons again."

"Father couldn't give a shit about me if he tried, Caine."

He grimaced. His sister was right, and they both knew it.

Peeling away from the doorway, Theodosia made a beeline for the blue velvet armchair by the window. She plopped into it and kicked her feet up on the ottoman. Her soles were caked with slush. Caine had stopped bothering to ask her not to put her feet up on his furniture a long time ago.

"I heard something interesting about your lovely bride today," Theodosia said, pretending to examine her nails, which were chewed to nubs.

"I thought I told you to stop listening to gossip." Caine cleared a space on the table with a sweep of his arm and settled on the edge, plucking a green grape from the bunch on a platter. "You've been hunting," he noted to change the subject. "You better not have used my crossbow."

"No, I used a real bow because I'm not a lazy bastard."

"Crossbows are practical," Caine argued, bristling when she rolled her eyes. "Where did you hide your catch?"

"Sold it. Stag, if you were wondering."

"I wasn't."

Theodosia dug into her pocket and produced a drawstring purse. She gave it a shake. It clanked with heavy coin.

"Thank the gods, now we can eat," Caine said dryly. Theodosia tossed him the bag. He caught it in one hand, frowning. "What are you giving it to me for?"

"Buy your future wife something nice. Or buy yourself some hex bags."

"Why the hells would I need hex bags?"

"Oh, I don't know," Theodosia said, storm-gray eyes glittering. For a moment, they looked so like the eyes of their mother it stole his breath. "Maybe because everyone thinks your bride is a witch."

Caine tossed the coin purse aside with a clang, his nostalgia snuffed. "Don't be ridiculous."

She threw her hands up. "Don't shoot the messenger."

"The Queen of Galesborough isn't a witch."

"They say she spent years in the mountains with a coven," Theodosia went on, adopting a mysterious tone.

"A convent," Caine corrected her wearily. He plucked another grape. "It was a convent, Theo."

"Whatever, but even if she isn't a witch, the Vaettir are still brutes."

Caine frowned. "You shouldn't talk about them like that."

"Why?"

"Because I'm about to marry one of them."

"Fine." Theodosia reclined in the armchair, resting her head on the upholstered cushion. A glob of slush dripped from her boot onto the ottoman. "On the bright side, I bet she'll be wild in bed."

Caine almost choked on the grape he had popped into his mouth. It went down like a fat pebble.

"Have you ever once shut up?" he demanded in a strained voice.

"Not recently, no." Theodosia got to her feet, stretching her arms over her head. "I should get to my lesson."

"Now that you've finished harassing me?"

"Now that I've warned you." She looked at him with a soberness he rarely saw about her. It was enough to disperse his annoyance. "Keep your wits about you, brother. This queen won't go down easy."

Keen discomfort slithered through Caine, raising the hairs on the back of his neck. "I'm marrying her, not breaking her."

"I guarantee that isn't how she'll see it, and you know that isn't how Father will, either."

Caine was silent. She was right again, as much as he hated to admit it. Theodosia started toward the door, walking backward to maintain eye contact as she bid him farewell.

"Watch your back, and remember, hex bags."

She gave him a sloppy salute and slipped out the door, leaving it wide open in her wake. Caine stared after her, the voice of his father pounding through the halls of his mind.

We take the Vaettir, we take the world.

☽○☾

The day was in full swing by the time Caine trudged downstairs. The snow had stopped, but the forest beyond the crystalline windows was robed in white. Servants fluttered through the warm, bright halls of Caer Sidi, carrying garlands and stacks of their finest dishes. He swiped a pear from a passing bowl and sank his teeth into it.

"Caine!"

Caine spun with his teeth still hooked on the fruit to see Ma Hendricks bustling toward him. Her eyes were as sharp as raven beaks, her fair skin creased with age. Stuffing the pear into his pocket, he swept into a gallant bow.

"Madame Hendricks," he greeted her. "Delightful, as always."

She swatted him on the head with a rag.

"Ow," Caine feigned, straightening up and massaging the back of his skull.

"Fer good luck." Ma Hendricks gave him a quick once-over. Her furry brows drew together to form a gray thatch. "Ye look terrible, boy."

"Thanks."

Ma Hendricks was one of two living souls who could get away with calling him *boy*, the other being his father. Caine far preferred the word from her. Coming from his father, it was always drenched with condescension.

"I knew ye'd be needing this," she said with a cluck. She dug into her apron and produced a vial of crushed herbs, holding it out to him in her rumpled hand. "Monk root fer yer head. Red lily fer the nausea. Snakeroot fer an extra kick."

Caine thanked her, and this time he meant it. He slipped the hangover remedy into his empty pocket.

"I gave Lady Viola a brew of her own," Ma Hendricks

continued, lowering her voice. "Ye must be more cautious going forward."

"If the legends of the Vaettir are true, I expect my wife would disembowel me if she caught me with another woman." He shook his head and changed the subject. "How are preparations for the wedding? I imagine you're in need of a break."

Ma Hendricks waved him off. "No need fer that, Caine."

"I was just—"

"Being polite, as I taught ye." Ma Hendricks patted his cheek and gave another admonishing click of her tongue. "Ye need to shave."

"I need a lot of things," he replied, watching a pair of servants bearing an evergreen wreath pass. "Mainly more than a week to get to know my future wife."

Ma Hendricks sighed, tucking her cloth into her smudged apron. "Steady on, boy. Marriage is a gift."

"Arranged marriage is a curse."

"It can be," Ma Hendricks conceded. "Or it can be a blessing. Ye and this Queen Ila already have something in common." When Caine shot her a questioning look, she returned a rueful smile. "Neither of ye is making the choice te marry the other."

Caine chuckled. He was oddly comforted by the thought. Neither he nor Ila was a willing participant in this game. Hopefully, they both sought to make the best of a situation that was less than ideal.

"Promise me one thing, will ye?"

"That depends," Caine answered, noting her abrupt shift in tone.

Ma Hendricks took him by the hand and guided him to an alcove with a statue of a dead king whose name he had long forgotten. She tugged him down to her level. Despite his confusion, he offered his ear.

"Promise me ye'll treat her right," she said, her voice barely a whisper. "Never raise a hand to her. Be gentle with her on yer wedding night. She may be inexperienced, if ye take my meaning."

"Of course," Caine assured her. Defensiveness and nausea surged in his gut. "What do you think of me?"

Ma Hendricks released his hand. The blood rushed back to his fingertips. He had not noticed how hard she had been gripping him.

"Ye are a gentle soul, Prince Caine," she answered after what seemed an age. "It is a rare thing fer the men in yer line."

Before Caine could respond, Ma Hendriks patted his arm and hurried away, her skirts rustling like the wings of a barn owl. He was left with the statue of the dead king whose apathetic eyes drilled into the opposite wall.

Shaking off the chill that now prickled under his skin, he started off again at a brisk pace, pulling the pear from his pocket to find his appetite had vanished. He set the fruit on a passing platter and wove through the crowds until he arrived at a tapestry chronicling some ancient fable beside an overgrown fern. Skirting the frilly leaves, he brushed the wall hanging aside and ducked into a narrow dry passageway.

Darkness buffered by periodic torches stretched ahead. When they were young, Caine and Theodosia used to play chase in the catacombs threaded through and below Caer Sidi. He always let her win. Until she got cocky, at least.

Caine walked until he reached a fork in the passage and turned left, brushing aside another tapestry to reveal the daylight. This wing of the castle was older, quieter. Dust motes courtesy of the many wall hangings turned lazy circles in the air. A group of noblewomen had congregated farther down the hall. They tittered like sparrows behind their hands. Probably about his betrothed.

Theodosia's words brushed the surface of his mind.

Everyone thinks your bride is a witch.

Caine shrugged off his unease and entered the throne hall.

Even after twenty-four years, he still found himself in awe of the room. Stained-glass windows detailing the history of Wolfhelm soared two stories high, spilling prisms across the floor. The banner of House Fallon, a lone wolf with iron teeth, hung from the vaulted ceiling. The gold and velvet throne loomed at the far end. Its legs were carved to resemble the claws of a wolf.

Upon the throne was his father, King Warwick of Wolfhelm.

"Caine," he called, his voice steeped in vexation. "I appreciate you taking a moment of your valuable time to see me."

Even seated, Warwick had a commanding presence. Caine found himself pushing his shoulders back as he approached. When he reached the steps leading to the throne, he dropped to one knee.

"I apologize for my tardiness, Father. I have no excuse."

"I drank myself into a stupor the night before your mother arrived in Wolfhelm."

Caine nearly sagged with relief. His father smiled, blue eyes glittering with sharp mirth. His once-dark hair had gone gray and hung around his shoulders. The bone crown, woven from the remnants of the wolf that protected the first King of Wolfhelm, rested on his brow.

One day, Caine would wear it.

"How is your head?" Warwick inquired.

"Fine," the prince lied, getting to his feet.

"Are you prepared for the arrival of our guests?" For an instant, Caine hesitated. Anyone else might not have noticed. Anyone else was not his father. The ember of humor in his eyes guttered. "You understand the importance of this alliance, Caine."

"Yes."

"Galesborough is the last kingdom on the continent that evades our control. Once you and Queen Ila are united, we will command the Vaettir forces. We take the Vaettir..."

"We take the world," Caine finished mechanically.

Warwick gave a sober nod. "The people of Galesborough are backward, uncivilized, but their queen is cunning. She will no doubt try to bend you to her will. You must be cautious."

"Of course."

"The sooner you put a child in her, the better." Warwick smiled again. This time, it was wolfish. Caine felt his stomach twist. "I hear she is a rare beauty, so I imagine this will not be a chore. Assuming, of course, she does not require persuasion."

Another roll of his gut.

"Is there a problem, Prince Caine?"

Caine forced himself to lock eyes with the king. "No, sir."

The smile sloughed from his face as Warwick appraised his son. A warning seeped into his weathered face, creeping into his tone like black ice. "If you take issue with this alliance, speak now."

"I don't take issue with it," he lied. "But I mean to foster trust with my wife."

"She is not someone to be trusted. She is a conduit to greater things, and she will bow if it means your boot on her spine."

Caine felt his eye twitch, but his tongue was frozen, as it often was in the presence of his father.

"You are my only heir, Prince Caine," Warwick continued. "You take no interest in joining me at the front lines, a strand of cowardice I have chosen to overlook. All that is required of you is to bed one girl, and still you balk."

"I don't balk," Caine snapped. "I will do what needs to be done for Wolfhelm."

Warwick stared at him like he could see into the basin of his soul. The cavernous throne hall amplified the silence. Caine felt his mouth go sour, his throat bone-dry. Then the king jerked his chin at the archway through which Caine entered.

"Go, then. Enjoy the festivities and remember what we have to offer the realm: peace and order."

The prince gave a shallow bow and spun on his heel, retreating as quickly as he dared through the curtains of vibrant light pouring from the stained glass.

He prayed his father could not see him shaking.

4
Alaric

"She should be here by now," Mica said for the third time in ten minutes. She shifted gingerly on the crate she was perched on. The waterlogged wood groaned in response.

"She'll be here," Alaric replied, peering out of the alley into the muddy streets of Black Root.

The silver Reverie sun was high above them, but it only exposed the ugliness of the soggy little village. Steam lifted from the swampy roads, creating a veil over the squat buildings.

Tattered kips squelched through the streets, avoiding eye contact with vexes. The kips appeared human. They were the unremarkable background characters in the dreams of humans, and most lived their lives as such.

The one thing kips and vexes shared was their mortality. They could be killed with a blade or be taken by sickness, but all would eventually die of old age, just like their human dreamers.

Mica and Alaric were both immortal, but that was where the similarities ended. Mica was a luminae, lovely and pure as the dream she was woven of. Alaric was forged of a nightmare, and it showed in his wicked horns and imposing stature.

"This is a stupid plan," Mica continued, fidgeting with the fabric of her goldenrod skirts.

"Those are the best kind."

"I mean it. This kip is going to get herself killed."

Alaric leaned against the wall, observing her with soot-dark eyes. Her brown skin was faultless, but her gaze betrayed centuries of life. Beneath her hood, he knew her bat-like ears fluttered anxiously.

"She has no connections to the rebellion," he reminded her. "Para Warwick has no reason to suspect her."

"Until he finds her snooping around for—"

Mica broke off and looked to the mouth of the alley. Alaric followed her line of sight. A figure was silhouetted against the drab light.

"Told you," Alaric muttered. Mica hopped off her crate, elbowing him as the figure hurried over to them. "Were you followed?"

"N-no," Solene answered, squelching to a stop.

Alaric gave the kip a quick once-over. She was a plain, slight thing with flaxen hair and deep-set hazel eyes. She smelled of earth and exhaustion but appeared to be in one piece. This was something of a feat, considering where she had just come from.

"What have you got for us?" Alaric inquired.

Solene paled, worrying the end of her braid. He knew that look all too well. It went with the territory, being a nightmare. Kips had every reason to fear the nightmares who stalked the Reverie, taking what they pleased from the mortal dreams they deemed beneath them.

Mica nudged Alaric aside and took Solene by the hands.

"You've shown great courage, Solene." Her face was full of the sort of grace only a luminae could muster. "The rebellion is in your debt. Tell us, have you found the weapon?"

"Not exactly," Solene mumbled. "But I think I know where it is."

"Where?" Mica and Alaric asked in the same breath. Solene threw a glance over her shoulder at the dream beings shambling past their hiding place.

"No one is listening," the nightmare assured her. If someone was lurking, he or Mica would have sensed them by now.

Solene nodded, though she was clearly not convinced. "A servant told me of a place beneath Caer Sidi. He called it the sanctum." She lowered her voice to a breathy whisper. "I think the weapon is down there."

"What makes you say that?" Mica inquired.

"He said the entrance was unguarded until recently, but now they watch it all the time. Nobody goes in or out but the Para."

Alaric bristled at the mention of his creator. Almost a quarter of a century had passed since he last faced Para Warwick, and still, the thought of the night terror sent his pulse sprinting. He tugged his cowl lower on his brow to hide his notched black horns as a pair of soldiers with the heads of rats marched past the alley, no doubt headed for the castle just beyond the wood to the east.

Mica tapped Alaric on the arm. "You said Para Warwick used the sanctum as a prison."

"He does," he said absently. "At least, he did when I was there."

His hand drifted to the back of his neck, feeling for the knot of scar tissue there. It had long since healed but still twinged with phantom pain now and then.

"He could be interrogating someone," Mica proposed.

Alaric looked at Solene again. She was now kneading the fabric of her threadbare dress, her eyes unfocused. "Is there screaming?"

"Wh-what?"

"If someone were being interrogated, you would hear it."

He should know. He was once the orchestrator of those screams. He swore Caer Sidi had been designed to amplify the sounds of torment.

Solene began to finger her plait again. "No, there's no screaming."

"Keeping the weapon down there would be wise," Alaric muttered, returning his attention to Mica. She stared at the wall like the answer was carved into the layers of grime. "Even before it was guarded, no one went in willingly. Not with Bloodreaper skulking around."

Solene made a noise close to a squeak at the mention of the infamous nightmare. Alaric had never met him and had no plans to change that anytime soon.

"What am I supposed to do?" the kip rasped. "How am I supposed to get this weapon out without anyone noticing?"

"You're the thief," he replied. "Figure it out."

The words came out harsher than he intended, but there was no sense coddling the girl. Kindness would not protect her. Fear would keep her sharp.

"Do you still have your fever stone?" Mica asked her, shooting Alaric a dirty look in the process. Like the vast majority of dream beings, he did not have a mother. With Mica, he often felt he did—for better or for worse.

Solene reached down the front of her dress and pulled out a small pouch hanging from a length of twine. Inside was the egg-shaped fever stone they had given her a week ago. It glowed orange when squeezed, growing brighter as its counterpart drew nearer. Mica kept theirs in the inner pocket of her cloak.

"Good," Mica said briskly. "Stay safe. Contact us with the stone when you have the weapon."

Solene pursed her lips. For a moment, Alaric thought she might challenge them. He would be impressed if she did. Instead, she gave a curt nod and turned on her heel, marching toward the main street.

"Remember, Solene," he called after her. "We know who you are."

Solene froze at the lip of the alley. Her fingers curled into shaky fists. Then she vanished around the corner.

Mica swatted Alaric on the arm. "Was that really necessary?"

He rubbed his bicep, pretending it hurt. "The more motivated she is, the faster we get the dreambreaker."

"The child, Alaric. The dreambreaker is a child."

"And an unfathomably rare being with the ability to move between worlds and possibly level cities, but go on."

"Whatever," Mica grumbled. She shoved past him and made for the street, wet skirts slapping against her legs. "We can't stay here."

Alaric adjusted his hood and followed.

The buildings observed through foggy windowpanes as they stepped into the open. A kip pushing a cart of wilted vegetables cursed at Alaric when he cut her off. He started to apologize, but Mica dragged him away.

"You're awfully polite for a 'mare, you know that?" she said, seething. "This is why I told you not to come. Someone is bound to recognize you."

"No one will recognize me. I promise."

The last time he was in Black Root, no one would have dared look him in the face. As long as he kept his horns covered, they would be safe.

"Still," Mica muttered as they wove through the sluggish streams of dream beings. "You coming so close to Caer Sidi isn't worth the risk. I could have taken care of this myself."

"This place is crawling with soldiers who would love to get their hands on a rebel luminae," Alaric reminded her in a low voice, eyeing the knot of armored vexes loitering outside a tavern.

Two were indistinguishable from the average kip, but he could sense the subtle viciousness lurking beneath their skin. The other was what could only be described as rotting, his skin blackened and sloughing off his skeleton in clumps.

Their chest plates were branded with the crest of Para Warwick, a wolf with two heads and two frothing mouths.

"I'm four hundred and twelve," Mica reminded Alaric as they passed the vexes, her tone clipped. "I can handle myself."

"And that means you get to have all the fun?"

He spoke lightly but hoped she grasped his true meaning.

He would never allow her to enter enemy territory alone. She was too small, too tenderhearted, and burned far too bright.

Thankfully, the luminae dropped her face to hide a smile. It faded the second she returned her eyes to Alaric.

"This *is* a stupid plan, though. You know that, right?"

"I know."

"For all we know, the Para has already killed the girl. Just like..." Mica took a steadying breath. "What if it happens again?"

Alaric felt his fingers flex at his thighs, his magic prickle in his rib cage. Memories steeped in shame threatened to puncture the careful barriers he had placed around them.

"We won't let it."

Even as Alaric spoke the words, they felt hollow.

The crowds thinned as they approached the edge of Black Root. A swathe of trampled brown snow separated the village from the Tanglewood, which was already thick with shadows at dusk.

Alaric was not keen on traveling the eerie forest at night, though he supposed the creatures that haunted the skeletal black trees were no more vicious than he.

As they arrived at the tree line, a hulking vex with gray skin and a scar across his face lumbered into view. His tiny beetle eyes lingered on Mica as they passed. Alaric slung an arm around her, which was somewhat difficult given he was over a foot taller.

He and the vex locked eyes. Alaric fought the urge to call magic to his hands. Perhaps he and this vex had crossed paths when Alaric served as the Hand of the Para all those years ago.

Shit, maybe Alaric had given him that scar.

Even if he wanted to, he could not recall all the faces of the dream beings he had tortured and killed in service of Para Warwick.

There were far too many to remember.

☽○☾

Unease dogged Alaric as he and Mica rode on horseback through the Tanglewood. They met few travelers on the path, just a handful of kips and a luminae faun whose body appeared to be wrought of wood and stone.

Still, Alaric felt his magic twitch and shiver in his chest periodically. It seemed to sense something out among the crush of black trees, but all he saw was snow, brambles, and a vanity robed in moss that must have dropped in from a dream. Lifeless objects rarely manifested in the Reverie, but Alaric could think of little other reason for the furniture to be so deep in the forest.

"Alaric."

He glanced at Mica sidelong. She considered him with a tilted head, silky ears and coiled curls silhouetted against the purple twilight. Warmth seemed to radiate from her, clashing with the desolate landscape.

"Yes?"

"I asked what you were thinking about."

"I'm fine."

"That isn't what I asked."

Alaric frowned, returning his eyes to the path. Befriending an insatiably curious luminae had its advantages and its pitfalls. He had yet to decide if their acute empathy was the former or the latter.

"What do we know about her?" he asked to distract her. "This weaver protecting the dreambreaker."

Mica sighed, her breath mushrooming in the air. He wondered if she was reconsidering befriending a nightmare.

"She broke her weaver vows a year ago to become queen of some kingdom in the Wake. Gainsborough, I think? Something like that."

"Who knew you could just leave the Weaver Order."

Alaric had not encountered many weavers, but those he came across over the years were cold and arrogant. Their abilities were intriguing, he supposed. The only other being he had met with power over the Boundary was Para Warwick.

"Weavers are supposed to despise dreambreakers and forbid their creation," Mica said, adopting a puzzled tone. "Their existence is said to be a threat to the Boundary."

"You'd think they'd be more critical of the Para, then."

Thud.

The magic at his center gave a shuddering kick. Alaric brought his horse to a halt, rubbing its dappled neck when it whickered nervously. Mica brought her own mount to a stop, her tawny bat ears pricked. A frigid breeze slithered through the trees. Nothing else moved.

"Did you hear that?" Mica whispered.

"I felt it," Alaric answered.

Thud.

Mica clutched her reins. "It sounds like wings."

Another pulse sent power sprinting through his veins. A warning.

Hide.

Alaric swung his leg over his horse and jumped down. Mica did the same, landing in the snow with a crunch. He grabbed her hand and dragged her into the trees, abandoning the horses and slipping into the drifts. They crouched with their backs to a gnarled trunk, partially shielded by a net of brambles.

"Alaric—" Mica squeaked.

He pressed a finger to his lips and conjured a sizzling bolt of magic in his free hand. It was the ebony color of skysteel and just as lethal. It would sear anyone it came into contact with to the bone but was merely warm against his skin.

Thud.

A storm of feathers, a rush of wind, and a black streak across the sky. Uncanny silence settled in the wake of the winged creature, the sort that only followed something deadly.

"Was that who I think it was?" Mica breathed.

Alaric nodded grimly, letting his bolt dissolve with a gentle hiss. "Nightstrider."

He had never met her, the winged nightmare Para Warwick created to replace him after he defected to the rebellion, but her name cast a shadow across the Reverie. All manner of dream beings whispered it as a warning and a curse.

They said she was dreamt without a heart. They said the same about him. At least, they used to, when he lived and fought under another name.

"Come on," Alaric said, getting to his feet. Mica followed suit, brushing snow off the back of her wool cloak. "We've got a lot of ground to cover."

By the time they reached their destination, an inn perched atop a hill just beyond the gloomy sprawl of the Tanglewood, Mica was fading. Alaric had never met an immortal who needed so much sleep.

"Are we sure he'll be home?" she asked through a yawn as they tethered their horses to the hitching post.

Smoke billowed from the twin chimneys at either end of the whitewashed lodge, but the windows were dark. It was as unassuming as an inn could be, but that was the point.

It served as a haven for kips and luminae who found themselves in the crosshairs of Para Warwick and his legions. Ultimately, they would be shepherded to Marrowrun, the last free city in the Known Regions of the Reverie.

"Only one way to find out," Alaric answered.

Together, they slipped around the back of the inn. They had no trouble finding their way in the dark. One of the three moons had swollen to three times its usual size, bathing everything in a gory glow. If Alaric was superstitious, he might have been alarmed, but he knew it was just the way of the Reverie skies. There were no cycles to the heavenly bodies; they simply appeared as they wished each night.

Mica slumped against the stack of firewood while Alaric rapped on the back door. The rolling click of tumblers, the thud of a deadbolt, and it opened.

"Alaric. Mica."

"Morthil," Alaric greeted the luminae. "Good somnia, brother."

Morthil smiled, white eyes blazing against his bluish-black skin. He and Alaric shook hands, then Mica threw her arms around Morthil. He laughed and spun her in a quick circle, depositing her on the packed snow.

"I've missed you," she said, pulling away to grasp him by the arms. "Do you know how hard it is to find anyone old enough to remember how to play echo stones?"

"The curse of immortality, my dear." Morthil spoke softly, but his words reverberated as if they stood inside a cavern. His milky eyes cut to Alaric. "Perhaps you can teach the youngling to play."

Alaric stepped around them deliberately as they laughed. Warm, aromatic air enveloped him as he entered the lodge. The back hall was cramped but tidy, the walls lined with cloaks, tools, and a longbow.

"I had one of the girls prepare a room for you," Morthil told them as he and Mica joined Alaric inside. "You'll have to share, I'm afraid."

"Fully booked, are you?" Alaric asked.

"Officially, no. Unofficially, always."

Morthil led them to the dining room. The space was bare and clean with a chandelier of antlers hanging from the rafters. There were no guests at the bar or the thick wooden tables, but Alaric could hear two female voices through the swinging kitchen doors. It was dark save for the firelight peeking through the slats.

Mica dropped her bag and dropped into the nearest chair, letting her head loll over the back with a drawn-out groan.

"Any word from your weaver friend?" Alaric asked, taking a seat beside her. "What was her name?"

"Ila—Queen Ila." Morthil sat down opposite them,

moving with effortless grace. He snapped his fingers, and the trio of sagging candles on the table ignited. "She received my last message but never answered."

"How is it you know her?"

"I knew her mother first," Morthil explained, crossing one leg over the other. Alaric had forgotten how penetrating his pupilless eyes could be and found it difficult not to glance away. "She was a skilled weaver. We met years ago when she was patching a breach in the Boundary."

A bittersweet smile wandered across his waiflike features.

"Before she died, she asked me to look after her daughter whenever she was in the Reverie."

"May she bloom in another dream," Mica murmured. Morthil dipped his chin in solemn thanks.

"How did a weaver end up protecting a dreambreaker?" Alaric asked. "And why send her to the Reverie in a matchbox?"

"It was a jewelry box, and I enchanted it months ago as a fail-safe. Neither of us anticipated having to use it," Morthil answered. "As to why Ila sent her to the Reverie alone, I cannot say, but I do know she would never have parted with her had she any other choice."

"Do we know what Para Warwick wants with this girl?" Mica inquired. She sat forward, resting her elbows on the varnished table. "What power does she possess that he does not already have?"

"Ila has not divulged this, but she assures me it would be ruinous for both worlds if the Para bends her to his will." His blank eyes shifted from Mica to Alaric. "This child may be more powerful than Luken."

Mica flinched. Alaric stilled.

"Ah," Morthil murmured. "It was this time last year."

Mica patted him on the hand in confirmation and absolution, her eyes unusually bright and her throat clearly too thick to speak.

"Three days."

Alaric only realized he had spoken aloud when both luminae looked at him. He swallowed the stone in his throat and continued in a near growl.

"In three days, it will be a year since Para Warwick murdered Luken, and we're no closer to killing him."

"Retrieving the dreambreaker will deal a considerable blow," Morthil reminded him.

"Not that you'll be any help."

"Alaric!" Mica gasped. He ignored her.

"You know why I can't return to the rebellion." Morthil spoke evenly, but Alaric had known him too long to be fooled. There was a tightness at the corner of his mouth, a bulge in his jaw. "I will continue to do what I can to aid you from afar."

"Like you aided Luken when Warwick took him?"

The ancient luminae narrowed his eyes fractionally. "Do not put the blame on me. You know it is not mine to bear."

"He came through here a day before he died, did he not?" Alaric gritted out. "You knew the Para was after him and you did nothing."

"Luken was a grown man, Alaric. The choice was his."

Black sparks exploded when Alaric slammed his fist into the table. Mica yelped. Morthil stared him down, unmoved.

"What about *your* choices? Our supply lines have been cut. Our camps are being burned. The rebellion is dying, the Reverie is suffocating, and you want to sit here playing innkeeper?"

"This is more than an inn, and you know it," Morthil shot back, the phantom echo in his voice bouncing off the white-washed walls.

Mica glanced up the staircase that led to the guest rooms and touched his arm in warning. He placed his hand over hers and continued in a more measured voice.

"I have been alive longer than you can fathom, Alaric. I have lost and won more wars than I can count. I am finished fighting. I do what I can here to aid the vulnerable."

"You can aid the vulnerable by helping us take down the Para," Alaric snapped.

Morthil shook his head. Slow, resolute.

"If Para Warwick falls, another will rise to replace him. When that happens, there will still be kips and luminae who need passage to Marrowrun. I can get them there."

Alaric weighed his words in stony silence.

"Whatever you've faced," he finally said. "Whatever evil you've known, it is nothing compared to Para Warwick. Killing him is the only way. Until he is dead, the rest is inconsequential."

Morthil bared his teeth, anger roiling in his bottomless eyes. "The lives of innocent dream beings are inconsequential?"

"You know what I mean."

"Do I? Would you feel differently if the dream beings I was helping were not mostly kips?"

The air between Morthil and Alaric crackled with tension. Mica looked back and forth between them, fuzzy ears pressed to her curls.

"Morthil," the nightmare murmured. All the fight had ebbed from his voice. In its place was a pleading tone that it almost shamed him to take. "We've lost so many. We need you home, brother."

For the briefest moment, he thought he saw something flicker behind the unshakable resolve on Morthil's face. Then it was gone, and when the luminae spoke, it was with finality impossible to ignore.

"You will always have safe harbor here." He got to his feet, radiating cold, insurmountable distance. "The third room on the left is yours. Good somnia."

Mica murmured a farewell as Morthil breezed across the dining room, disappearing through the swinging kitchen doors in a flurry of firelight.

5

Ila

The snow in Wolfhelm was wet, clumpy, and relentless. Ila was accustomed to harsh winters in Galesborough, but this was a different sort of cold. It seeped straight through the flimsy cloak she had purchased at the border to replace the furs she wore the night the Skysteel Guard tracked her down.

"Just a little farther," she promised Ailo. Her horse snorted, sending up a puff of steam as they followed the meandering road.

Nine days had passed since Ila sent Saoirse to the Reverie in her tiny vessel. She had not received a reply to the fire message she sent, but with Morthil, no news was generally good news.

At least, that was what Ila kept telling herself.

The smell of smoke and seasoned meats drew her gaze to the horizon. Three stacks climbed the gloomy sky just over the hill. Her heart leaped into her mouth. Ila clicked her tongue at Ailo, who picked up the pace. They crested the rise.

Ila could not resist a smile.

Nestled in the valley of stripped trees was a campsite dotted with tents and smoldering cookfires. Men and women clad in dyed wool and furs moved between them. Ila cracked the reins, and she and Ailo sailed down the hill toward the Vaettir. Toward her people. Their heads flew up at the approach of their queen.

Ailo and Ila trotted to a halt at the brink of the campsite. The queen dismounted swiftly. No sooner did her boots grace the ground than she was swept into a bone-crushing hug.

"Nils," Ila wheezed, patting him on the back. "Put me down."

"You're late," her guardian whispered in her ear. He set her down and stood back to examine her with angular blue eyes. Nils was tall and rugged with an air of kindness that clashed with the axe at his side.

"Barely."

"What happened?"

"Nothing." Ila stepped around Nils pointedly. Eleven Vaettir warriors tapped their hearts in greeting. All were originally hunters and herders who had taken up arms to defend their borders against Wolfhelm's grabbing hands, hands Ila was now forced to embrace. "Takja, min liern, for making this journey without me," she said, thumping her own chest. "May your sworn god bless your hearts and swords."

A woman in her fifties with a severe gray braid stepped forward. The antler necklace at the hollow of her throat marked her a general.

"It is our honor, Queen Ila," she said.

"Takja, Ashild. Walk with me."

Ila could feel Nils staring at her back as the crowd parted for her and Ashild. They passed a cookfire, a cluster of circular tents, and a wagon loaded with trunks and crates. One held the gown her late mother wore on her wedding day, altered to fit Ila only weeks ago.

It was a traditional Vaettirin garment, white and bottle blue with red and yellow accents and gold adornments that jingled when she moved. How many times had she tried it on growing up, the bodice drooping on her tiny frame and the wool skirts threatening to drown her? Her mother had laughed, nuzzled her nose, told her she could wear it when she married if she wished.

Ila had scarcely looked in the mirror during the fitting and intended to keep it that way.

"Are you unwell, Queen Ila?" Ashild inquired as they arrived at the royal tent.

"No, takja." Ila brushed aside the flap and motioned for the general to follow her inside. The tent was mercifully warm with a bed of furs, a washbasin, and the blue trunk from her home in Galesborough. A fire blazed at the center, the smoke curling through the hole in the ceiling. "Please, tell me of Wolfhelm."

Ashild locked her hands behind her back, standing dagger straight as she answered. "We arrived three days ago as you ordered."

"Any trouble with the locals?" Ila unlaced her cloak. It dropped with a splat.

"No. We observed from afar."

Ila shrugged off her vest next and cast it aside, resisting the urge to collapse face-first onto the bed of furs.

"Go on," she urged Ashild.

"It is as you predicted. Heavy military presence even in the smallest villages. Their armor and weaponry are undeniably superior." Ashild sucked her teeth and rested a gloved hand on the hilt of her sword. "The soldiers are mostly male. Well compensated and fiercely loyal to King Warwick."

Luxury, loyalty, and masculinity. A dangerous combination made worse by the fact that at the helm of this army was a tyrant unlike any the Wake or the Reverie had ever seen.

The weavers were at a loss to explain the existence of a night terror capable of traversing the Boundary, and had not the numbers nor the will to stop him. His movements between worlds were surgical, causing no lasting damage to the barrier.

As long as the Boundary was safe, they would not get involved in politics.

This was one of the reasons Ila cut ties with the weavers, and why she now faced a life in the clutches of this impossible para—and his son.

"What of the prince?" Ila asked, struggling to keep the trepidation from her tone. "What have you heard about him?"

A sound like the crack of a whip stopped Ashild from answering. Ila lurched to her feet as a spark ignited in midair, belching tendrils of white smoke.

"Go," she commanded Ashild, who had drawn her sword. "Now."

"But—"

"Ashild, hest."

Ashild hesitated, threw one more alarmed glance at the spark, then ducked outside. Ila focused on the budding fire message. Singed parchment unfurled from nothing, floating in midair. The smoke dissipated as the letter materialized. She plucked it from the air while it was still hot.

Ila,

We were too late. Para Warwick has the child. The box remains sealed. I have enlisted the help of the rebellion to retrieve her. Do not leave the Wake. We will find her, I swear.

Morthil

The letter slipped from her grasp. Ila clapped her hands to her mouth to smother a sob, a scream, a curse. Stupid. How could she have been so stupid? She should have fought the Skysteel Guard to her last breath. Anything but send Saoirse to the Reverie alone.

Now the rebellion was involved.

"Rakk," she cursed, her voice thin and quavering.

If she had to choose between Para Warwick and the rebellion, she would choose the latter. Still, the rebel dream beings were as sloppy as they were intrepid in their crusade to take down the Para and his legions. If they got their hands on Saoirse, they would undoubtedly try to use her for their own purposes.

A hand touched the space between her shoulder blades. Ila jerked and spun around. Nils stood behind her, a hand outstretched. His tanned face was wrought with confusion and concern.

"What is it?" he asked.

Before she could answer, his eyes found the letter at their feet. The queen snatched it up and stuffed it into her pocket.

"Nothing."

Nils seethed.

"Nothing I can share with you," Ila amended.

Few humans knew of the Weaver Order. Fewer still knew that Ila, like her mother before her, was one of them. Her father and brothers knew, of course, but they were with their sworn gods now, scattered ash in the Faeyenval Sea.

"We shared everything once," Nils said, sullen and not struggling to disguise it. "Has your trust in me failed?"

Ila felt her heart twinge. She stilled it at once. There was no room for regret or longing, not now.

"We're not children anymore," she answered softly.

Nils set his jaw. For a moment, Ila feared she had kindled his temper, which rivaled hers, but when he spoke, his voice was gentle.

"Tell me what has happened and how I can aid you."

A knot formed in her throat. Her will crumbled. She leaned her brow against his chest, inhaling his familiar scent. He smelled like childhood, like frost and firewood and nights spent under the stars.

"I wish I could," she whispered into his furs.

He brought the flat of his hand to her back. When he spoke, she could feel the words vibrating through his chest.

"Does this have something to do with the girl who lives under the hill outside the village?"

Ila stiffened, pulling away from him to look him in the face. "How do you know about her?"

"You're not as sly as you think," Nils replied, his lips twitching into a smile. "Don't worry, no one else knows."

Tears welled in her gaze. Ila blinked them back, glancing away from Nils. She could not afford to fall apart.

"Is she yours?" he asked, taking her hand. His skin was

warm despite the chill, his palms rough from years of training. "You know it makes no difference to me."

"No, she is not mine." She swallowed thickly, half wanting to retract her hand, half wishing to embrace him. "But she is special. I sent her away to protect her, but someone has taken her, someone who means her harm."

"Then we will get her back."

"If I leave, Wolfhelm will come for Galesborough."

Nils took Ila by the shoulders. She looked up to see thunder rising in his eyes. "You do not have to marry this dasak. We are prepared to march on this shit stain of a kingdom at your command."

She could hear the longing buried beneath his protectiveness. Her mind threatened again to wander back to the two years they spent together before their duties pulled them apart, making love in his tent, hunting in the forest with snow up to their hips. Ila anchored herself in the present stubbornly.

Reminiscing would only hurt them both.

"It is not so simple," Ila told him. "Even if it were, we're outnumbered. They would take Galesborough in a month."

She expected Nils to argue, but instead, he released her and reached behind his back.

"I may not know precisely what you face, but I know you."

Movement pulled her eyes downward. In his hands was the dagger that had belonged to her eldest brother, Morten. She had left it with Nils for safekeeping when she fled with Saoirse, worried the Vaettirin inscriptions on the blade would be recognized were they captured.

"The strength of your people is here..." Nils set the knife in her hands. The wrapped leather hilt was warm to the touch.

"And here." He touched her heart with two fingers. "You will find a way. You always do."

She wanted to believe him, but it was impossible with the letter burning a hole in her pocket.

"I am not sure what good this will do me in a castle," Ila said to change the subject, turning the dagger over in her hands. She knew as well as any daughter of Galesborough how to use it to skin a deer or split a branch, but from what she knew of the aristocracy in Wolfhelm, neither task would be considered appropriate for her status or sex.

Nils grunted. "I can think of one or two uses."

"I can't cut his throat while he sleeps, Nils."

"A man can dream."

Ila almost smiled.

Two short blasts of a horn shattered the moment. Nils glared at the tent flap.

"Go," Ila said. "I'll be fine."

He did not move, his jaw working beneath his sandy stubble. "I am here, Ila. Whatever you need."

She took a step back and curled the dagger to her breast. "I need you to do your duty."

Another horn blast, this one snappish. Nils sighed, then tapped his fist to his heart and trudged from the tent. As soon as he was gone Ila collapsed onto her furs, tossing the dagger aside and whipping the letter out of her pocket. She traced the curling script with her thumb as if she could rearrange the characters by sheer will.

We were too late. Para Warwick has the child.

Hoste, what had she done?

6

Wren

Wren slept like the dead but did not feel rested when she woke. She lay in bed for a long while, watching the silver sun crawl across her silken bedspread. She had read somewhere that the sun was golden in the Wake; that when the water caught its rays, it looked to be aflame.

How could one ever rest in a world on fire?

Eventually, Wren heaved herself from bed. She stretched her wings and arms with a groan. Fully extended, her feathers almost brushed the walls. She gave them a shake and collapsed them, shuffling to the washroom. It was still scattered with melted candles and splotches of wax from her tryst with Ondine.

She winced when she saw her reflection in the mirror. Her black hair was limp and tangled. The jagged white scar sprawled across her torso stood in stark contrast to her warm brown skin. Every other wound she had sustained over the years had sealed itself without a trace.

This one was different.

Wren grabbed her robe off the hook on the wall and donned it, fussing with the slits in the back that allowed her wings through. Her clothes were altered by a seamstress in the castle. Wren used to bring her pieces she had picked up in markets across the Reverie to be customized, but that was a long time ago. She did not waste time on such frivolous things anymore.

After running a comb through her hair and washing the crust from her face, Wren returned to her bedroom. Out of the corner of her eye, she caught a glimpse of blond hair and the shimmer of crystal.

"Eek!"

Wren snatched the falling goblet from the air just before it shattered against the floor. She offered it back to the servant who had dropped it.

"I-I'm so sorry, Nightstrider. I'm so c-clumsy." The girl fumbled her words, oblivious to the glass Wren still held out to her wordlessly. A film of tears formed over her eyes as the tip of her nose turned pink. "Please, I—"

"You're new."

Wren set the goblet on the table. Her gaze flicked to the silver breakfast tray the girl had delivered. A sweating pitcher of juice stood beside it. She could not imagine how this scrawny girl had hauled it all the way up to her chambers from the basement kitchens.

"Y-yes, Nightstrider," the servant answered, fear squeezing her voice into a higher octave.

"Do you have a name?"

"Solene."

Clearly, Solene expected to be beaten. Killed, even. The

other servants had doubtlessly told her of the nightmares who stalked the halls of Caer Sidi, creatures of violence and wrath. Nothing resembling mercy was to be expected of them.

"When did you manifest?" Wren inquired.

"Six years ago, near Frost Hill."

Though she possessed the mind and body of a young woman, she was as inexperienced as a child. Wren felt her stomach clench. How the hells did this girl end up at Caer Sidi? Only the most desperate kips sought work in the house of the Para. Solene appeared neither starved nor battered.

"Who was your dreamer?" Wren pressed.

Solene fidgeted with the hem of her apron. Sweat beaded on her brow.

She was terrified, Wren realized, but that was for the best. Better the girl fear her than try to befriend her. That never ended well. Wren was about to dismiss her when she spoke.

"He was a farmer in Wolfhelm."

Wren raised her brows at the mention of the kingdom Para Warwick presided over in the Wake. She could not remember the last time she had heard anyone but the Para himself mention it.

"He was dancing with his wife," Solene went on. "Strangers were dancing around them. I was one of them. The farmer looked at me, and I manifested. I was the only kip to come to life. The rest were lost to sleep."

Kips were funny that way. One glance from a human dreamer and they hurtled into existence. They were blank slates, capable of both good and evil. For this, Wren had always envied them.

"How did you end up here?" Wren asked.

Solene chewed her lip. Her eyes were glazed with terror. Wren realized abruptly that she had been interrogating the poor girl. She was not even sure why.

"You're dismissed," Wren said, turning from the kip and pretending to inspect the breakfast she had delivered. In her peripheral vision, she saw Solene sag with relief.

"Can I do anything else for you, Nightstrider?"

"No."

Solene bobbed a curtsy and scampered to the door.

"Solene," Wren called after her. The kip froze with her hand on the cast iron knob. "Be careful. Other 'mares will not be so forgiving."

The kip blanched and darted away like a frightened rabbit. The door clicked shut behind her.

Sighing, Wren dropped into the nearest chair to examine her breakfast in earnest. The kitchen had been generous today, sending up fresh fruit, two hard-boiled eggs, and a loaf of bread. She grabbed an orange and pierced it with a razor thumbnail. Juice bubbled from the wound as her thoughts wandered.

No manifestation was ever easy.

It was disorienting, terrifying, to one moment exist within the bounds of a dream and the next awaken in the impossibly vast Reverie.

Most kips found comfort in the arms of their own kind. Their lifespans were comparable to those of humans, but here at Caer Sidi they often died young. They were easy targets for nightmares and vexes looking to blow off steam.

Wren plucked a plump orange slice from the bundle and stuck it in her mouth.

Nightmares like her were born of the darkest dreams. The kind that made humans wake up screaming. The kind that made them never want to sleep again. The kind they felt compelled to immortalize in ink in an attempt to understand them.

Wren would live as long as her name was written in the Wake, as long as Para Warwick held the journal to which her existence was anchored. Unless somebody chopped off her head or reduced her to a pile of ash. She doubted she could survive that.

Wren popped another orange slice into her mouth, closing her eyes to savor the sweet tang. A knock rang out.

"Fuck, *what*?"

The door opened at her rancorous call. A vex whose face looked like it had been kicked in by a battering ram—teeth caved, nose crushed, and bloodshot eyes crossed—answered. Wren was not sure if he had manifested that way or if he had gotten into a fight with a troll in the last hour.

"Para Warwick summons you," he announced, his words a bit slurred.

Wren nodded. He retreated.

The second he was gone, she wilted in her chair, her head tipping over the back. This was not how she had wanted to start her morning, but when Para Warwick called, she answered.

It had been that way since the beginning. She had been nothing. Unthinking, unknowing matter suspended in oblivion. Then a voice wrenched her into being.

Rise, Nightstrider.

She manifested in dark water, a tangle of limbs and feathers and terror. Her brain had blazed with her first thought, her only thought, the only thing she knew how to do.

Rise.

She broke the surface. Her first breath flooded her lungs, but the relief was fleeting. She thrashed in the water, clawing for something, anything, to hold. Her hand struck craggy rock, and she knew pain. Instinct seized her. She clawed for the stone and heaved herself onto solid ground.

It might have been seconds, minutes, or hours that she lay there on the rock. She folded in on herself, wrapping her arms and wings around her. Everything was too much. The bite of the cold stone against her virgin skin. The deafening roar of what she would come to know as the Evendark Sea. The echo of her own pulse deep in her bones.

"Get up."

She blinked the world into focus. Standing over her, black eyes gleaming and power radiating from his every pore, was Para Warwick. She knew nothing of gods, but the reverence that filled her should have been reserved for one.

Perhaps he was a god. What was a god if not a creator and ruler?

"I said *get up.*"

A gloved hand gripped her by the hair, dragging her to her feet. Para Warwick released her and stepped back while she peered around.

They stood in the basin of a massive rock formation. Twelve towering stone spears rose around them, battered from the outside by monstrous waves. The pool at their center, the one she had crawled from, was undisturbed by the violence of the sea. There had to be a bottom, but she could not see it. Instead, she felt the abyss itself stare back with a thousand eyes.

"You are Nightstrider."

She ripped her eyes from the depths to gaze at the Para. The corners of his mouth tilted upward. Warmth tingled down her spine. She had been forged to please him, forged to want to please him.

"You and I are going to change the worlds."

The distant chime of a clock bell wrenched Wren away from her invasive memory. Her hand was sticky. She swore when she found that she had squashed the remains of the orange in her fist. Throwing it onto the platter with a soggy *splat*, she wiped her hand on her robe and crossed to the wardrobe.

Wren removed her soiled robe and selected a fitted green tunic and simple leggings. She dressed quickly, aligning the slits in her tunic with her wings, then stomped on her boots with more force than necessary and rushed out the door without braiding her hair.

Para Warwick did not like to be kept waiting.

The hall was deserted when Wren arrived. She had expected Para Warwick to be on his throne. Forged of skysteel, it matched the spindly chandeliers that drooped from the ceiling like great spiders. Wren paced beneath them, half wishing one would descend and devour her whole.

The fine hairs on the back of her neck prickled. She

whirled, dropping to one knee in the abrupt presence of her Para.

"Para Warwick." She bowed her head. Her hair slipped forward to shroud her face. "I did not hear you arrive."

"Rise, Nightstrider."

Bracing herself, Wren climbed to her feet and lifted her chin. Pain exploded across her face, knocking her to the floor. Blood burst in her mouth.

She did not wince. She did not cry out.

She swallowed the shame and rose again.

"You dare return to me with nothing?"

Para Warwick stood well over seven feet tall and wore scarred armor too heavy for any mortal to don. His eyes were black from pupil to lid, somehow infinitely darker than sky-steel, and ringing his brow was a circuit of bone that sprang from his flesh. The crown could not be parted from him any less than he could be parted from the Reverie throne.

"Answer me," Para Warwick barked.

Wren started to do as he bid, but he backhanded her again, sending her sprawling. She stayed down longer this time. When she got up, she kept her eyes down.

"Souldrinker tells me you killed the rebel by mistake," Para Warwick continued bitterly. "You do not make mistakes."

Ondine. Anger rippled through Wren, but it was quickly muted by reality. She should have known better than to admit her failures to Ondine. She would always use them to her advantage. Wren couldn't blame her. It was not so long ago that she herself would have done anything to get ahead, anything to be favored by their creator.

"Forgive me, my Para," she said through the blood in her mouth. "He was more breakable than I anticipated."

"Kips are weak, just like luminae and their bleeding hearts. I would have thought you knew that."

"It won't happen again."

"No, it won't."

"I'll find out what the rebels are up to, I swear on my anchor."

"That won't be necessary."

Para Warwick swept past Wren. His armor groaned and clanged like rusted machinery as he mounted the steps to his throne. Wren turned to face him, arms loose at her sides.

Slowly, the Para sat. He observed her for a charged moment. It felt as if he was peeling back her skin.

"I am relieving you of your duties beyond Caer Sidi until I return from the Wake in a week."

"Sir, please—"

"Souldrinker will take your place in the field. Bloodreaper will assume command of the castle in my absence."

Ondine's biting words in the bath returned to Wren again.

You get every good mission, every worthy kill, while the rest of us just sit here waiting for you to come back and act like you don't love every second of it.

"Are you listening to me?"

"Yes, my Para."

Para Warwick drummed his fingers on the arm of his throne as he studied Wren. She was a bug tacked to a square of cloth in his devouring gaze.

"Do you know why I created you, Nightstrider?"

"To kill," she answered without hesitation.

"To do anything and everything I ask without hesitation or remorse. I created you to be ruthless, loyal, and brutal." He reclined on his throne. His void eyes never wavered from hers. "You are my sword and my lever, more than any other 'mare who walks these halls." His words should have made her glow. Not long ago, they would have. "That is why I treat you harshly, so you may learn."

"Yes, my Para."

All at once, Para Warwick was an inch from her. She struggled not to recoil, keeping her eyes on his chest. He caressed her cheek with a too-gentle knuckle. She held utterly still, willing one or both of them to disappear.

"You have disappointed me." His gloved fingers drifted to her collarbone, tracing the edge of her scar that peeked out from under her tunic. "A shame to further mar such a beautiful creation, but you leave me no choice."

Para Warwick snapped his fingers. The air around them rippled, and a leather journal with singed pages appeared in his palm. Wren felt her throat constrict. Her instincts begged her to run, but running would not save her.

Nothing would.

"Remind me, Nightstrider, of the last time you saw your anchor." Para Warwick opened the journal her existence was tied to, riffling through it lazily. A shiver passed through Wren. She could feel his hands on her though he no longer touched her body. "Answer me."

"A year ago," she rasped.

"Then you recall what happens when I do this."

The tip of his pointer finger ignited with a blue flame. An involuntary whimper slipped from Wren as she backpedaled, but it was useless.

She could flee across the Reverie, and he could still burn her.

Para Warwick brought the flame close to the pages of her anchor. Itching, burning heat kindled beneath her right shoulder blade. Subtle at first, but rapidly escalating.

"Please," she begged hoarsely.

Her vision snapped into razor-sharp focus, and she knew her eyes had gone black, just like his. It happened when she was at her most vulnerable, her most afraid. It was nothing more than an instinctual reaction, but it only made her feel more like him.

"Will you disappoint me again?" The flame was only a breath from the paper. A brown circle bloomed on the white expanse. The patch of flesh on her back bubbled and seared. Wren bit the inside of her cheek to keep from screaming. "Well?"

"No, sir. Never."

Para Warwick considered her. The smell of her own flesh burning made her want to retch. The scent dragged with it memories of the night she had long since cast into the deepest trenches of her mind. She struggled to pin them down, to keep them from surfacing.

The Para snapped the journal shut and snuffed the flame at his fingertip.

"I'm glad we understand each other."

Wren trembled silently. Her burn throbbed, stung, smoldered.

"You will not cause trouble while I am away. My son is to

marry in less than a fortnight, and I will not miss the ceremony on account of you."

Through the fog of agony, Wren felt a flicker of pity for whatever poor human girl was being forced to wed his son.

"When I return, you and I will have a more detailed conversation about your responsibilities beyond these walls. Behave yourself, and I will not be forced to resort to such crude measures again."

A lethal smile and he was gone. Back to the Wake. Back to Wolfhelm.

Wren wrapped her arms around herself, somehow freezing and sweating in the silence of the throne hall.

There had never been another being like Para Warwick. An immortal who moved between worlds like breathing, a dream who created other dreams.

Wren did not know how he did it. No one did.

All she knew was that she hated him with every fiber of her being.

7

Caine

Caine waited at the edge of the pale gravel drive, shivering beneath his cloak. The wind sent snow spiraling through the bitter air. A quarter mile ahead, the gates of Caer Sidi were open to reveal the forest beyond the grounds and the manicured path that sliced through it.

There was no sign of the Vaettir.

Caine threw a glance over his shoulder. Thomas stood beside the other nine members of the Skysteel Guard, black armor and rapiers glinting proudly in the evening light. The captain passed him an encouraging smile, which he returned halfheartedly.

"Eyes forward, Prince Caine."

Caine glanced at his father. King Warwick was dressed in a stiff velvet jacket with ornate fastenings and a high collar. He radiated poise, but despite the cold, there was a thin sheen of sweat on his brow.

His skin was pallid, almost gray.

Before Caine could ask if he was well, Warwick continued. "What was the first lesson I taught you?"

"Never turn your back on your enemy," Caine answered mechanically. He shifted, the frozen dirt crunching beneath the soles of his boots. "Am I to consider my future wife my enemy?"

"It would be foolish to presume her anything but."

A sharp elbow jabbing his ribs caused Caine to turn to his other side. Theodosia, who had been wrestled into a plum gown and matching cloak lined with white fur, rolled her eyes and opened and closed her hand like a flapping mouth.

"I will send you back, Theodosia," Warwick said mildly. "Your presence is not required."

Theodosia deflated, folding her skinny arms and scowling at the packed snow. Before Caine could try to cheer her up, the savage cry of a horn lanced through the air.

A flock of crows launched from the bare trees. Out of the maw of the forest, a white shape bloomed—a rider streaking toward them at breakneck speed. A dozen more trailed him, fanning out in perfect formation.

Warwick placed his hands behind his back, standing tall in the face of the charge. Caine mirrored him, and Theodosia observed with eyes flown wide.

Moments later, the rider arrived, skidding to a halt some ten paces ahead of them. His horse reared. The rider, his face obscured by his white hood, calmed it with a few foreign words. The language was rough, yet musical. The rider dismounted and swiped back his hood.

Caine lost his breath.

Her skin was nearly translucent. Her white-blond hair was woven into a frayed crown braid. Her hooded eyes were as cold as the Faeyenval Sea. She was clad entirely in white from her cloak to her boots and was staring at Caine with venom that could sear skin from bone.

Gods, she was beautiful.

"Holy shit," Theodosia whispered.

Clutching at poise, Caine offered a shallow bow.

"Queen Ila," he began. "I'm honored to make your acquaintance. My name is Prince Caine. I—"

"My horse, Ailo," she cut in. Her accent was coarse, though not unpleasant. Her tone, however, was razor-sharp. "He will need water and rest, as will the other horses."

Nice to meet you, too, Caine thought sourly.

His irritation was doused as he beheld the riders behind her. Vaettirin warriors, straight from the legends. Caine counted seven men and five women. They were dressed in wool and pelts decorated with ornaments of metal and bone. Most were blond and fair like their queen, though some had shiny dark hair and cool olive skin. Their clothing was far more vibrant than that of their white-clad leader, but their expressions matched hers, stitched with loathing.

"Of course." Caine raised his hand, and a stable boy scurried out from behind the Skysteel Guard. The prince clapped a hand to his bony shoulder. "Please assist Queen Ila with her horse."

"Yes, sir."

Ila smiled like snow melting off a mountainside and leaned down toward the boy. "It has been a long journey. Please ensure he is well cared for. Can you do that for me?"

The boy bobbed his head eagerly and began to lead Ailo toward the stables. Ila watched him depart with natural fondness.

Caine cleared his throat. "You ride well."

Ila returned her attention to him, her expression snapping into a frown. "For a woman, you mean?"

"For anyone."

"I like your knife."

Every eye found Theodosia, who seemed to have lost the war against her own impulsivity. Caine looked to the sheathed blade at Ila's belt. What he presumed were Vaettirin runes were stamped into the leather.

"Thank you." The queen laid a gloved hand atop the hilt. "It belonged to my brother."

"Can you use it?"

"Theo," Caine warned quietly.

Ila observed the princess with waxing interest. "Well enough."

"Could you teach me?" Theodosia asked, now somewhat breathless. "We're to be sisters, after all."

"Sisters," Ila repeated distantly, her arm falling to her side.

"Queen Ila."

The little color Ila had bled from her cheeks as she turned to face King Warwick, her body taut as a bowstring. She did not so much as nod or curtsy. He offered nothing in return.

Tension sizzled between them, potent enough to make Caine itch.

"My deepest sympathies for the loss of your family," the king continued tonelessly.

Ila lifted her chin. "Thank you."

"I hope you will find peace here at Caer Sidi. I can assure you, there is no place like it in this world."

It might have been his imagination, but Caine could have

sworn he saw Ila stiffen. Warwick regarded her with a peculiar look, one the prince could not place. A wayward thought darted through his mind.

Do they know each other?

Before he could decipher their exchange, Ila switched her gaze to Caer Sidi. Caine followed her line of sight, twisting to look over his shoulder.

"Is it to your liking?" he asked.

Ila nodded curtly.

The castle truly was a sight to behold. Its twelve ivory towers were silhouetted against the rosy winter sky. In the spring, flowering vines would scale the walls. Now the battlements were only dotted with sentries. Caine could not see their eyes beneath their visors but knew every pair was trained on the mounted Vaettirin warriors.

"We are most grateful for your hospitality," Ila said, finally ripping her gaze from Caer Sidi.

Caine turned to face her again. "The pleasure is ours, Queen Ila."

He offered her his hand. She blinked at it mutely. For a split second, he wondered if she had any idea what to do with it. Then she placed her hand in his. He raised her gloved knuckles to his lips. Their eyes locked. Caine forced himself not to pull away as gooseflesh raised on his arms.

It was as if she saw straight through his skin to the very foundation of his soul.

He released her. She took a step back.

"It has been a long journey," Ila said. "I would like to rest before the feast."

"Of course," Caine answered. "I can show you to your chambers."

"That won't be necessary." Ila looked to Theodosia, who lit up like a beacon. "Perhaps your sister can accompany me."

Out of the corner of his eye, Caine saw his father jerk his chin at Thomas. The captain stepped from the ranks with a militant snap.

"It would be my honor to escort you both," he said with a gallant bow.

Ila dropped her chin abruptly as if to make herself smaller. Theodosia had other plans.

"The only thing we need protection from around here is boredom," she huffed, locking arms with Ila and tugging her off toward the castle. Thomas fell into step behind them, one hand on the pommel of his rapier.

A heavy *thwump* and stomping footfalls pulled Caine around in time to see one of the Vaettir, a man about his age with wild blond hair and prominent cheekbones, stalking after Ila and her minders. He locked eyes with Caine as he passed, staring down his nose as if the prince were some foul slug. Caine met his gaze unflinchingly despite the tensing of his stomach.

The Skysteel Guard moved to block the man from going any farther, but Warwick made a dismissive gesture with his hand.

"Let him go. He has no power here."

He spoke loud enough to let the words float over to the remaining Vaettir, who shifted on their mounts.

But as Caine watched Ila recede across the lawn, a brilliant speck against the drab landscape, he could not help but wonder who would have power over whom.

8

Ila

Ila was not sure what she had expected.

Perhaps a towering monstrosity with guts in his teeth or a demon with smoldering red eyes. Para Warwick was unnervingly human down to the age lines bunched around his mouth and the gray in his hair.

Plenty of dream beings appeared human on the outside, but they could not hide the fabric of their souls from a weaver. The souls of all dream beings were knit with the silver threads of the Reverie.

But when Ila called on her weaver sight to view the Para, his threads were golden.

Human.

The same was true of Prince Caine and Princess Theodosia. The children of a para and a human should have glowed white as a product of two realms, but both were stitched with gold. Worse, she would be lying if she said she did not find her betrothed handsome. Loose chestnut curls, bright eyes caught between green and blue, a little on the skinny side, but not scrawny.

And no doubt just as abhorrent as his father.

There is no place like it in this *world.*

A new brand of fear shivered through Ila as Theodosia led her through the brilliant halls of Caer Sidi. She turned the Para's words over and over in her mind like a strange coin. Was it a slip of the tongue? Had he meant to say *the* world? Was it a mistake, the result of his darting back and forth between the Reverie and the Wake with such regularity? Or was he gauging her reaction to the subtle implications of those two little words?

"Sorry."

Ila glanced at Theodosia as they continued to walk arm in arm. She was a lanky thing in her early teenage years with dark hair and round gray eyes. Despite her being the daughter of a para, there was something charming about her breathless eagerness.

"Sorry?" Ila repeated blankly.

Theodosia grimaced, releasing her elbow. "I thought you would be...different. I said some nasty things about you before you got here."

"I see."

Ila tossed a glance at Nils over her shoulder and immediately wished she had not. Her guardian tailed her from several paces back, his hand twitching for the axe the sentries at the entrance had relieved him of.

Beside him, tall and dignified in his obsidian armor, was the captain of the Skysteel Guard. The very man who had watched her split open the sky then dive over a cliff less than a fortnight ago.

The captain caught her eye and offered a reserved, though not unkind smile. Ila twisted around again, her insides knotting.

It was dark, she chanted to herself. *My hair was dyed. My head was covered. He cannot know.*

"Are you all right?" Theodosia inquired, her brow crumpling with what appeared to be genuine concern.

"Yes," Ila answered too quickly. "Fine."

"You're really pretty, by the way. Could you teach me how to do my hair like that?"

Ila lifted an absent hand to her circuit braid. It was far less intricate than the ones her mother used to weave, but it served her well enough.

"Perhaps."

"You don't want to be here, do you?" Theodosia spoke with that matter-of-fact cadence that came with childhood.

It reminded her of Saoirse so much that it made her chest ache.

"I am grateful for a chance at peace between our kingdoms," the weaver replied.

The princess sighed. "How political."

They retreated into mutual silence, the footfalls of their guards dogging them. For the first time, Ila allowed herself to soak in Caer Sidi.

The weavers had told her of echopoints, exceptionally rare mirror image places that existed in both the Reverie and the Wake, but she had never seen one until now.

This Caer Sidi was built of sugar-white stone. Its counterpart in the Reverie was said to be carved of volcanic rock.

The corridors were flanked with marble statues of dead nobility, loping garlands, and tapestries depicting heroic battles. Ila wondered what images adorned the walls of the castle in the dream realm. The heads of the Para's enemies, perhaps? That seemed the most likely option.

This Caer Sidi, at least, was beautiful. That only made Ila hate it more.

"Here we are," Theodosia announced.

They had arrived in a thoroughfare lined with broad windows and heavy oak doors. Golden sunlight tumbled through the glass, casting shifting patterns on the floor. The captain stepped around Ila and Theodosia and approached the nearest door, opening it and standing aside to allow them passage.

Ila hesitated. Sensing her anxiety, Nils stepped up to stand beside her.

"Liv tel lien?" he mumbled.

"Apologies, Queen Ila." Ila felt her blood run cold as she turned to the captain, but to her surprise she found him looking rather uncomfortable, more like a messenger with awkward tidings than a deadly soldier. "King Warwick respectfully requests you speak the common language within the walls of Caer Sidi."

Nils let out what could only be described as a growl while Theodosia scoffed indignantly.

"What is your name, sir?" Ila asked the captain, using his embarrassment as a foothold.

"Captain Thomas Hendricks at your service, Your Majesty."

"Thank you for your kind escort, Captain Hendricks."

This time, his smile crinkled the corners of his brown eyes, and Ila knew he did not recognize her. The kernel of relief gave her the courage to enter her new chambers, and she did so with her head held high.

The room was larger than the entirety of her home in Galesborough. A vaulted window overlooking the grounds stood beside a sprawling bed with rich sapphire hangings. Opposite the bed was a pair of armchairs and a roaring hearth. The crest of House Fallon hung above the mantel, and fresh flowers had been placed on the table.

Nils began to pace the perimeter of the room. Ila let him, knowing it would calm him to ensure there were no lurking adversaries.

"Your room is bigger than mine," Theodosia proclaimed as she strode in, gazing around with her hands on her hips.

Ila began to unlace her cloak, unsure how to respond or how to tell this girl she wished to be alone.

"Are you a witch?"

The weaver snapped her eyes to Theodosia, keenly aware of Thomas watching from the doorway. Thankfully, the captain looked as if he was battling the urge to disparage the princess for her outburst.

"Excuse me?" Ila asked, praying she had injected the appropriate amount of reproach into her tone.

The princess went white. "Never mind. Nice to meet you."

Ila opened her mouth, but Theodosia had already scampered away, ducking past Thomas and disappearing into the hall. Charged silence lingered in her wake, made worse by the captain lingering in the doorway.

"You're not to leave me alone, are you?" Ila inquired.

"I will be right outside, Your Majesty."

Nils crossed his arms, leaning against the bedpost to size him up through narrowed eyes. "How welcoming."

"Enough, Nils," Ila muttered.

When the Skysteel Guard cornered her on that clifftop, they called her *witch* and ordered her to hand over the child. It stood to reason they had believed they were doing a good deed, rescuing an innocent child from the clutches of evil, and that they knew nothing of the Reverie or the true nature of their king.

Besides, it was not *his* fault she had been forced into this marriage.

"There is a bell at your bedside. You may ring it for assistance day or night," Thomas said, gesturing to the braided velvet cord hanging beside the bed. "My mother is in charge of the staff; she will ensure your comfort." He looked to Nils, clearly sizing him up. "There are quarters for your guards in the servants' wing. I'll call someone to escort you."

"No," Nils said tersely.

"I can't leave you alone in a room with the future Queen of Wolfhelm," Thomas replied, irritation pricking his tone.

"Nils is my guardian," Ila answered, calling on the tact her mother had impressed upon her. "Measures have been taken to ensure he cannot defile me."

"Ah." Nils turned red, then a worrying shade of plum as Thomas dropped his eyes to his crotch and grimaced empathetically. "I will leave you to settle in, then. Your Majesty."

Thomas departed, shutting the door behind him. He did

not lock it, but perhaps there was no need. Where could she run?

Ila turned to face the bed, unbuttoning her vest and folding it atop her cloak. Nils approached the opposite side of the mattress, fuming.

"Did I miss someone cutting off my balls, or were you planning to do the honor yourself?" he spat.

"If they think you a eunuch, we can be together in private," she explained patiently. "These people are obsessed with virtue."

"I am *not* a eunuch."

Ila snorted. "I am well aware."

"But—"

"I have far greater concerns than your bruised ego."

At once Nils became solemn, his face darkening like a curtain pulled across the sky. "Do you have a plan to save your friend?"

"Saoirse," Ila said quietly.

"Do you have a plan?" Nils pressed.

"No." Standing abruptly became overwhelming, and she sank onto the lip of the bed. Hoste, the coverlet was so soft and smooth it was almost cool to the touch. "But there is something you can do for me."

Nils rounded the bed to face her. "Anything."

"I need you to spy on Prince Caine."

A loaded pause as he considered. A log snapped on the fireplace, sending up a plume of sparks and smoke.

"What does he have to do with the girl?" he inquired, spitting out the word *he* like bile.

Ila hesitated on the precipice, chewing the inside of her cheek. How was she to explain that she was a weaver who walked between worlds, that King Warwick was a night terror, that he was the one holding Saoirse hostage, and her betrothed might be involved?

"It is better for now that you know as little as possible."

Nils frowned. "How can I help if I do not know what to look for?"

"Look for suspicious behavior, things you can't explain."

"Things I can't explain?" Nils repeated, his nostrils flaring with frustration. "What the hells does that mean?"

"Look for anything that presents a threat to me," Ila snapped. "I need to know if he is dangerous before…"

The words caught in her throat. Images of her future swelled in her mind. A cold ceremony in this opulent cage surrounded by strangers, the prince sweating over her, thrusting into her once their vows were sworn at the altar of a god that was neither Vaettirin nor weaver. She fisted the comforter, fighting nausea.

"Please, min liern," she begged Nils in a rasping voice.

His eyes softened, his voice dipping low as he spoke. "I will not fail you."

And despite everything, warmth flickered through Ila, because she knew he spoke true.

9

Alaric

Alaric was having a nightmare. He knew it was a nightmare because he had been here before, and it felt like he belonged. Oblivion surrounded him, filled him. He was alone. In dreams, he was always alone.

Until something was born of all the nothing.

They arrived one by one, forming a rippling circle around him in the pitch-dark. Their faces were blurry, their bodies vapor. He could hear them speaking but could never understand them.

He was not afraid of them. They could not hurt him.

He made damn sure of that.

The last of the apparitions drifted in, and the ring went still. Quiet. Crushingly quiet. Alaric held his breath, waiting.

"Good somnia, brother."

A man had materialized before him. Unlike the apparitions, he was solid. Whole. His blond hair was unkempt, his eyes liquid gold. He carried no visible weapons, but Alaric knew better.

An easy grin lit his face, the sort only mortals wore.

"Luken," Alaric greeted him.

The dreambreaker stuck out his arm. Alaric knew what happened after they clasped hands. The same thing that happened every time he returned to this place. Still, he found himself reaching out. They grasped each other at the forearm.

"You look like shit," Luken said as they let go. "When was the last time you slept?"

"Ask them." Alaric jerked his chin at the horde of ghosts surrounding them. They radiated a sick sort of glee. They knew what happened next, too.

"Who are they?" Luken asked.

"You know who they are."

Luken scanned the faceless watchers. His smile was gone, like it had never existed in the first place.

"The people you killed." His gaze returned to Alaric. It was empty. "Why am I not among them?"

The nightmare did not answer.

"Do you think you're innocent just because you did not wield the blade?" A sneer warped his features.

"You chose to leave the rebellion," Alaric reminded him, but there was no fire behind the words.

"What about your choice? I asked you for aid before I left. You could have helped me."

"Morthil had just run off," Alaric shot back. "And you expected me to help you abandon the rebellion, everything we fought for, for some girl?"

Luken shook his head pityingly.

"A 'mare could never understand. You only understand violence. I should have known that from the start."

Again, Alaric held his tongue. This was not the real Luken. The dreambreaker had never judged him for his origins—or anyone for that matter.

Still, each word from the lips of his likeness was a kick to the teeth.

"Go on, then."

Luken reached behind his back and pulled a slim blade from the blackness. He tossed it to Alaric, who caught it by the handle on instinct. The specters drew closer with a vicious jeer, eager to watch what happened next.

"No more blaming Morthil or Warwick," Luken said. "Finish it properly."

Alaric cast the blade aside. Instead of clanging against the ground, it slipped into the void.

"I won't," he growled.

"But you do. Every time."

A glint of silver caught the corner of his eye. Alaric looked down to find the blade clenched in his fist again. A calloused hand shot out and snatched him by the wrist. He lurched back, but Luken anchored him in place.

"Do it," the dreambreaker snarled.

"No."

"Stop fighting your nature." Luken brought the tip of the blade to his chest. A thin trail of blood oozed from his mortal skin, seeping into his white tunic. "You're a monster, Alaric. Act like it."

"You saved me because you thought I was more." The nightmare spoke through gritted teeth. His arms trembled with exertion as he fought to draw the blade away from Luken. The dreambreaker was so much stronger than him in this place. "You brought me to the rebellion because you saw the good in me."

"I was wrong."

Luken jerked the dagger forward, plunging it into his own heart. Alaric released the hilt with a shout and stumbled back. The apparitions keened and yowled with delight as Luken swayed on the spot. His mouth opened, and blood bubbled over his bottom lip.

"I—told you," he sputtered.

His eyes rolled back into his skull. Luken fell backward into oblivion, disappearing like a coin in dark water. Alaric screamed and grabbed for him, but he was too late.

He was always too late.

The apparitions flew at him on the wings of an otherworldly screech, and—

Alaric jolted awake. His magic thundered in his chest, so loud he feared it could be heard all the way in Black Root.

He sat up in bed and squinted around the plain little room. Mica slept peacefully on the opposite side of the mattress, her hair wrapped in a soft yellow scarf. He pressed the heels of his hands to his aching eyes, drawing colors from the black.

"The nightmare again?"

Alaric dropped his arms to see Mica sitting up in bed. Though hooded with sleepiness, her eyes were embers in the semidarkness.

"No," he answered.

Mica gave him a sour look. "Why do you bother lying to me? You know I can hear your heartbeat."

Well, at least she could not hear the din his magic was making.

"Slow learner, I guess."

"Luken freed you from Para Warwick for a reason, Alaric,"

Mica told him, her expression softening. "He would not want you to waste your time feeling guilty for something that was not your fault."

"Where do you think they go?"

Mica cocked her head to the side. "What?"

Alaric shifted on the straw mattress to face her fully. "Humans dream us in the Wake. We manifest in the Reverie. What about our dreams? Where do the dreams of dream beings go?"

Mica studied him in the red moonlight streaming through the partially curtained window. She looked troubled.

"No one knows, Alaric."

Thud.

Alaric was on his feet in an instant. Mica whipped her head toward the door.

He raised a finger at her and called a bolt of energy to his hand. He padded over to the door on the balls of his feet. Mica slipped off the bed, putting her back to the whitewashed wall.

With a steadying breath, Alaric raised his weapon and jerked open the door.

A plump girl with a birthmark on her cheek leaped back, bracing herself against the banister.

Alaric relaxed his fist. The conjured spear dissolved in a shower of sparks.

"What is it?" he asked.

"Soldiers," she squeaked. "Close. We must hide you."

Mica appeared beside Alaric, wrapping a shawl around her shoulders. "Lead the way."

The girl scampered away in stocking feet, beckoning them

to follow her down the stairs to the dining room. The rebels exchanged a glance and went after her. The dining room was dark save for the sheets of light coming through the slatted kitchen doors. The girl burst through them, holding one open to allow Alaric and Mica through.

Thud.

Sweet hot air washed over Alaric as he passed into the kitchen. He caught a glimpse of copper pots simmering on the stove and dried herbs hanging from the ceiling before he noticed Morthil crouched in the corner.

A slab of stone had been pushed aside to reveal a hole in the floor. Wooden steps descended into darkness.

"Get in," Morthil ordered.

Mica complied at once, touching his shoulder before plunging into the cellar. Alaric lingered at the top of the stairs.

"These are not just vexes," he warned Morthil in a low tone. "They have a 'mare with them. I felt it." He tapped his sternum with two fingers. "Let me take him out before he gets here."

Morthil smiled, so fleeting Alaric wondered if he had imagined it.

"Bravery and recklessness are a lethal combination, youngling. I have seven kips and a luminae in my care. I can't risk them. This must be handled with precision, not brute force." Morthil rose from his crouch, an unfortunate reminder of his substantial height. "Get in the cellar. I won't ask again."

Deafening knocking rattled the foundation of the inn. The kip girl, who Alaric had all but forgotten, let out a whimper. Morthil stepped around Alaric and crossed to her at once.

"Laurel," he said calmly. "See that the cellar entrance is covered, then go to your room." He pressed a kiss to her reddish hair. "I won't let them harm you. Do you understand?"

"Y-yes."

Another round of ruthless knocking. A voice followed, rough, male, and unfamiliar to Alaric.

"In the name of Para Warwick, Lord of the Reverie, King of the Wake, I demand you to open this door."

Thud.

"Alaric!" Mica whispered shrilly from halfway down the cellar steps. Her eyes were wild with panic, knifing through the dark. "Come on!"

"Morthil," Alaric said, ignoring her. "I'm sorry."

The ancient luminae clapped him on the shoulder. "Another time, brother."

Alaric nodded once, then followed Mica down the rickety stairs. The stone was shoved into place over the hatch, and they were plunged into absolute darkness.

☽○☾

"Can you hear anything?"

"Not if you keep talking."

Mica sat cross-legged on one of the two cots in the cellar, eyes closed and ears poking out from the folds of her scarf. The candle on the bedside table cast quivering shadows across her face and the earthen walls.

Alaric slumped in the chair across from her, useless. His hearing was better than the average kip's, but there were at least ten feet of earth between them and the inn, not to mention the crate Laurel had shoved over the entrance to the cellar.

His magic sputtered and whirred in his chest, alerting him to the threat upstairs. Such warnings were not especially helpful at times like these when there was nothing he could do except wait.

"They're inside," Mica muttered. Alaric held his breath as she screwed up her brow. "Morthil is talking to them."

"How many are there?"

"Shhh."

Alaric bit the inside of his cheek. Mica flexed her fingers and then curled them into fists, a nervous habit.

"They're asking him about his connections to the rebellion." Her lashes fluttered. "They're searching for someone."

"Who?"

Mica just shook her head.

"A woman is speaking. She sounds angry." Mica opened her eyes. "Nightstrider?"

"No, I don't think so."

The warnings Alaric received from his magic were rarely specific. They did not distinguish between threats, only alerted him that there *was* a threat. But when Nightstrider flew over them in the Tanglewood, something was different. The signature of the nightmare upstairs was formidable, but it paled in comparison to hers.

Nightstrider was in a category of her own.

"Oh gods..."

Alaric snapped his attention back to Mica. The luminae was staring at him, terror warping her features.

"What?"

"Alaric, they're asking about a rebel 'mare."

A distant crash rang out, the soldiers destroying the dining room. Alaric lurched to his feet, a crackling shard of magic already in hand.

"Alaric," Mica whispered shrilly. "Sit down."

"But—"

"Shut up and listen to me!" Mica popped to her feet and jumped in front of him, her hands raised like she was calming a rabid dog. "They don't know who the 'mare is, but if you go up there with that thing..." She jabbed a finger at the conjured weapon in his hand. "They will."

Shit. She was right.

"Fine." Alaric made a show of letting the bolt of magic disintegrate. "What are they saying now?"

Mica shut her eyes again, concentrating. He waited on the edge of a razor.

"The vexes are searching the rooms. The woman is staying with Morthil." Mica furrowed her brow. "Wait—"

A terrible scream lanced through the quiet, echoing despite the thick layer of dirt and stone between them.

Morthil.

Alaric gritted his teeth, reeling against the urge to charge up the steps and burst through the cellar door. His horns alone could shatter the stone, and the vexes would drop like mayflies to his hands. He would not even need magic to take them down.

The other nightmare, though...

"I don't understand." Mica opened her eyes, tears blooming

in their corners. "They're not fighting, but Morthil is in so much pain."

Icy dread flooded Alaric's stomach. He should have known. If Nightstrider was at Caer Sidi, there was only one nightmare Para Warwick would trust for a mission like this.

Souldrinker.

The last time Alaric saw Ondine was over two decades ago. The two of them were among the first nightmares Para Warwick created, and for a time, they were close as kin. She was the last person he spoke to before leaving Caer Sidi for good.

He'd been her only friend.

Another scream, louder this time. Mica covered her mouth with her hands, horror eclipsing her face.

"She won't kill him." Alaric could scarcely hear his own voice over the ringing in his ears. "It would ruin her fun."

He had never been on the receiving end of her strange magic, but he had seen it in action more times than he could count. When insurgents were brought to Caer Sidi for interrogation, he and Ondine were the first to see them.

Alaric tortured their bodies. Ondine tortured their minds.

Mica inhaled sharply.

"What is it?" Alaric demanded.

"Someone is in the kitchen."

"Get behind me."

Mica complied. He could feel her breath scraping his back as he snuffed their only candle. The chilling crunch of wood scraping stone came out of the black. Someone was moving the crate. The cellar door blended with the floor, Alaric reminded himself.

But would it be enough?

"They're just standing there," Mica said in a near whimper.

Alaric pivoted on his back foot to brace himself and raised both hands with his palms facing the stairs. He called on the well of power at his core, drawing it to his hands. His nerves crackled with concentrated energy as he prepared to blast whatever came down the stairs to the tenth hell.

Mica touched the space between his shoulder blades. "Wait. The woman called them. They're leaving."

Silence.

The sizzling heat in his veins dissolved. Mica plopped onto the nearest cot. Alaric sank down next to her, and she lay her head on his shoulder. He patted her leg awkwardly. Even after all this time, he was still not entirely comfortable with the casual closeness of most luminae, but he let her lean on him anyway.

Eventually, the telltale sound of stone grinding stone pulled them to their feet. Warm light flooded the cellar. Alaric squinted up the staircase. A silhouette blotted out the patch of light.

"They're gone," Laurel called softly. "Morthil, he needs help."

Mica leaped to her feet and took off up the stairs. She and Laurel disappeared, and a moment later, Alaric heard the squeak of the swinging kitchen doors. He sat in silence for a while, thoughts churning.

He had always known there would come a day when word of a nightmare fighting for the rebellion alongside luminae and kips would reach Para Warwick. In fact, he was surprised it had taken this long.

Now Ondine was stalking him, and sooner or later, she would know who it was she hunted. She would know that the Para had not, in fact, razed her old friend to ash.

Alaric rose from the cot and trudged up the stairs with leaden limbs. When he reached the dining room, he was surprised to find it full of flustered guests in their nightclothes.

He was less surprised to find it partially destroyed.

Kips and a handful of luminae were clustered around the remaining upright tables. They spoke in hushed tones and clasped steaming-hot drinks. Scattered about were the splintered remains of the furniture Ondine and her vexes had demolished.

A dream being with the body of a kip and a head that could only be described as a knot of green tentacles with a beak stood behind the bar talking to a luminae who resembled a satyr. He turned his slimy, writhing head toward Alaric and jerked it at the door to the left.

The nightmare stepped over a broken chair to knock on the door. It opened as soon as his knuckles graced the wood.

"Come in." Laurel beckoned. She was still pallid but seemed to have mastered her fear. "Quickly."

Alaric followed her into a bedroom with paneled walls draped in silks, muted light, and a low ceiling. Morthil sat on the edge of his bed, his head in his hands, a quilt wrapped around his slender shoulders. The air around him shivered like a mirage. Mica was perched beside him. She rubbed his back in steady circles, her expression pinched with worry.

"There is nothing wrong with him physically," she told them as Alaric shut and locked the door.

"It isn't that kind of injury," Alaric explained. "Souldrinker tortures the mind, not the body."

Mica inhaled sharply. "Souldrinker?"

"Yes."

Mica, Laurel, and Alaric stilled when Morthil spoke. His voice, usually characterized by a surreal echo, was flat and dissonant. He lifted his head from his hands. His eyes flashed between blue and white, sputtering like failing flames.

"What did she do to you?" Mica asked, cupping the back of his neck with a gentle palm.

"Never mind that." Morthil put his hands on his knees and rose with a grunt. Mica steadied him by the elbow. "Para Warwick knows a 'mare is working with the rebellion."

"We heard," Alaric replied, folding his arms across his chest. "They don't know it's me, right?"

"Not yet."

Relief flickered through Alaric. It guttered almost at once. "Who the hells tipped them off?"

"I told you coming to Black Root was a bad idea," Mica muttered, nailing him with a brittle stare. "Someone probably recognized you."

"The very concept of a 'mare working alongside kips and luminae is a threat to Para Warwick's reign," Morthil broke in. "Even if you were not his creation, he would have you hunted off the edge of the Reverie."

Alaric nodded.

Para Warwick relied on fostering the division between dream beings and the hierarchy that placed nightmares at the top. It had been this way since before Alaric manifested, and he doubted it would change anytime soon.

"We have to get you back to base," Mica said. "You need to lay low."

"No, we're not leaving until we have the dreambreaker."

Alaric cut his gaze to Morthil. Though his eyes had stopped flickering blue, he still looked in desperate need of a drink. "Any word from your weaver?"

Morthil shook his head. It seemed the simple movement made him ill. "No, though I'm sure she is not pleased with me."

Alaric raised a brow. "Why?"

"She distrusts the rebellion. She won't be happy I involved you."

"She will be when we get her kid out of Caer Sidi."

"I'm afraid I have not made things easier for you in that regard," Morthil said with an apologetic wince. "I warded her vessel against nightmares. Touching it could kill you, Alaric. Mica will have to carry it."

Alaric grunted. *Just what we need, another complication.*

"You must move quickly," the male luminae continued. "My wards will keep Warwick out, but she cannot survive in there forever."

"Does she have a name?" Mica asked.

"If she does, I do not know it."

"The poor thing," she whispered, ears flattening against her silk scarf. "She must be terrified, all alone in the dark."

"How do we get the box open once we have it?" Alaric cut in.

"Only Ila knows the password," Morthil replied. "Send a fire message when you have the girl, and I will contact her."

Alaric nodded gravely, the gears of his mind whirring. "How much longer can she survive in there?"

"I'm not certain. It could be days or weeks."

"Then there's no time to waste." Alaric set his eyes on Mica.

She swallowed, the skin of her throat rippling in the low light. "We're getting her out of the castle tomorrow night."

"What if Solene isn't ready?" Mica asked.

"She isn't, but we're not losing another dreambreaker to Para Warwick."

10
Wren

Wren spent a half hour cleaning her anchor burn with a bottle of whiskey and a rag. The cut on her cheekbone and the black eye would heal by morning. The burn would linger for the rest of her days.

She used a mirror to guide her hand. The wound was just under her right shoulder blade. She had to extend her wings fully to get at it. It was roughly the size of an apple, jet-black with jagged edges. Though smaller than the one stretched across her abdomen and chest, it was just as painful.

One shattered bottle of whiskey and three soiled rags later, Wren gave up and slipped on a fresh tunic. Despite the dull roar of agony, she was brimming with chaotic energy. She left the mess for someone else to sweep up and stalked from her bedroom, slamming the door on her way out.

There were many ways to blow off steam. Hacking her enemies to bits was one of them. Sex also worked, but if Wren knew anything about Ondine and her ability to hold a grudge, she would not be partaking anytime soon.

Training was the next best thing.

Wren moved through the castle with her eyes trained dead ahead. Kips and vexes alike skittered out of her way. She ignored them all.

She smelled the training hall before she saw it: sweat, blood, and rage. Wren ducked inside as a vex slammed his opponent into the wall to shouts of approval.

Clusters of vexes dotted the expansive room, their pungent stench overwhelming. Leather mats were laid out across the floor, and an armory of steel racks on the far side of the space held every weapon imaginable. There were no windows, but many torches lined the walls, bathing everything in a shuddering glow. The whole place looked like it had not been scrubbed clean in decades, which might have been true.

"Nightstrider."

Silence as thick as sap drowned the room. Sparring matches were abandoned as dozens of vexes scrambled to salute Wren.

"At ease," she muttered.

The vexes returned to their matches with amplified fervor, fighting for approval she would never deign to give them. Dust shook from the ceiling as a man with the head of a bull threw a vex covered in some sort of putrid green fungus to the ground.

Wren started across the room with her shoulders squared. She used to relish the mixture of fear and awe the soldiers regarded her with. Now she just found it irritating.

She reached the armory and began to browse the selection of weapons. Calm settled over her as she perused the gleaming instruments. Weapons did not tend to beat or betray her, she found.

A slender blade caught her eye. She plucked it from the rack to test the balance.

A chill scampered down her back. Wren spun, poised to stab whoever thought it wise to sneak up on her.

"Nice eye, Nightstrider."

"Spineripper." Wren lowered her blade, her lip curling in distaste. "You're supposed to be in Ironmoor."

"Don't sound so disappointed."

Spineripper could pass for a kip in his forties at first glance, but she could smell the darkness lurking in his bones. He was one of the few nightmares Para Warwick employed that he did not create personally.

A bounty hunter by trade, Spineripper and his band of mercenaries came and went as he pleased, something he reminded Wren of at any opportunity.

"We finished up early," he drawled, leaning against the nearest rack. "Thought I'd come see what my favorite flying cunt was up to."

Wren shouldered past him and swore when he materialized in front of her with a faint *pop*.

"Stop doing that," she snapped. Spineripper possessed the ability to disappear and reappear a short distance away. He was not nearly as powerful as Para Warwick in that regard—the Para could travel vast distances in a heartbeat—but it did make him even more of a nuisance.

Wren tried to step around him again, but Spineripper gripped her by the arm.

"Let me go."

"I take it you're the reason Para Warwick is in such a bad mood." His breath smelled of ale and something rotten.

Probably his personality, Wren thought.

"What did you do this time?" Spineripper pressed.

"Fuck off."

"I was going to talk to him about a raise, but maybe I'll hold off. I'm not looking to become his new punching bag."

Wren knocked his hand away and jabbed the blade under his stubbly chin. The vexes nearest to them froze. Spineripper clucked admonishingly.

"You know what your problem is, kid?" he asked. "You can't take a joke."

"Jokes are supposed to be funny."

"And the 'mares of Caer Sidi are supposed to be disciplined, but here you are, falling from favor."

Wren flicked her eyes to their audience, which had tripled in size. Another *pop* and Spineripper disappeared. She jammed her elbow back on instinct. It nailed him in the gut as he rematerialized behind her. He doubled over as the breath whooshed out of him.

Wren took him by his oily blond hair and rammed her knee into his nose. He stumbled with a gurgling curse.

The vexes looked on, silent as trees.

"Out," Wren barked at them.

There was a great clamoring as the vexes obeyed, shuffling over the leather mats and out the door in a horde.

"Did you need something, or were you just trying to get a

rise out of me?" Wren asked Spineripper as the last of the soldiers trickled out.

The bounty hunter grinned up at her, pinching his gushing nose. "Gods, you're beautiful when you're angry." Wren started to walk away, but he sprang to his feet and caught her by the bicep again. "Easy, kid. I just wanted to pick your brain."

"You should have opened with that."

"Please, I could smell your temper across the room. I know better than to talk to you when you're like that."

Wren jerked her arm from his grip again. His bloody fingerprints smeared across her skin. "So you *were* trying to get a rise out of me. Was it worth it?"

Spineripper took the skewed bridge of his nose between his thumb and forefinger and locked it back in place with a crunch and a groan.

"A small price for the right information," he said thickly.

"Masochist."

"Funny, I usually get the opposite."

"What do you want?"

Spineripper leaned against a shelf stacked with leather gauntlets and helmets, blood still oozing from his nostrils. If he felt the pain, he was doing an excellent job masking it.

"In all your contact with the rebels," Spineripper began, "have you ever come across any weavers?"

"What the hells is a weaver?"

"You know, that order of human women with some sort of power over the Boundary. Sanctimonious as luminae, the lot of them. One of them is supposedly working with the rebellion. The Para wants her found."

"Is this some sort of joke?" Wren growled, glancing toward the door to make sure no vexes were lingering. This was not the sort of conversation she wanted anyone to overhear. "Para Warwick is the only one who can cross the Boundary."

Spineripper wiped his upper lip with his sleeve. He sneered, his already disgusting teeth stained with ribbons of blood. "I see. Clearly, this was a mistake."

This time Wren caught him by the arm before he could depart. She wheeled him around and drew him down to her level by the front of his tunic.

"What are you talking about?"

"Forget it. If the Para wanted you to know, he would have told you by now."

Wren clenched her jaw and thought hard. Para Warwick had never even uttered the word *weavers* to her.

"Interesting," he purred. His lips twitched when his eyes dropped to the scar that peeked over the neckline of her shirt. "As I said, discipline."

She released Spineripper, revolted and prickling with rage. "Like you know anything about discipline."

"I'm not the Hand of the Para." Spineripper prodded her in the sternum with a slick finger. "And if you're not careful, you won't be, either."

"Is that a threat?"

"A promise."

The abrupt soberness in his voice set her nerves on fire.

"There's something else," she said. "Something you aren't telling me."

Spineripper shrugged. "Maybe."

"You're a fucking bastard."

He grinned, a bloody conniving thing that made him look every inch a nightmare. "Guilty."

Pop.

Spineripper evaporated again. Wren cursed at the dully gleaming flecks of blood he left behind on the floor.

The silence in the training hall was deafening.

Wren grabbed the nearest knife and hurled it at the wall. It embedded itself in the stone with a crunch and a plume of dust. She stared at the still-vibrating hilt, thoughts humming.

Weavers.

Spineripper could be lying, of course, but what would he have to gain by crafting a fictional race of human women with power over the Boundary?

And if one of these *weavers* was working for the rebellion, the very organization Para Warwick had tasked her to bring down, why had he not told her?

11

Caine

The sustained buzz of celebration filled the hall, mingling with the aroma of heady wine. Caine could see everything from his seat at the high table. The blue and silver banners embroidered with their crest, the sow roasting on a spit, the chattering nobles and the servants in their pressed uniforms weaving between them.

The Vaettir had carved out a nook for themselves in the far corner. They still wore their vibrant winter clothes along with their deep scowls. Even ample drink was useless against their mistrust, not that Caine blamed them.

Queen Ila, seated next to Caine, had exchanged her riding clothes for an ornate wool dress with a flared skirt and a high collar. Tiny charms that reminded him of coins were stitched into the bodice, matching her earrings that appeared to be made of both pewter and bone. Her hair tumbled down her back like sea foam. She had not uttered a word since they sat down half an hour ago, and even then, her greeting was brief and brittle.

Caine cleared his throat. "How was your journey?"

Ila stabbed a seasoned potato with her fork. "Uneventful."

"Your chambers, are they to your liking?"

"Yes."

"How—"

Ila set down her utensils with a clatter. The guests nearest them fell silent. Caine shot them a placating smile.

"Your letter showed me who you are, Prince Caine," Ila said. "You need not pretend with me."

Caine took a bite of his food, mostly to buy time and avoid her penetrating gaze. "I assume you're referring to the proposal."

Ila snorted bitterly. "*A proposal.* Is that what you call it?"

"Well, what would you call it?"

The queen pursed her lips, her only response.

"My father wrote that letter," Caine continued. "I was not aware of it until it was already sent."

Ila picked up her fork and knife again and began to saw at the slab of pork on her plate. Its juices pooled on the polished face of the silver platter.

"Regardless," she said without looking at him. "I would request you not lie to me, at least about our arrangement. In return, I will not lie to you."

"I'm not lying. I want to get to know you."

Ila sniffed, raising her crystal goblet to her lips. The wine rippled, sloshing against the walls of the vessel.

She was trembling, Caine realized with a pang.

"Ila," he said quietly, shifting toward her. Her eyes flashed to his. Now he glimpsed the fear lurking behind the malice. "I have no more choice in this than you."

"Is that so? Are the lives of *your* people at stake?"

Shit.

So that's what was in the letter.

"My father can be harsh, but he is also reasonable. No harm will come to you or your people as long as you are by my side."

Ila impaled a chunk of meat on her fork. Instead of eating it, she examined it with glassy eyes.

"How many rulers has he promised the same before taking their heads?" she inquired flatly.

"Keep your voice down." The prince tossed a wary glance at his father, who sat only a few feet away. Thankfully, Warwick was deep in conversation with a dignitary from Sandmere.

"I thought you said I was safe."

"I can't protect you from yourself," Caine warned through his teeth. "So please, do us both a favor and shut up."

Ila blinked. An ounce of ire drained from her stormy eyes. Caine leaned toward her, and to his surprise, she did not pull away.

"My father could raze Galesborough to the ground if he wanted to, but he chose diplomacy."

The queen made a strained noise close to a laugh. "How courteous."

"I expect you to show me the same respect I extend to you."

Caine studied Ila in the drunken glow of the party. The skin around her eyes was pink. He wondered if she had been crying.

"I have known men of Wolfhelm before," she finally spoke. "Killers and conquerors with fragile egos where their consciences should be."

Caine felt a flush spread from his neck to his face. "I'm not like that."

"Men who feel the need to say that usually are."

"You can't speak to me like that," Caine said, his voice low and tense. "Not in public."

"Is that so?"

"Yes." He tossed another fleeting glance at his father, who was still occupied with the dignitary. "We have appearances to keep up."

"Appearances?" Ila sniffed in distaste. "Such as?"

"Such as you being a grateful, dutiful bride." Anger flared in her eyes, but Caine was not finished. "I don't expect you to feel that way, but things will go a lot smoother for both of us if you could just pretend while we're in public."

Ila swiped the silk napkin from her lap and threw it down on the table.

"You just proved me right," she whispered in his ear.

Before Caine could cobble together a retort, Ila shoved back her chair with a screech of wood on stone and swept away, the little charms on her dress tinkling like sleigh bells as she moved. Silence rolled over the room as every head swiveled to follow her progress.

Caine locked eyes with Theodosia, who was seated at one of the lower tables with a few of her friends. She mouthed a word at him that looked suspiciously like *witch*.

The prince was about to mouth *Shut up*, but then he caught sight of his father. Thunder roiled beneath the king's calm visage.

"She was feeling ill," Caine told him, loud enough to cut

through the critical drone rising around them. "I'll check on her."

The prince popped to his feet and started after Ila. His father caught him by the arm as he passed. His fingers were a vise.

"Keep her on a tight leash, boy," he muttered. "She belongs to you."

Caine nodded reflexively. His body was oddly distant as he jogged after Ila, who had disappeared through the side door. Passing into the dim corridor, he looked left and right.

"Ila!"

The queen jerked to a halt. Moonlight poured through the windows, giving a luminous quality.

"What do you want?" Her words wobbled like loose wheels.

The heat and noise from the feast dissipated as he approached. "I told you, I want to get to know you."

Ila rounded on Caine. It was not hard to imagine where the rumors of her witchcraft originated. She was ethereal, otherworldly.

"This isn't ideal for either of us," he went on. "But we're here now. We might as well make the best of it."

Caine extended his hand, praying it was not slick with flop sweat. Ila stared at it, something like uncertainty kindling in her eyes.

"You're being genuine." She spoke as if she could not quite believe what she was saying, a notch of confusion between her brows.

"I am," Caine confirmed.

She folded her arms, but her posture did not imply a challenge. It was as if she hugged herself in the face of a bitter wind. She still did not move to take his hand.

"You know I do not wish to be here," she said softly.

Caine finally dropped his arm, which was now somewhat stiff. "I know."

"You know I am not..." She swallowed, the faintest pink tingeing her cheeks.

"What?" he asked, cocking a brow. "Not a virgin? Neither am I."

Ila blinked. "I heard men of Wolfhelm find it distasteful when a woman is not untouched."

"Perhaps men who lack confidence."

Caine winced at his own crudeness, but to his shock Ila managed a brief laugh. The sound was like the faintest patter of rain on a glass roof.

"I don't know what you've heard about me, but I want you to know I've no intention of forcing myself on you."

"I...appreciate the sentiment." Ila took the smallest step toward him. Her stormy eyes were fixed on him with unnerving intensity. "You said you had no choice in this, that we are both trapped. Is there nothing you can do?"

Caine felt his expression harden along with his heart, which had been stirring against his better judgment. "I can't go against my father. Or my kingdom."

"Even if you believe it wrong to force my hand?"

"If it is for the good of our kingdoms, yes."

"The good of our kingdoms?" She let out a hollow, mirthless laugh that bounced down the empty corridor. "How in the name of Hoste does this benefit my kingdom save from staving off the wrath of yours?"

Caine bit his tongue. She was right and they both knew it.

Her shoulders sloped down as if she was wilting. Then her lip curled, and she took a generous step back.

"You may believe you are different, Prince Caine," Ila said quietly. "But in my experience, passivity is as deadly as any blade."

She spun on her heel and marched away, wading through pools of moonlight until she turned the corner. Her words echoed through Caine's mind long after she had disappeared.

12
Ila

Ila slammed the door to her chambers, kicking off her boots. One landed in the middle of the floor. The other disappeared under the bed. She crossed to the hearth in her stockings and dropped into one of the armchairs, resting her head in her hands.

It was nauseating, breaking bread with the monster holding Saoirse hostage. Warwick had all but ignored Ila for the duration of the feast, scarcely stooping to offer a nod when she arrived.

Caine was a different story entirely.

I don't know what you've heard about me, but I want you to know I've no intention of forcing myself on you.

It was a mercy she did not wish to appreciate, but she could not help it. The accounts she had heard of Wolfhelm's armies raping and butchering as they claimed new lands were enough to keep her awake at night, and no doubt they were true.

But that did not mean Caine was so cruel.

It did not mean he was her ally, either. No, he was her enemy, who at the very least sought to cage her and her kingdom.

Ila shook off the thought spiral. All that mattered was finding Saoirse and protecting Galesborough.

She raised her head and called on her weaver sight. The fabric of Caer Sidi unfurled around her. The threads of the echopoint were utterly unlike those of the Reverie and Wake. It was not silver or gold but white like the light of the Boundary. The threads seized with chaotic energy.

Just watching it made her sick.

Ila pushed past the queasiness and began to scan the castle from the top down. Individual nodes of life drifted through the pale meshwork. She sensed people, cats, mice, even a slumbering hound on the third floor. The feast was a bonfire of golden human souls.

Ila scanned all the way to the ground floor, then dove beneath the castle in her mind. To her surprise, a network of tunnels burrowed through the soil, culminating in a massive circular chamber deep beneath her feet.

A chill passed through her when she realized the chamber was completely devoid of life. Not even a lone spider scampered across the floor.

Strange, she thought distantly.

Ila allowed her weaver sight to dissolve.

Part of her had clung to the hope King Warwick had brought Saoirse back to the Wake for safekeeping. She had hoped she might save her without leaving the Wake, but Saoirse was not here, and the choice still hung over her like a blade.

Soft knocking pulled her to her feet. She went to the door and opened it cautiously. Her insides turned to slush.

"Good evening, Queen Ila. I'm sorry to disturb you, but I felt compelled to check on you personally."

"King Warwick," Ila greeted him, keeping her voice low so it did not shake. "I apologize for my sudden departure. I was weak from my travels."

Warwick was a portrait of humanity. Ruggedly handsome with age lines and sharp blue eyes. She would have preferred he manifested as a demon from the mouth of the hells.

Somehow, that was less unsettling.

"Are your chambers to your satisfaction?"

Ila had no choice but to stand aside as the Para swept across the threshold. She left the door wide open behind him.

"Yes," she answered. "I am most grateful for your hospitality."

Warwick rested a ringed hand on the armchair Ila had occupied only a moment ago.

"I would prefer you not pretend with me, Queen Ila."

Paranoia squeezed her chest like a pearl snake. The Para was engaged in another conversation when she asked the same courtesy of Caine. Had he overheard them? Had Caine told him what she said? Worse, had the Para invaded her mind?

Could he?

"Forgive me," Ila answered. "I'm not sure what you mean."

Warwick splayed his fingers before him, examining his rings. Gems the size of acorns glinted in their beds. A ruby, an emerald, and a pale sapphire.

"Do you know what these are?" he inquired.

"No."

"Gems from the crowns I have claimed. Veltspar." He

touched the emerald. "Rookrun." The ruby. "Mistrun." The sapphire. Warwick raised his eyes to hers. Ila willed her expression to remain cold, indifferent. "But Galesborough has no crown for me to claim."

"We have no need of such trinkets. If I recall, you yourself wear a crown of bone, not gold."

Warwick smiled, raising the hairs on her arms. "A tradition my ancestors would be devastated to see me abolish. Surely a daughter of Galesborough could understand the importance of tradition."

Ila did not respond.

"Besides, you have already given me something far more valuable than any jewel."

She felt her throat constrict as Warwick closed the gap between them and laid a hand on her shoulder. She resisted the urge to slap it away. Even through the thick fabric of her dress, the rings dug into her.

"What is that?" she asked.

Her heart thudded in the caverns of her skull as his lips curled into something resembling a smile. When he spoke, his voice was almost sugared.

"Your obedience." Ila exhaled as he let his hand fall from her shoulder and stepped away. "Good night, Queen Ila."

Ila bid him farewell and shut the door behind him. She pressed her ear to the keyhole, listening to his retreating footsteps. Eventually, the sound disappeared. Ila backed away from the door. The room tilted on its axis.

You have already given me something far more valuable than any jewel.

Hoste, he knows.

Ila careered across her bedroom and swiped her bag from under the bed. Her vision blurred as she began to pack haphazardly. Clothes, flint, and steel, the package of dried food she had purchased on her journey. She only paused when she found Morten's dagger still in its sheath. The guards at the entrance hall had allowed her to keep it either because they had not noticed it at her hip or because they did not deem her capable of wielding it.

"What are you doing?"

Ila whirled, unsheathing the blade and flourishing it clumsily. Nils batted it aside like he was swatting a fly. He looked ready to rip the life from someone with his bare hands, but when he took her by the shoulders, his grip was gentle.

"Ila, what is it? What happened?"

"Nils—"

"Tell me what happened."

Ila looked up at her protector through glazed eyes. She could not cry, but she already was. Fat tears rolled down her cheeks as she bowed her head.

"This was a mistake," she whispered, her voice thin and quavering. "Coming here was a mistake."

"We can still leave," Nils said firmly. She felt him seeking her eyes, but refused them. "You don't have to do this."

"No . . . that isn't . . ." The weaver drew a shuddering breath and peered up at her guardian through sticky lashes. "This was a trap. Hoste, how did I not see?"

"I don't under—"

"King Warwick has Saoirse."

Nils went still, his fingers tensing at her shoulders. Dull pain twinged where Warwick had dug his rings into her.

"What reason would he have to take a child hostage?"

"She has gifts."

Memories flooded Ila: teaching Saoirse to ride in the meadow beyond the village, her shrieks of delight as a reindeer calf ate sugar from her tiny palm, telling her stories before bed, her eyelids fluttering as she struggled to stay awake.

"Magic, you mean," Nils said, finally letting go of Ila.

"He wants to use her as a weapon of conquest."

Her breath was coming in strained gasps. Her face was numb. Nils pried the dagger from her clawed fingers and tossed it onto the bed, leading her to the nearest armchair. Ila sank into it as he crouched before her. Shame poured from her mouth.

"This is why I'm here. Not to foster an alliance. I'm a hostage as much as Saoirse. He knows... Hoste, he knows who I am, what I am. He knows—"

"That you're a weaver?"

Ila ceased to breathe.

"I pieced it together over the years." Nils answered her unspoken question with a bittersweet smile. "Letters I glimpsed, conversations I overheard between you and your mother. I can't say I understand all of it, but I know enough to know ours is not the only realm you frequent."

Hot tears budded in her already burning eyes. Hoste, when had she become so tenderhearted?

"Can you contact the other weavers?" Nils asked. "Could they not aid the girl?"

"They think her an abomination. I cannot allow them to have her any more than I can Warwick."

"Are you . . . ?" He trailed off, trepid, but she prompted him with a nod. "Are you certain she can be saved?"

Ila swallowed the lump of doubt in her throat. "Yes."

Nils got to his feet. He towered over her, the firelight crowning him with a flickering halo. "Then I will go."

Ila rose, head spinning, and lifted her palm to his bristly cheek.

"Where she has gone, you can't follow. Only I can reach her."

"So take me with you."

She withdrew and rolled her fingers into a fist. "How many ways must I say it? I cannot leave without sacrificing Galesborough."

"You said the king intends to use her as a weapon of conquest, did you not? Perhaps to save her would be to save Galesborough."

Ila fell silent as she absorbed his words. He studied the planes of her face until, finally, she nodded.

"Perhaps," she murmured.

"That settles it," Nils said, fire sparking in his mouth and eyes. "We will leave before dawn."

"No. If we're actually going to try this, we need a plan, and to form a plan we need the right information."

"The prince," Nils finished her thought.

"I must know if he is involved in this. If he is, we can use him." She began to pace, chewing her thumbnail as she had when she was a child. "It seems he is already fond of me, or at least he wants to be. If I can earn his trust, I can learn what he knows."

"We will need an exit," Nils said, following her progress across the room with his eyes. "I can find us one."

Ila waved him off without looking in his direction. "I know how to get out."

That answer, at least, was simple. She had sensed it only minutes ago beneath the castle like an empty tomb. Yes, that chamber—whatever its original purpose—would serve her just fine as a place to breach the Boundary. She could do it from anywhere, but not without waking everyone in the castle.

"Then what do you need from me, Ila?"

She scuffed to a stop before Nils and let her arm fall limp at her side. "I don't know," she admitted. "Just stay with me until I figure it out."

He raised his hand to his heart and bowed, reverent and tender. "For as long as you'll have me."

13

Wren

Wren did not remember walking out of Caer Sidi, but she found herself on the path to Black Root as dusk bled into the sky. The violet moon would dominate the skies tonight from behind gathering storm clouds, it seemed. A mournful wind slithered through the naked trees of the Tanglewood, tugging at her cloak.

Her fingers drifted to the raised cut on her cheek. It still ached distantly, but it was nothing compared to the anchor burn. She had one of the servants prepare a salve, which she sloppily applied herself. It scarcely took the edge off.

In the years since her manifestation, Wren had learned that pain and teaching were kin.

A burst of noise from the brush stopped Wren in her tracks. Her hand flew to the blade at her hip. She scanned the woods in the failing light. Nothing but bony trees. She sniffed the air. Her fingers tightened around the hilt of her knife.

Ash and dust. The unmistakable scent of a nightmare. And judging by its potency, a powerful one.

"Show yourself," Wren growled. "I know you're there."

The trees watched her with bored reproach. She inhaled through her nose again. Her stomach bottomed out. The scent had disappeared. Had she imagined it? No, she could not remember the last time she sensed another 'mare outside Caer Sidi. Vexes certainly, but this was not the smell of some lowlife. It blistered with power.

Whatever it was, it was gone.

Wren started off again, her mind racing ahead to the pint of cider that awaited her at the tavern. She did not make it three steps before a piercing scream sliced through the twilight. Her blade was drawn before it cut off. She shot off the path into the trees. Another scream. She followed it and exploded into a clearing.

Three men, vexes by the reek of them, were clustered around a girl with her back to an ancient pine. Two were at least eight feet tall with ghastly white skin and heads like boulders. One was a man with receding red hair and fingers like the talons of a rooster. Wren did not recognize them, and they did not appear to recognize her.

If they did, they would be running.

"Get out of here," Wren said, jerking her chin in the direction of Black Root.

"Mind your business, girl," one of the tall ones snapped. His meaty hand matched his rotting stench. He grinned to reveal three rows of ragged teeth. "Unless you want to join us. We were just getting started."

The girl whimpered. Wren clenched her jaw. It was Solene, the new servant, her dress torn and her lip split.

"That is my servant you have there." The winged nightmare

spun her blade, making eye contact with each lowlife in turn. "Leave now, and I'll consider sparing your lives."

The vexes gawked at her. Then they erupted into uproarious laughter. Solene began to cry, heaving sobs that racked her entire body.

"Get out of here, bitch," one of the vexes barked at Wren.

"Nah, I think she should stay," another countered, his jaundiced eyes raking up and down her body. "What you got under that cloak, girl?"

Wren released the clasp at her throat. The garment cascaded to the ground. She snapped her wings out, ignoring a dizzying stab of pain. Muted light skimmed her coal-black feathers. The vexes crashed to their knees, discarding their weapons as if tainted with plague.

"N-Nightstrider," the man with rooster talons stammered. Terror beaded on his skin. She could smell it halfway across the clearing. "We didn't know it was you. If we had, we would—"

"Have tried to violate some other girl," Wren finished for him. He made a noise like a mouse caught in a trap. He was little more, in truth. "I understand."

Wren darted forward and sliced the throats of the big ones in a swift arc. They crumpled before they could scream. She rounded on the man. He scrambled backward, his scaly talons and feet slipping in the snow.

"No, please," he begged. "Please!"

Her knife nailed him between the eyes with a satisfying crunch. Silence rushed to fill the Tanglewood.

"You killed them."

Wren glanced at Solene. She had peeled herself from the tree trunk. Her eyes were on the bodies of her attackers.

"I saved you," Wren corrected her. She stepped over the steaming puddle of blood and collected her blade with a squelch. The stench made her want to gag. "Did they—"

"No."

Wren looked the kip up and down. She carried nothing with her, not even a coin purse. The nightmare narrowed her eyes, prickling with suspicion.

"What were you doing out here?"

The kip swallowed audibly. The foul vex blood had nearly reached the tips of her boots. She shuffled back onto the roots of the tree to escape it.

"I was running an errand for Souldrinker."

"Ondine has a personal servant, and that is not you."

"Ondine," Solene repeated. "I thought her name was Souldrinker."

"To you, it is. What were you doing out here, Solene?"

Solene stared at Wren, her pupils dilated with terror. The last shreds of daylight were withering around them. They lengthened the shadows on her face and made her appear even more gaunt.

"I have a friend in town. I was going to see him."

"That so?"

"Yes."

"Does this friend have a name?"

"Of course." Solene licked her cracked lips, looking anywhere but Wren. "Lee. His name is Lee."

Wren advanced on her, splashing through the sludgy blood and backing her into the tree.

"Lie to me again, and I'll deliver you to Bloodreaper," she warned. The kip inhaled sharply at the mention of the infamous torturer. She did not know Wren avoided him at all costs, that saying his name made her stomach lurch. "Last chance. Tell me why you're out here."

"I can't."

"If you don't tell me what you're up to, I'll have to bring you in. Bloodreaper hasn't had anything to play with for months." Wren took Solene, whose eyes were glazed with panic, by the shoulders. There was no way for her to escape. "I don't want to see you suffer."

She was startled to find it was not a lie.

"Please. They'll kill me if I tell you."

"Who?"

The kip blinked back the wet sheen in her eyes. Wren could feel her pulse sprinting beneath her fingers.

"The rebellion," Solene said, her voice scarcely more than a whimper. "I'm working for the rebellion."

Solene burst into tears.

Her hiccupping wails were muffled by the snow-padded clearing. Wren barely registered them. Her thoughts spun webs in her skull. The rebellion. The only faction of the Reverie with the courage, or stupidity, to defy Para Warwick. She had failed to determine what they were searching for.

Now, after weeks of fruitless hunting, she had a lead.

"Solene." The kip continued to sob, her face buried in her knit gloves. Wren took her by the wrists and forced her to look at her. Snot bubbled from her nose. "Solene," she repeated firmly. "What did the rebellion ask you to do? Why did they send you?"

"They were looking for s-something. Something Para Warwick stole from them."

Wren frowned. That was not what she expected to hear, nor did it make sense. Why would Para Warwick send her after the rebels if he already had what they were looking for?

"What did he steal from them?"

"Some sort of weapon. They never told me what it was."

Solene sniffed, crossing her arms against the cold. Wren turned to collect the cloak she had discarded.

"Here," she said gruffly, offering it to the kip. After a brief hesitation, Solene took it gingerly and wrapped it around her slight frame. "Start at the beginning."

"They found me a month ago. They knew all about my past—they threatened me. They knew I was a thief." Shame crept across her plain features.

"Do I look like the kind of person who would be offended by petty thievery?"

For a moment, Wren thought Solene was going to smile, but the moment passed. She sighed.

"Go on."

"They needed someone without connections to the rebellion. Someone who could move around Caer Sidi and not be noticed."

"A kip," Wren muttered. "Smart. Tell me about the rebels you met."

"There was a girl, a luminae. She had golden eyes and ears like a bat."

"A bat?"

Solene nodded eagerly. "She was kind."

Kind enough to send you to your death, Wren thought. "Was there anyone else?"

Solene bit her cut lip until it started to bleed again. The smell of metal pricked Wren's nose through the thick stench of the vex blood.

"There was a man," Solene went on. "He was tall. Handsome. Dark eyes and hair."

"Tall, dark, and handsome. Is that the best you can do?"

"He was a 'mare."

Wren went still, her pulse stuttering. Solene bundled the cloak tighter around her as the cold air slithered through the trees, drawing moans from their petrified forms.

"A 'mare is working for the rebellion," Wren repeated.

She did not phrase it as a question, but Solene answered anyway. "Yes."

"A 'mare is working against Para Warwick alongside luminae and kips."

"Yes."

"You understand how that sounds."

Solene gave a sober nod. "It's the truth."

Her words rang clear and true. The world seemed to tilt as Wren let her vision drift from focus.

"Tell me more about the weapon," she heard herself say. "Anything you can think of."

"It's in a skysteel box that could fit in the palm of your hand. There are runes on its face, and it shines like starlight."

Wren blinked Solene back into focus to find frustrated tears welling in her gaze. She knew that look well. The kip didn't want to talk. She didn't want to die, either.

"Keep going," Wren coaxed her, more a threat than a suggestion.

"They said the weapon could destroy Para Warwick."

The world narrowed until there was only Solene staring up at her with dizzying dread.

"What is it?" Wren asked.

"I don't know, I swear." Solene began to worry the end of her straw-colored braid.

"Did they tell you where it would be in the castle?"

"No, I was supposed to find it."

"Have you?"

"I—I think so." Solene paused, frightened or unsure. "I think it is being kept in the sanctum."

Solene flinched when Wren barked a curse. The 'mare backed away and turned her aggression on the nearest dead vex. His ribs cracked like dry twigs when they met her boot.

"Nightstrider?"

Wren waved her off, pinching the bridge of her nose between her thumb and forefinger. A migraine stirred in her skull.

"How are you supposed to get this weapon out of the sanctum?"

"I was supposed to figure it out myself."

Wren grunted. "Figures. Fucking idiots."

Solene stared at her with eyes round as pockmarks. "I don't understand."

Something long dormant stirred within Wren. A hunger she had stifled for years, knowing it could never be satiated. But something had changed. The fabric of the universe had shifted. She could smell it. She could taste it sizzling in the air like ozone before a lightning strike.

Revenge.

"I'm going to help you steal the weapon," she said. "But first, you're going to steal something for me."

14
Alaric

Mica and Alaric left the inn at dawn. They rode back toward Black Root through the Tanglewood in silence, their horses weighed down by the provisions Laurel had packed for them. Both rebels were pensive.

Until now, Alaric had only known one dreambreaker, Luken. Mortal, but blessed with a long life and devastating power. Alaric had yet to meet anyone who rivaled him in terms of his abilities. Except Para Warwick, of course.

Even then, Luken could do things the Para could only imagine.

Alaric touched the back of his neck out of habit, running the pads of his fingers over the lump of scar tissue there, a reminder of what would have been—had the dreambreaker not altered his fate.

If what Morthil said about this young dreambreaker was true, that she was more powerful than Luken, and the only thing stopping the Para from accessing her was a rogue weaver and a warded box, they were in serious trouble.

Mica spotted Black Root in the early evening, a gray smudge through the black bars of the trees. They skirted the village, heading for Caer Sidi. Alaric felt his magic begin to shiver as they drew nearer. Getting so close to Para Warwick felt like tempting fate, but what choice did they have?

Eventually, they halted in a clearing of twisted mirewood trees a mile or so from the castle. Alaric lashed their horses to a tree as Mica cleared a stump of snow with a sweep of her arm. She sat gingerly, digging into the inner pocket of her cloak to produce a stone the size of an egg, the sister to the fever stone they had provided Solene.

Alaric observed as she clasped the fever stone with both hands and curled it to her chest. She closed her eyes as if in prayer. The wind wandered through the glade, teasing her deep brown curls.

Mica opened her eyes and hands. The fever stone now glowed like a steady ember.

"Now we wait," she said, more to herself than Alaric.

The nightmare tossed his pack into the snow beside her stump and sat heavily. "Now we wait."

☽○☾

An hour passed, then two. Mica alternated between clenching her fists and chewing her nails ragged. The fever stone blazed all the while. Eventually, Mica looked in the direction of Caer Sidi with pricked ears. Alaric picked up the rhythm of boots crunching snow a moment later.

They rose in unison as Solene slipped into the clearing. She wore a cloak too flimsy for the frigid weather, and judging by the bluish shadows under her eyes, she had not slept since their last encounter.

"Why are you here?" Solene asked tightly, lingering on the opposite side of the clearing. "You told me to contact you when I was ready."

Mica and Alaric exchanged a glance. For once, the luminae let him lead. "Things have changed. How much time do you need?"

"As long as you can give me."

"How about a day?"

Solene went as stiff as the drab mirewood trees surrounding them. "I can't."

"Can't, or won't?"

The kip clenched her jaw, her only answer. The tip of her nose was red with cold, her chapped hands wrapped in rags.

"Lives depend on this, Solene," Mica broke in. Her voice was firm but not unkind. "We chose you for a reason. We know what you're capable of."

Solene glared at the ground.

"You have one day," Alaric told her. "Squeeze your fever stone when you have the weapon. We'll meet you at the clearing beyond the southern wall."

"What if I'm caught?" Solene lifted her eyes to his. Angry tears glinted like skysteel from their depths. "What then?"

When he was the Hand of the Para, Alaric would have discarded her without a second thought. It would be the wise choice, certainly the less dangerous one. For better or worse, two decades with a bunch of luminae had permanently adjusted his moral compass.

"We'll get you out."

Solene blinked up at him, stunned. Clearly, that was not the answer she was expecting. She glanced over her bony shoulder. "I should get back before they miss me."

Mica dipped her chin, her expression grave. "Good somnia, Solene, and good luck."

"Wait."

Solene, who had started to walk away, paused as Alaric stooped to dig through his bag. He found what he was looking for, a pair of evergreen gloves Mica had knit for him, and tossed them to the kip. She caught them awkwardly, her throat bobbing as she examined the gift.

"Thanks."

Her eyes flicked to Alaric, then to the gloves again. Then she turned around and began to follow her own tracks back to Caer Sidi, slipping on the gloves as she went.

The rebels waited until the crunch of her footfalls disappeared to speak.

"That was kind," Mica said quietly.

Alaric forced a smirk. "Not really my style, anyway."

The luminae huffed, then soberness overtook her. "Do you have a plan for when she gets out?"

"I have part of a plan."

"Brilliant."

"You got any bright ideas you want to share?" When Mica did not reply, Alaric pressed on. "Horses won't be fast enough once they start tracking us. We need something faster. We need to fly."

Mica made an exasperated noise at the back of her throat. "And how do you propose we do that?"

"Don't get upset."

The luminae squinted at him. He saw the gears click into place behind her golden eyes. Her face curdled. She held up a single finger.

"Absolutely not."

"Give me a better idea," Alaric countered.

"Anything."

"Come on, Mica," he pleaded as she retreated to her stump with her hands on her hips. "You know he's our best option, and he's not far."

"Don't remind me," Mica grumbled. She sat with a huff, glaring at the blanketed forest floor. Alaric half expected the snow to start melting from the heat of her gaze. Then her eyes softened, and she spoke without looking at him. "How are we supposed to get Solene out if she gets caught?"

"We won't be able to alone," Alaric answered. "We'll head back to base and regroup. Come back with reinforcements."

"Reichart will never go for that."

"Then we better hope she gets out on her own, and we'd better have a ride."

Mica lifted her eyes to his again, revealing the fear cowering beneath her ire. "Fine," she huffed. "Be quiet; I need to focus."

Relief poured over Alaric. As he watched, Mica closed her eyes and sat up tall, tilting her face toward the sky. The setting sun bled through her semitranslucent ears, highlighting the delicate veins there. Her lips parted, but no sound came out.

At least, none Alaric could hear.

A flock of iridescent pink birds exploded into the air

beyond the clearing, squawking indignantly. The air around Mica shivered, the rippling waves blurring her image until she herself seemed to vibrate.

The luminae closed her mouth, opened her eyes. The rumbling ceased at once.

"Did it work?" Alaric asked.

"Yes, but it will take a while for him to get here."

"How long is a while?"

An earsplitting scream lanced through the Tanglewood. *Solene.* Alaric's body reacted before his mind, conjuring two shards of energy in his hands. Before Mica could stop him, he tore off in the direction of the scream, blood howling in his ears.

Thud.

The force of her power slammed into him like a battering ram. Alaric skidded to a halt, carving a path of dark earth in the snow.

Nightstrider.

She had Solene.

It took everything he had not to charge ahead recklessly, but Nightstrider could kill Solene in an instant if he startled her. Calling on his last shred of restraint, Alaric crept forward and crouched at the base of an ancient tree.

He peered around its knotty trunk.

Cowering against a pine some thirty paces away was Solene. Blood ran from a cut on her lip. Her clothes were torn, and she still wore the knit gloves. Three vexes were clustered around her, but their attention was fixed on the nightmare across the clearing.

The way the rebels spoke of her, Alaric expected Nightstrider to be a beast akin to Bloodreaper. The last thing he expected was for her to be beautiful.

Regal features. Dark hair and darker eyes framed with lush lashes. Warm brown skin that seemed to gleam in the dusk. She didn't look like a monster, but then, monstrous things didn't always look monstrous.

"...should stay," one of the vexes was saying. "What you got under that cloak, girl?"

Nightstrider smiled like steel in sunlight.

She released the clasp at her neck. Her cloak pooled around her feet. Snow gusted as she snapped out her wings. They were wider than she was tall and black as coal. The vexes plunged to their knees and discarded their weapons.

Faster than Alaric could track, Nightstrider lunged at the vexes and sliced two of their throats in a single motion. Solene let out a squeak of terror as her attackers slumped to the ground. The remaining vex tried to scramble away, but Nightstrider stabbed him through the eye with brutal precision.

For a moment, nothing moved but the blood of the vexes creeping from their bodies.

Alaric watched, paralyzed with indecision and shock, as the nightmare spoke to the little thief. Logic urged him to cut her throat while he had the element of surprise, to save Solene before their only hope was butchered. Yet there was something about the way Nightstrider appraised the girl, flecked with gore though she was, that stayed his hand.

Then the nightmare bent down and retrieved her discarded cloak, offering it to the kip as if they were friends.

Alaric felt the hair on the back of his neck stand on end. Half a beat later, a hand was clapped to his mouth.

"You idiot," Mica whispered in his ear. She removed her hand. "We have to go."

"But—"

"Look."

Alaric looked back to see Solene stumbling toward Caer Sidi behind Nightstrider, wrapped in the cloak that was far too big.

"Let's *go*."

With a final glance at Nightstrider, Alaric let his spears dissolve into the snow and took Mica by the hand, slipping back the way they came.

15
Ila

The first night in Wolfhelm was the worst. Her bed was too soft, the castle too cold and stoic. She longed for the round birch walls of her home in Galesborough, for furs against her cheek and crisp, clean air rolling down from the mountains. When sleep finally claimed her, it was brief and restless.

As a weaver, she had long since learned to suppress her dreams, thus preventing any unfortunate beings from manifesting in the Reverie on her account. That did not stop formless foreboding from worming into her brain, tossing her about like a rudderless ship.

Then the door to her chambers was opening, and a small army of maids headed by a stout aged woman with a pale complexion and a mop of gray curls was pouring in. The maids bore trunks Ila did not recognize and colorful boxes, which they began to deposit around the room. The weaver climbed from bed in her shift and watched, too bewildered to stop them.

"Apologies for the intrusion, Yer Majesty, but we're to prepare ye for breakfast," the elderly woman said briskly.

"Breakfast?" Ila asked as if unfamiliar with the concept.

"Aye. Come now, a hot bath will do ye good."

The woman took Ila by the hand and coaxed her toward the washroom with gentle insistence. She moved quickly despite her advanced age.

"Ye may call me Ma Hendricks, Yer Majesty. Everyone does but my son."

"What does he call you?"

"Mama, or Mother when I've pressed his nerves." She gave a throaty chuckle. "Ye met him yesterday, aye?"

"Yes," Ila answered, putting two and two together as they passed into the spacious sunstruck washroom. Someone had already slipped in and filled the porcelain tub with steaming water. "Captain Hendricks."

"Handsome lad, aye? He takes after his father, rest his soul." Ma Hendricks suddenly turned to face Ila fully, patting her hand with her own rumpled one and peering at her with round eyes full of empathy. "I was very sorry te hear of yer loss, Queen Ila. Te be without a family in a strange land is a terrible thing."

Ila felt a lump balloon in her throat. She nodded through it. Kindness was the last thing she had anticipated at Caer Sidi, and she did not know how to accept it. Thankfully, a pair of maids a few years younger than Ila flitted through the door.

Despite her protests, they helped her peel off her shift then guided her into the seething bath. Nakedness was not a source of shame in Vaettir culture, but she could feel the younger maids eyeing her body, taking stock of the prize their prince had snared.

She was not much to look at in terms of breeding stock, Ila thought as she sank into the hot water. She had always been a wisp, narrow at the hips and forever waiting for the full breasts many of her weaver sisters had been blessed with.

But then, she was not truly here to produce an heir, was she?

"Such beautiful hair ye have," Ma Hendricks said as the younger maids dipped porcelain bowls into the bath. "Does it come from yer mother or yer father?"

"My mother," Ila answered.

"She must have been a rare beauty."

"They called her starlende doniven. The radiant queen."

Ila could not suppress a gasp of surprise, then pleasure as hot water was poured down her back.

"She must be proud of ye," Ma Hendricks said, the creases around her eyes deepening as she smiled.

A pit formed in Ila's stomach as she was bent double and more deliciously warm water was poured over her, soaking her hair. She could not imagine her mother was proud of her if indeed she watched her beyond death. She had been naive and selfish. Now Saoirse was in danger, and the fate of Galesborough hung from a precarious thread that frayed with each passing moment.

And she still did not have a plan.

Ma Hendricks and the other maids washed her body and hair with perfumed soaps that made her nose itch. Then they helped her from the bath and dried her with fluffy towels and guided her back to the bedchamber, where two more maids had laid out a gown and accessories.

They were clearly expensive but decidedly not Vaettirin.

Past the point of arguing, Ila allowed them to dress her in the silken mauve gown trimmed with delicate lace. Its bodice was encrusted with pearls and had laces in the back that pulled so tight it made breathing a chore. It did, however, give her bosom the illusion of fullness. Rouge was dotted on her cheeks as her hair was combed, then twisted into a style she had seen at the feast the previous night and pinned in place with pearly combs.

"Ye are a vision, Yer Majesty," Ma Hendricks cooed, leading her to the gilded mirror in the washroom.

Ila smiled mechanically.

She looked pretty, she decided, like a moth trapped in amber. How anyone was meant to move in such a contraption was beyond her, but perhaps that was the point.

"Right, off we go."

"I am not hungry," Ila lied.

"Nonsense." Ma Hendricks shooed the flock of maids away. They scattered like chickadees, bobbing curtsies as the Vaettir queen was ferried back across the opulent room and into the hallway.

They walked in silence, a mercy Ila was grateful for. Her stiff slippers pinched her toes, and she could feel the beginnings of a blister forming on the back of her heel. After only moments, they reached another door similar to the one that led to her chambers, and Ma Hendricks opened it.

"Here ye are, Queen Ila."

"Thank you, Madam Hendricks."

Ila froze.

Caine stood at the head of a round table set with porcelain dishes heaped with food. He was dressed in a simple tunic that brought out the blue in his eyes. A large window overlooking a wintery courtyard crowned him with golden sunlight. Bookshelves lined the walls of the little room, and a small marble hearth housed a merry fire.

"I thought we could try again," he said as Ma Hendricks ushered her into the parlor. "Or I could, at least."

Ila looked away, keenly aware of the sting at her heels and the pressure against her chest each time she drew breath. Ma Hendricks shut the door behind her with a soft *click*.

"Please, sit."

He gestured at the dining chair opposite his. Ila sighed and sat gingerly, worried one wrong move would split the sheer fabric of her gown. Once she was seated, Caine joined her, smiling cautiously at her across a spread of pastries, fruits, meats, and cheeses.

"I don't know what you like," Caine said. "So I had them bring a spread. Please, help yourself."

Ila reached for the nearest item, a flaky golden pastry the size of a large egg with some sort of berry filling, and set it on her plate ringed with blue flowers. Caine reached for the matching teapot and lifted it to her askance, steam coiling from its spout. She shook her head, and he poured himself a cup.

"We had a bad start," he said, setting the teapot aside. "I was hoping we might have a better middle."

"That may be difficult. I am not here of my own volition."

"As you've said," Caine acknowledged. "I'd prefer to wed

someone who does not hate me, or not to marry at all, but people like us are not often afforded such luxuries."

Ila sniffed. She grabbed a serving spoon and scooped a portion of mixed fruit she had no intention of eating onto her plate.

"Tell me about yourself." She glared at Caine, who was now nursing his cup of tea. "Work with me here," he said over the rim.

"There is nothing to tell."

"Nothing to tell?" He shook his head in disbelief. "You're one of the youngest queens in the history of Galesborough. You speak at least two languages, which is one more than me. You ride like you were born to, and you showed up to meet me armed. Not to mention you're beautiful." He took another sip of his tea and returned it to its saucer, a smile lifting one corner of his mouth. "I barely know anything about you and you're the most interesting thing that has ever happened to me."

Ila almost smiled back. Hoste, his words were sweet, his cadence honest and true. She locked her weaver sight into place again, scanning his threads for any trace of his true parentage, but there was nothing.

"Careful, you'll make my blood run cold."

Ila blinked the mundane back into view. "What?"

"You did that yesterday, too. Like you're trying to see right through me."

"You notice a great deal," she replied tepidly. Caine shrugged, taking a bite of bacon. "Three," Ila said. "I speak three languages. Four if you count the Forgotten Tongue."

"The Forgotten Tongue?" The prince lifted his brows, clearly impressed. "Does anyone *speak* the Forgotten Tongue?"

Her lips twitched again. "It is mostly written."

"I see. And the other three?"

"Vaettirin, Sandmeren, and the Common Tongue."

"Where did you pick up Sandmeren?"

"From my friend." From a weaver visiting from the southern continent, in fact. Their temples had joined forces to seal a sizable fissure in the Boundary, and in the months spent together, she and Ila had grown close as kin. "It is a beautiful language."

"My mother spoke many languages," Caine said. "I wish she would have taught me."

She recognized the way he spoke of her. It was the way she spoke of her family. "I am sorry for your loss."

"And I yours, Queen Ila." The prince hesitated. "May I ask—"

"I do not want to talk about my family."

Caine nodded. "I was going to inquire about your dress. It reminds me of our fashions."

Ila frowned at her untouched plate. "I expect so. You chose it for me, did you not?"

"Why would I choose your clothes? You're not a child."

Silence bloomed in the parlor, buffered only by the mockingly cheery crackling of the fire. Bitter understanding took root in Ila. It was not Caine who had chosen the dress for her; it was Para Warwick.

Just another way he would exercise control over her. Why even bother marrying her to his son? He may as well have just taken her himself, but no. No, he would not sink so low.

"Don't let them boss you around," Caine said with a flippant wave of his hand. "Please, wear what you like. Besides, if I'm being honest, I preferred what you wore last night."

Ila studied him. Not his threads, but his face. There was not the slightest flicker of evil there. Her body relaxed slightly, and she became aware of the hunger gnawing at her stomach. She took a small bite of her pastry. It was delicious, the buttery flakes melting on her tongue.

Caine offered her tea again, and this time she accepted.

"I have questions," she said as he filled her cup.

"Anything," he answered, replacing the teapot on its tray and flopping back into his seat. "I'm an open book."

"Did you really not know you were to marry me?"

"Not until after the letter was sent. I was angry, too." He paused, a tentative smile wandering across his mouth. "Less so after meeting you."

Hoste, but he was charming.

"What have you heard of the Vaettir?" she inquired, raising her porcelain cup to her lips. "Your sister said—"

"Please don't listen to anything my sister says," Caine groaned. "I've met frying pans with more tact."

Her laugh surprised both of them. Ila sipped her tea to collect herself. The prince continued.

"She had some ideas about your people, as does my father."

"They tell stories of our warriors," she said. "That we're brutal and violent, but we are not. We only fight to protect our home."

Caine stilled. "Is that so? We were told—"

"That the Vaettir ride the north wind into battle? That we

are the most bloodthirsty army in the realm?" Ila scoffed. "We are fierce, but we are not conquerors. My father was the first to give us a formal army, but only to guard our borders from the machine of your kingdom."

The prince drummed his fingers on the table, brow furrowed with tension as he appraised her. "My father is under the impression that our marriage will earn him your warriors."

"You have earned nothing," Ila replied, the chill that had receded fractionally from her heart setting in again. "My people will not fight for you. If I asked them to, they would renounce me."

"They are loyal to you, are they not?"

"They are loyal to Galesborough."

Caine leaned forward and spoke in a low tone. "It is in your best interest and mine that this stays between us. You are valuable to my father because of your army. If he learns it is not his to command, you will be of no use to him."

He does not know.

Though they spoke of politics and not dreams, his sincerity as he said his father would have no use for her without her army was impossible to ignore. The prince knew nothing of the Reverie. His world was contained in the white walls of this Caer Sidi, where his father was just a king and she was just a reluctant bride from a distant kingdom, not a disgraced weaver seeking a stolen dreambreaker.

He could not help her save Saoirse.

Hot tears misted her vision, and worry eclipsed Caine's face.

"Did I say something?"

"No," she whispered, wiping her eyes with the scratchy lace of her dress. "No. You surprised me, that is all."

"In a good way?"

Ila smiled faintly. "I suppose it must be good."

She rose without meaning to, and Caine followed her to her feet.

"I am not feeling well," she said. "I would like to return to my chambers."

"Queen Ila—"

"Good day, Prince Caine."

As fast as her vise of a dress would allow, she slipped out from behind her chair and out the door, careful not to meet his eyes on her way lest she feel a twinge of sympathy.

16

Caine

"We received word from General Sokovo this morning. They have quelled the uprising in the southern reaches of Mistrun."

Thomas stood at his place before the sprawling table, every inch of which was covered in intricate maps. The captain spoke directly to Warwick, who sat in the high-backed chair at the head. A dozen noblemen, most of them from Wolfhelm, observed with scarcely veiled apathy.

Caine, seated to the right of his father, listened to the best of his ability. Images of Ila still glazed his eyes, though he had not seen her since they shared breakfast three days prior, her voice still knocking about in his head like an echo in a cave. He had not seen her since, nor had he seen any of the Vaettir.

I suppose it must be good.

What could she have meant? How the hells could his being less awful than she anticipated be anything but good?

Gods, she was an enigma, one that wrapped tighter around his mind with each passing day.

"The general assures us that any remaining agitators will be dealt with swiftly."

"Thank you, Captain Hendricks," Warwick said. His tone was as inscrutable as his expression.

Thomas bowed and took his seat.

"Lord Dowling," the king continued, switching his attention to the balding man in burgundy robes sitting across from Caine. "I trust all continues to go well in Veltspar?"

Lord Dowling rose, the legs of his chair squeaking against the floor.

"Yes, my lord. Any lingering hostility from the locals has died since your shipment of grain arrived. It is most welcome in the face of this... *unlucky* blight."

Caine shifted uncomfortably. What Lord Dowling had failed to mention was that it was their forces that brought the blight to Veltspar in the first place.

"Something to say, Prince Caine?"

Caine looked to his father. Warwick was staring at him, a warning blazing in his eyes. Ila's scorching words flared in the prince's mind.

Passivity is as deadly as any blade.

"No," Caine answered. The weight of every gaze in the room beat down on him. "Nothing."

"In two days, you will be wedded to the Queen of Galesborough," Warwick proceeded, raising his voice to ensure everyone heard. "Once Galesborough is secured, and the last corner of this continent is unified under my reign, we will begin the invasion of Sandmere with the help of the Vaettirin forces."

Caine spoke before he could think better of it.

"To what end?"

Lord Dowling coughed to disguise a gasp. Out of the corner of his eye, Caine saw Thomas go stiff. Slowly, Warwick returned his attention to his son. The king did not look angry. In fact, he appeared almost detached.

That was never a good sign.

"To whatever end I wish," Warwick said. His voice matched his expression, dangerously level.

"Queen Ila may resist our using them—"

"She will not resist if she wants her barbarian kingdom to see spring, and if she does resist, you will discipline her accordingly. Is that clear?"

Caine felt his ears grow hot. He rolled his fingers into fists under the table. His father condescended to him as if he were a child or some lowly pawn. He was the only son of the king, loyal and ever compliant. Did that not afford him an ounce of respect?

"Is that clear, Prince Caine?"

"Yes," Caine heard himself say.

The meeting shuddered to life again. Warwick inquired about the state of another conquered kingdom. Another lord answered, but the prince scarcely noticed. His father did not acknowledge him again, nor did Caine speak again.

After what felt like hours, the meeting concluded. Warwick departed, and the nobles began to meander toward the exit. Caine rose and made for the door, still lost in the forest of his thoughts.

"I could lose a finger for saying this, but you have a point."

Caine looked up to find Thomas walking beside him.

"What does it matter?" the prince asked as they passed into the sunlit hallway. "He'll never listen to me."

"You and he are..." Thomas paused.

"Speak freely."

"You and your father are different men. You have never possessed a hunger for power outside the bounds of Wolfhelm, and I believe the king knows this."

Caine scraped to a halt in the middle of the corridor, which was now nearly deserted save for a pair of noblemen conversing farther down.

"Careful," the prince warned. "You are treading on dangerous ground."

"I meant no offense." Thomas bowed his head. "I am loyal to King Warwick, but I am also loyal to you as your subject and your friend. I simply seek to remind you of the divergence between yourself and the king and how it may affect your perception of each other."

Thomas raised his head again when Caine clapped him on the shoulder. "I asked for the truth, and you gave it. Thank you, my friend."

Movement in his peripheral vision tugged his gaze around. Caine looked in time to see a figure retreat around the corner.

"What is it?" Thomas asked.

"Nothing," Caine replied, snapping his eyes back to the captain. "What do you think of her?"

"Queen Ila? She is beautiful, intelligent. I imagine she will make a good wife once she has acclimated."

"Do you think she will acclimate?" Caine asked, leaning

one shoulder against the wall as a pair of middle-aged noblewomen breezed past, skirts rustling and heels clacking.

"In time, I imagine." Suddenly, Thomas grinned. "Hang on, are you *nervous*?"

"Of course not."

Thomas blew a low whistle through his teeth at the bite in his words. "The Prince of Wolfhelm, weak in the knees for a girl. Never thought I'd see the day."

"Goodbye, Thomas," Caine said loudly before striding away, headed anywhere.

Unfortunately, he was not fast enough to miss the captain laughing.

That night, Caine found himself drawn to the library. He could always find peace among the stacks, and the scholars were good company in that they rarely bothered him. He found the book he had been paging through the day before, and began to make his way to his favorite corner. He did not wait to start reading.

> *The Vaettir are polytheistic. When they reach the age of thirteen, children pledge themselves to the deity of their choice. While there are dozens of gods to choose from, the four most ubiquitous are Somma, Varae, Vin, and Hoste, each of whom is associated with one of the four seasons. Somma, often depicted as a maiden with healing hands, is tied to summer. Hoste, the god of winter and death, carries a hammer forged of starlight . . .*

Caine stopped in his tracks. Sitting at the head of a table, her nose in a fat book, was Ila. Her hair was loosely plaited, and she wore a simple gown with yellow flowers sewn into the neckline. The antler earrings she had worn the night of the feast dangled from her earlobes. A quill and inkpot rested on the table before her.

Caine hesitated, then approached.

"Queen Ila."

She looked up, startled.

"What are you reading?"

"Nothing." Ila closed the book, but not before he saw an illustration of Caer Sidi inked on the page. The word *sanctum* was scrawled in the margins. It seemed he was not the only one reading up on the home of their betrothed. "Did you need something?"

Caine gestured at the chair to her right. "May I?"

"I suppose."

He sat before she could change her mind, setting his own book on the table. Her brows pulled together. She slid the text closer to her.

"*The Traditions of the Vaettir?*"

"Since we're to be married, I figured I ought to have an understanding of your customs," Caine said with a shrug.

Ila opened the book and began to thumb through it. She landed on an elaborate illustration of the four central gods. She caressed them like they were portraits of old friends.

"So have you pledged yourself to a god?" he asked.

"Yes," Ila answered. "Hoste."

"Right, the god of winter and death." Caine cocked a brow. "Should I be concerned?"

A smile twitched on her mouth. "Death is not always unkind."

"When is death kind?"

"Often, Prince Caine. Though not in the way your father inflicts it."

"Keep your voice down," Caine murmured, his eyes darting to a bespectacled scholar lingering nearby. The scholar ducked his head when he realized he had been spotted and bustled away, disappearing between two soaring stacks. "I will admit, his tactics can be excessive."

"Have you told him you feel this way?"

Caine pressed his lips into a thin line. "He won't listen to me."

"Is that so?"

"Never has, never will." He spoke with more venom than he had intended.

Ila sighed. Her eyes wandered to the shafts of light tumbling through the windows. Their glow drew out the rosy undertones in her skin. The next words Caine spoke caught both of them off guard, the prince most of all.

"I'm sorry."

Ila blinked.

"I'm sorry my father forced your hand, and that you don't want to marry me."

"Prince Caine—"

"I can't promise the conquests will stop while my father is on the throne, but I can promise that, as your husband, I will always shield both you and your people from harm."

Ila stared at him, and for an instant, he wondered if anything he had just said made any sort of sense. Had he been blabbering like an idiot?

"You truly are unexpected, Prince Caine," she finally said.

"Am I?"

It might have been a trick of the light, but Caine swore he saw her blush. "I may have had one of my guards follow you."

"Ah, the eunuch. I thought I saw him this morning. How romantic." Ila smiled, revealing a small gap between her front teeth. It only made her lovelier. "What was his verdict?"

"He told me you are respectful to those around you, no matter their status. That you are entitled, cocky."

"Fair enough."

"He told me you don't appear to be a monster."

This gave Caine pause. He scanned her round features for a moment, searching for something nameless.

"And what is your verdict, Queen Ila?" he inquired.

"That perhaps I was a bit of a dasak."

"Do I want to know what that means?"

Ila snorted, and for a moment, he thought she was going to say more. Instead, she gathered her materials and got to her feet. Caine followed suit.

"I should go," Ila said.

"Of course." Caine scratched the back of his neck, looking away to hide his disappointment. "I'll be here late if you can't sleep."

He kicked himself internally. *Stupid. You sound stupid.*

If Ila agreed, she did not let on.

Instead, something else passed across her face like a tendril of fog, something Caine could not place. Before he could decipher it, Ila dipped into a curtsy, the first she had ever given him, and glided away.

☽○☾

The scholars snuffed the torches after sunset, leaving Caine alone with a candelabra and a hefty stack of texts on Galesborough. After Ila left, he migrated to his usual hideaway, a window seat in a neglected corner of the library. His eyelids grew heavy as the moon scaled the skies beyond the frosted windowpanes.

Vaettirin women are encouraged to practice both archery and self-defense. In the days when their society was nomadic, following the migration patterns of reindeer, women were required to hunt alongside their male counterparts.

Caine felt his lips quirk into a smile. *Theodosia would like this*, he thought. Perhaps such practices could be implemented in Wolfhelm when he was king and Ila his queen.

"What have you learned of my homeland, Prince Caine?"

The prince nearly jumped out of his skin. Ila stood a few paces from him. He got the feeling she had been there awhile. She had traded her gown for the riding clothes she had arrived in, her dagger at her hip. Alarm bells echoed through his mind as he stood, his eyes on the weapon.

"What are you doing here?" Caine asked.

"You told me you would be here. I wanted to see you."

His heart flopped like a fish on deck. "Oh?"

"There is something I need to say."

Ila stepped closer, her blue-gray eyes never straying from his. Her gaze kept him rooted on the spot; it would have been less effective if she had chained him to the floor.

"Someday," she began in a soft voice, "you will have a choice to make about the kind of king you want to be. You have a gentle soul. Armor it against wickedness and apathy. Promise me."

Silence rang out in the library, buffered only by the murmur of the wind outside.

"I—I promise."

Ila raised up on her tiptoes, angling her mouth toward his. Caine leaned down and she pressed her mouth to his. Shock and euphoria roared through his veins. He embraced her, his hand sliding down her back. Her cold hand found his cheek . . . then she broke away.

"I truly am sorry. I have no doubt you would have made a fine husband."

"What?"

The world tilted. Somehow, the books did not tumble from their shelves, and the candelabra did not topple. Caine staggered. Ila backed away, regret radiating from her indistinct form.

"This is for the best." Her voice sounded very far away.

"What did you do?" Caine demanded, but the words never left him.

"Goodbye, Caine."

The last thing he heard before the blackness engulfed him was the echo of the warning Theodosia gave him.

Everyone thinks your bride is a witch.

17

Ila

Ila did not look back as Prince Caine hit the floor. She used her sleeve to wipe away the soporific moon sap lingering on her lips as she exited the library. The corridors were deserted in the middle of the night, but the statues seemed to breathe as she passed.

She followed the route she had memorized to avoid the patrols, peeking around every corner with her heart beating in her throat.

Eventually, she arrived before an expansive tapestry near the throne hall. A battle full of warriors run through by swords and studded with broken arrows poured across the cloth.

Charming, Ila thought.

She looked left and right down the vacant hall. If their intelligence was correct, the next patrol would not pass for another ten minutes.

She reached out to touch the tapestry. Cool air moved beneath it.

"Nils," she breathed.

A hand shot out from behind the cloth. She took it and was pulled behind the fabric, into a hidden hole that led to a black tunnel. They carefully made their way down the darkened path.

"Did you do it?" Nils asked out of the shadows.

Ila called on the aura of Caer Sidi. White light collected in her palm, bobbing like a bottle at sea. Nils gaped at it, and she realized with a jolt that he had never seen her use her abilities.

"Yes," she answered. "He's unconscious."

"Remind me why that was necessary," Nils said, ripping his eyes from the knot of energy in her palm. "Not that I'm opposed to knocking him out, but..."

"He saw me reading about the sanctum. When he wakes, his memory of the day will be erased. It was the only way to be sure."

"Fair." Nils leaned against the wall. His eyes drifted back to the radiance cupped in her hand. It cast dense shadows across his face. "Your room is torn apart. We left the window open and threw blood across the sheets."

"Ashild?"

"Drank her moon sap. Passed out on the floor of your room." Nils winced. "She made me break her nose. I have a feeling I'll pay for it later."

Silence settled between them as reality set in. There was nothing else to discuss. The only thing left to do was part ways.

"Are you sure you'll be able to cross over to this...other world from this sanctum?" Nils asked, striving to keep the conversation from ending.

"Yes. You must trust me on this."

"I do."

Ila smiled weakly. "If everything goes as planned, I'll return with Saoirse in a week. Leave as soon as you can after the search ensues, and wait for us—"

"At the inn outside Greenbrooke, I know."

The queen gazed up at Nils in the quivering light she held. The weight of his unspoken words was almost tangible. She cleared her throat to bid him farewell, but he wrapped his arms around her and drew her in. Her eyes stung as she inhaled his familiar musk. He kissed the top of her head.

"Sol liv hjent warren, Ila."

"Sol liv hjent warren." Nils pulled back, still holding her by the arms as if to keep her in place. Ila took a shaky breath and continued. "Nils, if I don't return—"

"Ila—"

"If I don't come back, Wolfhelm may march on us. You must return to Galesborough to warn them. Promise me on your sworn god."

Nils clenched his jaw, his grip tightening around her biceps. His blue eyes gleamed brighter than usual.

"I swear on the name of Somma, I'll return to Galesborough should the need arise." The way he spoke the words, Ila knew they were a bolt to his heart.

"Takja."

"Go," he said, finally releasing her. "Saoirse is waiting."

"I will see you soon," Ila promised, her voice echoing softly as she started to back away down the tunnel. The ground sloped gently downward, luring her toward the sanctum. Toward Saoirse. "Goodbye."

Before fear or longing could stop her, Ila turned from Nils and walked into the darkness.

☽○☾

The deeper Ila descended into the catacombs, the more her pulse climbed. She had no doubt she would die in the labyrinth were it not for her weaver sight.

She was able to follow the energy pathways to the sanctum. The pinprick souls of insects and mice skittered through the rivers of light, gold flecks in the juddering white threads of the echopoint.

Far beneath them, the sanctum loomed like a black moon.

She had sensed it the night she arrived in Wolfhelm. It was rare to find a place utterly devoid of life in the Reverie or the Wake. It did not necessarily spell evil, but it was certainly unusual. The events of the past days had sent the strangeness of it to the back of her mind until she needed a place inside Caer Sidi to open a portal without waking the entire castle.

She just hoped she would not bring the ceiling down on herself in the process.

After what felt like an eternity, Ila sensed her destination approaching. She slowed her pace and rested her hand on the hilt of her dagger.

The smooth walls of the tunnel widened as she walked. The light of the threads revealed a towering entrance ahead. She came to a halt, craning her neck to view its heights. To her surprise, the stone was engraved with the curling runes of the Forgotten Tongue.

"Pan fyd... hael yn estide yn...," Ila read aloud. Her

clunky words disturbed the sober air. She was seized by the urge to apologize, as if she were bothering someone while they slept. "... sythrio, fel bydn ni gyd."

Chills crawled down her spine as understanding rolled over her. Ila knew those words. She had heard them repeated thousands of times at the weaver temple, the final words of a legend meant to teach young weavers of their sacred duty to protect the Boundary.

When the twin suns fall, so will we all.

It was a warning, a promise that if the Boundary were to fall, if the silver sun of the Reverie and the golden sun in the Wake were to collide, it would unravel the fabric of reality.

The legend should not have been written anywhere. It was an oral tradition unique to the weavers, protected from outsiders.

So, what the hells was it doing carved into the entrance of a sanctum beneath a castle in Wolfhelm? An echopoint, no less?

Focus.

Ila hurried into the sanctum. The vast circular chamber expanded around her, crosshatched with shivering energy currents. She tipped her head back to view the domed ceiling, spinning in a slow circle.

Yes, this would do just fine.

She knelt on the floor and folded her hands in her lap. Her weaver sight bloomed again, drawing the threads of the echopoint into sharp focus. She reached out to test them, pinching one between her thumb and forefinger. The threads were not taut the way they were in the rest of the Wake. They were anxious, unsteady.

One wrong cut could unravel the entire echopoint.

Ila grasped a single thread and tugged gently. A shock wave rippled down her arm. She released it with a curse. Opening a portal alone was hard enough. Opening a portal alone inside an echopoint was madness.

Her hands began to tremble. She closed her eyes. Saoirse was painted on the backs of her lids. Her gap-toothed smile, her impossible curls, her lone dimple.

"Sol liv hjent warren, min stjern," Ila whispered.

She snagged the thread that had shocked her and snapped it in half. Light erupted from the tear in space. She made another incision, then another. Icy air poured into the sanctum through the portal taking shape above her, but she did not dare look and risk losing focus.

She began to sing, a rich and melodic sound from deep in her throat. There was no tune devised by any poet or bard, nor did it involve words, only the sounds that sprang naturally from her tongue, as if her very soul was gracing the air. It was a tradition that had bound the Vaettir for as long as any could recall, nearly as long as the weavers had guarded the Boundary.

The last time she sang was the day she cast her family to the sea. Then, her song was grief embodied.

Now, it was a path to focus.

Keening built in her ears, nearly drowning out her own voice. The smell of rust clogged her nostrils. The portal widened above her head, volatile and unbearably bright. She snuck a glance at it and glimpsed the silver Reverie sun.

Ila pinched one final thread between her fingers, her vocal cords stilling. The wind rose, whipping her hair.

Hoste, help me.

She ripped the string in half.

The portal shivered, moaning like the hull of a ship, and stilled above her.

Ila released a relieved breath. She scrambled to her feet, adjusting the straps of her bag and reaching out for the portal. Frigid wind spiraled down to greet her, drawing her in.

Despite everything, a spark of anticipation flickered in her chest. It had been nearly a year since her last journey to the Reverie. As dangerous as it was, the dreamworld was intoxicating, pure creation.

The portal was about to claim her when a desperate cry rang out across the sanctum.

"Wait!"

Ila lost her grip on the portal.

18

Caine

Caine's tongue felt like raw cotton. He forced his eyes open. The stacks dangled from the library ceiling like stalactites. He rolled onto his stomach and coughed up bile. Wiping his mouth with his sleeve, he clambered to his feet.

The library was eerily quiet. Outside, the sky was strewn with stars.

Ila was gone.

She drugged me, he realized through the lifting haze. *Fuck.*

He lurched forward, using the shelves as a crutch. He made it five steps before his knees gave out. Strong hands caught him just before he hit the floor.

"Caine, what happened?"

"Thomas, thank the gods." Thomas hauled him to his feet and drew his limp arm around his shoulders. The captain was fully dressed in his uniform, his ceremonial sword at his belt. "Ila drugged me."

"What?" They started across the library. Caine moved with

the grace of a newborn fawn. If he had the energy, he would have been mortified. "How?"

"Never mind," Caine replied a bit too quickly. "How did you know I was here?"

"I was on patrol."

They exited the library, moving into the torch-lit corridor. Nothing moved but the shadows on the walls. "We have to find her."

"I'll alert the Skysteel Guard," Thomas said with a nod.

"No!" The captain looked at Caine like he had lost his wits. *Maybe I have*, he thought grimly.

"Why the hells not?"

Caine's reply caught at the back of his throat. Try as he might, he could not shake the feeling of Ila's caress, her mouth on his, her words in his ear.

Someday, you will have a choice to make about the kind of king you want to be.

"We need to figure out what she's up to first," Caine reasoned. "If they kill her, we'll never know."

"Fine," Thomas conceded, dragging the prince onward like a sack of flour. "But how do you expect us to find her while you're like this?"

"Your mother gave me a snakeroot tonic a few days ago for a hangover. I never took it." He swallowed thickly. Even the reflexive motion was difficult. "It should be enough to keep me upright."

"Where is it?" Thomas asked dubiously.

"My chambers."

The captain heaved his arm over his shoulder hard enough

for Caine to bark a curse. "We'll go and get it then. But if it fails, I'm calling the Guard."

☽○☾

"So?"

Caine grimaced as he set the drained vial on his bedside table. The tonic had resembled swamp scum in both taste and texture, but the tar that seemed to coat his muscles and the fog in his brain were both beginning to recede.

"I prefer wine," the prince replied, glancing up at Thomas from his seat on the bed. "But it is working."

"What are we doing, Caine?"

The captain stood with his back to the door, thick arms folded across his armored chest. The only light came from the low-burning fire across from his bed and the solitary candle at his bedside.

"Look," Caine said. "I don't know what she's doing, but I don't think she meant to hurt me. She could have killed me, but she knocked me out instead."

"Maybe she did mean to kill you. Maybe you got lucky." His eyes narrowed, and he drummed his fingers on his opposite bicep. "Why would she run two nights before the wedding? Why come all the way here only to leave?"

"Cold feet?" Caine proposed.

"No offense, but her feet were freezing when she got here, and cold feet don't usually lead to poisonings. Something…" He trailed off. Then his eyes flared wide. Caine sat up straighter, head sloshing. "Gods, Theodosia was right."

"What do you mean?"

"I knew there was something familiar about her."

"Spit it out, Thomas."

Thomas shook his head. "I can't say anything, by order of the king."

Caine lurched to his feet, anger burning away the lingering effects of the drug. "What the hells do you mean you *can't say anything*? I'm the fucking Prince of Wolfhelm."

"I was sworn to secrecy." Thomas was stone-faced, but there was a pleading look in his eyes visible even in the low light. "You will have to trust me when I tell you Ila is not who she says she is. She may not even be Queen of Galesborough."

Understanding clicked into place in his mind. "This isn't about that rumor, is it? About her being a witch?"

Thomas pursed his lips.

Caine exploded. "Gods, not you, too. This is ridiculous."

"Is it? She knocked you out and disappeared, not to mention..."

"What?" Caine snapped. "Are you going to tell me now?"

"I'm sorry, Caine. I have to warn the king."

Thomas put his hand on the knob, but before he could twist it the prince had gripped him by the other arm. Stars swam in his vision, but he held his ground.

"I am ordering you to *stop*."

"Your word does not outweigh his."

"Then I am asking you as your friend." Caine leaned in, tightening his grip on Thomas's forearm. "Please, Thomas. I just want to talk to her."

He should not have been fighting for her. He knew it, as did Thomas. The captain thought him a lovesick fool, and perhaps he was right. Thomas was stoic for a long moment. Then he sighed, his gloved hand slipping from the wrought-iron knob. Caine released him.

"How do you propose we find her?" Thomas asked tightly. "She could be anywhere."

"She could," he agreed. "But what if she never left?"

☽○☾

By the time they reached the catacombs beneath the castle, the effects of the moon sap were almost a memory. Thomas and Caine crouched at the base of the stone stairs, peering out into the labyrinth. The tunnels were cool and dry with bowed walls. A morbid sort of silence hung in the air.

Caine had not been this deep since childhood. He and Theodosia used to go ghost hunting in the tunnels when it was too cold to play outside. Ma Hendricks always warned against it. *That place reeks of dark magic*, she would say. She was not alone in her assessment.

"Too quiet," Thomas said under his breath.

Caine did not respond, still drinking in their surroundings. The ceiling was lower than he remembered. The torch Thomas held burned low, making the cobwebs glimmer like fresh snow.

"Move fast, stay alert," the captain ordered. He was, of course, fully dressed in his leather and skysteel armor, his rapier at his belt. Caine still wore his lounge clothes and slippers, only pausing to grab his velvet dressing gown off the hook as they left his chambers.

Every moment they wasted was another moment Ila slipped closer to her assured destruction.

They crept through the catacombs for what felt like hours. The occasional mouse scampered across their path, but there was no sign of the queen. Then Thomas threw up a fist. Caine ground to a halt. He started to ask why they had stopped when he heard it. A voice pure as spring rain singing in a foreign tongue.

Ila.

"Ten hells," Thomas breathed. His knuckles blanched as he gripped the hilt of his rapier. "She is a witch."

Caine did not respond, hypnotized by the ethereal notes rolling through the catacombs like distant thunder across the sky. She returned to the same sounds time and time again, following some inscrutable melody that raised gooseflesh on his arms.

"Caine."

Thomas motioned for him to follow and headed off. Caine fell in behind him. The song grew louder as the soaring entrance to the sanctum came into view. Ancient runes he doubted anyone alive could read were scrawled above it, etched directly into the stone. Thomas jerked his chin to one side of the arch. Caine slipped over to it while the captain darted to the opposite side.

Scarcely daring to breathe, they peered inside the sanctum.

Unlike the catacombs, the sanctum was just as Caine recalled. The fires had not been lit for centuries, but everything was illuminated by the light pouring from the girl at its center.

Ila knelt with her back to them, her head bowed as she wove her hypnotic song. Every inch of her was robed in white light.

It shone through her clothes and hair, pulsing and writhing with each note.

A rumble struck up beneath them. He braced himself against the wall. The stone was warm to the touch. High above Ila, an orb of light blossomed from nothing. Its edges shuddered like a heat wave.

The queen got to her feet, reaching for it.

"Wait!"

The word exploded from Caine before he could bite it back. Ila whirled, her hand flying to the dagger at her side as he burst into the open. The pocket of light above her shivered and warped. The air crackled, setting his teeth on edge.

"Get back!" Ila cried. "Get out of here!"

"Stop this!" Caine shouted back, advancing on her again. With each step his body felt lighter, as if he was about to be lifted from the floor. "Whatever this is, stop it!"

"Caine!"

The prince turned to see Thomas spring out. Ila swore and took her dagger from her belt, twirling it expertly. She looked like a young god, brutal and radiant.

"Get out of here!" she bellowed. The knot of light above her seized. "I can't hold it much longer!"

"Ila—"

Ila shrieked in agony and folded to her knees. Caine raised his arm to shield his face as the light above her grew brighter. Her glow dimmed as if in response. He pressed forward, reaching for her. Thomas shouted after him, but his words were lost to the howling wind.

"Ila!"

Her eyes were screwed shut. Her face was pallid, and blood ran from her nose.

Caine grabbed Ila by the shoulder. Her skin was as hot as a forge through her clothes. Her eyes snapped open and locked with his. Her lips curled around a single word. He could not hear it, but he knew the shape.

No.

The world was lost in a soundless surge of white.

☽○☾

It was not the cold that woke Caine, but the light. Like someone had harnessed the moon and dragged it closer. He struggled to blink the world into focus. A face filled his vision, pale and furious.

"Get up!"

Caine sat bolt upright, his brain sloshing like water in a bucket. They were in a snowbound clearing. Inky trees pressed in on them from all sides. Everything was bathed in an unnerving silver light. He squinted at the sky. He could not see the moon through the dense clouds.

"You dasak."

Ila stood over him, fuming. Blood had crusted on her upper lip. Her ethereal glow was extinguished, but she still palmed her dagger. Caine glanced around the clearing again. Thomas was nowhere to be found.

"Where is Thomas?" he growled, sounding steadier than he felt.

"Back in the Wake, thank Hoste. I was able to contain the portal before it swallowed the whole castle. It was supposed to take me straight to the sanctum beneath the other Caer Sidi, but thanks to you, we're in the middle of the fucking Tanglewood!"

"I—what?"

"And now I've broken *another* vow bringing you—whatever the hells you are—through the portal with me," she ranted. "You should have been knocked out for the day; that was enough moon sap to take down a bull." Ila narrowed her eyes at him accusatorily. "How are you conscious?"

"How the fuck am I supposed to know?" Caine shouted, getting to his feet. His legs felt like jelly, but he refused to lean on the nearest tree. If it could be called a tree; it looked more like a memory of one, shadowy and warped.

"Well, how did you find me?" Ila demanded.

"I saw the notes you were taking in the library, and I heard rumors."

Caine tensed. He had half a foot and fifty pounds on Ila, and even with her dagger, he could overpower her in seconds, but gods only knew what sort of dark magic she was capable of.

"They say you're a witch. Ma Hendricks always said the sanctum reeked of black magic. Seemed like a safe bet you'd be there."

Ila barked a laugh.

"I'm no witch." She drew herself to her full height, which was not particularly impressive. "I'm a weaver."

Caine stared at her. Ila let out a noise of frustration and jammed her dagger into its sheath.

"I'll explain later," she said. "Right now, we have to go."

"Go where, exactly?"

She gestured to his feet. "You'll freeze. We need to find shelter."

Caine looked down at his slippers. The snow had already soaked through them. Somehow, he had failed to notice. Shock did wonders for frostbite, he supposed.

"Right."

Ila grumbled something under her breath in Vaettirin and stalked off across the clearing. She made it two steps before Caine snatched her by the arm and whipped her around to face him.

"Let me go," she snarled.

"You're going to tell me what the hells is going on. Now." Ila opened her mouth, but Caine was not finished. "I don't care if I lose all ten of my toes; you're going to tell me who you are, where you've taken us, and why."

"I—"

His grip tightened around her arm. "Now."

Ila swallowed thickly. Her eyes darted to where Caine held her in a vise. He took a deep breath, drawing on the last shreds of his patience, and released her. She covered her arm where he had grabbed her, and even in the midst of it all, he found himself hoping he had not hurt her.

"Are you really Ila of Galesborough?" he asked.

"Yes," she answered at once. The truth burned in her eyes like the tip of an iron brand. "I am."

"You said you're a weaver. What does that mean?"

Ila licked her lips. They were already cracked with cold. "We protect the Boundary between the Wake and the Reverie."

"The what?"

"Caine," Ila pleaded. "We're in danger out here. You do not want to be caught in the Tanglewood after dark."

"The sun will be up soon, right?"

His eyes drifted skyward. The clouds had parted, revealing the source of the cold light. It was not the muted glow of the moon as he had assumed. It was not the familiar radiance of the yellow sun, either.

"What in the name of the gods . . . ?" Caine began.

"We are not in Wolfhelm anymore," Ila broke in, her voice as gentle as he had ever heard it. It was the same voice she had used to speak to the stable boy the day she arrived at Caer Sidi. Any other time, Caine would have been irritated, but right now, he felt like little more than a child. "I know you want answers, and I swear I'll give them to you, but right now, we need to go."

The strange trees held their breath while Caine stared at Ila, waiting for him to make a decision.

"Fine," he said. "Lead the way."

PART TWO

FEATHER AND BONE

19

Wren

They left the bodies of the vexes for the foxes and crows. Solene moved at an excruciating pace, her labored breaths frosting in the air. Wren struggled to mask her impatience as they walked.

The plan she'd cobbled together was unlikely to succeed. It was far more likely that she and Solene would meet a brutal end before they got out of the castle. Dread slithered through Wren as she recalled the fate of the nightmare who came before her, Bonehunter. He served as the Hand of the Para for decades, until he deserted. He was hunted down like a dog and tortured for weeks before his anchor was mercifully destroyed.

"Nightstrider?"

"What?"

Solene slipped along an icy snowbank. Wren grabbed her by the arm before she could topple over.

"Thank you," the kip squeaked.

"We're almost there."

Solene squinted into the dusk. "You can see Caer Sidi from here?"

"Yes."

Through the stripped trees and brush, Wren could just make out the glint of the torches at the gates. A shiver passed through her, rustling her feathers. She would rather walk into the mouth of the hells than return to the castle. Then again, perhaps they were one and the same.

"Nightstrider, a-are you all right?"

"Call me Wren."

Solene passed her a blank look. "Not Nightstrider?"

"What did I just say?"

"Sorry, Wren." Solene handled the name like a child picking up a sword for the first time, uncertain and clumsy.

They trudged on in silence. Wren kept her eyes on the torchlight in the distance but could feel the kip watching her intently. She sighed, producing a small cloud of steam.

"You have questions. I'll answer five. Choose wisely."

Solene scrambled to collect herself, lashes fluttering. Her eyes were still fogged with shock.

"Why did you help me?"

Wren stepped over a felled tree, pausing to watch Solene clamber over it. The tips of her fingers were raw with cold. Still, she did not complain, brushing snow off the front of her dress like flour.

Wren headed off again. Cushioned footsteps struck up behind her.

"There are crimes even I won't stand for," she answered in a flat tone. "Rape is one of them."

Solene jogged to catch up with her, hiking up the borrowed cloak to avoid tripping over it. "Why?"

"Is that your second question?"

"Um, no." Solene swallowed, the bruised skin of her neck rippling. "One of the other servants told me you killed a seamstress for pricking you with a needle. Is that true?"

The kip flinched when Wren barked a laugh. It fell flat, muffled by the snow. "No."

The rumors that circulated about her were almost as bad as the ones about Bloodreaper. Some of them were true, but most were not.

"Why are you helping the rebels?"

Wren came to an abrupt halt at a bend in the trail. The wind lifted, coaxing strands of dark hair from her braid. "I'm not. Para Warwick took something precious from me. I intend to make him pay."

"You hate him." It was not a question, so Wren did not answer. "If you hate him so much, why not just kill him?"

Wren bit the inside of her cheek, wondering how much she should tell this frail girl. Ten hells, she could snap her spine with her thumb and forefinger. Still, the rebellion chose her for a reason. Perhaps there was more to her.

"I'm not strong enough," Wren answered. "He would end me in an instant."

"Because he has your anchor."

"Who told you that?" the nightmare asked sharply.

Solene dug the toe of her boot into the snow, refusing eye contact. "One of the rebels."

Foreboding took root in Wren. How much did the

rebellion know about her? The only contact she'd had with them was at the end of her blade. Were there other spies inside the walls of Caer Sidi?

"So, does he?"

Her attention snapped back to Solene, who looked up at her with fearful awe. "Yes. He does."

"But if he has your anchor, he can kill you at any time," Solene pointed out, her brow wrinkling. "If you betray him, you'll die. What are you going to do?"

"That was five."

"Wait, no! Please, I just have one more."

"Gods, what?"

"What did Para Warwick take from you?"

All at once, the wide path felt oppressively narrow. The freshly dark sky pressed down on Wren from above, the ground up from below. When she spoke, her voice was scarcely a breath.

"My home."

Before Solene could respond, the nightmare walked away.

"Wren."

Wren peered over her shoulder, daring the kip to test her. Solene looked soft and vulnerable in the twilight. The blood on her lip had crusted, and a nasty bruise crept across her cheek.

"Yes?"

"Thank you."

"Keep up," Wren grumbled, turning back toward Caer Sidi, her anchor burn pulsing. "We have work to do."

Morning rolled in like distant thunder. Wren rose with the bluish dawn after a near sleepless night. She forced herself to eat the food the servant, a kip named Alma with auburn hair and a disposition far too sweet for Caer Sidi, brought on a gleaming platter.

"Where's the new girl?" Wren inquired casually as Alma refilled her goblet with juice.

"Solene?" Alma asked, drawing back the pitcher with a frown. "She fell ill this morning. I can send for her if you like."

Wren shook her head, taking a sip of her drink to disguise her satisfaction. Solene was not thrilled when Wren handed her the vial of crushed pearl snake fangs to induce vomiting, but Wren knew she would follow through. The symptoms would last half a day, long enough to ensure word of her illness would sweep through the mob of servants with nothing better to talk about.

"That will be all. Tell the others I'm not to be disturbed."

Alma curtsied and departed. Wren picked up a roll and split it open, reaching for the butter knife. The door banged open. She did not so much as flinch. Instead, she smeared a clump of jam onto her bread.

"Enjoying your sabbatical?"

"Ondine," Wren greeted her coolly, finally looking up. Ondine looked unfairly beautiful. She wore a black gown that hugged her curves and made her porcelain skin glow. Her vibrant hair fell to the base of her ribs in waves.

"I hear the Para took you out of the field. Such a shame." Ondine leaned against the doorframe, observing Wren with thinly veiled ire.

"I hear you've taken my place." Wren set her roll aside and got to her feet. She was still in her pajamas at the late hour. "I'd congratulate you if it was earned."

Ondine gave a brittle smile. "You have no ground to stand on, Nightstrider."

"Stop calling me that."

Ondine prowled toward Wren, her dress whispering against her legs. "What are you going to do about it? Strike me?"

"No."

Ondine stopped a breath from her lover. They had been this close many times, closer. This was different. This was not affectionate or even passionate. This was Souldrinker, and she was hunting.

"You used to be so strong." Wren stilled as Ondine lifted a deceptively tender hand to her cheek, running her thumb over the remnants of the bruise Para Warwick gave her. She wondered if Ondine knew about the anchor burn on her back. It still throbbed with each beat of her heart. "But you slipped when you met that luminae."

Wren jerked away with an animalistic snarl. "Leave him out of this."

"Does it sting?" Ondine purred. "To know you're the reason he's dead?"

Wren clapped her hands over her ears when a terrible keening struck up, but she knew it was in vain. The sound came from the hollows of her mind. It was the sound of Souldrinker ransacking her memories.

"You buried it so deep." Ondine grabbed Wren by the back of her neck, knotting her fingers in her hair and drawing their foreheads together roughly. She let it happen, too disoriented to fight back. It was too late, anyway. Souldrinker had sunk her claws into her. She was pawing at the fabric of her soul.

Pulling, tugging, ripping, unraveling. "I can feel them, your memories of that day."

"Please," Wren rasped.

Steel at her wrists and ankles. Air thick with the stench of seared flesh. A hand gripped her by the hair, forcing her to look up.

You killed him.

With a roar, Wren shattered the hold Ondine had on her, shoving her lover off with all her strength. Ondine flew back, her body cracking against the far wall with a fractured cry. Wren crashed to her knees, panting. Her eyes were jet-black. It felt like someone had yanked out her insides and stuffed them back in.

She heard Ondine get up.

"You're a disgrace," she spat. "Thank the gods I'm not the only one who sees it anymore."

Wren collapsed onto her side as the door slammed. She drew her knees to her chest and bundled her wings around her to shun the cold. The trouble was it came from inside her.

Ondine had always had a vindictive streak. Hurt her, and she would come back ten times harder. They had their fair share of shouting matches over the years resulting in broken bottles and days of splintered silence.

It wasn't love, but Wren was not foolish enough to believe she deserved better.

Using the table as a crutch, she went to the wardrobe and collected her empty pack from its hook. She stared at it, kneading the leather between her fingers. It had carried weapons, provisions, even the occasional severed head. Para Warwick liked to mount them on the ramparts, a warning for those who dared move against him.

You killed him.

Wren cleared the table with a violent sweep of her arm. Glass shattered, plates rattled, wine found the cracks in the flagstones. Slamming the bag down, she began to dress methodically. Leather leggings. A movable tunic. Her light leather gauntlets and chest plate. A cropped jacket lined with jet-black fur. She wriggled her wings through the slits in the back, wincing as her burn cracked and stretched.

Snatching her sword belt from its hook, she strode over to the trunk in the corner. She popped the lid with the toe of her boot. Sleek throwing knives and savage daggers sneered up at her from their velvet beds.

How many lives had been scrubbed clean from them? Hundreds? Thousands? She stopped counting so long ago. She grabbed her favorite long knives and tucked them into her belt. Four shorter blades followed. Her hands shook as she strapped two to her thighs and slipped the others into her boots.

Getting to her feet, Wren returned to the mirror beside the looted wardrobe. Her wings loomed behind her like an oncoming storm. She looked ruthless, lethal.

Just as she was created to be.

☽○☾

The day crawled by. Wren only left her room once to grab a quick meal in the drafty basement kitchen. She could not gather provisions without raising alarm, but she had plenty of coin. Not that she would need it. How many meals could she have left?

A soft purple dusk was soaking into the horizon when a knock rang through her chambers. She was at the door before the sound cut off, opening it to find Solene dressed for the cold. Her swollen lip and bruised neck were looking better, but she was faintly green around the edges.

"I vomited thirteen times," she informed Wren wearily. "Could I not have just pretended to faint?"

"Did you get it?" Wren asked.

Solene nodded. The nightmare stepped closer.

"Show me."

Solene reached into the pocket of her apron and withdrew a rusted key the length of her index finger. Wren took it, holding it up to the light. It was as unsuspicious as a key could be but opened the door to something more valuable than all the weapons in her possession and twice as deadly.

"Did anyone see you take it?"

"No. No one."

Wren glanced at Solene over the iron ridges of the key. The confidence in her voice was difficult to ignore.

"Well done," the nightmare said, tucking the key into the breast pocket of her jacket. "Do you remember your part?"

"Go out the south gate ten minutes after you leave, then wait for you off the path to Black Root by the split mirewood tree."

"And if anyone asks where you're going?"

Solene reached into her apron again and pulled out a skysteel dagger. It was dull, a touch of rust near its base.

"I'm taking this to the smith for you."

"Good." Wren went to the table to collect her bag. "If I'm

not there in an hour, go to the rebels and tell them you failed. Offer them information about me in exchange for protection."

Gods know it won't matter what they know when I'm a pile of ash.

"Can't I come with you?"

Wren thrust her pack at Solene, who caught it with an *ooof.*

"You'd just slow me down." She brushed past the kip, making for the door. "Besides, you don't want to go where I'm going."

"Wait!" Solene yelped. Wren paused, her hand hovering over the handle. "Be careful, Wren."

Wren blinked. A reply built on her tongue. She swallowed it and departed without a backward glance.

The nightmare kept her eyes forward as she moved through the castle halls. Everything seemed brighter in the absence of Para Warwick. Even the vexes were in better spirits. Servants and nobles chatted among themselves, but wherever Wren went, a hush followed.

She sped up, veering off the central corridor into a narrow passage. It was deserted save for two vex guards flanking a door halfway down. Wren pushed her shoulders back and walked tall.

The vexes snapped to attention at her approach.

"At ease," she said as she arrived before them. "Let me through."

The guards, one with a head like a yellowed gourd and the other dishwater gray with stubby tusks, looked at each other.

"We're not 'sposed to let anyone through," the gray one answered.

"I'm not anyone."

"The Para said—"

"I'm here on business for the Para." Wren took a half step forward. The jaundiced vex swallowed. The gray one looked like he wanted to melt into the floor. "Now, let me through before I go through you."

The vexes did not waste another second. The gray one fumbled with the keys at his belt while his partner stepped aside. Wren waited, her expression flat.

"Here ye go," he said, opening the door with a moan of rusted hinges. "Er, good luck, Nightstrider."

Tendrils of shadow seemed to reach for her beyond the door. No one went into the catacombs of their own free will, and no one came out alive.

Well, almost no one.

Wren steeled herself and walked into the abyss. The door slammed behind her, the sound bouncing down the stone steps. She started down the stairs at a jog. Damp cold slammed into her. It swelled with each step she descended.

The stairway ended as the tunnel came to a fork. She looked both ways into the darkness, though even her keen eyes struggled to penetrate the shadows. She turned right and prowled forward, both hands on her long knives.

After what seemed an age, Wren scuffed to a stop, squinting into the gloom. Up ahead, puncturing the black, was a light, one warmer than the silver sun, softer than flames.

Nightstrider.

Her knives were out before she could think to draw them. She pressed her back to the slick wall.

"Who's there?" Wren snarled. The only answer was her echo.

Keeping her blades drawn, Wren peeled from the wall and started toward the light, toward the sanctum. The air grew steadily warmer. *Strange.* She paused at the arched entrance to the sanctum, eyes trained on the knot of light. It seemed to hover at the center of the room, radiant and unyielding.

Nightstrider.

She did not hear it as much as she felt it in the hollows of her ribs. Her legs drew her forward. The immense sanctum unfurled around her. Despite its size, it was intensely claustrophobic. The walls were lined with manacles, splintered bones collected around the edges. The smell of decay was heavy in the air.

But all Wren could focus on was that ember of light. She arrived before it, hypnotized.

It was just as Solene described, a skysteel box no larger than her fist. She could scarcely see it through its glow. It did not float, as she originally thought, but was perched on a stone dais. Faint whispering radiated from it, nearly drowned out by the thud of her pulse. She sheathed her blades and reached for it.

"Nightstrider. What a pleasant surprise."

Wren closed her eyes as dread sank its teeth into her.

"Bloodreaper."

She turned slowly, putting her back to the box. Bloodreaper hovered just beyond the boundary of its aura, a hunched, indistinct mass dripping with rags soaked in blood and piss by the reek of them.

"You look well." Familiar words were made foreign by his mouth. He skirted the edge of the light. Though she could not see them, she knew his eyes were drilling into hers. "Better than last I saw you."

Wren clenched her jaw as the scar across her torso twinged painfully. "Maybe you're losing your touch."

Screee . . .

Bloodreaper's laugh sounded like iron scraping stone. "It would seem I'm not the only one."

Wren smiled thinly. He was trying to bait her, but it would not work.

"To what do I owe the pleasure?"

"Para Warwick asked me to check up on you," Wren replied, examining her blackened nails.

"Did he, now?"

"He said something about a conniving rat skulking around the sewers."

"Come now, Nightstrider. Don't go lying to me. We're old friends, are we not?"

Wren's heart kicked as if trying to free itself from its cage. "We're not friends, and I'm not lying."

Bloodreaper lifted his cowl to reveal his eyes, murky and lidless. His skin was like wax paper, and there was a gaping hole where his nose should have been. His lips rolled back to reveal multiple rows of splintered teeth as he inhaled, a wet, rattling sound amplified by the expansive chamber.

"You forget, I know the smell of your lies," he said. "Just as I know the sweetness of your truths."

"Don't know how you can smell anything with that crater in your face."

Bloodreaper grinned, baring his mottled gums. "You're out of your depth, girl."

"Perhaps, but I'm also out of your reach."

Her eyes dropped to the halo of light that poured from the box. Bloodreaper snarled, spittle flying from his jaw. Wren laughed with a bravado that did not reach her core.

"Now I understand why Para Warwick hid it down here. He knew you could never get your greedy hands on it."

"I would never betray the Para. I—"

Wren snatched the box from its stand and thrust it high into the air. Bloodreaper shrieked and scuttled back into the shadows. "How?" he hissed. "How are you touch—"

His words dissolved into another gurgling scream as Wren barreled forward, holding the box before her like a shield. The smell of his sizzling flesh engulfed her, triggering that familiar memory.

She stumbled.

Steel at her wrists and ankles. Air thick with the stench of seared flesh. A hand gripped her by the hair, forcing her to look up. The face of her Para filled her vision. She could scarcely see him through her streaming eyes.

You killed him.

A prick of pain anchored Wren. She looked down to see blood oozing from a shallow cut on her bicep. *Shit.* She had forgotten about his claws. Coated in the venom of an infant sugar snake, a single cut from one could fell a being twice her size.

Wren lifted the box higher to scatter the dark. Bloodreaper was nowhere in sight.

"Stay back, you fucking parasite!" she bellowed.

Wren launched into a dead sprint. Out of the sanctum, down the tunnel, past the staircase to the castle. Trails of blood raced down her arm as her heart pumped faster. Her vision was already beginning to fade. She pushed herself harder, deeper into the catacombs, guided by instinct.

Then she heard it.

The bone-chilling yowl of the uilebheistan in their cell ahead. Chills skittered down her spine. She had not seen the demons in years, not since Para Warwick sicced them on a vex attempting to desert. The uilebheistan tore the vex to ribbons before he reached the gates of Caer Sidi.

Hopefully, they would keep Bloodreaper and the others busy long enough for her and Solene to disappear.

Still running flat out, Wren dug into her jacket and produced the key Solene had stolen.

"Nightstrider!"

Bloodreaper's voice frothed with rage, almost as animalistic as the horde of demons ahead. Wren was panting, her lungs struggling to combat the poison. With a roar of frustration, she slammed into the iron door that contained the uilebheistan. The scent of rotting meat enveloped her as she groped for the lock.

Nightstrider.

Time slowed as the key slipped through her fingers. It glanced off the ground with a delicate ping and skidded under the door. The uilebheistan continued to throw themselves against the exit, hissing and screeching. Wren closed her failing eyes. She could hear Bloodreaper galloping toward her on all fours. She could smell his skin smoking, bubbling.

She could feel her death.

Not yet. Her grip on the box tightened. *Help me.*

A solitary pulse radiated from the skysteel box.

The breath was stolen from her lips. Frigid wind rolled over her, banishing the scent of seared flesh.

Wren opened her eyes.

Black branches like a net cast across the sky. Falling snow and the call of a lark. A faceless figure leaning over her. The smell of ash and dust.

Then nothing.

20

Alaric

Night settled swiftly over the Tanglewood. Alaric and Mica sat on opposite sides of their low-burning campfire, which did little to stave off the cold. The luminae nibbled on a piece of bread slathered in jam while the nightmare stared into the flames with void eyes. The fever stone sat between them in the snow.

With any luck, it would soon blaze orange.

"Alaric?"

Mica was watching him over the crust of bread, curious and perhaps a bit cautious.

"Yes?"

"What are you thinking?"

Alaric flicked his eyes skyward. Two of the three moons were visible through the snarl of branches, one red and one silver. The stars were so thick tonight he could scarcely see the spaces between them.

"I was wondering when our ride was going to show up," Alaric answered.

"He'll be here." Mica kicked a clump of snow into the fire. The flames guttered, then devoured the snow with a sizzling hiss. "He better be. But that wasn't what you were thinking about."

Alaric chewed on her words. In truth, he was not entirely sure where his mind had been. His head felt foggy and rattled.

"You were thinking about her."

"Who?"

"Nightstrider."

Alaric did not confirm this. There was no need. When he spoke, he kept his eyes on the fire.

"Do you remember when Luken brought me to the rebellion?"

The silence that followed his question was deafening. Mica shifted on the cloak folded beneath her. Her ears fluttered anxiously.

"Yes," she answered. "Of course."

"You remember what I was like, then."

Mica nodded, slow and grave.

"Para Warwick forged his 'mares without empathy. It took me years to develop any real sense of it. You, Luken, Morthil, and the others guided me. Without your friendship, I would have stayed a monster for the rest of my days."

Mica did not speak.

"Nightstrider shouldn't have any concept of morality, but she saved Solene and punished her attackers without hesitation. She did what was right." Alaric raised his head. Mica beheld him with glistening eyes. "Why? How?"

"I don't know, but you're wrong about one thing."

"What?"

Mica offered a melancholic smile. "Whether or not the Para intended it, you were not manifested without empathy. Or did you forget why you deserted in the first place?"

Alaric grimaced. "That was different."

"Was it? If I remember correctly, you disobeyed direct orders because your conscience would not allow you to carry them out."

He scowled at Mica. This did not deter her.

"I've been alive a long time, Alaric. If there is one thing I've learned, it's that no dream being is entirely good or evil. The lines between nightmares and dreams are rarely as stark as they seem."

Alaric grabbed a branch from their pile of kindling and snapped it in half, tossing the pieces onto their fire.

"For some, maybe," he replied, watching as the flames lapped up the fuel. "But not for Nightstrider, and not for me."

"Alaric—"

"One good deed does not erase a lifetime of evil."

Memories slipped through the bars of his mind, flashes of splintered bone, blood-slick skysteel, adrenaline, and black magic rioting in his veins. He clenched his fists to hide the sparks that popped at his fingertips.

"You've forgotten who I was, Mica."

Who I am still.

Mica started to respond, but a brilliant orange glow lit up her features. She dropped her snack and scooped the blazing fever stone from the snow. It had pulsed once and now burned steadily.

"Solene got out," Mica said breathlessly, popping to her feet. She tilted her head back to scan the skies. Nothing but the multicolored moons and a crush of brilliant stars. "Gods, where *is* he?"

Alaric rose, slinging his pack over his shoulder. "Worry about that later. We have to go."

He kicked a mound of snow onto the fire while Mica grabbed her bag. They took off into the trees, leaving the doused embers hissing and steaming. Alaric had to slow considerably to allow the luminae to keep up with him. It would have been faster if she let him carry her on his back, but he knew better than to suggest it.

They ran in silence, ducking and weaving through the droves of slumbering trees. The snow was eerily red in the moonlight. Twice Mica nearly slipped and fell, but Alaric was able to catch her.

All the while, his magic prickled beneath his skin, alerting him to the danger they willingly ran to.

"We're close," Mica panted, sliding to a stop and bracing herself against a gnarled tree choked with bulging green fungus. The stone in her hand seemed to glow even brighter than before. "Very close."

"Cover it," Alaric said. "She might have company."

Mica closed her fist around the fever stone. He called his magic to his fingertips, conjuring a spear of snapping energy. They slowed their pace slightly to cover their tracks. Every move they made was far too loud.

"Wait." Mica halted again. "I hear something... It sounds like crying."

"Where?"

The luminae pointed. Alaric stepped around her and started into the trees, calling back to her over his shoulder. "Stay here."

"Alaric!"

But he was already gone. His breath fogged in the air as he ran. The thunder of his pulse and his magic nearly drowned out the sound of snow crunching and twigs snapping.

It was not loud enough, however, to mask the sound of a girl crying.

Alaric sank into a crouch behind a mirewood tree, peering around it.

Holy gods.

"Solene."

The kip jerked her head up as Alaric stepped into the open. Another sob, this one of relief, tore from her throat.

"I—I don't know what happened. She was—we were—she told me to wait here, and then she just appeared—"

Alaric stared.

Solene was kneeling in the snow. A pack far too heavy for her hung from her narrow frame. She had removed her cloak and tucked it around a body lying on the ground.

The woman's eyes were closed, her skin ashen. Her hair and feathers were ink stains against the snow.

"Nightstrider." Alaric looked at Solene, dumbfounded. "How the hells did you manage to take her out?"

"No!" Solene threw her hands up. "No, she was helping me escape."

"What?"

Mercy in the face of an unspeakable crime was one thing, but this?

"She told me to wait for her here while she got the weapon," Solene continued.

"Touching the box should have killed her." Alaric paused, his eyes flitting up and down Nightstrider in search of vital signs. "*Is* she dead?"

"No, but—" Solene pulled her cloak off Nightstrider. "I told you, she just appeared like this."

Alaric let his energy bolt dissolve and crouched before the nightmare. Her jacket was partially removed to reveal a muscular arm. A cut on her bicep oozed green pus, and black spidery veins crept from the wound.

"Bloodreaper," Alaric muttered.

His eyes darted to her abdomen. His heart seized. Her free hand was splayed on her stomach. Beneath it was a small box that radiated white light.

The dreambreaker.

She was still holding it.

"Is she going to be okay?" Solene squeaked. Another haunting knell swept through the forest, drawing Alaric to his feet. He squinted into the dark. The torchlit gates of Caer Sidi peeled apart in the distance like a great iron jaw.

"We have to go now," Alaric said. "Take the box. Don't let go of it under any circumstances, understand?"

Solene bit her lip, which Alaric now noticed was split, then took it from Nightstrider with tender hands. A shudder rippled through the winged nightmare, and she fell still. Alaric scooped her up in his arms. He expected her to be heavy between her wings and her muscles, but she was built for the skies. Her head lolled over the crook of his elbow.

Thud.

Alaric swore when his magic gave a telltale pulse. A haunting toll of a bell swept through the forest, followed by the bloodthirsty shouts of soldiers.

"Run."

They bolted but only made it three steps before a shadow blotted out the moons. Alaric swore, preparing to drop Nightstrider and defend them.

Solene screamed when an enormous dragon landed between the trees, blowing their hair back with a gust of hot air. It was ten feet tall, with milky eyes, flaky ivory scales, a bulging belly, and talons like scythes. Great leathery wings with pink veins were folded against its back. Sitting behind its head was a man with locs and a radiant grin. Two bat-like ears stood atop his head, identical to those of his sister. Mica sat behind her brother, scowling.

It was rare for siblings to be dreamt together. Most bonds in the Reverie were forged in time, not blood. And as Mica and her brother proved, being manifested as a family unit did not guarantee closeness.

"Need a ride?" Nico shouted.

Alaric could not help it. He beamed.

"Good somnia, Nico," Alaric called back. "Nice of you to show up."

Mica gasped when her eyes found Nightstrider. "Is that—"

An arrow whistled past Alaric's head and embedded itself in the tree with a hollow *thwunk*. Torchlight and savage cries bled through the trees.

"Solene," Alaric barked. "Go!"

Thwunk. Thwunk.

Two more arrows narrowly missed Alaric. Another hit the armored flank of the dragon with a *ping* and fell to the snow. The beast let out a roar like the shattering of steel and released a jet of green flames, whipping his head in the direction the arrows came from. Screams flew up as the approaching soldiers were engulfed in emerald fire along with the black trees.

"Here!" Nico reached down an intricately tattooed arm for Solene to grasp while his dragon crouched low.

Solene reached out hesitantly, the box cradled to her breast. She shrieked when he and his sister clasped her forearm and yanked her up like a rag doll, then helped her crawl into place behind Mica.

Alaric lifted Nightstrider higher with a grunt. Mica and Nico took her by the arms and heaved her over the armored spine of the dragon between them. Her legs and wings flopped uselessly.

"Go!" Alaric shouted, leaping to grasp one of the spikes behind Solene and swinging his leg over.

Nico kicked his behemoth mount, and it spread its wings. Solene let out another earsplitting screech when they shot off the ground. Alaric shielded his face as branches scraped past.

They exploded into the open sky.

Nico let out a whoop. Though he could not see her face, Alaric knew Mica was rolling her eyes. He twisted in his seat. A shrinking blotch of torchlight studded with vexes stained the Tanglewood.

Alaric turned to find Mica staring back at him with a

combination of confusion and fear. Her hand rested on Nightstrider, who was slung over the spine of the dragon like a fresh kill. The wind had unraveled her braid, her dark hair rippling in the stinging wind.

"Did you get the dreambreaker?" Mica shouted over the wail of the wind.

Alaric just nodded. He did not take his eyes off Nightstrider until they began to water with cold.

Gods, what was she?

21

Caine

Caine had lost all the feeling in his fingers, toes, and face by the time Ila spotted the inn. Perched atop a snow-cloaked hill beyond the Tanglewood, it was painfully idyllic. The windows glowed with docile firelight, and smoke curled from two chimneys on either end of the building.

"Hurry up," Ila called over her shoulder. Caine glared at her back but was too miserable to vocalize anything.

The hike up the hill took longer than it should have. Ila was born into the ice and snow and was dressed accordingly. Caine was not so lucky. His slippers offered zero traction. Twice he nearly found himself face down in the drifts.

They reached the inn as a haunting bloodred twilight settled into the sky. The stars and the moons, the *three* moons, provided ample light. Part of Caine still wondered if he was dreaming.

But his dreams were never this cold or strange.

"Keep your mouth shut, understand?" Ila said as they approached the front door. The dull rumble of conversation filtered through the wood slats. "Don't draw attention to yourself. Some of them may be able to tell we're not from here."

Caine bit the inside of his cheek to keep from snapping at her. Ila opened the door. Warm air engulfed them. His skin stung at the sudden shift in temperature.

He froze.

Serving girls in evergreen dresses wove between a dozen round tables. A chandelier of bleached antlers dripping with wax hung above the dining room. All this would be rather unremarkable were it not for the guests. Half of them appeared human. The others were anything but.

Three satyrs leaned up against the bar, drinks in hand, their thick, fuzz-covered legs ending in hooves that clacked audibly against the floor when they moved. Wiping down the counter was a man with blazing white eyes and midnight skin. Two girls with shimmering mint complexions whispered to each other nearby, their gazes trained on Caine. A man Caine *thought* was human stood up from his table to reveal two extra, fully functional arms growing out of his sides.

"Come on," Ila muttered. Caine allowed her to lead him to the bar, doing his best to keep his expression neutral in the presence of the satyrs.

They looked straight out of the legends.

"Well, well, well," the bartender greeted Ila. "I was wondering when you would show up." His voice had an echoey quality that further unsettled Caine. "I should have told you to come; then you might have stayed put."

"Good somnia, Morthil." Ila smiled. Morthil responded in kind, flashing ivory canines. "You look tired."

"Thank you," he replied, resting his elbows on the counter. His eyes flashed to Caine. "Who's your friend?"

"Nobody," Ila answered with a dismissive flutter of her hand. "My servant."

Caine felt his ears grow hot as Morthil appraised him. "Your servant is severely lacking in clothing. I'll see he gets what he needs."

"Thanks," Caine answered before Ila could. She shot him a warning look, which he ignored. Morthil chuckled and beckoned with a willowy hand. A serving girl with reddish hair and a birthmark on her cheek hurried over.

She appeared human, but Caine had the distinct feeling that in this place—whatever it was—looks could be deceiving.

"Prepare a room for Queen Ila and find some bedding and clothes for her servant," Morthil instructed. The server bobbed her head. As she departed, one of the satyrs pinched her backside. She flushed as he and his companions dissolved into crude laughter. Caine rounded on him, but Morthil was faster.

"Keep your hands to yourself, or I'll relieve you of them."

The echo in his voice sounded like rolling thunder. It cast a hush across the room. The satyrs shifted uncomfortably.

"C'mon, Morthil," one complained. "It was just a joke."

"Do you see me laughing?" A heated pause, then the satyrs shambled away, muttering in a language Caine did not recognize. "You must be hungry," Morthil continued smoothly. "I'll bring you something to eat while Laurel prepares your room. I apologize for not having anything ready. There was an incident yesterday."

"What do you mean?" Ila asked, worry flickering across her face, which was still tinged pink with cold. "Is it . . . ?"

"I've not heard anything new, but we'll speak later in private."

"Takja, my friend."

Ila took Caine by the arm and steered him to a table in a relatively isolated corner of the room. He sat heavily, exhausted.

"How are your feet?" Ila asked flatly, taking the seat opposite him and beginning to unbutton her fur vest.

"Intact."

"I know you have questions. I'll tell you what I can while we eat."

Caine did not respond, transfixed by a man with the horns of a ram ambling across the dining room.

"Here you are." The prince nearly jumped out of his skin when Morthil appeared bearing a tray of food. He set it on their table. "Something has come up. We'll speak in the morning. Try to stay out of trouble until I return."

"I'll endeavor to," Ila replied.

Her words were nonchalant, but Caine could see the tightness at the corner of her mouth. Morthil departed. Caine appraised their meal. Four slices of brown bread, two bowls of stew, and two tankards of what he sincerely hoped was something strong.

"Spiced cider. Morthil brews it himself." Ila picked up a tankard with both hands and inhaled deeply. "Have some." Caine ignored her advice, staring at her with flat eyes. She set the cider aside with a sigh. "Ask what you want. I'll answer what I can."

Caine wasted no time.

"Where are we?"

"The Reverie." Ila grabbed a bowl of stew and began to stir it, coaxing ribbons of steam into the air. "You would call it the dreamworld."

"Dreamworld?"

"Hoste, I need to start at the beginning." Ila set down her spoon regretfully. "Have you ever seen a ghost?"

"What?"

"Have you ever seen a ghost?" Ila deadpanned.

"Uh, no. I mean, my sister and I used to go looking for them in the catacombs when we were kids, but neither of us actually thought we would find anything."

"You might have if you knew what to look for." Ila grabbed a piece of bread from the platter and used it to gesture at him. "Eat."

This time, Caine did as she insisted, sliding the remaining bowl toward him. He was relieved to find the broth full of carrots, potatoes, leeks, and what appeared to be chicken. He was not sure what to expect from a kitchen that catered to creatures from fairy stories.

Ila continued.

"The apparitions humans call ghosts are fragments of half-remembered dreams. Here, they're called splinters."

"Splinters," Caine repeated lamely. "Right."

"Occasionally, splinters slip through the Boundary between this world and our world, but they rarely manifest for long. Hence the tales of disappearing apparitions."

Caine took a bite of his stew. The meat was not chicken after all, but whatever it was, it wasn't half bad.

"So, these worlds—"

"The Wake and the Reverie. We live in the Wake. The Reverie is home to the dreams and nightmares of humans."

The prince swallowed another mouthful of stew. It settled in his stomach like a hot stone. His eyes swept the dining room. He could not have plucked a stranger scene from a fairy tale.

"These people—"

"Dream beings," Ila corrected.

"Are you saying these *dream beings* aren't real?"

"They're just as real as us."

A strange chill passed through Caine.

"Could I have created a dream being without knowing it?" he asked, his eyes darting around the room again.

Ila hesitated just long enough to prick his suspicions. "Yes."

Caine started when a deep guffaw burst through the hum of conversation. Morthil, now wearing a deep emerald cloak that dusted his ankles, was talking to a dream being covered in woolly brown fur. Caine could not even see its eyes through the tangle of hair. The two dream beings embraced and slapped each other on their backs.

"What about Morthil?" Caine inquired. "What sort of dream is he?"

"Morthil is a luminae, a powerful good dream." Ila raised her spoon to her lips and blew on the broth. "Luminae are ageless and difficult to kill, but not invulnerable."

"What makes a dream good?"

Ila hummed through a bite of stew, tilting her head from side to side. "The way the weavers explained it to me was that a luminae is often the hero or protector in a human's dream, whereas a nightmare is the villain or aggressor."

"But you said dream beings are not beholden to their dreamers, so would they not have a choice on their actions in this world?"

Perhaps it was the low light or his reeling brain, but he could have sworn a smile pricked the corner of Ila's mouth before she answered. "Maybe you do have something rattling around up there."

"What about you?" Caine said, ignoring her backhanded compliment. "Are you a dream, too?"

"No," Ila replied with a slight laugh. "I'm a weaver. Weavers are human. Our purpose is to maintain the Boundary between the Wake and the Reverie. If ever it were to fall, the worlds themselves would disintegrate."

The prince wanted to ask more, but something in her tone staved him off. Instead, he asked a question that took them in another direction entirely.

"Why did you really come to Wolfhelm?"

Laughter erupted from a table of dream beings who had clearly had a round too many. Ila fixed Caine with pensive eyes, her mouth pressed into a thin line. The second she opened it, the serving girl with the birthmark appeared.

"Your room is ready, Queen Ila."

"Thank you, Laurel." Ila hopped to her feet a bit too quickly, grabbing her vest and beckoning at Caine. "Come, servant. We have much to do in the days ahead of us."

22
Ila

Ila did not truly expect to fall asleep when she went to lie down on her straw mattress. She stared at the whitewashed ceiling, watching the bruised moonlight wander across it.

She was under the same sky as Saoirse again, yet she had never felt so far away.

She rolled onto her side, glaring down at Caine asleep on his bedroll. How he had overcome the effects of the moon sap, she did not know. Although, his utter confusion in the face of the Reverie had all but convinced her of his innocence. If he had any para blood in him, it had been diluted by his humanity. He was still a problem, though.

"Dasak," she mumbled, flopping onto her stomach to bury her face in her pillow.

"You or me?"

Ila grimaced. "I thought you were asleep."

"Not likely."

The queen sat up, brushing her mussed hair from her face. Caine lay on his back with his hands behind his head. He had changed into the loose sleep shirt one of the maids brought him. Ila could not help but notice the way it exposed the lean muscles of his chest.

"Are you going to answer my question, or do I have to guess?"

Ila knit her brows. "What question?"

"I asked why you came to Wolfhelm... only to leave two nights before the wedding. You never answered."

The wind gusted outside. The walls of the inn groaned in reply.

"It is complicated, Caine. There's so much you don't understand."

"Then tell me," he bargained, sitting up on his bedroll. His eyes were wide and keen. "You owe me that much."

Ila considered him for a moment in the dimness. Something stirred in her chest, an ache she thought she had laid to rest. "You remind me of my brother."

Caine frowned, looking vaguely as though she had just likened him to a catfish. "Oh?"

"He was also irritatingly persistent."

"Were you close?"

"When I was young, yes." Ila dropped her eyes to the quilt stretched across her lap. "It was harder when I left for Llyr."

"Llyr?"

"The weaver temple north of Galesborough." She glanced at Caine. He was bursting at the seams with questions. Ila had to admit there was something endearing about his curiosity. "There's a story we were taught growing up at Llyr. It may help you understand. Would you like to hear it?"

"I can't remember the last time someone told me a bedtime story," Caine said with a wry smile. "Does it have a name?"

" 'The Legend of Everloom.' "

Ila felt her stomach twist. She was no longer part of the Weaver Order, but the vows were still deeply embedded in her. As far as she knew, no one outside the Order had ever heard the legend.

But she had already broken most of her vows. What was one more?

"It is a long story, so I'll shorten it." Ila laced her fingers in her lap. "Long ago, in the realm of the gods, there lived a goddess called Everloom. Everloom was the goddess of thread. Many sought her affections, but her heart belonged to Foxheart, the goddess of the hunt."

Caine gazed at Ila from his bed on the floor, rapt.

"One day, Foxheart brought Everloom enchanted golden thread. *Weave whatever tale your heart sings and it will be so*, the goddess of the hunt told her. And so, for thirty days and thirty nights, the goddess of thread worked tirelessly to weave a tapestry like no other. Between its wefts and warps, a world awakened."

Ila was rushing, leaving out the lovely gleaming bits that made the tale so memorable—but she was exhausted and not in the mood for storytelling. Caine, however, was hanging on her every word.

"A universe was born of the Tapestry. Everloom called it the Wake. It was filled with plants and animals and brilliant creatures with thunderous hearts. Everloom called them humans."

"Wait," Caine interjected. "Is this real?"

"That depends who you ask," Ila answered. "Some weavers call it a metaphor. Others take every word as gospel."

"What do you believe?"

Ila considered, familiar doubt stirring in her gut.

"I don't know," she admitted. "I was raised to worship the Vaettirin gods, but not even Hoste has answered my prayers. I suppose you could say there is more evidence for Everloom's existence, though no one I know has ever seen her or heard from her. Whatever the case, her story will help you understand the Reverie and the Wake. If you allow me to tell it, that is."

Caine threw his hands up. "Okay, okay. Sorry."

"For generations, the Wake prospered. The Tapestry began to grow of its own accord. Each night, the humans dreamed wonders Everloom herself could never have fathomed, and in the yet-untouched reaches of the Tapestry, these dreams stitched themselves into reality. Their threads gleamed silver, not gold, and they formed a world of their own. Everloom called this world the Reverie."

Caine made a quiet noise of intrigue in the back of his throat.

"The Wake and Reverie were intimately entwined. Humans manifested dream beings, dream beings inspired humans, and both worlds prospered in a virtuous cycle. Meanwhile, a shadow grew in the heart of Gallowglass, the god of chaos. He had long sought the affections of Everloom, but her heart belonged to Foxheart."

Ila began to sink into the rhythm of the tale. Warmth spread from her chest to the tips of her fingers and toes as she wove it.

"One fateful night, Gallowglass stole into the home Everloom and Foxheart shared, determined to take something from them. He discovered the Tapestry stretched across the loom."

"Oh gods . . . ," Caine muttered.

"Gallowglass whispered chaos into the threads of the Tapestry, corrupting the minds of the humans while they slept. Their hearts and dreams soured. Their nightmares began to manifest in the Reverie."

Ila paused here, struggling to recall the path of the story. It had been so long since she had heard it, much less told it.

"Foxheart came upon Gallowglass corrupting the Tapestry. The goddess of the hunt fought valiantly to protect it, but the god of chaos prevailed. Everloom arrived to find her lover dying and Gallowglass collapsed on the loom, his blood soaking the Tapestry. In desperation, Everloom used a blade to cut the Tapestry down the middle, preventing more nightmares from manifesting in the Reverie."

"Where did she get the knife?"

"Caine."

"Right, sorry."

"Everloom cut the Tapestry down the middle to prevent more nightmares from manifesting in the Reverie, separating the Wake and Reverie. Gallowglass moved to embrace her, but his blood that soaked the Tapestry snared him, pulling him deep into the heart of the dreamworld. Everloom then stitched him a prison that could only be opened by the darkest of means."

"A little vague."

Ila huffed.

"With the god of chaos gone, Everloom stitched Foxheart's wounds with the enchanted thread. The goddess of the hunt was saved, but the threads pulled her into the Wake. Everloom wove her lover a paradise there. She longed to join her, but the rest of the Tapestry threatened to unravel. Alone beside the frayed remains of her universe, Everloom wept. She cried until there was nothing left but resolve."

Finally, the prince had settled into solemn silence. His greenish eyes were fixed on the floor, his brow furrowed.

"And so, the goddess of thread began to mend the Tapestry. She stitched a wall between the Wake and the Reverie to prevent any more nightmares from poisoning the dreamworld, but both worlds were already corrupted. Wars spilled across the Wake, and the existing nightmares ravaged the Reverie. The Tapestry was beyond repair, but Everloom could not destroy it without destroying Foxheart."

"Shit."

Indeed, Ila thought.

"Dismayed, Everloom blessed twelve human women with the gift of weaving so that they could maintain the Boundary. She told them to keep secret their duties and allow knowledge of the Reverie to die out in the Wake. She left the sacred few with a single warning. *When the twin suns fall, so will we all.* Then Everloom vanished."

Silence settled in the little room. Even the faint noise from the dining room below seemed muted.

"So . . . ," Caine began after a moment. "The weavers protect the Boundary."

Ila dipped her chin. "Yes."

"And the Boundary separates the Reverie and the Wake."

"Correct."

"If the Boundary is supposed to keep them separate, why do new dreams still manifest in the Reverie?"

"It has degraded over time, allowing new dreams to slip into the Reverie and manifest. If it were to unravel completely, it would be catastrophic." Ila cocked her head to the side, pensive. "It is better to think of the Boundary as an energy field instead of a simple wall. It exists all around us, a veil between worlds."

"I see." Caine, who had until now kept his eyes on the floor, now raised them to Ila. "Why did Everloom choose women to guard it?"

The queen arched a skeptical brow. "Why not?"

"I meant nothing by it. I was just curious."

"Perhaps Everloom felt more kinship with women, or trusted them more. Whatever the case, the gift of weaving has always been passed from mother to daughter."

"Your mother was a weaver, then."

"Yes." Ila blinked rapidly when her eyes frosted over. Each brush against a memory of her family left her bristling with agony. "She left the Order to marry my father and become queen."

"What about you?"

"I left, too." She began to pick at a loose thread on her quilt. "Weavers don't take sides, and I took the side of my kingdom. I was naive to think a queen could remain neutral. My mother tried to tell me, but I did not listen."

"Your stubbornness isn't new, then."

Ila almost smiled. "No."

"You still haven't told me why you came to Wolfhelm. Was it to kill me?"

"No."

"My father, then?"

"No." *Not directly.* Ila pinched the bridge of her nose between her thumb and forefinger, squeezing her eyes shut against a lurking headache. "If I tell you, you must promise not to interrupt me until I am finished."

"On my honor."

Her straw mattress crinkled. Ila snapped her eyes open to find Caine perched on the edge of her bed. He left a solid foot of space between them. She wondered if it was purposeful.

"I was never meant to rule," Ila began. "I had three older brothers. Morten, Henrick, and Anders. Morten was first in line for the throne. He would have made a great king; any of them would have. Then the plague came."

She kept waiting for the ache to dull, but it never did.

"Traders from Veltspar arrived in our harbor with a strand of rust fever we had never been exposed to. By spring, a third of our population was dead."

"I'm sorry," Caine said. His voice was heavy with empathy. "How did you survive?"

"I was at Llyr, far to the north. By the time word of the plague reached us, my family had been dead for weeks. When I returned home, the dead were piled high in the streets."

She could still smell them, the droves of bodies stiff with frost and death. There were too many to build individual funeral pyres. Thousands too many. They were blessed in piles and burned outside the village. The skies were choked with smoke for days.

That winter, the snow fell black.

"They told me my family died within three days of falling ill."

"At least they did not suffer long."

Ila nodded, hollow.

"They had already been burned when I arrived. Their bodies were crawling with plague. Their ashes were scattered to the sea."

Silence grew between them. Laughter swelled from the dining room below.

"What happened then?" Caine asked.

"There was no one left to take the throne. No one except me. I sent a letter to Llyr voiding my vows and was crowned queen that night."

It was a brief and somber ceremony, nothing like that of her mother's and father's. There were no choirs, no feasts, no dances or blessings or poems. There had been only Ila and a priestess at the shrine of her sworn god, the solitary moon looking on as Ila pricked her thumb with the thorn of an ashwood tree and smeared it across the stone altar.

"That must have been terrifying."

"Yes," Ila agreed. "But I was determined. Not just to help my kingdom recover, but to assist our allies. For years I watched my father allow our neighbors to be invaded by Wolfhelm, stripped of their sovereignty and culture. I promised myself I would not be remembered as a queen who bowed—but it's complicated."

"For people like us, it usually is."

"When I left the weavers, I was not alone. There was a child."

Caine went stiff. "Your child?"

"No, not mine." She paused. Caine betrayed no signs of the dark power his father possessed, but that did not mean she could trust him. But he was here with her now and she could use all the help she could get. She steeled herself with a deep breath.

"Her name is Saoirse. She's a dreambreaker."

"A what?"

"Rarely, a child is born of a weaver and a luminae. They're known as dreambreakers, and their creation is forbidden."

"Why?"

"They're extraordinarily powerful, and they can cross the Boundary at will like their mothers," Ila explained. "It is forbidden for weavers to lie with luminae for this reason. Their children are viewed as a threat to the Weaver Order and the integrity of the Boundary."

Ila glanced over at Caine. He observed her keenly.

"Saoirse was brought to Llyr to be detained and studied as an infant. When I met her, she had little control over her powers. She would have remained locked in that temple for the rest of her life, or worse, if I had not smuggled her out with me."

"What? Why?" Caine balked.

"Weavers care only for preserving the Boundary. The movements of dreambreakers through the Boundary are often erratic and can cause massive abrasions. I have trained Saoirse to cross with precision and to close every door she opens, so she is not a threat to it."

"Why are the weavers after her, then?"

"Her other abilities are..." Ila weighed her words carefully. "Coveted. There are those who would use her as a weapon of war, the weavers included."

"Who would they wage war on?"

"On the night terror who defies the laws of nature and wreaks havoc not only on the Reverie, but on the Wake." Ila locked eyes with Caine, though all she wanted was to look away. "Your father."

The prince went utterly still. His face was stripped of emotion save for a telltale glint in his eye.

"You're lying," he said, his voice dangerously low.

"When your father sent the proposal, I knew there was a chance he was not just after Galesborough. There was a chance he had discovered my weaver past and knew I was hiding Saoirse. I fled Galesborough with her, hoping to get her to a friend in Mistrun, but the Skysteel Guard found us first. I was forced to send Saoirse to the Reverie alone. I'd hoped she might be safe for a time, but your father found her and now holds her hostage."

Caine stared at Ila, visibly numb. She knew he was not really seeing her face. It twisted her gut more than she thought it would.

"I came to Wolfhelm hoping your father had brought Saoirse back to the waking world, but she was not there. He's keeping her in the—"

"Stop."

"He's keeping her here in the Reverie."

"No."

"Caine—"

Ila reached out to touch his knee, but he shot to his feet, raking a hand through his hair. He paced across the room, then turned to face her again. His eyes sparked with chaos and dread.

"This is ridiculous. This is some sort of trick to turn me against my father."

"What would I stand to gain?" Ila shot back, her voice rising with her temper.

"You tell me!"

Before Ila knew it, she too was on her feet. "Look around you, Caine!" She jabbed a finger at the frosted window, through which two of the three moons could be seen. "You're in a world you did not know existed this morning. You believed every word I spoke until now. Why would I lie about your father?"

Caine was breathing hard. The tendons in his neck strained. Fear flickered through Ila. Even if he had none of the powers his father possessed, he was still considerably larger than her, and her dagger was across the room on the dresser. She shoved down her fear and pressed on.

"Even if your father was human, he would still be a monster."

"I don't need to listen to this," Caine barked. Grabbing the boots and jacket Laurel had left on the nightstand, he stalked across the room, making for the door.

"Where are you going?"

"Anywhere."

"Caine!"

The prince wrenched open the door. Warm light and rowdy conversation from the drunken guests below filled the room. The noise cut off when Caine slammed the door behind him, leaving Ila alone in the semidarkness.

23
Alaric

The last time Alaric flew was five years ago, on the back of a manticore. He disliked it now as keenly as he did then. He was not alone. Solene kept her eyes glued shut for the first hour of their flight, clinging to Mica until the luminae gently told her she had lost feeling in her arms. As soon as she let go, Solene vomited over the side of the dragon.

Alaric did not blame her.

Still, he could not ignore the ecstatic beauty of the Reverie from above. The moons painted the snowbound land red and violet. Orange and yellow pockmarks dotted the landscape, little towns coming alive in the night. Softly gleaming rivers were threaded through the terrain. It all looked so peaceful from afar, though life on the ground was grim.

Kips bound in servitude, luminae forced into hiding, vexes and nightmares taking what they pleased from them.

Eventually, they reached the edge of the flatlands and crossed into the Shadowrise Mountains. The craggy peaks crept higher and higher, glinting like black shards of glass in the starlight.

All the while, Nightstrider remained unconscious, slumped over the back of the dragon like a carcass, her hair wild and unbound. Mica checked the wound on her bicep periodically. The blackened veins that crept from the gash seemed to be receding, but still, she did not wake.

"We should be getting close!" Nico called over his shoulder after some time. He was taller and leaner than his sister but shared her velvety ears and rich brown complexion. "Any rooms open at the base? Think I'll crash with you for a few days."

Mica whistled. "You? In one place for more than a day?"

This time, Nico twisted at the waist to smile at his sister. "I missed you, too."

"You could visit more, you know," she muttered. Alaric could scarcely hear over the howling wind but knew the twin luminae had no trouble.

"I've been busy," Nico said defensively. "I came when you called, did I not?"

Mica sighed, shoulders sagging. "Yes, you did."

Nico roped her into a hug made awkward by his twisted position. "I always will."

Alaric found himself smiling as Mica hugged her brother back. It faded when he spotted something beyond their silhouettes. He gripped the scaly spike in front of him.

"There!"

They were suspended over a plunging ravine with craggy black walls. Magnificent peaks ringed the chasm, capped with snow and skirted by evergreens. Built directly into the tallest of the peaks was a castle; ancient, looming, and weathered, with countless towers and windows without glass.

Caer Bheinn, the headquarters of the rebellion.

Nico shouted something to his dragon in the musical language Alaric used to hear him speak with Mica back when they were joined at the hip. The beast came to a near halt, flapping in midair.

"Do they know you're coming?" Nico asked, twisting to lock eyes with Alaric. The nightmare gestured with his hand. Nico turned to face the castle again.

A blazing pink spark had ignited in midair. As they watched, it ballooned to form a ring large enough for the dragon and its riders to pass through. It crackled with chaotic energy.

Nico chuckled. "Shit, I missed this place."

He kicked the sides of his dragon, and they roared forward. Solene gasped, clutching Mica again. Alaric shut his eyes as they passed through the barrier. One lick of the pure energy would knock him out cold.

The barrier was built to keep out nightmares. He was only welcome inside because the commander allowed it.

They soared down toward Caer Bheinn, landing gently on half of a wide stone bridge that led to the grand entrance. The rest of the bridge, which was flanked by behemoth headless statues, had been lost to time and war. Their remains were crumbled somewhere in the abyss below.

Nico slid off the back of his dragon, then spun to assist Solene. The kip, who was still green around the edges, took his hand and allowed him to help her. Alaric dismounted swiftly. His legs nearly caved beneath him when he hit the ground, and he braced himself against the beast's side.

With a mournful groan, the doors to the castle parted. Firelight spilled down the steps with three men on its heels.

"Commander," Alaric said, straightening up.

"Alaric," Reichart greeted him as he came to a halt. Two kips Alaric knew by sight but not by name stood off to the side, eyeing the pale dragon suspiciously. "Did you retrieve the dreambreaker?"

Commander Reichart was short of stature but intimidating nonetheless. The luminae kept his straight black hair in a knot at the base of his neck and was rarely seen without his leather armor.

"We did."

Alaric gestured at Solene, who was hovering on the sidelines, still looking ill and clutching a bunched-up cloak to her chest.

"Give it here, child," Reichart said, not unkindly.

Solene hesitated, her eyes darting first to Alaric, then to Mica. Alaric offered a nod while Mica forced a smile, her expression still drawn. The kip passed the cloak to Reichart. The commander took it in his hands tenderly and unfolded it. The white glow of the skysteel box sliced through the night as it was revealed.

Nico blew a low whistle through his teeth. Reichart glanced at him, a subtle smile pricking his lips.

"It has been a while, Nico," Reichart said as he covered the box again. "How have you fared?"

"I was in Marrowrun on business until a few weeks ago," Nico answered, leaning against the side of his dragon. The beast twisted its great head to nuzzle him, white smoke curling from his nostrils. "Lucky I was in the area when my sister called."

Mica smiled.

"Holy gods."

Alaric looked to Reichart again, only to find the commander staring at the dragon. Or rather, the girl slung over the side of the dragon. Nightstrider was still limp and pallid and showed no signs of waking. Mica had attempted to fold her wings into her back, but the result was crooked and awkward.

"Is that—"

"Nightstrider," Alaric answered. "Yes. She's alive, or she was when we left the Tanglewood."

"How the hells did you manage to capture her?"

"She was unconscious when we found her," Mica cut in.

"Incredible," Reichart murmured. His dark eyes glinted with adrenaline, the dreambreaker still in his hands. "This is a great victory for the rebellion. Well done, all of you."

The commander snapped his fingers at the two guards who had been watching the scene unfold from the sidelines. "You two, get her down and take her to one of the cells."

"No!"

A pale blur rushed past Alaric. Solene had leaped in front of Nightstrider and was now shielding her from the approaching guards. Reichart blinked at the kip, perplexed.

"D-don't hurt her," Solene continued. "Please, she saved me."

Reichart threw up a hand. The guards paused.

"What do you mean she saved you?"

"There were three of them, vexes. They cornered me in the Tanglewood. They were going to rape me. She killed them."

"She's telling the truth," Alaric said. "And she helped Solene escape Caer Sidi with the dreambreaker."

"A trap?" Reichart asked, arching a brow as he flicked his eyes between Nightstrider and Alaric.

"Could be."

Reichart considered, then after what seemed an age, spoke in a smooth tone. "Take Nightstrider to one of the cells. *Alive.*"

24
Wren

Steel at her wrists and ankles. Air thick with the stench of seared flesh. A hand gripped her by the hair, forcing her to look up. The face of her Para filled her vision.

You killed him.

A wail tore from her. He laughed, high and cold, and let her collapse. She crawled on her stomach through pools of blood, dragging her chains. Her leg was broken just above the knee. She dragged that, too. All the while, she was screaming beyond the bounds of her hearing, a single name on her lips—

"Wake up."

Wren crashed back into her body. Panic seized her when she heard the familiar clink of chains. She shot to her feet and threw a wild punch, but her arm was jerked back. She was blind, a strip of cloth tied over her eyes.

"Get this thing off me, you fucking cowards," she spat.

"Pretty, eh?" came a male voice. Wren whipped her head in his direction, inhaling sharply through her nose. The musk of a kip flooded her senses.

"So is a pearl snake," came the bored response—another kip.

"Where is Solene?" Wren growled. "What have you done with her?"

"She is none of your concern." Booted footsteps tapped toward Wren. She curled her fingers into fists, the tendons of her wrists chafing against the metal cuffs. "You should be more worried about yourself."

He slammed his fist into her jaw. She stumbled in her chains but managed to stay on her feet. Spitting out a wad of blood, Wren grinned in his general direction. "Is that the best you got?"

Her lungs emptied as he rammed his knee into her gut. He grabbed her by the throat and slammed her into the wall, lifting her from the floor. The anchor burn on her back screamed as it ground against stone.

"You killed my brother, you bitch!" he roared, hot spittle flecking her face. "I'll make you wish you never manifested!"

"Too late," Wren wheezed. He released her. She slumped against the wall, gulping down air.

The other kip drew nearer. They reeked of anxiety. "Save it, Hodge."

"Yeah, Hodge," Wren parroted. "Save a little for someone who can throw a punch." She was expecting his fist this time, but stars still cracked in her vision when his knuckles collided with her temple. "Better."

"Someone needs to gag you," Hodge snarled.

"Hodge, control yourself. She's not worth it."

Wren was no longer listening.

The air was bristling with power.

A chill skittered down her spine. A new smell had invaded her senses. Ash and dust. The door banged open.

"Out." His words were tinted with anger, but strangely, it did not seem to be directed at her. "Now."

Hodge cursed and spun, stalking back across the cell with the other kip on his heels. Wren spat after him. The door clicked shut, and she was alone with the 'mare.

"You're shorter than I expected."

Wren blinked, her lashes scraping the blindfold. "Excuse me?"

In an instant, a nightmare was an inch from her. His resting heart rate was nearly as fast as hers—*nearly.* She could feel his eyes scouring her. Then he lifted the blindfold with careful hands. Wren squinted through the flood of light.

He towered over her; that was the first thing she noticed. From a distance, she would call his eyes black, but this close, she could see the dark brown lurking in his irises. Through the haze of his power, the sharp scent of winter clung to him. Black horns curled from his wild hair.

The nightmare smiled, just a little wicked around the edges. "Nightstrider. Pleasure to meet you."

"Where is Solene?"

He gave an inquisitive tilt of his head. "Why do you care?"

"None of your business."

"I think you'll find it is." His words rang with nonchalance, but he shot a pointed look at her shackles, which she now noticed were forged of skysteel. He took a step back, appraising her. "Solene is safe. She will be compensated for her troubles and relocated."

"You were her contact, I assume."

"Why do you say that?"

"Solene mentioned you after I saved her from a bunch of vex bastards."

"Why did you save her?"

"Why didn't you?"

"It looked like you had everything under control."

"You were there." Wren narrowed her eyes. "Why didn't I smell . . . ?" She trailed off as the realization slammed into her. "The vex blood."

"Guess it was my lucky day."

Wren's nostrils flared. Over his shoulder, she took her first glimpse at the room in which she had been placed. It was borderline claustrophobic with a low ceiling and damp walls. Torches flanked the lone door. It was ancient, by the looks of it.

"So, tell me, Nightstrider."

Wren snapped her gaze back to the nightmare when he tilted her chin up with two fingers. Her teeth slammed together, but she refused to look away. His touch was surprisingly gentle, but there was a certain hardness lurking behind his eyes, a quiet viciousness she was all too familiar with.

"What were you planning to do with the dreambreaker?"

Silence settled over the cell, thick as blood.

"What?"

"Coy doesn't suit you." He leaned down so that their noses nearly brushed. Wren fought the urge to bite off the tip of his. "I know you're built to withstand torture, but I think you'll find I can be very persuasive, and we do have an eternity."

Wren laughed through the blunt pain in her abdomen. Hodge did more damage with his fists than she cared to admit.

"Maybe you do, but I'll be dead in a fortnight." The words filled her with a reckless sort of confidence. She pushed on, suffocating caution with her heel. "Do whatever you want to me. I got what I wanted."

"And what was that, exactly?"

There was no sense holding back now, not with her end looming like a full moon. Wren strained against the bite of her shackles.

"Revenge," she spat.

"I see." The nightmare straightened, observing her with an inscrutable expression. "It was never about the dreambreaker, then. It was about betrayal."

"Yes."

"You're unhinged."

"What do you care? You have your weapon now. Your *dreambreaker.*" Wren offered a grim smile, which he did not return. "Who knows, maybe you'll get in a few hits before he eviscerates you."

"I was like you once." He crossed his arms over his broad chest. "I believed Para Warwick was untouchable, but I was wrong."

"Any particular reason you insist on insulting me? Compensating for something?"

Her irritation piqued when he cracked a boyish grin, the corners of his eyes crinkling like parchment. "You sound like Ondine."

Wren stiffened in her bonds. Her name was not the only

one that inspired fear throughout the Reverie. Souldrinker, Bloodreaper, and the other nightmares Para Warwick created were equally infamous.

But as far as she knew, Wren was the only person alive who called Souldrinker by her chosen name.

"I suppose I ought to introduce myself." The smugness radiating from him made her want to smack him. "My name is Alaric, but you would know me as Bonehunter."

Wren's field of vision shrank to the head of a pin. The room tilted on its axis, but somehow, she remained upright. "No," she heard herself say. "Bonehunter was executed for desertion. His anchor was burned."

"Yes, I suppose it was."

The cell door opened with a screech of rusted hinges. Wren flinched, her heart scaling her throat. She had not sensed anyone approaching; the scent of the nightmare in front of her was overpowering. Alaric stood aside.

A stranger had appeared in the doorframe. He was short and slim with guarded brown eyes and black hair drawn into a knot. A scarf obscured the lower half of his face. At his hip was a blade with a polished hilt.

"Commander," Alaric greeted him.

"Alaric," the commander replied. His voice was smooth as glass. Wren sniffed. Beneath the blistering scent rolling off Alaric was something else. The smell of fresh water and earth warmed by sunlight.

"Does it bother you, luminae?" Wren drawled with renewed bravado.

The commander cocked his head. "Elaborate."

"That your subordinate is more powerful than you."

Alaric glared at her. The commander was unruffled.

"Power is only half the battle," he replied, starting toward them. "Power without leadership is of little consequence." The commander paused beside Alaric and locked his hands behind his back. "Why are you here?"

"You tell me. You magicked me out of the catacombs and dragged me here. Wherever *here* is."

The rebels shared a blank look.

"Come again?" Alaric asked after a pause.

"Coy doesn't suit you," Wren said sweetly.

Alaric glossed over her snide retort. "I found you in the Tanglewood. Not the catacombs."

"Don't fuck with me. I was in the catacombs, then I was in the forest holding your stupid fucking box. Now I'm chained to your wall. You expect me to believe you had nothing to do with that?"

Thunderstruck stares met her exasperation. If this was a new interrogation tactic, it was only succeeding in annoying her.

"Solene said she appeared in the forest holding the dreambreaker," Alaric said, speaking to the commander with his eyes still fixed on Wren. "I didn't think she meant literally."

"We should discuss this elsewhere," the commander replied.

"Is no one going to tell me what the hells is going on and why your weapon was talking to me?" Wren broke in.

The commander cut his eyes to Wren. "The dreambreaker spoke to you?"

The genuine shock in his voice made her hesitate before answering, but there was no sense holding back now.

"Yes."

"She had sugar snake venom in her system from Bloodreaper's claws," Alaric said. "She could have been hallucinating."

"I was *not* hallucinating."

The rebels exchanged a loaded glance. The tension in the cell was suffocating. Then Alaric and the commander turned their backs on their prisoner and started toward the exit. Sudden panic gripped Wren.

"Wait!"

Alaric looked at her over his shoulder. The commander disappeared out the door without a backward glance.

"You're just going to leave me here?" *In chains?* Fear pitched her voice into a higher octave.

It made her want to ram her head against the wall.

"What did you expect?" Alaric asked, more curious than malicious. He offered an almost apologetic shrug and followed the luminae out.

Wren shrank into the wall when the door slammed, scarcely registering the sting of her anchor burn. Silence engulfed her. The weight of her skysteel chains doubled, tripled, in the absence of distraction. It dragged her to her knees.

And she was alone, neck-deep in her nightmares.

25
Ila

Ila was on the verge of sleep when Caine slunk back into their room like a scolded hound. She remained on her side with her eyes shut as he trudged to his bedroll and sat heavily. She could feel his eyes on her. She wondered if he would speak.

Then he went to lie down and did not stir again.

She must have dozed off at some point because when she opened her eyes, a cold sunfall was crawling across the bedroom. Caine was sleeping on his bedroll, one arm thrown across the floorboards. Even in sleep, he looked troubled.

Ila shoved back her quilts and climbed from bed, dressed and packed her bag. Taking her boots in hand, she padded across the room and slipped out the door.

The inn was quiet in the sleepy morning light. The queen tugged on her boots in the hall and hurried down the staircase, skipping the last three steps. The kitchen doors swung open the moment her feet touched the dining room floor.

"You're up early," Morthil said by way of greeting. He wore a pale blue tunic that brought out the cool undertones in his skin.

Ila rarely used the word *beautiful* to describe a man, but it suited him. He had confided in her long ago that while he manifested in a female body, he found solace as a male. His current manifestation was ethereal, though Ila supposed her opinion mattered little—Morthil was over a thousand years old and mainly interested in men.

Besides, she was technically engaged to the stubborn, infuriating prince still asleep on the floor upstairs. The one she was about to leave behind.

It should not have stung her, but for reasons she could not fathom, it did.

"As are you," Ila replied. She let her pack fall to the floor and plunked down in the nearest chair, crossing one leg over the other.

"Mornings are less relevant when you don't sleep," Morthil said.

"I suppose."

Morthil pulled out the chair opposite her and sat, his expression grave. "I told you not to come, Ila."

"You don't dictate my actions. I can't just sit by and wait while Saoirse is in danger."

Grief welled in her chest. It must have registered on her face because Morthil reached across the table and took her hand. His skin was cool and as smooth as a river stone.

"You did right by Saoirse, sending her to the Reverie," the luminae said. "But coming here was a mistake. If Para Warwick captures you—"

"He won't."

"He will find a way to make you open the box."

Ila's lip curled. "I'd rather die."

"That is precisely what concerns me," Morthil shot back, releasing her hand rather abruptly. His tone reminded her of her brothers, protective and a tinge frustrated. "I told you we will get her back."

"When you say *we*, I assume you mean the rebellion." Ila folded her arms across her chest, a challenge. "You know I don't trust them."

"You forget I was one of them."

"You left for a reason."

"I left for many reasons," Morthil corrected her, a warning stirring in his expression. She had trod on a sore subject. "But not because I didn't trust them. Besides, you don't need to trust the rebellion. You only need to trust me."

"You know I do."

"And I trust the rebellion. They won't harm her."

"I'm not worried about them hurting her," Ila explained. "I'm worried about them using her. Her power is beyond anything I've ever seen. Greater than yours, perhaps greater than—"

"Para Warwick?"

Ila shut her mouth. Morthil observed her intently. She had never understood how his faultless white eyes could be so expressive.

"I don't know," she admitted. "All I know is that everyone in both realms either wants to kill her or use her." A wave of nausea rolled over Ila. She swallowed hard. "But if we don't get her back soon, it won't matter."

"I have some news regarding that."

Morthil reached into his pocket and drew a square of

parchment with scorched edges. A fire message. He offered it to Ila. She snatched it up at once.

The box was delivered to Caer Bheinn along with Nightstrider. Likely a trap.

"I received it from Commander Reichart an hour ago." His voice and posture tensed at the mention of the commander. There was history there that went back further than Ila could fathom.

"Nightstrider," Ila murmured, pinching the fire message between her fingers. "Why do I know that name?"

"She's one of the 'mares Para Warwick created. Not someone you want to cross."

"I suppose I'll find out." She folded the singed paper in half and got to her feet, slipping it into her vest. Morthil followed suit, radiating concern.

"You're leaving?"

"Saoirse is at Caer Bheinn, so I'm going to Caer Bheinn."

"You can't traverse the Shadowrise Mountains alone."

"I can and I will."

"What about your *servant*?"

Ila flushed. "He is inexperienced in the Reverie. He will only slow me down. Unless you wish to accompany me, I'm going alone."

A shadow passed across his waiflike features, his shoulders sloping downward. "You know I would if I could."

"You've already done more than I could have asked of you," Ila said firmly, placing a hand on his arm.

Morthil removed her hand and kissed it. Their fingers twined.

"I swore to your mother I would watch over you," he said softly. "I break that vow by letting you go alone."

"You're needed here. There are kips and luminae who need your protection far more than I do."

"Perhaps." With his free hand, Morthil brushed a stray lock of hair from her forehead. "You have your mother's light in you, starlende doniven."

Ila felt her throat tighten. That name was a mantle she did not deserve. But to hold it close was to hold her mother again, so she let it be.

"There is something you can do to help me from here," she said to change the subject. "Watch over Caine."

Morthil took his hand back, abruptly stern. "A quarrel between lovers is no reason to brave the Shadowrise Mountains alone."

"We're not lovers, and this is not a quarrel." Ila grabbed her pack off the floor and stood, heaving it over her shoulder. "As I said, Caine will only slow me down."

"There's something you're not telling me."

"Morthil, please."

The luminae sighed, sounding as weary as Ila felt. "Fine. I will look after him."

"Takja."

Morthil grunted. "Your horse is waiting for you in the stable. Laurel packed her with enough rations to support you and Saoirse for a fortnight."

"Takja," Ila repeated. She adjusted the straps of her bag but did not move for the door. "I am in your debt."

"And the realms are in yours." Morthil shook his head when she scoffed. "I've never once seen a weaver go against the Order for the sake of a dream being, much less a dream-breaker. Not even your mother."

She waved off his praise, unable to process it. "I'll send a fire message when I reach the rebellion."

"What should I tell the boy upstairs?"

Ila glanced over her shoulder, half expecting to see the prince coming down the stairs. Perhaps half wanting him to.

"Tell him the truth."

"Which is?"

"That bringing him along was too big a risk. He'll understand."

Morthil cocked a skeptical brow. "Will he?"

"No." The queen started toward the door. Her feet seemed hesitant despite her resolve. "But do what you must to keep him here."

"Good somnia, my friend."

Ila bid him farewell, opened the door, and stepped into the dawn.

26

Caine

When Caine woke, he lay still for a long time, staring at the ceiling. In the light of the moons, it had appeared faultless, but now he saw the ceiling's ridges and divots. He tried to focus on the textures, but it only distracted him for so long. He finally had to face the wild thoughts in his mind.

Had it all been a dream? He supposed so, in a way. If this was truly the dreamworld, were not all his experiences dreams?

Last night certainly felt real.

After he'd stormed away from Ila, Caine had gone downstairs to the dining room and claimed a table in the far corner, hoping in vain for a bit of peace. What he found was anything but. The rabble had died down at the late hour, but simply by existing, these creatures—these *dream beings*—sent his pulse sprinting and his thoughts spinning.

He tried not to stare at those who looked as if they had crawled out of fairy stories. The men with tattoos covering every inch of their skin, the bartender with what appeared to be a ball of tentacles for a head, the giant slug that oozed inside sometime after midnight (the serving girl with the birthmark, Laurel, served it a washbasin of mead, to its blubbering delight), but it was impossible.

Eventually, it became too much, and Caine stepped outside in the threadbare woolen socks Laurel had given him to find the night sky illuminated by towering violet clouds greater than any storm he had ever seen. The land itself was quiet, but in the distance, he could see the lights of a town no doubt just as strange as the inn.

Thinking about it made his head ache.

Sighing, he shoved off his blankets and got to his feet.

Caine froze in the middle of a yawn.

The bed was made with military precision. Ila was gone.

The prince dressed quickly in the spare clothes the maid had left for him. Tough leather boots were warming by the hearth. He stomped them on, relieved to find they fit, and hurried out the door.

When he arrived downstairs, the dining room was empty save for Morthil, who was wiping down one of the tables with his back to him.

"You just missed her."

"Sorry?"

Morthil tossed the cloth over his shoulder and rounded on Caine. His bottomless white eyes raised the hairs on his arms. "She left an hour past dawn. She asked me to keep you safe until she returned."

"What? She's *gone*?"

Morthil nodded, a pitying smile playing on his mouth. "I'm afraid so. I presume you're not truly her servant."

Caine dropped heavily into the nearest chair. "What gave it away?"

Morthil laughed. Like his voice, it echoed inexplicably. "You're not a very good actor, but neither is she."

"It would have helped if she had given me a little time to prepare." He rubbed his eyes with the heels of his hands. They throbbed from his fitful sleep.

"Ila seemed tired, too," Morthil commented, slipping his svelte hands into his pockets. "Up late, were you?"

"No," Caine replied too quickly. "I mean, yes. We were just talking."

"I see."

Caine flicked his eyes to the door as if he could pull Ila back through it. Shame darkened his thoughts as he recalled his behavior the previous night, like that of a spoiled child.

I really am a dasak, he thought. Whatever that meant.

No wonder she had left him behind.

The words she spoke the night of their first meeting seeped back into his mind.

You know I do not wish to be here.

He understood, gods knew he did, but to leave him alone in the belly of this bizarre world without a cent to his name or a way home seemed unnecessarily callous.

"Gods," he muttered, digging the heels of his hands into his eye sockets. "What am I supposed to do?"

"She would like you to wait for her," Morthil answered. "When she returns, I assume she will deliver you home to—"

"Wolfhelm," Caine finished for him, dropping his hands to look the innkeeper in the eye. He winced. "You probably don't know where that is."

To his surprise, Morthil nodded. "I have heard of it."

His tone suggested he was more than just vaguely familiar with the kingdom, but the question Caine asked next steered them in another direction.

"Morthil, are you familiar with a King Warwick?"

Morthil tensed. It was subtle enough that the prince might not have noticed if he were not looking for it.

"We in the Reverie know him as Para Warwick."

Though the definition of the word *para* escaped him, it filled Caine with a creeping sense of dread. "What do you know about him? And what the hells is a para?"

"Paras are the product of a human condition called parasomnia. Are you familiar with it?"

"Yes, actually."

Thomas suffered from sleep paralysis as a child. He often described waking up to a demon sitting on his chest, unable to move or speak. He was always gray-faced and sweating the next morning.

"Paras are the rarest and most powerful dream beings, even more so than us luminae, much as it pains me to admit." The corners of Morthil's mouth tightened, and for the briefest instant, Caine thought he saw a flash of blue in his white gaze. "Their kind have ruled our land for thousands of years."

"Has there ever been a para who could leave the Reverie?"

"None that we knew of until Para Warwick."

Shit. He had hoped to the gods that would not be his answer.

"Tell me about him," Caine heard himself say.

"Why the interest in the para?"

"Because I fell into this world less than a day ago and am curious as to why someone with the same name as my f—my *king* is lording over a bunch of fairy-tale creatures. Sorry," he added. "I don't mean to be rude, but I'm out of my depth."

Morthil did not respond at once, searching Caine's face with those haunting white eyes. "How did you say you knew Ila?"

"Does it matter?"

"It does."

"Look, I can't claim we're friends, exactly," Caine admitted. "But I mean her no harm. She brought me here mistakenly, and I need her to take me back. Until then, I've got to survive here, and I need to know more about this place."

Technically, it was not a lie, but it was not the whole truth, either. Regardless, it seemed to satiate Morthil enough to coax an answer from him.

"Para Warwick claimed the Reverie throne from Para Vega forty years ago," he explained. "I have seen dozens of paras rise and fall, all of them cruel, but I will admit Para Warwick is unusually formidable."

Caine felt his gut lurch. "How so?"

Morthil leaned on his table, considering Caine with unnerving intensity.

"All paras are power hungry and violent. Para Warwick is no exception, but both his abilities and his nature set him apart."

"What do you mean 'his nature'?"

Morthil leaned back slightly, drumming his long fingers on the table. "Paras are reckless, blinded by bloodlust. More often than not, this is their downfall. Yet Para Warwick is patient, calculating."

"Have you ever seen him in person?" Caine asked, heart thudding and mouth bone-dry. "What does he look like?"

"Not unlike a human. Not unlike you, in fact."

Fear spread through Caine like icy slush as Morthil rose. He readied himself for an attack, but then Morthil spoke again.

"Ila is headed for the rebellion in the Shadowrise Mountains. If you ride hard through the Bone Hills, you will be able to catch her."

Caine blinked. "I thought she wanted me to stay here."

"And I thought you were not her servant."

Caine could not help it. He grinned.

"I have duties here I cannot neglect," Morthil continued. "If I could, I would accompany Ila to the rebellion myself. She should not travel these lands alone. Your companionship is better than nothing." Caine bristled, his smile slipping at the backhanded comment. "I will have Laurel prepare some provisions for you. You can take my horse."

With that, the luminae swept away toward the kitchens, graceful as a wave.

"Wait," Caine called, getting to his feet. Morthil lingered in the doorway, peering back at the prince inquisitively. "Why are you doing this?"

There was a brief pause thick with tension. Then Morthil spoke.

"I sense you've not been entirely truthful with me, but that your intentions toward Ila are good. She needs an ally, and it seems it must be you."

Before Caine could formulate a response, Morthil passed him a bracing nod and disappeared into the kitchen.

27
Alaric

The wind thrashed and howled outside the window. Alaric did not feel it though the glass had shattered long ago. If he concentrated, he could just make out the raw pink shimmer of the shield that enveloped Caer Bheinn. He brought his knuckle close to the barrier but did not touch it. His magic recoiled from the purity.

Though he considered it home, it was here that he felt most like a monster.

"Was she telling the truth?"

Reichart stood with his hands behind his back, scanning the haphazard spread of maps and scrolls on the table. Despite his neat dress and organized mind, his chambers were a mess. Books with cracked spines were stacked like cairns around his bed, which had not been made in months.

"I think so," Alaric replied. He pulled out one of the high-backed chairs at the table and sat.

Nightstrider had behaved as he expected while he was questioning her. Brash and unafraid with barely checked anger sizzling beneath her skin. When he went to leave, however, something changed.

You're just going to leave me here?

She had been poisoned, beaten, and kidnapped, but it was being alone that scared her.

Why?

"Alaric," Reichart said, anchoring him.

"Sorry, what?"

"I asked for your opinion of Nightstrider."

Alaric allowed his vision to drift from focus as he stared at a flickering candle on the table.

"She's strong," he answered, blinking away the haze. "More powerful than Souldrinker and Bloodreaper."

Indeed, when she had awoken from her fevered state, the force of her power slammed into him like a hurricane. He followed the ceaseless thrum to the dungeons where they had left her restrained. The closer he got, the more his magic reacted, twitching like a caged animal in his ribs.

Even stranger, she did not appear to possess any physical magic like his or Ondine's psychic abilities.

Nightstrider simply blazed with unbridled strength, as if her soul was the heart of a forge.

"And?" Reichart pressed.

"And she stole the dreambreaker to punish Para Warwick despite knowing he could kill her from a distance. She has nothing to lose. There isn't much more dangerous than a 'mare with nothing to lose."

I should know.

Reichart pulled out the neighboring chair and dropped

into it. "How long does she have before the Para eliminates her?"

"He'll want to interrogate her before he destroys her anchor. He might try to cripple her from a distance by destroying it partially, but I doubt it."

Anchors were an inexact business. For all Para Warwick knew, a tear or chip in her anchor could be cutting off her head. In fact, that was probably the only thing keeping Nightstrider alive.

A knock came at the door. "Enter," Reichart called pensively. It opened at once. The commander smiled. "Quintus."

The kip in question beamed. He was easily a foot taller than Reichart, with red hair and a blizzard of freckles. Reichart rose and crossed to Quintus, who met him in the middle. They clasped hands and pressed their brows together.

Alaric felt his stomach knot. He wondered what it would be like to hold someone like that. Not with simple lust but with tenderness.

"Did you bring her?" the commander asked, adopting a formal air again as they parted.

Quintus stood aside. Alaric got to his feet. "Solene."

Solene hovered at the edge of the room, rolling the end of her braid between her fingertips. Guilt swept through Alaric. He did not get a good look at her in the Tanglewood nor on the flight home with Nico. There was a purple bruise around her throat to match her split lip.

If Nightstrider had not been there to stop those vexes, she'd be in a far worse state.

"Are you all right?" he asked.

"Am I *all right*?" Solene repeated in a wobbly voice. "No, I'm not all right. I could have died trying to get your stupid weapon for you. I was almost—" She cut herself off, flushed and teary.

"You knew the job was dangerous when you took it," Reichart pointed out.

"Took it? I had no choice!"

Reichart clasped his hands, something he often did when he was uncomfortable. "We thought you were experienced, skilled in the art of burglary. Perhaps we were mistaken."

"And I thought luminae were supposed to be good," Solene said, seething. "Wren treated me better than you have. At least she was honest."

Reichart cocked his head to the side. "Who is Wren?"

Solene folded her scrawny arms, looking more like a stubborn child than anything. "Why should I tell you?"

"Nightstrider." All eyes fell on Alaric as Solene went an even deeper shade of pink. "Wren is Nightstrider."

He did not know where the need to choose a name other than the ones Para Warwick crowned them with came from, only that almost every 'mare, himself included, had done so. Perhaps in its way it was a form of rebellion, a mark of something undeniably *theirs* in a life that did not belong to them.

Wren, he tested the name in his mind. It suited her.

"Solene," Quintus broke in. His gentle voice matched his disposition. He stood in stark contrast to Alaric and Reichart. "You owe the rebellion nothing. You've helped bring us a weapon of immeasurable value. I will escort you anywhere you want to go when you're ready. In the meantime, any information you could provide us about Nightstrider would be invaluable."

Reichart shot Quintus a grateful look. Alaric breathed a

mental sigh of relief. Of the three of them, the kip was certainly the most adept at de-escalation. Solene chewed on his proposition for a moment.

Then her narrow body sagged.

"Fine," she agreed gruffly. "What do you want to know?"

"I saw Nightstrider—Wren—save you in the Tanglewood," Alaric said. "Why did she save you?"

"She said there were crimes even she would not stand for."

Alaric nodded, grim.

He had never taken a woman by force, not even when he was the Hand of the Para. He had torn dream beings limb from limb, gouged out their eyes, uprooted their tongues, but that was one line he refused to cross.

Maybe the only line.

"Why did Nightstrider steal the weapon?" Reichart asked Solene, drawing Alaric back to the present.

"She wanted to take revenge on Para Warwick. She said he took something from her. Her home."

"Her home?" Alaric repeated blankly. "What home?"

Solene shook her head. "That was all she said."

Reichart and Quintus looked at Alaric in unison, the same question written on their faces. He just shrugged. When he was the Hand of the Para, he called Caer Sidi home. Caer Sidi, and the battlefield, of course.

As far as he could tell, neither of those things had been stolen from Wren so much as she had discarded them.

Reichart jumped back in before Alaric could continue. "Are you certain she was holding the box? Did she have skin-to-skin contact with it?"

"Yes." The sureness in Solene's voice was difficult to dispute. "She appeared in the forest holding the box. She was unconscious and wounded. I thought she was dead until I felt her pulse."

"It makes no sense," Reichart said, frustration coloring his tone.

"We're missing something," Quintus agreed.

Alaric maintained his silence. Questions circled in his mind like vultures. Each one opened the door for ten more. A pit settled in his stomach, followed by an inexplicable wave of dread.

Something told him the answers were not for the faint of heart.

Thud.

The other dream beings turned to Alaric when he inhaled sharply.

"Alaric?" Reichart asked.

The nightmare waved them off, listening to the frantic thrum of his magic. Something was different. Something was wrong. It was not pushing him away, telling him to run from something.

It was pulling him forward toward something.

Toward someone.

"I have to go," Alaric said in a scattered voice. Then, avoiding eye contact with the others, he ducked around Solene and made for the door.

"Alaric—"

But he was already gone, sprinting down the stairs to the dungeons at full tilt.

28

Wren

Breathe.

Minutes and hours crawled by, and Wren turned the word into a prayer. If she kept still, she would not hear the hollow clank of the chains at her wrists. Gods knew she heard it enough in her sleep, yet the sound was never isolated. Screaming and the unmistakable sound of sizzling flesh always accompanied it.

Breathe.

Wren knew her life would end in chains. She knew before Para Warwick destroyed her anchor, he would torture her, but it would be worth it knowing she took something of such value from him. She would steal the weapon, get it to his enemies, then fly until her lungs ached with all the free air they could breathe.

She would face her death with her head high. She would not be contained by a bunch of deluded rebels.

Breathe.

Wren twisted violently and yanked on her chains. The

skysteel links groaned, the manacles cut into her wrists, but they did not budge. She crumpled, panting.

You killed him.

"Shut up," she whispered. "Shut up!"

The cell door banged open. Wren lurched to her feet. Three kips, all men, trekked into the cell.

"What do you want?" Wren demanded.

The largest of the men stepped forward. He was as tall as he was ugly. A leering smile stretched across his face. He was missing his right front tooth, and the rest of his teeth were yellowed and crooked.

"Justice."

"Hodge," Wren greeted him, recognizing his gravelly voice. "Now I know why you blindfolded me."

Hodge barked a laugh, then nodded at his two companions. They filed out and shut the door with a clang.

"When they told me you were here, I barely believed it. The great Nightstrider, at the mercy of the rebellion." His watery blue eyes flashed to her manacles. "Do you like them? Reinforced skysteel. I always hoped to see you in them."

"You think you're the only one with a vendetta against me? Get in line."

"I don't see a line," Hodge drawled. He prowled her, wading through palpable anticipation. "Just you and me."

"Your funeral."

"You killed my brother. Murdered him in his sleep," the kip said, finally arriving half a step from her. His breath was hot and stale in her face. "We manifested together thirty years ago. He was a great man."

"Great enough to be murdered."

"Two years ago, he went on a mission for Commander Reichart and did not return," Hodge continued, unruffled. "Only one member of his party made it back alive. He died that night of his wounds, but not before he described their attacker. A 'mare with black wings sent by Para Warwick himself."

"I hate to break it to you, but I've killed a lot of people," Wren shot back. "I don't remember your brother, and I won't remember you once I rip your lungs out through your ass."

Hodge slammed his fist into her chin. Her head snapped back, bouncing off the wall with a crack. She staggered.

"Commander Reichart wants you alive," Hodge spat. Saliva flecked her face. "No surprise his pet 'mare agrees."

"I guess they'll both be disappointed," Wren said through her teeth. "I'll be dead in a fortnight."

"You'll be dead long before that."

Another blow to the temple. Wren stumbled in her chains, scarcely managing to stay upright.

Gods, when did kips get this strong?

"If you think you can beat me to death, you're wrong," she taunted. "Unless you happen to have my anchor shoved up your—"

Her vision scattered to black when his fist connected with her nose. Before she could curse, he grabbed her by the neck and pinned her to the wall. Her feet dangled an inch off the floor.

"Shut up!" Hodge roared.

Wren drove her knee into his groin. He howled and released

her. She whipped around, grasping her chains with both hands, and pulled with all her strength. The stone around the base cracked.

Searing pain lanced through her wing, plunging deep into the festering anchor burn on her back. Wren screamed in agony as Hodge yanked the knife. She collapsed on her side.

Hodge kicked her in the ribs, and she rolled onto her back. He straddled her, one hand crushing her throat, the other fumbling with his belt.

"They say if you cut a 'mare into enough pieces, they're as good as dead." Hodge leaned so close that she could see the capillaries in the whites of his eyes. "I'll test that theory when I'm through with you."

A pin dropped in the halls of her mind, and Wren was gone. Her mind fled to the only safe place she had ever known. A cabin beyond the Tanglewood where the grass was sweet and the water clean.

A place only they knew. A place they could be together.

A home.

You killed him.

Bang.

Wren rolled her head to the side, blinking through the haze of oxygen deprivation. The cell door had been blown clear off its hinges. Standing in the frame was a blurry horned figure robed in thunderous black magic.

"Get out of here, 'mare," Hodge snarled, the spit from his words flecking her face. "We're busy."

Silent as a wraith, the figure descended on then. Wren squeezed her eyes shut. Then the pressure was gone from her throat, the burning hands from her body. She coughed and retched, struggling to rise as hot blood coursed down her back. She collapsed again as blackness encroached on her vision.

"W-wait. She deserves it, you know she—"

Crunnnch.

"Wren."

Alaric stood over her. Blood sprayed his features, and his eyes were black from pupil to lid. She knew those eyes. They were her eyes. The eyes of their Para.

You killed him.

Leave me alone, she begged, but the words never left her. Her vision failed. Cool air kissed the skin of her wrists as they were released from the cuffs. The ground moved beneath her. A rapid pulse tickled her skin.

Then nothing.

29
Alaric

When he carried her body through the Tanglewood, Alaric thought that would be the last time he touched Wren without a weapon in his hand, but somehow, she was again warm and vulnerable in his arms. She was also losing blood. Fast. His hands were slick with it, and the front of his shirt was plastered to his skin.

"Killed him..."

Alaric glanced down at Wren. Her eyes were open, but only slightly. They were black from pupil to lid, just like his.

"Yes," he assured her. "I did."

Hodge's blade, still slick with her blood, was jammed in his belt. The kip would not need it, his head cranked around like a broken doll, his belt unbuckled and his pants halfway down.

Men like Hodge had no place in the rebellion, no place in any world.

Reichart could shout about restraint and justice all he wanted, but he would not cast out Alaric. Where would he find another nightmare to do his dirty work?

"Killed him..."

"Hold on," Alaric said, adjusting his grip under Wren's knees. "We're almost there."

He picked up the pace, weaving through the halls of Caer Bheinn, which were deserted at the late hour. The radiance of the night's heavenly bodies seeped through the shattered windows, tainted pink by the shield. The raw light had always unnerved him. It was as if they lived within the chambers of a petrified heart.

Alaric turned down a windowless corridor, arriving at the last door on the left. It flew open before he could shift Wren in his arms to knock.

"Ten hells, what happened?" Mica was in her shift, staring up at them with enormous lamp-like eyes.

"She was attacked."

Mica opened the door wider. "Put her on the bed."

Alaric did as he was told, turning sideways to fit Wren and her wings through. Mica shut the door behind them and bolted it.

Her room was one of his favorites at Caer Bheinn. It was warm and dim with a broad canopied bed shrouded in patterned quilts. Potted luminescent plants he could not name hung from the ceiling. Wooden shelves lined the walls, brimming with tonics, herbs, and surgical instruments. The windows were obscured by heavy curtains, and a fire roared green at the hearth.

"Here." Mica shoved several books off her bed with a sweep of her arm. "Put her on her side."

Alaric lay Wren on her uninjured side. She was as limp as a kitchen rag. Her blood was already soaking the sheets.

Something's wrong, Alaric thought. *She shouldn't be bleeding this much.*

Mica snatched a pair of shears from a jar on a nearby shelf. Wren twitched as the luminae cut away her tunic to reveal her skin and feathers. A stab wound cut straight through her left wing. Mica eased the wing aside. She froze. Alaric pressed forward to peer over her shoulder.

"Gods," Mica whispered.

The knife wound went straight through her wing into her back. Straight through *another* wound. This one was shiny and black as pitch with jagged branching arms. Alaric would have known it anywhere.

"An anchor burn," he muttered.

Mica grabbed a cloudy glass bottle and cloth from the shelf. She popped the cork and doused the rag in sharp-smelling liquid.

"No wonder she's so weak," she said, shaking her head. "This is fresh; she must be in incredible pain."

Alaric just nodded. The scar on the back of his neck twinged.

"The burn is impairing her healing." Mica began to dab at the overlapping wounds with the damp cloth. Wren shivered but did not wake. "Who attacked her?"

"That kip Hodge. He said she killed his brother."

"Did she?"

"Probably," Alaric answered absently, still hovering behind Mica with his eyes glued to Wren. "I killed him."

"Alaric!"

"He was going to rape her."

Mica, who had been swelling up to scream at him, went still. Hardness he did not often see about her eclipsed her face.

"Of course he was," she murmured. "What better way to destroy her? Now, go sit down; you're in my way."

Alaric went to the squashy armchair by the hearth and spun it around to face Mica and Wren. The luminae worked swiftly and methodically, retrieving needle and thread from her kit and starting in on the stab wound.

Still, Nightstrider did not awaken.

"What does Reichart have planned for her?" Mica asked, tying off the first suture with expert fingers.

"Not sure it matters," Alaric replied. "Para Warwick will finish destroying her anchor sooner or later."

Gods, why did saying it aloud feel like a gut punch? What was wrong with him?

Mica wiped her bloody hands on a cloth and started on the next stitch. "You said the same thing when you got here."

"That was different," Alaric said flatly. "We had Luken."

"And now we have a new dreambreaker."

"A child stuck in a box that only one weaver can open. We don't even know if either of them is still alive."

Mica glared at him over Wren's limp form, pulling the glistening thread taut. "You're exhaustingly pessimistic."

"You noticed, did you?" Alaric returned his attention to Wren. Even unconscious, she looked angry. "She told me she stole the dreambreaker to get revenge on Para Warwick."

Mica paused mid-stitch. "Revenge? For what?"

"I don't know." Alaric sat forward in the armchair, resting his elbows on his knees and lacing his fingers loosely. His gaze brushed over the sharp lines of Wren's jaw, the pointed tip of her ear.

"I was her, Mica. I know how deep the indoctrination runs. For her to do something like this, he would have had to do something unspeakably cruel."

The healer refocused on her task, a divot forming between neatly shaped brows. "He is a night terror. What do you expect?"

Alaric did not respond. He knew Mica meant nothing by her dismissive tone, but it still wore on his nerves. A luminae could not comprehend the horrors that festered inside the home and mind of a para. For her sake, he was grateful, but it would be a relief to have someone who understood his past.

His eyes settled on Wren again.

"What is it?" Mica asked.

"Nothing," Alaric lied unconvincingly. When Mica shot him a withering glance, he folded. "She's hiding something."

"Of course—*shit*," Mica cursed when her fingers slipped. She regained control of the needle and put another stitch in Wren, who twitched and gritted her teeth but did not wake. "Of course, she's hiding something. She's our enemy."

"There's more to it than that. There's more to *her* than that." Alaric shifted in his chair, rummaging around in his head for the right words. "Her energy—she does not feel like a 'mare, Mica."

That gave the luminae pause. She set aside her tools and put her hands on her hips to appraise him.

"What do you mean?" she asked.

"I spent half my life surrounded by 'mares at Caer Sidi, and her energy is nothing like theirs." Alaric shook his head, staring at Wren as if she were a fourth moon on the rise, unexpected and luminous. "Nothing like mine."

"What are you saying? That she's not a 'mare?"

"I don't know what else she could be." Alaric finally tore his eyes from Wren, switching his attention to a troubled Mica. "Para Warwick created her."

"You're not making any sense, Alaric." He started to respond, but Mica lifted a slick crimson hand. "I need to focus. Just keep Reichart and the others busy until I finish patching her up."

"Fine," Alaric agreed, getting to his feet begrudgingly. "Thank you, Mica."

The luminae nodded without looking up.

With one final lingering glance at Wren sprawled on the bed like a crow shot from the sky, he departed.

30
Caine

Peony, the russet horse Morthil had loaned Caine, was an enduring creature with an agreeable disposition. The prince pushed her hard into the afternoon, cantering down the broad path through the Tanglewood.

The woods themselves were even stranger in the midday light. The trees were slick as whetstones and dark as obsidian set against the snow. Once, Caine could have sworn he saw a manor house in a clearing farther in, but when he looked back, it was gone.

Most appeared human—kips, Caine assumed—though they did cross what he was fairly sure was a pack of ghouls on foot. Their heads were level with his calf as he rode past. They smelled like spoiled milk and looked as ghastly as the legends described with gaping jaws and chalky, sagging skin.

He wondered which came first, the stories or the dream beings. Or did they grow from one another, a ceaseless circle? To think his own nightmares were traversing the planes of this bizarre world made his hair stand on end.

Of course, nothing was as bad as imagining his father sitting at the helm of the Reverie.

He was endeavoring not to think about it, but with no one but Peony for company, it was rather difficult.

They exited the Tanglewood in the late afternoon, trading the mesh of branches for boundless skies. Caine tugged on the reins at the edge of the open lands.

Hills white as bone stretched almost as far as he could see. Rising among them were great stone monuments. At first, Caine thought they were mountains, but as he drew nearer, he realized the mountains were farther beyond the hills, standing like splinters against the horizon.

The stone behemoths among the hills were gravestones the size of ships.

Morthil had called this place the Bone Hills. The name was fitting for more than one reason, it seemed.

"Just a little farther, girl," Caine lied, giving Peony a bracing pat on the neck. She snorted. For a fleeting moment, he wondered if she could understand him. Nothing would surprise him at this point.

He switched the reins and dove into the hills.

No matter how Caine tried, he could not outpace the uneasiness that rode with him. Every valley seemed to swallow them whole. Every peak felt dangerously exposed. Wherever he went, he could see what he assumed were gravestones towering over him. Some were covered in moss and lichen; others were crumbling, their remnants bleached by the sun. All were inscribed with runes Caine did not recognize.

How big were the creatures laid to rest here? he wondered as he passed beneath a bridge formed by a headstone felled between two hills. Was this a graveyard for gods? Were there actual gods in this realm?

Ila would know.

If she was still willing to speak to him when he reached her, he would have to ask her.

Caine winced.

He had already made an utter ass of himself the night before, storming out like a petulant child, and now he had gone against her wishes and followed her where she did not want to be followed. Things were not exactly shaping up for a happy union.

"What the hells?"

Caine, who had been lost in thought, had nearly been thrown from Peony when the horse screamed to a halt at the mouth of a cavernous ravine between two leaning headstones.

"What is it, girl?" he asked, leaning forward to scratch her behind the ears.

Peony whinnied and dug at the dirt. Caine scanned the area. The walls of the canyon—the gravestones—were easily three stories high and capped with snow. It was quiet enough that he could pick out the delicate *ping* of melting ice hitting the ground. The only other sound was the forlorn gusting of the wind.

It felt almost alive.

Caine flicked the reins and squeezed Peony with his thighs. She whinnied, shuffling backward.

"Come on. We must be getting close."

When Peony refused to budge, Caine jumped down from

the saddle. The horse continued to stamp her hooves and toss her head. He shrugged off his pack and rummaged around until he found a round, lumpy fruit roughly the size of an orange with pale green skin and a soft fuzz.

"Here, want it?" he asked, offering it to her.

Peony regarded him with doleful eyes, her velvety nostrils quivering.

She made it half a step toward Caine before he was knocked aside with the force of a bull. The fruit flew from his hand and rolled across the road. Peony reared, shrieking with a fear that transcended language.

The prince struggled to his feet and drew the hunting knife Morthil had lent him. His vision was clotted with shadows. He tried to blink them away, but they only grew.

Second born . . .

Shadowspinner . . .

Second . . .

The whispers were like shards of glass jammed into his skull. Caine folded to his knees. His back arched, and his head cranked back as if someone had grabbed him by the hair. The sky was blotted out.

The shadows were circling him.

They moved with bizarre raggedness, jerking and staggering through the air like drunkards. Caine spun in a circle, still kneeling on the frozen ground and clutching the hunting knife.

Peony was gone.

The shadows tightened their ring. Caine slashed with his weapon. He might as well have been hacking at the air.

. . . spinner . . .

Second born . . .

The whispers were becoming yowls, pounding on the walls of his skull, threatening to shatter it. The creatures pressed closer. A scream died in Caine's throat. A distant part of him realized that this was the end.

He would never see his home, his world again.

Theodosia. Thomas. Even Ma Hendricks. They would never know what became of him.

He would never know the truth about his father.

Shadow . . . spinner . . .

Heat skimmed the top of his head, singeing his hair. Caine lifted his face in time to see a tongue of flames slice through the living shadows. They let out an unearthly screech, convulsing in midair.

"Go!" someone bellowed. "Stay low!"

Caine dropped and crawled on his stomach. Heat roared over his head again, punctuated by another blistering scream from the shadows. With a shout of exertion, he threw himself from the deadly ring.

"Stay down!"

He clamped his hands over his head as fire rolled over him once more. The wailing of the shadows crescendoed and died.

Silence blanketed the canyon.

"Do you have a death wish?"

Caine flopped onto his back, gulping down precious air.

"Ila," he wheezed. "Good to see you."

Ila stood over him with her hands on her hips, her dark stallion some twenty paces behind. Her hair was woven into a frayed braid, her round face flush with cold. In her hand was a flaming whip. Its end sizzled in the snow. Her expression was thunderous.

"What in the name of Hoste are you doing?"

"I could ask you the same thing," Caine shot back, clambering to his feet. His knees knocked as a bout of nausea hit, but he managed to remain standing. "You left me behind!"

Ila twisted the handle of the whip violently. The flames receded. She began to coil it with gloved hands. "You were acting like a child! You should have stayed at the inn. You would have been safe with Morthil."

"You're awfully preoccupied with my safety for someone who tried to poison me!"

"It was moon sap, not arsenic!" Ila clipped the whip to her belt on the opposite side of her dagger. Her eyes burned brighter than the flames that roared from it only moments ago. "You know, I was actually starting to like you. I thought you might make a good King of Wolfhelm, maybe do some good in the Wake, but I was wrong." She jabbed a finger into his chest. "You're reckless and entitled."

"At least I'm not a lying shrew."

A breathless laugh burst from Ila.

"Your entire life is a lie! You kiss the boots of a tyrant and ignore the atrocities he's committed."

"That isn't true."

"It is!" Ila jabbed a trembling finger at him. "You kneel in the blood at his feet, and you've become soaked with it."

"Shut up."

"No!"

"Enough!" Caine bellowed. The word echoed into the hills, so loud Ila took a step back.

He stalked over to her, his boots crunching the frosted dirt. Ila was even paler than usual. She held her ground, though there was a flicker of fear in her expression.

"I am not my father," he gritted out. "I've spent my life trying to evade the role he crafted for me. He would have me leading battalions, collecting kingdoms for him like trinkets—"

"As you've collected mine!"

"Because I ran out of places to run, Ila! Same as you." He dragged a hand down his face, trying not to scream again. "He would have me treat you as a prisoner, but even when you betrayed me, I protected you. I all but crawled after you."

Ila, whose lips had pressed into a bloodless line, opened her mouth. Caine did not let her begin.

"And now I'm doing it again, following you around like a dog after you ripped me from my home—"

A high, humorless laugh from the weaver. "*You* were ripped from your home? You forced me from mine!"

"I AM NOT MY FATHER!"

"THEN PROVE IT!" Ila screamed, her voice cracking from the strain, her pupils pinpricks. "Stand up to him! Dissolve our engagement! Let me go, Caine!"

Dense silence grew between them. It was heavier than the shadows that had descended on Caine only minutes before. There was no trace of them left in the overcast sky, but he could still feel their icy touch.

"Fine," he said hollowly. "When—if—we return to

Wolfhelm, I'll ensure you and your people return to Galesborough unharmed and that my father leaves your land untouched. In the meantime, consider our engagement dissolved."

"Caine..."

"You're right." He stood tall against the bitterness that threatened to bow his spine. "I've never been able to stand up to him, but maybe I can do it for you."

The fire guttered in her eyes, and Ila sagged. Perhaps with relief, perhaps with exhaustion. Either way, Caine was numb to it.

"Your horse went this way," Ila finally said, jerking her thumb over her shoulder where her horse munched on a tuft of brown grass poking up through the dirt. "We can catch her on Quora."

"Is there a *we* now?"

"You've made sure of that." Dressed entirely in white wool and furs from her boots to her cloak, Ila looked like she belonged between the monuments that framed them. The wind teased a strand of hair from her braid, and she tucked it behind her ears, which Caine now noticed stuck out just a little. For some reason, it made his chest ache. "I meant it, you know."

"What?"

"You would've made a good husband."

He waved her off like it meant nothing, like he could not still feel her poisoned kiss on his lips. "You don't have to say that."

"I mean it." Ila folded her arms, rocking back on her heels

to scan the planes of his face with her penetrating gray-blue gaze. "Under different circumstances."

Caine couldn't help but chuckle at that. "Is there *another* world where you'd want to try?"

It was her turn to laugh, but the musical little noise dissipated at once. "We should get going."

"To the rebellion?"

Ila sucked in a sharp breath, then her eyes narrowed to slits. "Rakk ve dah, Morthil."

Her tone was confirmation enough. "What do a bunch of rebel dream people have that you need?"

"Dream beings," she corrected him. "And because they have Saoirse."

"I thought you said my father had her."

"Not anymore." Ila started back toward her horse, calling over her shoulder. "Your friends will be back. Fire only disperses them for so long."

Caine tossed a furtive glance about. The road was empty for now, but his head was still pounding from the spirits' attack, and the ancient gravestones leered over them like silent gods.

He followed Ila, chest full of lead and skin prickling with the inescapable feeling that they were being watched.

31
Wren

Wren knew she was not dead. Hell could not smell of lavender and mint. Still, her eyes refused to open, and her muscles ached at the slightest motion. Her wing and shoulder throbbed with dizzying pain. Something soft was pooled around her waist. A blanket? Was she in a bed?

"You're awake."

Wren sat bolt upright, forcing her eyes open and snapping her wings out halfway. Big mistake. The world swam as a fresh wave of agony surged through her.

"Easy, easy. Draw them in slowly."

Too queasy to argue, Wren retracted her wings. They settled awkwardly against her back, which was smeared with something warm and sticky.

"Don't worry, it's just a salve," the buttery voice came again. "Your anchor burn was impairing the healing of your knife wound. I stitched it up as best I could. Probably the first time you've needed stitches, right?"

A laugh like the tinkle of a bell.

The room pulled into focus. Wren had been placed on a bed and tucked under a stack of quilts. The space around her was dimly lit and brimming with strange glowing foliage. Teetering towers of books rose between the potted plants, and shelves lined the walls.

The only door was ten steps away, and at the end of her bed was a luminae.

She presented as a young woman with dark honey eyes and lush curls. Her ears resembled those of a bat and were covered in brown fuzz.

Solene's other contact, Wren realized.

She had not been entirely sure what Solene meant when she described the woman as having *bat ears*, but she had not anticipated them suiting her so.

"You're safe with me," the luminae promised. Her ears twitched as she pondered Wren. "Am I safe with you?"

"What happened?" Wren rasped.

"You were attacked. I'm Mica, by the way."

Disjointed memories came crawling back to Wren, trailing with them intense nausea.

Nausea and shame.

How in the name of the gods had she let that kip get the better of her? Her body had locked up. Her mind had fled.

Then Alaric was there, blazing with magic.

He saved me.

"Why did Bonehunter help me?" Wren asked.

"You'll have to ask him." Mica got to her feet. She was shorter than Wren expected and undeniably pretty. "Commander

Reichart will want to question you soon. Alari—I mean, Bonehunter is going to stall him as long as possible."

Wren almost laughed at the absurdity of it all, but shame won out. The memory of her chains clanking blended with the sound of Hodge's belt buckle, drowning the soothing whispers of the fire at the hearth.

It should have filled her with vengeful ichor, but it did not. All she felt was exposed. It was not unlike the way she felt when Para Warwick touched her anchor, like he had reached inside her and left grimy fingerprints on her soul.

"It isn't your fault."

Wren grunted. "I let it happen."

"You're injured, badly. And had you not been, it would have still been wrong."

Mica made a noise of protest as Wren shoved off the blankets and swiveled to plant her feet on the woven rug. She had been stripped to her undergarments, revealing the branching white scar on her abdomen and chest.

"Keeping me here is a mistake," Wren said tonelessly. "The Para will be looking for me."

"We can protect you."

"Protect me?" Wren cut her eyes to the luminae, perplexed. "Why the fuck would you do that?"

"You brought us the one thing that can help us take down Para Warwick. I can't speak for the commander, but I'd wager that would at least buy you an audience."

"I don't want an audience." Wren rose arduously and hobbled over to the bench where her clothes had been folded. Her weapons and armor were nowhere in sight, but at least her soiled tunic had been replaced with a fresh one. Unfortunately, she would not be able to wear it without cutting slits for her wings. Tucking the stack of garments under her arm, she snatched her boots from beneath the bench and headed for the door. "I don't want any part of this."

"Wait!"

Warm fingers closed around Wren's wrist. Her body reacted like a trap springing shut. She dropped her things and whirled, twisting Mica's wrist until the tendons popped. The luminae shrieked, her knees caving.

The door burst open behind them. A crackling blade of energy was at her throat in an instant.

"Let her go," Alaric growled in her ear.

"Are you trying to save me or kill me?" Wren snarled back.

He only pressed the sizzling shard closer, his breath caressing the shell of her ear. Wren swallowed, hot sparks kissing her neck.

"Let her go." Wren released Mica with a snarl. The luminae danced away, her hand cradled to her breast. Alaric allowed his spear to dissolve. "You all right, Mica?"

"Yes, yes, fine." Her voice was high and tight with pain. Under different circumstances, Wren might have felt guilty.

"What happened?" Alaric demanded.

Wren rounded on him.

He had changed into a loose gray sweater and leggings, a simple blade at his belt. All at once, she was acutely aware of her own lack of clothing. His eyes, now brown rather than black, flicked to her chest. For a split second, Wren debated breaking his jaw.

Then she realized he was looking at her scar.

"Get out of my way," she snapped.

Alaric shook his head. "I can't let you leave, Wren."

Her resolve gave way to suspicion. Her eyes narrowed. "You know my name. How?"

"Solene."

Of course. She should have known the kip would not be able to keep her secrets. Then again, what did it matter now? "Get out of my way."

"No."

"Why not?" Wren exploded. "If you're not going to kill me, what do you want from me? I got your weapon. I even saved your thief. Do you want information?" She closed the gap between them. He met her gaze without flinching. "You were the Hand of the Para before me, so you know damn well he can't be killed. Why do you try?"

"Anything with a heart can be killed."

"Exactly."

Alaric smiled, just a quirk of his lips.

"I'll make you a deal," he said after a moment. "I'll tell you what I want, and if you still want to leave after that, you're free to go."

"Alaric," Mica gasped.

Wren narrowed her eyes to slits. She did not believe for one instant that he had the authority to release her, nor did she believe he would if he did. Still, despite her furious vexation, a part of her was curious what the hells he was going on about.

"Fine." She folded her arms, ignoring the groan of her wounds. "Spit it out."

"I want you to stay and fight for the rebellion. Help us destroy Para Warwick and end the rule of the paras in the Reverie."

For a moment, Wren just stared at him, waiting for him to bust out laughing. When he failed to, a bewildered laugh sprang to her own lips. To his credit, Alaric maintained his composure.

"Maybe I did not make myself clear, Bonehunter," she said through a sneer. "Para Warwick has my anchor." She pronounced each syllable with severe clarity as if speaking to a rather dense child. "He's going to kill me, and soon."

"If this is about Hodge, you don't have to worry about him anymore."

The image of the horned nightmare standing over her, eyes black and blood arching across is features, was conjured by the venom in his voice. She shook her head to clear it.

"It isn't about him. I'm not going to spend my final hours aiding your lost cause."

"What if I told you we could save you?"

"I would tell you I can't be saved." Wren swiped her boots and clothes off the floor. "And that I don't want to be."

Alaric opened his mouth to respond, but she knocked him aside with her good shoulder and made for the door again. She expected him to grab her, but it was not his hand that stayed her.

It was his words.

"We can separate you from your anchor."

32
Ila

They found Peony half a mile down the road. The horse was shaken but miraculously unharmed. Something of a feat given the bloodthirstiness of the splinters that attacked her and Caine.

The prince spent more time than they had calming Peony, feeding her from the palm of his hand and scratching behind her rusty ears. Every second they wasted was another second Saoirse was stuck inside that box.

Eventually, Caine hoisted himself into the saddle, and they headed off toward the Shadowrise Mountains.

Every moment was stitched with tense silence.

The relief she had felt when Caine released her from their engagement was undeniable, but she could not ignore the twinge deep in her ribs as hurt, honest and true as any she had witnessed, melted the rage from his face.

I've never been able to stand up to him, but maybe I can do it for you.

Guilt surged inside Ila, causing her to grip her reins tighter.

Had she been too hard on him? Had he not told her he had no more choice in the union than she? It was not the same, perhaps, but it was not wholly different.

It did not matter now, she supposed. When they returned to the Wake, they would both be free of the engagement.

The temperature dropped steadily as night closed in on the Bone Hills. Ila rode ahead of Caine for hours. The first moon had just started to rise when she heard him urge Peony faster. They slid into her peripheral vision.

She kept her eyes on the purple moon. It was small tonight, distant.

"Ila—"

Hoste, help me.

"I owe you an apology."

Ila glanced at Caine in the waning light. His cheeks were flush, but it might have been the cold. Dirt was smudged on his face and clothes from his encounter with the splinters. Still, he looked every inch a prince, sitting tall and proud astride his horse.

"You were right; I've behaved like a child, but this is all..." He gestured wordlessly to the bizarre landscape, the violet moon that gleamed like an amethyst among the stars. "You abandoned me in a strange world with no way home."

There was a strain of earnestness in his voice that was difficult to ignore.

"I understand," Ila said begrudgingly. "I'm sorry I left you behind."

Caine nodded his thanks.

Sudden thunder rolled across the darkening sky, drawing

both their gazes skyward. The violet moon had been blotted out by pregnant rain clouds as thick as a forest canopy and bristling with little flashes of lightning.

"Where the hells did that come from?" Caine asked, gawking at the storm.

"There are no weather patterns in the Reverie," Ila explained as she pulled her hood over her head. "Storms come out of nowhere, and sometimes they have purpose."

Caine swiveled to look at her. "Purpose?"

"Vendettas, if you will."

The prince looked to the thunderheads again, his mouth slightly agape. Ila felt her lips quirk into a smile.

"Is this one . . . ?" he started to ask.

"We would know if this storm was alive."

Caine nodded, visibly relieved.

They settled into silence again, this one more comfortable, as rain began to speckle them. The Shadowrise Mountains were draped in blues and purples ahead. The clouds themselves were backlit by the light of the gemstone moons, bright enough to light their way with ease.

Ila would never grow accustomed to the ecstatic beauty of the Reverie.

"How long until we reach Caer Bheinn?" Caine asked after a time.

"Three days if we make good time," Ila answered with a grimace. Saying it aloud made it worse.

"These rebels, are they friends of yours?"

"Not exactly." Caine raised an inquisitive brow. Ila heaved a sigh. "I have no real allies in the Reverie apart from Morthil and a few scattered contacts. The rebels and I do share a common goal, at least. We both want Para Warwick gone."

"But?"

"But I don't trust them. They would not hesitate to use Saoirse as an instrument of war."

Ila reached into her saddlebag for her waterskin. She took a quick swig of water and offered it to Caine. He shook his head.

"What is it that Saoirse can do that makes her so valuable to them?" he inquired.

Ila swallowed. Infuriating though he was, all she had learned of Caine thus far pointed to his innocence in the matter of Saoirse. Still, doubts flared when he spoke her name.

"Something no being has been able to do in generations," Ila answered.

"That clears it up."

The queen glanced at Caine sidelong to find him sporting a wry smile.

"Only I can open the box Saoirse is kept in," she explained in a dour tone. "But once I do, we'll be at the mercy of the rebellion. I won't allow them to use her."

"What about Saoirse? What does she want?"

The question was innocent enough, but it set her teeth on edge. Ila took another sip of water to evade answering.

"Saoirse wants to help people," she finally told him, slipping the waterskin back into the saddlebag. "She always has."

"If she is as powerful as you say, and she wants to fight—"

"Absolutely not," Ila snapped before he could finish. Caine shut his mouth. The queen inhaled through her nose and exhaled through her mouth. She loosened her grip on the reins, which she was still choking. "If she wants to fight when she is older, that is her choice. For now, it is my duty to protect her from those who would abuse her gifts."

"Fair enough."

"Saoirse is the only family I have left. She may not be blood, but she is a sister to me."

"Tell me about her."

"Oh." Ila blinked, caught off guard. "Saoirse?"

Caine nodded patiently despite the obvious answer.

"She is funny. Brave. Compassionate. Wise beyond her years, but still just a child." Ila pinned her gaze on the jagged horizon. "She deserves a childhood. I've failed to give her one."

"You did what you had to do to protect her," the prince corrected her. "I would have done the same for Theodosia, as much as she would have hated me for it."

"Your sister is . . . energetic," Ila said to change the subject.

Caine snorted. "One word for it, I suppose. I think she would be happier living in the forest than Caer Sidi."

"I hear she is a fine hunter."

"Don't let her hear you say that."

"She reminds me of my brother Anders. He brought down an ice bear when he was thirteen and never stopped talking about it." A smile, unprecedented by them both, surfaced on her chapped lips. "He made a necklace out of the claws and showed it to all the girls."

"Did it work?"

"Not when I told them he pissed himself in the process of getting them."

A laugh burst from Caine, highlighting his dimples. "Queen Ila, I'm shocked."

"What did you expect from the Vaettir queen?"

"Certainly not this."

He gestured at the vast dreamscape with a sweep of his arm. The red moon was now perched on the cusp of a mountain, its lower half peeking out from beneath the cloud cover. All around them, the snowbound hills and headstones were quiet.

"What are these?" Caine asked, nodding at a crumbling gray gravestone looming above a nearby rise.

"No one knows," Ila answered. "They've been here for as long as anyone can remember. Morthil remembers seeing them when he manifested over a thousand years ago."

Caine made a noise of disappointment in his throat. "So, you don't know everything, then."

"I never said I did."

"You certainly act like it."

Ila opened her mouth to snap at him but realized immediately he was teasing her. She looked away, her face heating.

"We should make camp soon," she mumbled. "There is a cave at the foot of Mount Anvil."

She pointed at the imposing cliff that embodied its namesake. The jutting ledge soared a thousand feet above them. It looked far too flimsy to support the boulders and trees perched atop it.

"Is it safe?" Caine inquired doubtfully.

Ila arched a pale brow. "Afraid, Prince Caine?"

"I will have you know I was prepared to take on an army of spirits with a hunting knife."

"Courage and stupidity are often confused." A smile split her mouth, more genuine than any she had ever given him. "Race you."

Ila cracked the reins before Caine could answer. Her horse plunged forward with a wild cry. The prince shouted something after her, but it was lost to the wind and the rising thunder.

33
Alaric

Wren froze a step from the door, her muscles tightening like the lines of a ship. Alaric stole a glance at Mica. She was watching the scene unfold from the other side of her bed, which was stained brown with dried blood. Her eyes were round, her ears tucked.

"You're lying."

Wren had not moved an inch. Her wings were flush against her muscular back. The feathers around her stab wound were bent and frayed.

"I'm not," Alaric answered calmly. "Death isn't the only way to be free of Para Warwick."

The winged nightmare wheeled around to face him. Her face was a war zone of emotion, and beneath it her sprawling scar blazed like a tongue of white flames. It was old, at least a year. Was it linked to the stolen home she spoke to Solene of, or just some other horror she had endured at the hands of their creator?

"Does playing savior make you feel like less of a monster?" Wren hissed.

Her words slipped through the cracks in his ribs and settled in his chest. She knew just how to make them hurt. Of course she did. Alaric was no different when he left Caer Sidi.

"You deserted for a reason," he pressed. "What was it?"

"None of your business."

"I know you, Wren. I *was* you."

Her eyes flashed like iron pokers. "You know nothing about me."

"I know your anger. I know what it is to hate your creator. To want him dead and know you're powerless to stop him." Wren fumed but did not argue. Alaric chose to see that as progress. "You're not the only one who has been gutted by Para Warwick, Nightstrider."

Wren flinched.

"Yeah, I never wanted to be called Bonehunter, either. It was the name he gave me, the one I used to torture and kill." He paused, studying her. Even broken and angry, she was beautiful. He could not help but notice the powerful lines of her body, her long legs and full breasts. Alaric fixed his gaze on her face stubbornly. "But I reclaimed it. You can, too."

Wren cast her eyes to the floor, her brow furrowed. Alaric stole another glance at Mica. Her face was full of pity he did not want

"Some things," Wren said in a near whisper, "cannot be reclaimed."

Before Alaric could respond, a shuddering horn blast sounded, shaking dust from the ceiling. Wren went stiff. Mica, who had plastered her sensitive ears to her curls, sprang to her feet.

The alarm.

Alaric felt his magic shiver to life. He pressed a hand to his chest to calm it. Mica began to dart around the room, collecting medical supplies in a sling bag. Wren dropped her clothes and boots unceremoniously and began to dress.

"What are you doing?" Alaric demanded, more an accusation than a question.

Wren shrugged on her jacket over her bandages, gritting her teeth as she inched her wings through the slits in the back. Two crumpled feathers tumbled to the floor.

"I told you they would come for me." She stomped on her boots. "Give me that blade."

"You're in no condition to fight."

"Please," Wren scoffed.

"You don't have to be a hero."

Wren straightened fluidly, tossing her midnight hair over her shoulder. The look in her eyes could sear skin from bone.

"You think I'm doing this for you?" she said, seething. "No, I'm going to finish this on my terms, and I won't let you get in my way."

"You—"

"One more word about me, and I'll rip out your fucking tongue." Another horn blast tore through the room. The jars on the shelves rattled like rain on a tin roof. "Stop trying to make me something I'm not. I'm not a victim, and I'm sure as hells not a hero. Try to stop me, and I'll prove it to you."

Alaric glowered at her. Power pooled in his hands. He clenched his fists to contain it, trying to formulate a response.

Then Wren moved.

Faster than his eyes could track, she darted forward and plucked Hodge's knife from his belt. Half a beat later, she was at the door. Wren flashed stark white teeth, and for the first time, Alaric noticed her canines were subtly elongated, closer to fangs.

"Don't hurt yourself, Bonehunter." Her eyes glinted with insatiable, volatile energy. The kind he knew all too well.

And she was gone.

Alaric lunged after her as the door slammed.

"No!"

The horned 'mare froze at the distressed shout and rounded on Mica. Her hands were on her hips, her sling bag hanging off her shoulder.

"You're not going out there," she said, raising a finger in warning. "For all we know, it could be the Para at our gates."

"He wouldn't come this far himself."

He started after Wren again, but Mica caught him by the hand and wheeled him around to face her.

"Alaric," she whispered desperately. "Para Warwick knows a 'mare is with the rebellion. If you go out there and he or one of his soldiers sees you, you're fucked. Besides, Nightstrider is stuck inside Caer Bheinn, just like you."

"What do you think will happen if Reichart sees her running around with a knife?"

"What if Reichart sees *you*? You just killed—"

"A rapist? Yes."

Mica chewed her bottom lip. "Then go—but if they break the shield, you hide. Understand?"

"Yes, Mother."

The luminae might have said something else, but Alaric was already out the door. Dream beings were filtering through the halls in their nightclothes, civilians and soldiers alike. Most were the former, kips and luminae who took refuge with the rebellion to escape the rising violence against them.

They made way for Alaric as he took off down the corridor. Whispers flew up in his path, but no more than usual. Those who had been at Caer Bheinn for a while had grown accustomed to him. Some he even considered friends. Those who arrived more recently were still wary of him.

It would be worse when Hodge's body was discovered.

Sidestepping a luminae with the wings of a dragonfly, Alaric came upon the entry hall with its soaring shielded windows and towering pillars. He sped up when he spotted Reichart and several armed guards crowded around one such window, staring out into the night intently.

Nightstrider was nowhere to be found.

"What happened?" Alaric asked as he arrived beside them.

Reichart did not even glance at him, nor did any of the others. The quartz light of the shield cast a rippling glow across their faces. Alaric followed their line of sight. His stomach dropped.

There, hovering over the maw of the ravine with Hodge's blade in her hand, was Nightstrider.

She was outside the shield, her back to them and her eyes fixed on something he could not see.

"Who let her outside?" Alaric demanded, staring daggers at Reichart. "We have to help her."

"No."

"Fine, then send someone else."

The commander finally locked eyes with Alaric. His expression was maddeningly calm.

"I won't risk any of my fighters to aid a 'mare."

Alaric bristled. "No, of course not."

"How exactly did she get out of her cell?" Reichart inquired, lowering his voice and turning to face Alaric more fully.

"One of your kips went rogue. I took care of it."

"You *took care* of it?" he repeated flatly. "Tell me that does not mean what I think it means."

"Would you rather I let her die?" Alaric shot back. "Did you not want to question her?"

Reichart cursed, dragging a hand down his face. "We'll speak later," he said through his teeth. "The only reason you're not halfway to the dungeons is—"

"There!"

The luminae and the nightmare looked to the window in time to see three dark winged beasts streaking toward Wren. She twisted her blade in midair, readying herself.

Alaric felt his insides drop. He knew those creatures even through the radiance of the shield, but he would have recognized them by their harrowing yowl alone.

He remembered when they were created by Para Warwick, the horrific keening as their eyes were burned out, ensuring their only sighted memory was the face of their creator, and forcing them to rely on him until they learned to navigate the world through smell and sound. Once, Alaric felt pity for them. He even tried to slip a bit of fresh meat through the bars of their cages.

He lost a finger for it, which was how he learned nightmares could regrow small portions of their bodies and that the demonic creatures knew only bloodlust.

Shit.

On the wings of an otherworldly screech, Wren and the uilebheistan collided.

34

Wren

Wren slammed the door on Mica and Alaric and hurtled down the corridor. She expected the nightmare to follow, but he did not. Seconds later, she burst into an unfurnished entry hall lined with towering windows shrouded in pink sheets of magic. The shields rippled like sunlight on the ocean floor. Through them, she could make out the ragged silhouettes of the Shadowrise Mountains.

Confused rebels in their nightclothes were filtering in, mostly kips and a few scattered luminae.

Wren skidded to a stop near the edge of the room, panting. Her stab wound pulsed agonizingly, and she felt blood begin to leak down her back, soaking into the waistband of her pants.

She locked eyes with a barefoot kip wearing a rumpled shift. Wren raised her hands to calm her, then realized she was holding the knife she had lifted off Alaric.

"Wait—"

The kip screamed.

More shouts were triggered as the rebels spotted first the kip, then Wren. A chorus of terrified cries joined the shrill note. The dream beings fled to the far corners of the entry hall, cowering behind its many pillars.

A luminae with catlike features tried to tackle Wren, but she sidestepped him easily. He staggered into the shield. It flickered and warped where he struck it, and he bounced off unharmed.

So much for the formidable rebellion.

The double doors opposite Wren blew open. Six armored rebels charged through. Two took a knee, their crossbows trained on her. The rest drew swords and maces.

All but one.

"Commander." Her voice should have echoed in the vast space, but shields muffled it like packed snow. "Nice to see you again."

Reichart had stripped his mask to reveal a razor-sharp jawline and a grim mouth. While he was the smallest of the group, their respect for him was plain. They shifted around him like worker bees.

"Was this your plan, Nightstrider?" he called. "To lead Para Warwick to our doorstep?"

Wren sucked her teeth, fingering the hilt of her stolen blade. She was surprised Alaric had not come up behind her yet. What was he playing at?

"You're the ones who brought me here," she returned. "All I did was steal what you were too cowardly to get yourselves."

"Watch your mouth, 'mare," a satyr barked. Wren smirked to stoke his fury. Another horn blast tore through the hall, the longest yet. They were close. She could not smell them through the barrier, but she did not need to.

She knew who Para Warwick had sent after her.

"I'll handle this," Wren said, already making her way to the nearest window. "Try to stop me, and I won't spare you."

Something whistled past her ear. She plucked the arrow from the air and split it with her thumb. The rebel who fired it blanched and made a noise like a field mouse. Wren tossed the broken arrow aside.

"I said *try* to stop me." She stepped up to the ledge beneath the window and faced the rebels again. The barrier hummed against her spine.

"Nightstrider," Reichart warned. "Don't touch—"

Wren fell backward.

The shield parted like water, and bitter mountain air slammed into her. She spread her wings, ignoring the agony that tore through her. With a powerful stroke, she launched herself higher.

The rebel base was built directly into the mountains, its dilapidated towers rising with the magnificent peaks. It looked as ancient as the land itself, as if it grew from the rock face along with the titan statues surrounding it. The barrier was invisible from the outside, but she could still hear its restless buzz. Stars were smeared across the sky, and the moons seemed close enough to touch.

A bone-rattling screech fractured the night.

Wren wheeled around in the air.

Three beasts streaked toward her on leathery wings. The uilebheistan had grown since she last saw them. They were now larger than horses, their veins and muscles bulging beneath their dark hides. The largest flew at the head of the flock, its hooked beak open in another scream.

On its back was an armored rider with brilliant red hair.

"TRAITOR!" Ondine bellowed.

She yanked the reins, and her uilebheistan came to a halt. The others followed suit, their wings wafting their rotting scent toward Wren. Bands of scar tissue marked where their eyes used to be.

"Ondine," Wren said, greeting her coolly.

"Para Warwick wants you back alive," Ondine shouted, drawing her sword. She rarely used physical weapons but was perfectly formidable with them. "But he never said in how many pieces."

"What are you waiting for?"

Ondine let out an unhinged scream and brought her sword down in an arc. The uilebheistan flanking her lunged.

Wren tucked her wings and dropped like a brick. A thunderclap echoed above her. She looked up in time to see the barrier materialize where one of the uilebheistan crashed into it, a pink blossom against the stars. She darted away as the beast fell, trailing smoke and a pitiful yowl.

"That all you got?" Wren called, struggling to disguise her labored breathing. Hot blood continued to ooze from the wound on her back, making the back of her leather jacket stick to her.

Ondine and her mount dove. Wren waited until she could see the freckles on her cheekbones to shoot skyward.

"The sky is mine, Ondine!" she yelled. The redhead craned

her neck to view her, snarling. "You should never have challenged me here."

Ondine shouted at the remaining uilebheistan. It streaked toward Wren with a screech. She slashed with her stolen blade. Foul blood splattered her face. She shot higher, then let herself plummet for a split second before landing on the back of the demon. With a cry of exertion, she drove the dagger into its skull.

The uilebheistan went lax. She uprooted her blade and pushed off. The beast plunged to join its kin in the canyon miles below.

Wren stared down at Ondine, breathing hard. Her face had gone white beneath her freckles.

"I don't want to hurt you," Wren called over the wind.

"Then come quietly." There was a hint of a plea in her tone. "Para Warwick showed you mercy before. He might again."

A harsh laugh burst from Wren. "Mercy? Is that what you call it?"

"You fell in love with a luminae, Wren! You abandoned us! You abandoned *me*!" Her voice cracked on the last syllable, giving Wren pause. She had never seen Ondine cry before. Part of her was surprised she was capable. "You don't belong here."

"I don't belong anywhere."

"You don't belong with the rebels, and you sure as hells didn't belong with—"

"Don't say his name!" Wren barked.

Ondine slammed her teeth together. It was more than rage behind her void eyes. It was heartbreak, or some mangled form of it. Whatever it was, it hurt Wren more than she cared to admit.

The sensation died with Ondine's next words.

"You're a nightmare, Wren. A monster. You don't get a fucking happy ending."

With a scream that could shake stars from the sky, Wren let herself drop one last time. She landed behind Ondine on the back of the uilebheistan, hooked her arm around her, and sank the dagger into her breast.

The noise Ondine made was broken, childlike.

"You're right," Wren breathed in her ear. "I'm a monster, and I care about you. Remember that when he turns me to ash."

She released her hold on Ondine, whose eyes were flickering between black and hazel.

"Wren—" she whispered.

Ondine slipped from her saddle and fell, a red-and-white star shook loose from the sky.

35
Caine

Firelight quivered on the bowed walls of the cave, bleeding out into the Bone Hills. The rain had turned to snow an hour ago, but Ila and Caine were warm in the hollows of Mount Anvil. The weaver stirred a tin of soup over the flames, pensive.

"Caine?"

The prince looked up from the map of the Known Regions of the Reverie he had been examining. The lands of the dreamworld were utterly unlike those of the Wake. There were no apparent borders to speak of, no kingdoms or territories. Only cities and towns speckled across the open lands. The largest of the cities appeared to be Marrowrun in the top-right corner of the map, what Caine naturally assumed was north, until he noticed the compass rose sketched on the parchment showing east was up. Even stranger, the edges of the map appeared to be shrouded in some sort of fog denoted by swirling clouds. Caine could not even begin to imagine what lay beyond.

"Yes?" he asked.

"What happened today when you were attacked by the splinters?"

"I was hoping you would know," the prince replied, folding the map and setting it aside. "We were riding, and Peony just stopped." He jerked his thumb at the horse, who rested at the back of the cave with Quora. "I got down to try to get her moving. Next thing I knew, I was being knocked across the road by a bunch of spirits."

"Splinters," Ila corrected him again.

She lifted the tin from the fire with a gloved hand and set it on the smooth dirt floor, pouring half of the steaming orange soup into a dish and passing it to Caine. He accepted gratefully.

"The half-remembered dreams," he spoke up, recalling her explanation at the inn.

"Yes. Most are innocuous, but some feed on the souls of fully manifested dream beings in an attempt to make themselves whole."

Caine took a sip of his soup. It was spicier than he expected. He coughed to hide his choking.

"Do they commonly attack humans?" he asked as the hot broth settled in his stomach.

Ila considered him through the haze of smoke and heat. Her steely blue eyes seemed to cut straight through him.

"A human in the Reverie is a rare thing, particularly one who is not a weaver. Even so, I have never heard of a splinter horde attacking one before." A twig snapped on the fire, sending up a plume of sparks. "So, why do you think they went after you?"

Her question sounded more like an accusation. Caine leaned back, propping himself up with his hands.

"What are you asking me?"

"Para Warwick is the most powerful dream being in a millennium." Ila spoke as if she walked on a sheet of ice ready to crack. "I find it difficult to believe his child would be entirely human."

"Hold on," Caine broke in, setting aside his meal. Orange soup sloshed over the lip of the bowl. "My father is an evil man, but you have no proof he and this Para Warwick are the same person. How would he have time to rule this world when he's been so busy—"

"Systematically bringing the kingdoms of the Wake to their knees?" Ila deadpanned over the lip of her soup tin.

Caine ignored the jab, honest though it was. "How would he have time to sneak off to another world in the midst of all that?"

"Plenty of people live double lives. Is it really so hard to believe your father would be among them?"

The prince opened his mouth to reply, but no words came out. Ila studied him intently.

"As far as we know, there has never been a para who could move between worlds at will. I myself doubted your father and the Para were the same person until he sent the Skysteel Guard after Saoirse and me."

Caine blanched in the quivering orange light. "The Skysteel Guard? When?"

"Nine days before I came to Wolfhelm."

"No," he muttered to himself. He continued, speaking to

Ila now with stiff certainty. "Thomas would never be involved in hurting a child—or a woman."

"In all likelihood, they were told they were rescuing a child from the clutches of a witch."

"And none of them recognized you the day you arrived at Caer Sidi?" Caine pressed.

"I was disguised as a trader the night they found us."

"Convenient."

Ila huffed. "Even if I laid all the proof in the worlds at your feet, you would still only see what you wanted to see."

Caine scowled, turning his gaze to the storm outside. The snow showed no sign of letting up anytime soon. If anything, it was thicker than last he checked. The glow of their fire glanced off the sheets of precipitation.

"Ila, I—"

Ila held up a finger, twisting to view the gusting snow. Her muscles were coiled. "Did you feel that?"

"Feel what?"

Her only response was to lay a hand on the dagger lying beside her. Caine caught sight of his hunting knife sticking out of his borrowed pack. He reached for it. The tips of his fingers kissed the leather hilt.

A blade cold as death pressed against his throat.

"Don't move."

Ila sprang to her feet, weapon in hand.

"Ah, ah, ah." At his side, Caine heard a gravelly voice chastising them. "Drop the knife, pretty thing, or he dies."

"Ila—" the prince started.

"Shut up." Caine swallowed with a dry mouth as the

stranger pressed the weapon closer to his jugular. "This blade is poisoned. If it cuts you, you're dead in seconds."

Ila hesitated. Her grip tightened around her knife, then relaxed. The weapon hit the dirt with a dull clatter.

"Good girl," the stranger drawled. "On the ground." She complied. Palpable rage buzzed beneath her skin. Had Caine not seen the look before, he would not have noticed the fear lurking beneath. "You look better on your knees."

"Don't talk to her like that," Caine snarled.

"You're going to be a thorn in my ass; I can tell already."

Caine heard the stranger lick his lips, then whistle through his teeth. The low, warbling note echoed into the night. Ila shifted on the cave floor. One of their horses let out a nervous nicker. The snow continued to blow. Nothing else moved but the twitching flames.

"How did you get in here?" Caine asked, trying to get a look at the stranger out of the corner of his eye. All he could see was the edge of a weathered hood. "There's only one way in or out."

"For you, maybe." His voice dripped with condescension. "You Wake dwellers are so unimaginative."

"Wake dwellers," Ila repeated. She and Caine locked eyes through the smoke. Her pupils were dilated. She had figured something out. Something he was missing. "What makes you think we're from the Wake?"

"Pretty, but dense." The stranger tsked. Caine drew in a deep breath when the blade at his throat disappeared. Across from him, Ila bit her lip. Her eyes were full of words she could not say. The stranger whistled again, three short blasts.

"Caine," Ila breathed.

He shook his head.

"Took you long enough," the stranger called.

Three figures caked in ice had appeared out of the storm. There was a stocky woman with gray hair and a boy a few years younger than Caine with a scar on his chin, both presumably kips. The third was a monster: eight feet tall with rotting skin, tusks, and a head like a misshapen pumpkin. The closest thing Caine could equate it to were the stories of orcs that he'd heard as a child.

"Sorry, boss," the boy answered. His voice was high and reedy. "Hard to keep up with you when you—" The woman jabbed him in the ribs with an elbow. "Ow," he complained, scuttling aside. "What the hells was that for?"

"Nice crew," Caine muttered. "Very professional."

The boy laughed when his boss kicked Caine to his knees. He hit the ground hard and could not hold back a wince.

"Tie them up," the leader barked, finally stepping around to look Caine in the face. He appeared to be in his forties with weathered skin and a nose that had seen more than one fist. He shouldered a sleek crossbow stocked with deadly bolts.

"Gag this one," he ordered. "The girl has some questions to answer."

The moment the leader moved, Caine grabbed for his hunting knife. His fingers closed around the hilt, but before he could strike, the leader nailed him in the chin with his knee. Ila screamed as Caine's head snapped back, and he collapsed. The knife flew from his hand.

"Nice try, princeling," the leader crooned.

Caine spat out a wad of blood. *"Princeling?"*

As soon as he spoke the word, icy dread trickled down his spine. It must have registered on his face because the leader grinned, exposing yellowed teeth.

"Your father would like to see you."

36

Wren

Ondine did not scream as she fell.

It was her uilebheistan that mourned her aloud, keening and circling as Wren hovered above it, silent as a guillotine before the fall. The knife slipped from her hand, joining her lover in the chasm below.

Gods, what had she done?

White scattered her vision to black as searing pain shredded her calf. Now Wren screamed, cursing and flailing as she was yanked down through the sea of stars. She grabbed helplessly for her lower leg and found a cold, thick metal hook embedded deep in her tissue. Gulping a breath, she ripped out the hook and cast it away.

"Surround her!"

Wren shot higher, but it was too late. Her vision swam as vague shapes bathed in red and purple moonlight swarmed her. Chains rattled, wings greater than hers, greater than the ragged flaps that held the uilebheistan aloft, stirred her feathers and hair.

"Come quietly and we won't have to hurt you," an unfamiliar male voice called.

"I've heard that before," Wren snarled in his general direction.

She forced her eyes to focus. Her stomach cinched.

She was surrounded by six beasts with the heads of lions and the claws to match. Massive wings with downy white feathers grew from their powerful backs. Manticores, if she remembered the fabled creatures correctly.

Seated astride each manticore was a rebel dressed in dark armor. She could not discern their species with the smell of her own blood clouding her nostrils, but the hardness in their eyes and the skill with which they spun their grappling hooks told her they were not like the rebels she had encountered before.

They were dangerous.

"Let me pass!" she demanded. "I just saved you from Souldrinker."

Hot blood trickled down her leg, which throbbed with pain that would pull her under again if she let it. The burn at her back stung. The manticores growled, drooled. The stars wheeled overhead.

Not like this.

"Take her."

Wren screamed as two more hooks stabbed into her, one in the hollow of her collarbone, one in her other leg. Wind whistled through her ears as she was dragged down by the chains attached to them. She would join Ondine in moments. Perhaps they could share a bed in the soil. Perhaps they would find peace together at last.

Perhaps, perhaps, perhaps . . .

The wind was knocked from Wren as ropy arms caught her awkwardly. Then they were moving. Her eyes rolled in her skull, and the next thing she knew she was kneeling in the dirt, gloves at her shoulders as her hands were chained behind her.

Don't underestimate her.

The tips of her boots dragged on the floor as she was carried through what appeared to be an endless maze of derelict castle hallways. Everything was bathed in that rosy light from the barrier. Her head was heavy and full of cotton. She could not hold it up, but the words of the men dragging her wormed their way in.

. . . found Hodge dead in her cell.

. . . was her . . . ?

. . . Bonehunter . . .

. . . nightmares will always come for their kind . . .

The boom of double doors opening sounded, and Wren was cast to the ground. Her knees struck the floor and she folded forward, but a warm hand intercepted her, heaving her upright.

"Was this necessary, Reichart?" His words were a baritone growl that raised gooseflesh on her arms.

"You're lucky I don't do the same to you. You killed one of ours for her."

"I killed a rapist, Commander. Did you really want that filth here?"

Wren tilted her chin up, fighting against leaden eyelids. A blurry face with dark horns swam before her, and beyond them an equally indistinct background. Vaguely, she was aware that the guards who had delivered her lingered nearby.

Footsteps tapping closer, then a distant *clink* reminiscent of a wine glass being set down. "Give her this."

"She needs rest."

"This has gone far enough. First, she held the box, and now she got out of the shield on her own. We need answers."

A sigh and the face before her shifted. "Sorry."

Wren blinked sluggishly as the unmistakable *thwop* of a vial being uncorked pricked her eardrums. A hand moved around the back of her neck, tilting her head back. She twisted away from the cold kiss of glass against her lips, then groaned as a sour liquid was poured down her throat.

Fingers brushed the sweaty hair from her face as she swallowed on instinct alone.

Then the world screamed into excruciating focus.

Wren shot to her feet with a shuddering gasp, pupils contracting to pinpoints, heart juddering in her throat, and blood on fire. She reeled back from Alaric, her hands still manacled behind her. The horned nightmare stood up, his hands raised partway. In one hand was a now-empty vial.

Behind him was Reichart, staring at her with the distrust one might reserve for a feral animal.

"What did you do to me?" Wren spit, but her words came out a jumbled mess. She was blazing, alight with unchecked adrenaline as her wounds bled freely.

"We need you awake," Reichart explained flatly.

"To torture me? I just saved you."

Rather than answering, the commander tossed a glance

over his shoulder. Wren flicked her eyes to the space beyond him and felt her blood run cold.

They stood in a cavernous space veiled in bluish mist and bristling with raw energy. As her focus sharpened, she realized she could feel its hum against her skin. They were indoors, they had to be, but she could not see the walls, ceiling, or floor. The only distinct features of the space were the towering white columns scattered throughout the fog and the circular inky pool in the floor a few feet behind Reichart.

"This is the Hall of Whispers," Reichart told her. "Caer Bheinn was built around it long before the paras took hold of the Reverie."

Wren swallowed, her mouth parched. She felt Alaric watching her intently, the vial still choked in his hand.

"Interrogating you would be inefficient. The Hall of Whispers reveals the fabric of your soul. Your memories, your fears, your desires. It will tell us what you are."

"I'm a nightmare," Wren shot back. "I just want to leave."

"This will not be a pleasant experience, but take comfort in the knowledge that you won't be in any real danger."

The commander motioned and the two guards who had dragged her here appeared at her sides, grasping her arms. She cursed and bucked against their grip and the cuffs at her wrists, but even awash with adrenaline her body refused to heed her. They began to haul her toward the columns beyond the dark pool.

Then a whip of pure energy lashed across the floor in front of them, scattering fog and stopping the guards in their tracks.

Wren stared at Alaric.

"This is wrong," the nightmare said in a low voice. His eyes were on her, but his words were clearly directed at the commander. "She helped us. At least give her a chance to explain herself."

"Fine," Reichart agreed after a tense pause. "Nightstrider, are you prepared to explain your abilities and motives?"

"Eat shit."

Reichart nodded once. "Just as I thought. Stand down, Alaric."

The nightmare gritted his teeth, sparks popping at his fingertips as he oscillated on the edge of reason. The strangeness of it struck Wren like a blow to the head, and she almost laughed. She had called him a pretender, a broken monster with a savior complex, but this was real to him. She could see it blazing in his eyes threatening to go black, that sense of justice she had only witnessed in one other.

Against all reason, against nature and their creator, he wanted to help her.

"Bonehunter," Wren said. He met her eyes and she almost smiled. "I'm not worth it."

Alaric let his arms fall limp at his sides. Slowly, he stepped back. The sentries flanking Wren walked her past him, past Reichart and the inky black pool, and right up to the edge of the endless maze of columns. They released her and pushed her forward. She stumbled but managed to remain upright.

When she turned around, her arms still locked behind her back, she was alone in the boundless forest of stone and mist.

Every step Wren took felt like it would be her last. She did not know how long she had been walking. She had lost all sense of time and space. The potion Alaric had given her had worn off hours or days ago. All around her was nothing but dense bluish fog, at once boundless and suffocating. The only saving grace was that she could no longer feel her wounds.

Rapid clicking struck up behind her, horribly close.

Wren spun, reaching for a weapon that was not there. That was when she realized the shackles at her wrists had disappeared. She flexed her fingers and turned in a slow circle. Uncanny stillness hung around her.

But she was alone.

She started off again. She did not know where she was going, but anything was better than staying in one place.

Her heart leaped into her mouth when the clicking returned. Wren spread her wings partway and sank into a crouch, sending coils of fog wafting.

"I know you're there," she growled. "Show yourself."

Nothing.

She held her position, tasting the air. She could not smell anything but that sticky sweetness.

Wren rose cautiously.

Blunt pain exploded at the back of her head. She was thrown forward and skidded across the invisible ground. Vision blurred, she sprang to her feet. Shock gripped her by the throat.

Looming above her like a thunderhead was a mammoth scorpion. Ten feet tall with a muddy red body and a stinger thick as a tree trunk. A ragged crack ran horizontally across its armored back, revealing the fragile skin beneath. Dozens of jaundiced beady eyes gazed at her with vitriol.

"Abdigor," Wren breathed.

Three weeks after her manifestation, Para Warwick took her to the fighting pits in the basin of the parched lake outside Black Root. The pits attracted nightmares, vexes, and even the occasional foolish kip looking to prove something.

The Para handed Wren a blade and pushed her over the edge. She had not yet learned to fly, so she landed face down in the muck. The crowd jeered as she struggled to her feet. She was still fumbling with her sword when the gates opposite her opened.

Abdigor exploded into the ring, clicking and whirring like a great clockwork. He was the beast they sent in when the crowds were getting bored.

When they wanted blood.

The audience expected her to be devoured. Instead, she had doused her blade in the corrosive blood of a vex and stabbed Abdigor in the back. A yawning crack split his armor, just wide enough for her to uproot her blade and plunge it into his spine. Wren jumped down to the roar of the crowds, elbow-deep in blood and grinning victoriously.

She lost focus just long enough for the dying scorpion to graze her with his poisonous stinger.

Para Warwick left her paralyzed in the ditch with a warning and a lesson.

If you bleed, you lose.

Abdigor let out a piercing shriek and stamped his many legs, his stinger bobbing above him like a mace. Wren launched herself into the air. There was no pain this time, but her limbs felt like they were made of lead. She climbed higher, but the space between the scorpion and her only seemed to shrink.

Swearing, Wren folded her wings and hurtled toward the ground. She landed on the broad back of the scorpion, one foot on either side of the crack. She dropped into a crouch, spinning on the balls of her feet to face his stinger.

"Come on, you stupid fucking bug," she muttered. "Come get me."

Abdigor jabbed with his stinger. Wren scrambled backward when it slammed into his armor, missing the old fissure by an inch.

"Come on!" she bellowed, plunging her hand into the crack and raking her nails across the spongy flesh there. The scorpion gave a terrible scream and stabbed again. Wren leaped from his back and landed on her feet. The unmistakable sound of crunching bone echoed behind her. She whirled, triumphant.

There was nothing there but listless fog.

Nightstrider.

Wren blinked.

In place of the scorpion was a child. She was short and waifish with wild dark hair and green eyes. She smiled like she had only just remembered how.

I've been waiting for you.

She did not speak, not with her mouth. Her words rang out in Wren's mind.

"Who are you?" Wren demanded. "What is this?"

The fabric of the Reverie is thin in the Hall of Whispers, the girl told her without speaking. She had a lilting accent, one Wren was unfamiliar with. *It was easier for me to contact you here.*

"Who are you?" Wren repeated.

I am like him.

"Like who?" Wren almost shouted.

Earnest green eyes blinked up at her before she answered. *I am like Bram.*

The name nearly brought Wren to her knees. It would have been better if she had screamed it. Instead, it bloomed with wrath inside her mind, spreading through her like wildfire.

"How do you know about him?" she managed to get out.

My name is Saoirse. I'm the weapon you stole.

"You're telling me this weapon, this thing everyone is tearing each other to shreds for, is a child?"

My caretaker hid me inside an enchanted box. Saoirse gave another melancholy smile. *I knew you would find me. I've known you since I was born. Your name is written in the stars and across the worlds.*

"What are you talking about?"

Everything will be explained, Saoirse assured Wren, an urgent note entering her voice. *For now, you must stay alive.*

"What?"

Stay alive.

"I heard you the first time."

Saoirse blinked up at her, unruffled. Her tranquility only fanned Wren's flames.

"Sorry, kid, but the Para will unmake me soon enough," Wren told her. "You've got the wrong person."

Bram has protected you.

"What the fuck is that supposed to mean?" Instead of waiting for her response, Wren barreled on. "Bram is dead. He can't protect me. No one can protect me, and even if they could, I have nothing to live for."

The will to live must come from inside you, Nightstrider. Wren flinched when Saoirse evaporated and rematerialized inches from her. The child took the nightmare by her bloody hands. Her skin was as warm as tales of the sun in the Wake. *It can't be given to you by someone else. This is not your time. You have a part to play in the battle to come.*

"Battle? What battle?" Panic mounted inside Wren. She jerked away from her gentle touch. "Get the fuck away from me."

She wheeled around and tripped into a sprint, jerking to a halt when Saoirse appeared in front of her again. Her eyes were at once pleading and stern.

Queen Ila was on her way to Caer Bheinn, but she was ambushed. She is at the foot of Mount Anvil. You must save her.

"But—"

Sol liv hjent warren.

"What does that mean?" Wren practically shouted.

A violent shudder rippled through Saoirse, causing her tiny body to flicker like a splinter.

I'm being pulled back. Repeat after me, Nightstrider: Sol liv hjent warren.

"S-sol liv hjent warren."

Wren fumbled with the foreign words. Saoirse guttered again. She began to fade into the mist. A wave of unprecedented dread washed over the 'mare as she was seized by the urge to reach out and anchor the child.

We'll meet again soon, Nightstrider. Stay alive. Promise me.

"I—I promise."

Saoirse grinned to reveal pearly teeth. Bram flared in Wren's memory like a dying star. His grin could start fires, too. Saoirse reached up with a translucent hand and pressed it to Wren's heart. Warmth spread from her core to the tips of her fingers. A strange calm settled over her.

Wake up.

Wren swallowed a lungful of water and burst through the seal. Two hands grabbed her and hauled her onto solid ground. She crashed onto her side. Her wounds pulsed with dizzying pain, and her hands were bound behind her back again. She smelled ash and dust through the blood and water in her nose.

"What happened?"

Alaric sliced through her bonds with a shard of his own magic. Her wrists sprang apart. She did not move except to curl into a pathetic ball, shivering uncontrollably in a cradle of fog. She looked up at Alaric through tangled hair. His face was wrought with shock and concern.

Strange, Wren thought distantly. She could not remember the last time someone had worried about her.

"What is this?" a male voice growled.

"Give her some fucking space," Alaric snapped. "Wren, what happened?"

"Dreambreaker," she croaked. "Dreambreaker."

37
Caine

After a considerable amount of bickering, their captors decided to ride out the storm in the cave beneath Mount Anvil. Ila and Caine were bound at the wrists and ankles. True to his word, the leader ordered one of his men to gag the prince with a strip of cloth. He was hauled to one side of the cave. Ila was dragged to another, shouting in Vaettirin.

"Can someone shut her up?" the woman with gray hair complained. For some time, she had been pawing through the bag Morthil lent Caine, but nothing seemed to interest her beyond the jerky she had pocketed.

"Cut out her tongue," the scarred boy suggested from the fireside. He looked a bit like a weasel with a pointed chin and lanky body. "That should work."

The orc gave a guttural laugh from the mouth of the cavern. Half an hour ago, he had removed what appeared to be the hind leg of some sort of animal from his bag and begun to devour it, fur and all. He now sucked the marrow.

"Hungry," he growled, his beady eyes on Ila.

The woman rolled her eyes, tossing aside a compass. "You can't eat her." She turned to the boy. "Where the hells did you find this thing?"

"Quiet, all of you."

The group fell silent at the command of their leader, who stood examining Ila's dagger with vague interest.

"This is a fine blade you have here," he commented.

"It will look better in your eye," Ila replied coldly.

The leader tossed it into the air and caught it. He advanced on her at an unhurried pace.

"Pity my boss wants you back in one piece." He dropped into a crouch before Ila and took her chin in hand. Caine began to struggle in his bonds. The scarred boy tossed him a taunting grin. "You would be easier to handle in several."

Ila spat in his face. He swore and released her.

"Rot," the queen spat. The leader backhanded her with a resounding crack, knocking her onto her side. Caine shouted through his gag. No one paid him any mind, not even the weaselly boy. He looked on gleefully as his leader dragged Ila into an upright position by her hair. Blood ran from her nose, dripping off her chin onto her vest.

"Do you know what they call me?" he inquired, tracing the tip of the dagger along her soft jawline. "Spineripper. Would you like to find out why?" Ila did not answer, but her lower lip quivered. "Now, tell me. How long have you been working with Nightstrider?"

The storm howled outside the cave. The orc fidgeted at the cave entrance, his clubbed fingers drumming against the handle of his axe. Ila made eye contact with Caine around

Spineripper, reflecting his own panic and confusion back at him.

"I—what?"

Spineripper sighed.

"I would hate to ruin such a pretty face." He twirled the dagger with expert fingers, then brought it back to her cheek. Ila stilled against the blade. "I'm going to give you one more chance," Spineripper said in a voice that was almost sugared. "How long have you been working with Nightstrider?"

"I have no idea—"

Her words dissolved into a sob when Spineripper dragged the tip of the blade across the delicate skin beneath her eye. Red seeped into Caine's vision as blood welled from the wound, rolling down her face.

Spineripper smeared the trail with his thumb.

"There now. The first cut is always the worst."

Ila squeezed her eyes shut when he lifted the blade to her cheek again.

"You know, I wasn't surprised when Para Warwick told me Nightstrider defected," Spineripper continued. "She was always reckless, emotional." Ila shuddered when Spineripper brushed a strand of sweaty hair from her brow. "But I was surprised to hear she was working with the rebels. She never played well with others."

"I swear," Ila repeated, her voice quavering. "I don't know a Nightstrider."

"You expect Para Warwick to believe his prized 'mare stole the dreambreaker with her bare hands and disappeared into oblivion all by herself?"

Ila went deathly still. "Nightstrider touched the box?"

Spineripper grinned, exposing too many teeth. "Ah, so you do know her."

"I—I know of her, but I'm not—"

Spineripper grabbed Ila by the throat, drawing her up before him as he rose. She twisted, aiming an awkward kick at his groin. It did not faze him. If anything, his smile widened.

"Such fire," he cooed. "We'll fix that."

Ila let out a strangled sob as Spineripper dug the tip of the dagger into the hollow of her collarbone. He dragged it inward, slow and indulgent. This time Caine could not hold back a roar of rage. Spineripper threw him a bored glance.

"Is that all you got, princeling? I expected more from the son of the Para."

Caine felt his blood churn to a halt. Every discernable thought flaked away save for one.

Help her.

Keening flooded Caine's ears. The cave pressed down from above and up from below. Bone-deep cold seeped into the space, far more bitter than any brought by the snowstorm.

The fire was snuffed like a wick between fingers.

"What is this?" Spineripper barked out of the maw. Caine heard him drop Ila with a sickening thud. "What are you doing, weaver?"

The boy struck a match, briefly illuminating his wan features. It died at once. Caine wrestled free of his gag.

"Ila," he called out, struggling to his knees. "Where are you?"

"Caine!" she cried.

"Splinters!"

Panicked screams punctured the suffocating blackness. Caine shuffled toward Ila on his knees, nearly falling on his face twice. *I have to get my hands free*, he thought desperately. Cold tendrils encircled his wrists and ankles. His muscles coiled with dread as the feeling of drowning enveloped him.

The ropes binding him snapped.

Caine shouted in surprise as his limbs sprang free. All around him, the splinters writhed like shadows on the ocean floor, their inhuman voices worming into his brain.

Second . . . born . . .

Shadow . . .

. . . spinner . . .

"Caine!"

The prince snapped out of his trance when Ila screamed. He crawled with one hand stretched out before him. His fingers closed around her bicep.

"Caine!" she screamed in his ear. "The whip! My bag!"

Caine spun on his knees, feeling for her pack. His bones creaked under the mounting pressure in the cave. The splinters tightened their circle. He could not see them, but gods, he could feel them.

Shadowspinner . . .

Second . . .

He kept moving. The pads of his fingers skimmed coarse material. *Yes.* Caine tugged the bag toward him and plunged his hand inside, flinging rations and tools aside until—

"I have it!" he bellowed, yanking the whip free and shooting to his feet. A wave of dizziness washed over him, but he forced himself to remain upright. "What do I do?"

"The switch!"

His thumb found the lever, and he ignited the whip. A tongue of flames unfurled from the handle. Splinters shrieked and fled to the boundaries of the cave, revealing Spineripper and his comrades again.

The orc and the woman were both unconscious. The boy cowered near the mouth of the cave, his hands over his head. Spineripper was the only one who managed to stay on his feet, but he looked disoriented. He and Caine locked eyes. He still palmed the dagger he stole from Ila, which was slick with blood.

Her blood.

Something base and feral stirred in Caine's gut. His grip tightened on the whip.

"Caine! The splinters!"

Caine raised the whip high and swung it in a wide arc. Inhuman screeches spiked, and the pressure in his head scattered. His lungs burned as they were flooded with oxygen. A roar tore from him as he cracked the whip again, dispersing the remaining splinters.

Shadow . . .

. . . spinner . . .

Silence settled around them like ash. The campfire flickered to life again, joining the light of the blazing whip. Spineripper glowered at Caine across the cave, still palming the stolen dagger.

"Drop the whip," Spineripper ordered.

"Are you really in a position to be making demands?" Caine gestured around the cave with his chin. The orc and the woman were still collapsed in the dirt. The boy with the scar on his chin was tucked into a ball, whimpering. "Drop the knife, or I swear I'll wrap this around your neck."

Caine did not have enough practice with a whip to do anything more than fling it around wildly, but Spineripper did not need to know that.

The nightmare grinned manically. "You've got balls, kid. Guess your father underestimated you."

Caine's knuckles bleached around the handle of the whip, which was starting to grow hot. He could feel Ila watching him but kept his eyes on his opponent.

"Sounds about right," Caine said bleakly.

It did, he realized with a swell of dread. It sounded exactly right.

"Unfortunately, a little pluck won't fucking cut it."

Spineripper disappeared with a faint *pop*.

"Over here."

Caine whirled and raised the whip partway. The nightmare had rematerialized at the back of the cave. He crushed Ila to him with a ropy arm, holding the blade to her throat with his free hand. Ila was gaunt. Blood was starting to dry on her face and chest.

"Drop it," Spineripper repeated lazily.

"How—"

"You asked me how I got into the cave. I believe you have your answer." He pressed the knife closer to her throat. Blood welled from a shallow cut. Ila shut her eyes tight. "Drop the whip, princeling."

"You said Para—" Caine swallowed the name. "You said the Para needed her alive."

"I can still make her wish she was dead."

Caine tightened his grip on the whip. The tongue of flames sizzled with anticipation. Then he cast it to the ground.

Spineripper smiled at him over the blazing coils.

"There, was that really so difficult?" Ila, still bound at the wrists and ankles, gasped when the man supporting her evaporated. She fell and landed on her side before Caine could catch her. "Tick, stop blubbering and get your ass up," Spineripper barked at the scarred boy when he reappeared at the fireside.

While Spineripper was distracted, Caine scrambled over to Ila and knelt beside her, hauling her into a sitting position and grasping her by the shoulders. Her pupils were dilated with fear, but he was relieved to see the gash across her throat was superficial. The wounds under her eye and above her collarbone were deeper.

"Caine," she said weakly. "Your father—I tried to tell you."

"You did." He brushed a strand of sweaty hair from her brow, surprised at how natural it felt to touch her. "I should have listened."

Ila gave a ghost of a smile. Her eyes drifted from his, settling on his wrists. They were rubbed raw from the ropes.

"How did you get free?" she asked in a whisper.

Caine could still feel the icy tendrils of the splinters gnawing at his bonds, could still feel their strange words worming into his brain.

Second born. Shadowspinner.

What did it mean? A warning? Had the others heard it? He had no idea. All he knew was that when he prayed to the gods for help, demons answered instead.

"The ropes must have been weak."

Caine was not entirely sure why he lied but could not ignore the relief that washed over him when Ila changed the subject.

"Something is very wrong," she murmured. "Spineripper said Nightstrider touched the box. That shouldn't be possible. But..." She trailed off, shaking her head at the cave floor. "If a nightmare could touch it, why not a para? And why would Nightstrider take Saoirse to the rebellion?"

"Who is Nightstrider?"

"One of the nightmares Para Warwick created."

Caine frowned, feeling even more lost than usual. "Dream beings can create other dream beings?"

"No. No, they can't. Your father is the first." Panicked frustration ate into Ila's tone. "Nothing makes sense anymore. None of this is right."

"We're going to figure this out, okay?" Caine promised in a whisper. "If"—he drew a steadying breath—"if my father truly is Para Warwick, maybe I can talk some sense into him. I told you I'd stand up to him, right?"

Ila mustered a weak smile.

Caine looked up when a hand clapped his shoulder. The boy, Tick, appeared to have gathered his wits, though he was still green around the edges. He carried with him a set of fresh ropes.

"If you two are finished," he said snidely.

"You have a lot of confidence for someone who just pissed himself over a bunch of shadows." That earned Caine a blow to the head. He swallowed another insult and stood, passing what he hoped was a reassuring glance at Ila. "We're going to be fine," he promised, surprised by how sure he sounded. "I swear."

Ila did not respond, but her eyes flicked to his naked wrists again. Tick grabbed him by the arm and led him away. The woman had been revived, though she looked shaken. She and Spineripper now spoke in hushed tones near the mouth of the cave. The orc was still unconscious.

Or better yet, dead, Caine thought.

Tick sat him down near the rough cave wall and set about tying him up again. Caine glanced at Ila periodically. She stared at the fire with empty eyes, looking even paler than usual.

"Ten hells, you've got it bad," Tick muttered as he finished the last knot. "Bet you didn't even bed her yet. Too bad you missed your chance."

Caine did not have the energy to come up with another retort. Instead, he closed his eyes and reclined against the wall. He knew sleep would not come, but at least he could rest.

Unfortunately, his mind had other plans. Living shadows swirled on the backs of his lids. With each twist of their smoky bodies, they seemed to whisper—*Shadowspinner.*

38
Alaric

"What?"

Collapsed on the floor of the Hall of Whispers, Wren regarded Alaric through her sopping hair. The whites of her eyes were laced with red. He shrugged off his jacket and helped her sit up, careful to avoid the puncture wound above her collarbone. She winced when he wrapped the garment around her shoulders.

"Stand aside, Alaric."

Alaric, still crouched beside Wren, looked up to see Reichart standing over them. The commander looked as shaken as he felt, his hand choking the hilt of the blade at his hip.

"I'm not going to kill her. I just want to speak with her."

Alaric hesitated, his eyes flicking back to Wren. She did not appear to be aware of what was happening. She still mumbled under her breath, shuddering and rocking slightly in the bed of fog.

"Another inch of insubordination and you won't see daylight for a decade," Reichart warned.

The commander had never been one to lie. With deliberate slowness Alaric rose and stepped aside. He turned to face Wren while Reichart squatted before her, balancing on the balls of his feet.

"You're an anomaly, Nightstrider," the commander said.

Wren stared past him into the forest of columns. Her eyes were as empty as fresh graves.

"This pool is a mirror," the commander went on, gesturing at the inky waters from which she had emerged. "It allows us to see what is happening in the fog. What it is *not* is a gateway. No one has ever come out through it."

Wren just blinked, bleary and drained.

"We saw you fighting the scorpion," Alaric prompted. "Then the water rippled, and you appeared under the surface."

Wren pulled the jacket tighter around her, her drenched hair slipping forward to curtain her face.

"Saoirse."

Her voice was so faint for a moment that Alaric thought he had imagined it. Then Wren raised her head, an ember of resolve burning through the haze in her eyes.

"The dreambreaker," she rasped. "Her name is Saoirse."

Alaric and Reichart traded a glance.

"She spoke to me in the fog." Wren raised a trembling hand to her temple. "She said her protector, Queen Ila, had been ambushed." She paused, her heavy brows pulling together as if she doubted her own words. "She wants me to save her."

The rebels stared at Wren. She seemed tired just holding up her head. Her spine bowed. Her blood had already soaked through the fabric of the jacket Alaric draped over her. The potion he had forced down her throat would be wearing off by now. She would crash soon.

"What else did *Saoirse* say?" the commander went on.

The nightmare lifted her head again, struggling visibly with the simple motion. "Sol liv hjent warren."

"Sol liv hjent warren," Alaric repeated, rolling the unfamiliar words around on his tongue. "What language is that?"

"Vaettirin," Reichart answered. "The language of Galesborough."

"Queen Ila is from Galesborough, is she not?" Alaric asked. "Do you speak the language?"

"Morthil taught me the basics many years ago," the commander answered. "The phrase is a Vaettirin truism. It means something to the effect of 'carry the sun in your heart.' Nightstrider, remove the jacket."

Wren jerked her head up, rivulets of blood streaming down her face.

"If you cooperate, you will not be harmed," Reichart assured her.

Wren made eye contact with Alaric. It reminded him of the look she had given him when they left her chained in the cell, like she was shattered. It pulled at something nameless deep in his ribs.

"Remove the jacket," Reichart repeated. "And stand."

Moving gingerly, Wren climbed to her feet. The jacket slid off her back. Mist scattered when it hit the floor. Reichart sucked in a shallow breath while Alaric took an involuntary step toward her.

Burning over her heart like a newborn star was the handprint of a child.

"Is that what I think it is?" Alaric breathed. He reached out to touch it, entranced. Wren flinched away. He pulled his arm back.

"A blessing," Reichart confirmed. His eyes never left the blazing mark on her chest. "From a dreambreaker."

Silence rang long and loud in the Hall of Whispers before Alaric broke it. "How?"

"It may be beyond knowing," the commander replied. "But a dreambreaker blessing is a mark of protection and trust. It cannot be forged or falsified. For whatever reason, this Saoirse trusts Nightstrider."

Alaric was scarcely listening, his eyes fixed to the glowing mark. Wren had faded again, swaying where she stood.

"What are you going to do?" he asked Reichart.

"Not me. You."

Alaric saw Reichart look to him out of the corner of his eye and finally ripped his gaze from the blessing. The commander regarded him with quiet solemnity.

"You will go with Nightstrider to aid Queen Ila. Return with the weaver alive, and you will be pardoned."

Alaric nodded, his jaw set and adrenaline already blazing in his veins. He turned toward Wren just in time to see her crumple, sending coils of fog wafting across the obsidian pool.

39

Wren

When Wren woke, she was lying on her back under a hanging pot overflowing with luminous green foliage. Panic kicked in her stomach. She tried to move herself upright, but her vision scattered to black.

"Oh no, you don't." Someone pressed her back into a spongy pillow. The scent of a luminae tickled her nose. "Don't think I won't knock you out again."

The world crept back into focus. Mica hovered over Wren, fuming. Her curls were wrapped in a blue scarf, her apron stained red and brown. Wren wet her lips, trying to remember how to talk.

"How long—" She dissolved into a coughing fit.

Mica grabbed a clay jug off a shelf and passed it to her. Wren propped up on her elbows and drank, the mercifully cool water dribbling down her chin. She did not stop until she had emptied the container.

"How long?" she gasped.

The luminae took back the empty container. "You slept for

two days, thank the gods."

Shit.

Wren struggled into a sitting position. Mica clucked in dissent but did not try to push her down again. Smart move.

The nightmare took stock of her body. She was worse off than she initially thought, with wounds in her calf, thigh, back, chest, and wings. Each one of them had been wrapped in fresh bandages.

"Thank you," Wren rasped.

Mica nodded. She set the jug aside and put her hands on her hips. "I know you heal quickly, but the dressings should speed things up. No flying for at least a week, though. The injury to your wings is serious."

Wren barely heard the luminae. Her hair had slipped aside to reveal the blazing handprint on her chest.

Saoirse.

The dreambreaker burned so brightly in her memory. Everything else—Ondine, the Hall of Whispers, her injuries—paled in comparison. It was as if the words the child spoke were seared into the fabric of her being.

Stay alive.

Her encounter with Spineripper in the training hall slunk back into her memory. She thought he'd been toying with her when he spoke of beings with power that rivaled Para Warwick's, but she could not help but wonder if she had just met someone who could match him.

A knock brought her out of the memory. The nightmare sat up straighter in bed as Mica popped up to her feet and slid back the deadbolt to the door. "What took you so long?"

Alaric shrugged. His eyes flashed to Wren, who looked away, fixating on one of the many lush potted plants. Gods, she had known him all of two days and had spent half that time passed out in his arms.

"I brought someone to see you," he said, oblivious to her mortification. Wren tensed. Alaric stepped aside.

"Wren!"

"Solene?"

Solene rushed forward and threw her arms around Wren, who disguised a wheeze of pain as a cough. Mica and Alaric observed from the door. Alaric leaned against the frame, an amused smile playing on his lips. Wren flushed and gave Solene an awkward pat on the back.

"Are you all right?" Wren asked when they pulled apart.

"Yes."

Wren looked Solene up and down. Her bruises had faded from blue to yellow, and the cut on her lip was healing nicely.

"Thank you, Wren," Solene said. "I never would have gotten out of Caer Sidi without you. You saved my life."

Wren fidgeted, caught in the spotlight of her gratitude. "It was nothing," she mumbled, looking anywhere but her face.

"Alaric said you can be separated from your anchor."

Wren looked past Solene, glowering at the nightmare in the doorway. Alaric gave another innocent shrug.

"Did he?" Wren asked flatly.

"If you do what this dreambreaker asks, you can be free of Para Warwick." Solene took her hands and squeezed, her face full of radical hope. "You can live."

Wren wrenched her hands back and shoved off her quilts.

Solene scampered out of the way as the nightmare got to her feet and stalked over to Alaric. White spots popped in her vision. Alaric peeled away from the doorway, a challenge in his eyes.

"You're unbelievable," Wren snapped.

"So they tell me."

"You're using Solene *again*."

"Wren—"

Wren laughed, an unhinged sound like an out-of-tune piano. "Save a human queen? Protect the child? Go off on some ridiculous quest to kill an unkillable monster? Why won't you just let me die in peace?!"

The last word punched a gaping hole in the room. Mica looked at her feet, her ears drooping. Solene quivered like a frightened rabbit.

Alaric stared into the basin of Wren's soul, unafraid. "You want to die."

Wren slammed her teeth together. Her hands trembled at her sides. She rolled her fingers into fists to stifle it.

"It's what I deserve."

"Whatever you did in service of Para Warwick—"

"You have no idea what I've done!"

"Have you murdered a son because his father disappointed the Para?" Alaric snapped. Black sparks rained down from his hands. Wren held her ground, but her feathers rustled against her spine.

"Alaric," Mica said softly.

"Have you burned villages to the ground? Tortured insurgents and rebels fighting for their right to live? Orphaned children?" Alaric closed the gap that remained between them in a single stride. Wren had to tilt her head back to maintain eye contact, which only stoked her anger. "Have you killed and liked it?"

Yes, Wren wanted to scream, but her words had dried up. She had never met anyone or anything that made her feel the way she did with a blade in her hand. That unbridled power set her bones on fire. Not even Bram could make her feel that way.

"What do you want, Nightstrider?" Alaric asked.

"Stop calling me that."

"What do you want?" he repeated, pronouncing each word with brutal clarity.

"I got what I wanted."

"Liar."

"Please, tell me more about myself, *Bonehunter*!"

Alaric bit his tongue. His pupils were dilated, nearly swallowing the ring of his iris. How hard would she have to push him before they went black? How far would she have to push him to bring out the beast? She wanted to know.

"Three days."

Wren stiffened. "What?"

"Give me three days," Alaric bargained. "Saoirse trusts you; prove her right." He nodded at the gleaming mark on her chest. "If in three days you're still alive and you still believe you deserve to die, I'll kill you myself."

"Alaric," Mica gasped. Behind them, Solene let out a squeak. Neither of the nightmares paid them any mind.

"You're serious," Wren said.

"It'll be preferable to anything Para Warwick has in store for you. I can do it quick and clean. You won't feel a thing."

Wren gritted her teeth; her nostrils flared. His confidence was infuriating and intriguing in equal measure.

"If I agree," she began, "and I'm not saying I will. What happens then?"

"We leave tonight." Alaric folded his muscular arms across his chest. "We find Queen Ila and bring her back to Caer Bheinn. She opens the box. Presumably, we save two lives." He paused, studying her with inscrutable eyes. "Perhaps more."

"And after?"

"That depends on you."

"You rebels are so fucking cryptic," Wren grunted.

Alaric grinned, displaying stark white teeth. "Keeps things interesting."

Wren narrowed her eyes at him. The dark matter in his eyes and hands had receded. He could pass for a kip were it not for the horns and the smell of embers radiating from his body.

Gods help me.

Wren stuck out her arm. Alaric grasped it firmly at the elbow. His skin was vividly warm, his pulse quick and steady.

"Three days," Wren said. "And then you end it."

"On my life."

PART THREE

SNOW AND ASH

40
Ila

"Keep up, weaver."

Spineripper yanked the rope that anchored Ila to his saddle. She tripped but managed to remain on her feet. Spineripper promised he would drag her if she fell, and she believed him.

"How are your wrists?"

Ila glanced over at Caine. They had been marching behind the bounty hunters since dawn. She was tied to Spineripper, who was riding Quora. The prince was bound to the female bounty hunter, who was slouched on Peony wearing the extra jacket Ila had packed. It was much too small for her.

"Fine," Ila lied. The ropes cut deep, grinding down the skin of her wrists. The wounds Spineripper inflicted on her had faded to a distant sting, but she was sure they would scar. "What about you?"

Caine offered a smile that matched the bleak sky. "I'll live."

"Quit talking," the boy, Tick, called from behind them. He rode a sturdy palomino, the only horse they appeared to have brought with them. The huge vex trudged along beside him, his elephantine footsteps setting the tempo of their march.

The silver sun peaked then began its descent, and still, they did not stop. The Shadowrise Mountains melted into the horizon. The Bone Hills and their enigmatic headstones swelled around them. They did not meet any travelers, though Ila doubted they would aid them if they did—all Spineripper had to do was name his boss to send them running.

The ragged party eventually halted at dusk. Spineripper led them to a shallow valley in the shadow of a broken gravestone fifty paces off the road.

Caine and Ila dropped where they stood, spent. They must have looked as poorly as they felt because their captors did not bother to bind their ankles. After the bounty hunters made camp, Tick dropped a waterskin and a packet of jerky wrapped in paper beside the prisoners.

"Enjoy," he said nastily.

Ila forced herself to eat and drink slowly to spare her churning stomach. She was halfway through her second piece of jerky, which had the taste and consistency of leather, when she noticed Caine had not touched his.

"Are you all right?" she asked.

Caine did not respond at once. His expression was vacant, as if his mind had fled his body.

"My father is a night terror," he finally said, looking anywhere but Ila. "My mother was human as far as I know. So, what does that make me?"

Ila glanced at their captors, who were clustered around the fire some ten steps away. They had been quarreling for the past half hour about the best route to take to Black Root, the tiny village outside Caer Sidi.

"Does this have something to do with the splinters?" she asked in a hushed tone.

Caine took a piece of jerky from the paper, but instead of eating it, he turned it over and over in his chapped fingers.

"Saoirse is the child of a luminae and a weaver, right? Are there ever children of humans and paras?"

"Well..." Ila frowned, taking a bite of her paltry meal. "That would be impossible under any other circumstances as neither a para nor a human—one that was not also a weaver, anyway—could cross the Boundary, but your father is the exception. In theory, he could father a child with a human. But—"

"But?"

Ila set her jerky on her knee, balancing it with care. She felt Caine watching her all the while.

"The weavers told me they expected the offspring of a para and a human was not likely to survive infancy."

"What? Why?"

Ila shot another discreet glance at their captors. The hulking vex was gnawing a hunk of stringy meat. Spineripper, who was reclining against his pack, took a drag of his pipe and passed it to the woman, tendrils of violet smoke coiling from his nose. Tick was sleeping with his arm thrown across his face.

"They said the strength of their para blood would overwhelm their human bodies," Ila told Caine. "That they would unravel."

"Then why am I alive?" Caine asked, staring at the frozen ground. "Why is my sister alive?"

"I don't know, nor did the weavers." Ila offered the waterskin to him, but he shook his head. "You and your sister confounded them."

"Well, what do you believe?"

"I believe that Para Warwick is not a normal para," she answered truthfully. "Perhaps there is something in his makeup that allowed you to survive. Whatever the case, I do know one thing, Caine."

The prince met her eyes. He looked lost, almost childlike, in the twilight.

"If it was your destiny to unravel, you would have died long ago, and if you contained power like your father, it would have manifested by now."

Caine paled. Guilt gnawed at Ila. She had wanted to see his reaction when she brought up the possibilities of his bloodline, but now she almost wished she had kept her mouth shut.

Almost.

"What happened, Caine?" she murmured.

"I don't know." He looked away, his brow creased with acute distress. "It all happened so fast. I was thinking that I needed to get my hands free so I could reach you, then the ropes snapped, and I heard these voices."

Cold foreboding swept through Ila. "Voices?"

"I think the splinters were trying to tell me something, but none of it made sense." Finally, he returned his gaze to hers. His eyes were achingly human. "Is that normal?"

Slowly, Ila shook her head.

She almost told him the truth, that not only was it abnormal to hear a splinter speak, it was impossible. They were without mouths or minds. Instead, she set the waterskin aside and took his bound hands in hers. He blinked down at them as if seeing them for the first time.

"Look at me, Caine."

The prince raised his eyes to hers again. His pupils were dilated, swallowing all but a sliver of his irises.

"You're an ass, but you're not evil. Any fool could see that."

Caine snorted, though it was clearly forced. "You sure I'm not a dasak?"

Ila gave his hands a squeeze. "I never said that."

Smiles flickered across both their faces, then they fell quiet. Their captors had ceased bickering, subdued by fatigue or whatever Spineripper packed into that pipe. Only the wind and the whisper of the fire were left to beat back the hush.

"We can't run from blood."

Caine spoke so softly that, initially, Ila thought she might have imagined it. The look on his face told her otherwise.

"No," she replied. "I suppose not."

She knew that better than most. Wherever Ila went, her blood followed. Her royal blood had followed her to Llyr. Her weaver blood followed her back to Galesborough, then to Wolfhelm.

"But maybe our blood matters less than our choices."

Caine leaned back, still holding her hands, and studied her in the waning silver sunlight. "Do you really believe that?"

"I try to."

Silence grew between them. After a time, Caine moved

to retract his hands, but Ila held on tighter. They locked eyes again, and for once, it was not tinged with malice or vexation. It was as steady and warm as the sun in the Wake.

"Do you have a plan?" she asked quietly. "For when we reach your father?"

Finally, they released each other.

"I've been thinking about it all day," Caine told her, cutting his eyes to their captors. "He wants us both alive; Spinerripper confirmed that."

"He needs me to open the box. The rebels have it for now, but he'll be doing everything he can to get it back." Ila swallowed, clenching her fingers into fists despite the sting of her chafed wrists. "I won't do it, no matter what he does to me."

"I won't let him harm you or Saoirse."

Ila considered him, pensive. There was *something* behind his eyes, a steadfastness that had not been there the day they met in Wolfhelm.

But in the end, it did not matter.

"You said it yourself, Caine. He won't listen to you."

"I'll make him. I swear, I will do whatever needs to be done to keep you and Saoirse alive."

A haunted sort of smile drifted across Ila's face. She wanted nothing more than to believe him, to relax into his sureness, but she knew it was in vain.

The Para took what he wanted, and from her, he would take everything, no matter what his son did.

41
Alaric

"Are you sure about this?" Mica asked.

Alaric dropped his pack onto his neatly made bed. The luminae sat in his threadbare armchair by the hearth with her feet tucked underneath her. His room was tiny compared to hers, but he liked it that way.

At Caer Sidi, his chambers were massive and chronically disastrous. Here, he kept his space neat and ordered. The only pieces of furniture were his bed, desk, two chairs that did not match, and a wooden chest that held most of his belongings.

Dozens of charcoal sketches were nailed to the smooth stone walls. There were landscapes, portraits, messy likenesses of creatures he encountered both awake and asleep, and even the occasional plant that piqued his interest.

Now that Luken was gone, the only soul who knew of his affinity for drawing was Mica.

It was the first thing Alaric discovered he enjoyed besides killing.

"Not sure I have a choice," Alaric replied, folding an extra shirt and tucking it into his bag. "Reichart gave the order."

"I mean about your pact with Wren. Are you really going to kill her?"

"Preferably not."

"I'm serious, Alaric."

You always are, he thought. He sank onto the edge of his bed, and the frame creaked.

"The dreambreaker wants Wren to rescue Queen Ila. Not Reichart, not the rebellion—Wren. She clearly sees something in her." Alaric flopped onto his back, frowning at the low arched ceiling. "If she, *we*, can save those two, maybe our dreambreaker friend will separate Wren from her anchor."

"Assuming she wants to be."

Alaric rolled his head to the side, raising his eyebrows at Mica.

She sighed, bringing her knees to her chest and wrapping her soft arms around them.

"You heard what she said, Alaric. She wants it to end."

"So we should just let her die?"

Mica gave an exasperated click of her tongue. "Of the two people in this room, which of us spent the last two days patching her up, and which of us made a suicide pact with her?"

"Point taken." Alaric sat up again so he could continue to pack. "I guess I thought if I had a bit more time, I could change her mind. If anyone in the world understands what she's going through, I do."

"I know what you're trying to do, Alaric," Mica told him gently. "I'm proud of you, and Luken would be, too." The nightmare focused intently on rolling up his woolen sweater and stowing it. "But you can't save someone who does not want to be saved."

Alaric just bobbed his head, still fixated on his task.

Then Mica was across the room, her arms around his neck and her curls tickling the side of his face. He froze, then patted her on the back.

"Be careful," she whispered. "Promise?"

He let his head melt onto her shoulder and wrapped his arms around her, drawing her close. "Promise."

Mica pulled away with a sniff and smoothed the front of her dress. Her eyes were even brighter than usual.

"I have to go get Wren ready. Her bandages need changing," she said, making for the exit. "Pack an extra pair of socks. See you soon, right?"

With one last smile, she ducked from the room and disappeared around the corner, footsteps tapping down the hall.

"Right," Alaric murmured, knowing she could hear him. "See you soon."

☽○☾

Alaric waited before the main entrance to Caer Bheinn, gazing out through the barrier at the barren landscape. Nothing grew at this altitude save for tufts of stumpy grass. Mica found it depressing, but he liked it.

The mountains, the stars, they all looked like freedom. Even through the sheen of the barrier.

The echo of two sets of footsteps drew him around. Reichart and the luminae Vrut approached across the vacant entry hall. The commander was dwarfed by his companion, who wore a surcoat over his furry goat legs. Stubby horns grew from his brow, and a set of floppy rounded ears matched his lower half.

"Alaric," Reichart greeted him curtly.

"Commander."

Hello, Bonehunter, Vrut signed with his hands.

Thank you for coming, Alaric responded in kind.

Vrut flicked his ancient yellow eyes to the barrier. *This will not take long.*

The luminae moved off toward the front door, leaving Alaric and Reichart alone in prickling silence. Alaric let it grow, unruffled.

"Hodge has been disposed of," the commander finally said. "No funeral, no honors."

Alaric bobbed his head in acceptance.

"His behavior was unacceptable, but do not let your empathy for Nightstrider cloud your judgment. She is still the enemy."

The commander reached into the pocket of his jacket and produced a bundle of rags, offering it to Alaric.

"Just what I wanted," the nightmare said flatly.

"This is the dreambreaker," Reichart said with a withering look. "Don't let it touch your skin, and don't let Nightstrider know you have it."

Alaric accepted the parcel with ginger hands. Warmth radiated from the knotted fabric. He dropped to one knee and shrugged off his pack, tucking the dreambreaker safely inside. He wondered if the child could feel the box moving, if it made her dizzy or ill. Gods, he hoped she would be all right jostling about in his bag.

"Would she not be safer here?" Alaric asked, climbing to his feet again.

"Perhaps, but our intelligence suggests she can't survive inside much longer. Best to get her to Queen Ila as soon as possible."

Alaric nodded again. Reichart shifted on booted feet, abruptly breaking eye contact with him.

"You saw Morthil, did you not?" the commander inquired. "How did he seem?"

Alaric had wondered when the subject of Morthil was going to crop up. He shrugged, feigning nonchalance.

"He seemed fine."

"Did he...?" The commander trailed off. "No change, then?"

"He isn't going to budge." Alaric shouldered his bag again and slipped both arms through the straps. "If he wanted to come back, he would have by now."

The commander started to say something else, but the murmur of featherlight footsteps interrupted him.

He and Alaric looked around.

Wren walked with the kind of confidence that could level cities. All traces of the fractured girl Alaric had scooped off the floor of the Hall of Whispers were gone. Her hair was braided, exposing pronounced cheekbones and flint eyes. Most notably, her weapons had been returned to her. Two long knives were strapped to her hips, and two more were flush against her thighs.

"Who gave you those?" Reichart asked her, his tone deceptively even.

"Does it matter?" Wren answered, laying a loving hand on one of the blades as she arrived in front of them. "Would you have me face whoever kidnapped this Queen Ila unarmed?"

"You're capable regardless, I'm sure."

"I'll take that as a compliment." She leveled an expectant look at Alaric. "Ready?"

A tap on the shoulder kept Alaric from answering. Vrut, whom he had all but forgotten about, stared openly at Wren. He looked more like a lovestruck teenager than an ancient luminae.

Is she the one who got through the barrier? he signed.

"Yes," Wren answered aloud, simultaneously kneading the word with her fingers. Vrut beamed in palpable delight. Reichart raised a brow. Alaric could not help but smile. *But do not ask me how,* she continued with her hands.

A 'mare of many gifts, Vrut returned. His silent words rang with esteem. *I would like to speak with you when you return.*

Wren stiffened subtly. The luminae did not appear to notice, still grinning ear to ear.

We should go, Alaric signed, nodding at the sealed exit.

Vrut bobbed his head, floppy ears wobbling. He spun to face the barrier and cracked his knuckles.

Wren strode up to stand beside Alaric, leaving a good three paces between them. Quiet fascination sprawled across her features as she watched Vrut raise a hand to the barrier. The translucent quartz wall began to melt, ushering in fresh air and unaltered moonlight. The mountains were bruised black and purple save for their snowcapped peaks, which were powder blue.

"Shall we?" Alaric inquired as if asking her to dance.

Wren made a vexed noise at the back of her throat, adjusting her bag. "This would be much faster if I could fly."

"Mica said it would be a week before your wings heal. Besides, Reichart wants you to stay with me."

"Do you not have horses?" she pressed. "Or those things those bastards with their little fishhooks were flying on?"

"The path to Mount Anvil is too treacherous for horses. We'll be faster on foot, and the manticore riders are our last line of defense. They can't abandon their posts."

Wren grunted, returning her gaze to the freshly unveiled landscape. The wind teased strands of hair from her braid and coaxed color into her cheeks. For a moment, Alaric thought he could see something behind her eyes, something too gentle for a nightmare.

He blinked, and it disappeared.

"Try to keep up, then," she said in a voice that highlighted her doubts. Without another word, she darted off down the crumbling steps of Caer Bheinn to the treacherous mountain pathway.

Alaric threw a final glance at Reichart and Vrut. The luminae still held the barrier open with a hand. He winked, his coat flapping in the abrupt wind. The commander watched him with calculating eyes.

She is still the enemy.

Alaric tucked away the warning and tore off after Wren.

42
Wren

Wren raced down the twisting path through the Shadowrise Mountains, skirting the sheer rock face. Pebbles skittered beneath her boots, diving into the oceans of clouds below. Alaric was hot on her heels. He was faster than she anticipated, keeping pace with her for over three hours, but he was starting to fade. His breathing was ragged, his pace uneven.

Still, he did not ask for respite. In fact, he had not uttered a single word since they left Caer Bheinn, not that she minded.

The moons followed their arcs through the brilliant night sky. Wren and Alaric dipped below the tree line. The landscape was studded with ancient pines, their impossibly vast trunks ornamented with bulbous blue fungi shaped like paper fans. Amber pine needles peeked through the snowdrifts.

Wren would have found it beautiful was she not steeped in cold focus. If there was one thing she knew for certain, it was that she thrived with purpose. It did not matter if that purpose was to save a queen or kill a bastard. As long as she had a tangible goal to cling to, she could survive anything, though that did not mean she deserved to.

Her nose twitched.

She slowed her pace, looking down the planes of her body. She cursed and scraped to a halt. Alaric skidded to a stop behind her.

"What is it?" He was winded and trying valiantly not to show it. Unfortunately for him, she could hear his heartbeat. "Are you all right?"

"Fine," Wren barked, turning off the path and crossing to a great leaning pine tree, the branches of which nearly brushed the snow.

Keeping her back to Alaric, she undid the clasps of her jacket and slipped her hand under the tunic Mica had altered to accommodate her wings. She swore again when she found a swath of sticky blood. The wound above her collarbone had split, soaking the bandages.

Opposite the wound, the dreambreaker blessing still glowed. It showed no sign of guttering anytime soon.

What good is a blessing if I can still bleed out?

"Let me see," Alaric offered, coming up behind her.

"I'm fine." She snapped her jacket back into place and wiped the blood on her leggings. "I've had worse."

"Well, you're not allowed to die for three days, so let me see."

Wren rolled her eyes at the roof of tree boughs. A patch of stars was visible through them. Bram would have known which constellation they belonged to. He seemed to know everything about everything, even her.

Especially her.

"Fine," she said with a sigh, turning to face Alaric. "Try anything and I'll throw you off the cliff."

"Noted."

Wren turned her head to the side, and he stepped closer. She swallowed, staring intently at a shelf of that blue fungus growing from a boulder. Up close, it seemed to pulse slightly.

Gross.

Alaric eased the flap of her jacket aside. The radiance of the dreambreaker blessing bloomed along with the sharp smell of blood. He teased apart the bandages and hissed through his teeth.

"Gods, how have you been running with this?"

Wren shrugged, still fixated acutely on the boulder and trying not to notice that he smelled of winter and embers. It was the scent of a nightmare, yes, but there was something else beneath it.

"It'll heal overnight," she said gruffly.

"Not if you keep pushing yourself this hard."

"Is this what you call hard?"

Finally, she noticed a smirk hanging on the corner of his mouth. He stepped away from her and dropped his bag with a muffled crunch of snow.

"You may have me beat on speed, but can you do this?" He produced a thread of dark matter with a flick of his wrist. It curled around his pointer finger like a serpent. Wren stared at it, curious despite herself.

"Pretty," she commented, her voice dry. "Can you do anything besides make ribbons?"

"You've seen what I can do."

"Eh."

Alaric grinned and opened his palm. The thread morphed into a spear, twice the length of his forearm and black as pitch.

In a fluid motion, he spun and hurled it at the boulder across the clearing. The rock cracked like an egg, belching a cloud of dust and releasing a plume of periwinkle spores from the fungus. The bolt dissipated along with the debris, the spores cradled by the breeze and whisked away into the ravine below.

"Impressive," Wren admitted. "Are we done comparing shoe sizes, or should we jump off the cliff and see who hits the ground first?"

"No thanks. Now, are you going to get the firewood, or should I?"

"What?"

"You need to rest," Alaric said firmly. "I'm not going any farther until you do."

"Are you serious?"

His expression answered the question.

"We're wasting time," Wren snapped. "I just want to get this over with."

"Odds are whoever took Queen Ila is going to put up a fight. If you rest now, you'll be in better shape to fight them later."

Wren scowled.

"Fine," she agreed, slipping off her own bag and tossing it to the ground. The simple motion brought her more pain than she cared to admit. She turned from Alaric and headed deeper into the forest. "If you're too tired to go on, we can stop for the night. I'll get the firewood."

"Whatever you say, magpie."

Wren froze, swelling up like a bird about to screech. Behind her, she heard Alaric chuckle under his breath. She squared her shoulders and marched away, indignant and fuming.

It took longer than she expected to find the firewood. The forest seemed to be full of everything but dry wood. She came across all manner of creatures, from deer with crystalline antlers to lizards the size of cats with barbed violet tongues and plumes of feathers around their necks. They did not look like they belonged in the snow and hissed at her as she passed their burrows.

Eventually, she stumbled across a felled tree that appeared to have been struck by lightning. Snapping off a bundle of branches, she made her way back to Alaric. His scent was a knife through the maze of trees.

"Took you long enough."

Alaric had laid out their bedrolls on opposite sides of a patch of earth he had cleared. Wren dropped the firewood in its cradle and crossed to hers. He watched as she sat and grabbed her bag, riffling through it in search of the flint and steel Mica assured her she packed.

"Are you always this pleasant?" Alaric asked, plunking down on his bedroll. Wren ignored him. She found the flint, but instead of using the steel, she used her thumbnail to produce a shower of sparks over the kindling. "What was it, then?"

"What was what?" She struck the flint again and the kindling ignited, spreading like a rumor through the twigs and branches.

"What was it that made you leave Para Warwick?"

"Why do you insist on getting to know me? You promised to kill me in three days."

"I try to be a little optimistic." Alaric smiled crookedly. "You think I'm unhinged."

"I think you're a fool," she corrected him, stoking the flames with the tip of a branch. "Why did *you* leave?"

Alaric did not respond at once. Firelight collected in his dark eyes. The blessing on her chest gave a kick, or perhaps it was the traitorous organ beneath it.

"You're deflecting," he accused.

This time, Wren did not answer. There was no need. Alaric reclined against the towering tree behind him. She studied the lines of his face. He was quite the looker, in truth. Strong jaw, gleaming olive skin, unruly black hair.

And his horns...

Stop it. She dropped her gaze to the fire, ignoring the sting of the heat and smoke. *What the fuck is wrong with you?*

"I was sent to punish a lord." Wren lifted her head. Alaric was avoiding her eyes. "A kip who had climbed the ranks. He refused to pay his tithe. I thought I would be killing him, but this time, Para Warwick wanted something else. He wanted me to kill his daughter."

"Was she—"

"His daughter by blood, yes." Alaric dragged his fingers through his hair, still refusing eye contact with her. "She was seven, maybe eight."

Wren grabbed another branch, brushed off the snow, and threw it on the flames. They rose to devour it.

"I knew the girl. She sometimes accompanied her father when he came to Caer Sidi. Gods know why he brought her. She was always happy, though. Nearly everyone liked her, even Ondine."

"Ondine hates children."

"She liked her."

Wren stared at Alaric. He stared at the fire. Shadows shivered on his face as a restless wind cut through the campsite, toying with the flames. A faint blue shimmer caught her eye, and she realized the fungus clinging to the tree trunks around them had begun to glow as night set in. It was almost beautiful.

"What happened?" she asked.

"When I got to their home, the girl was prepared to die for her family. Something broke in me. I told them to run, then I fled. I expected to die like you." His eyes darted up to hers. She shifted uncomfortably. There was more emotion in them than she was accustomed to seeing in a 'mare. "That was when I met Luken."

"Who?"

"A dreambreaker. He became a brother to me." Alaric took a deep breath. "He separated me from my anchor and brought me to the rebellion. I never looked back."

"How is that possible?" Wren asked with a shake of her head. She did not know if she was asking about his separation from his anchor or his being taken in by the rebellion. Either way, Alaric did not answer, so she asked another question. "What happened to him? Luken?"

"Ah." Alaric held up a long finger. "Your turn."

Wren cocked her head to the side. "What was that you said about deflecting?"

"Can you blame us?" He laced his fingers behind his head

and reclined against the tree again. "Caer Sidi is hardly a nurturing environment."

Wren snorted, surprising both of them. It chafed her, the laughter, as if it was not something that belonged to her.

"We should sleep," she said abruptly.

The 'mare lay on her uninjured side, facing away from Alaric. She rested her head in the crook of her elbow, her boots still laced and her blades in close reach. She pretended not to feel his eyes on her.

"Wren?"

She heaved a loaded sigh. "What?"

"I owe you an apology."

Wren went stiff. The forest hummed around them, teeming with life though it was choked with frost. "Why?"

"Because what you've been through, whatever happened to lead you here, is my fault."

Wren rolled over to face him, pushing herself upright. He was still sitting in the same position, his face sober and his eyes darker than the spaces between stars. "What the hells are you talking about?"

A twig snapped on the fire, sending up a plume of sparks. Somewhere in the forest, an owl—or something like it—gave a morose *whoo*.

"You were created to replace me," Alaric answered. "If I'd done what the Para commanded, if I'd stayed at Caer Sidi, you never would have endured whatever he put you through. If I hadn't been such a coward..." He trailed off.

The words Wren spoke next came from a soft place in the deepest part of her chest, one she thought had rotted long ago.

"You're the last person in this entire fucking realm who needs to apologize to me. You helped me when you did not have to. Only one person has ever done that for me."

"I—"

"Just stop before your sentimentality makes me sick."

Alaric closed his mouth. She looked away, prickling with vexation and something else she did not wish to examine.

"You said someone else helped you," the other nightmare finally said. "Who was it?"

"Someone long gone."

"Someone you loved?"

"Yes," she snapped. "If 'mares are capable of love, then yes."

Alaric hummed thoughtfully. He rested his head against the tree again. "I don't think I thought about love while I was the Hand. Things are different now, of course."

Something ugly and foreign twitched in Wren. "You have a lover, then."

"I have people I love, like Mica and Luken."

"I thought you said he was dead."

"Who said love ends with death?" Wren blinked at him. He changed the subject. "What about you? Is this person who helped you the only one you've loved?"

"I don't know." Wren grabbed a branch from the dwindling pile of kindling and broke it in two. Sparks fled as she tossed the pieces onto the fire. "Ondine and I were together."

Alaric had been reaching for his waterskin, but his fingers froze an inch from it. "Are you serious?"

"Is that a problem?" Wren asked in a flat tone.

"No, I just can't imagine her with anyone."

Wren snorted. "Sounds like you knew her pretty well, then."

"We manifested within a year of each other. For a long time, it was just the two of us. That was back before Para Warwick had expanded his reign past Ironmoor. Ondine and I were on the front lines of that conquest."

"She never talked about that time." For a split second, Wren felt her eyes frost over. She blinked, and they were clear again. "She never talked about you, either."

"Not surprised. When I deserted Para Warwick, I deserted her, too."

"So did I." Wren bowed her head, her braid slipping forward over her shoulder. "I don't know if I love her, but I know I care about her, and I don't want her dead."

The image of Ondine falling into the abyss, a blade hilt-deep in her chest, flashed in Wren's mind. She smothered it at once.

"She survived," Alaric assured her. "We're all cockroaches, the lot of us."

Wren did not respond. It was as if there was a splinter in her throat. She heard Alaric get to his feet and remained motionless. The snow crunched under his boots as he rounded the fire. He knelt beside her and rested a hand on her back. She did not flinch away.

"I don't think monsters waste much time worrying about being monsters," he told her.

Wren squeezed her eyes shut against a well of tears. She would not show them. She refused. Alaric sighed and took his hand away.

"Don't."

He froze, his palm still hovering over her. He lay his hand on her spine again. She leaned toward him, her head sagging onto his shoulder.

She did not look at him. He did not look at her. Neither of them dared disturb the moment with clumsy words. They remained this way until the fire devoured itself, two nightmares trapped in the amber of a daydream.

☽○☾

Wren awoke to the smell of sizzling meat, a blanket she had not fallen asleep with tucked up to her chin. She blinked groggily, eye level with the revived fire. Through the flames, she glimpsed a pair of boots.

"Morning, magpie."

Wren sat up with a groan, rubbing sleep from her eyes. "How long did I sleep?" she asked, reaching for her bandaged shoulder. Distant pain flared beneath her hand, but she did not smell any fresh blood.

"A few hours," Alaric answered in a voice far too cheery for the early hour.

Memories of the previous night slammed into Wren. His tender words, the smell of his skin, the heat rolling off his muscles as she leaned on him. She shoved off the blanket and popped to her feet, raking escaped strands of her braid out of her face.

"Hungry?" Alaric asked, gesturing at the skinned rabbit roasting over the flames.

Her stomach grumbled in response, but she shook her head, backing away. "No. I need to wash."

Alaric blinked. "Where are you going?"

"I smell a creek nearby."

Wren jogged off into the throng of pines before he could respond. She only slowed when she could no longer smell Alaric or the smoking rabbit.

It took a good ten minutes to reach the stream, but when she arrived, she was not disappointed. Clear water cascaded into a pool before rambling down the mountain. Spongy moss collected around the basin, lush green against the snow. The air was clean and crisp, so different from the smoggy atmosphere around Black Root. Steam rose from the surface of the pool.

Wren smiled. She had stumbled across a hot spring.

She shed her clothes and set about unwinding the bandages Mica had painstakingly wrapped around her wounds. She was pleased to see most of them were covered with pink tissue. Reaching over her shoulder, she prodded the knife wound Hodge managed to put through her anchor burn. The sutures were a prickly spine that itched with every motion.

Gods, was this what it was like to be a kip?

Wren combed out her braid with her fingers and approached the pool. The earth beneath her soles was warm and porous. She tested the water with her toe. It was hot as bathwater.

Perfect.

She stepped into the pool and walked until it closed over her head.

Warm bubbles skittered up her body. Her eyelids parted slowly. Jets of sunlight lanced through the water. Coin-size fish with bulbous eyes and royal blue scales examined her, baffled. She released the air from her lungs and the fish scattered. Pushing off the mushy floor, she resurfaced.

Wren screamed.

Hello, Nightstrider.

"Shit, kid!"

Saoirse was perched at the edge of the pool, her bare toes an inch above the water. Her semitranslucent figure absorbed steam and sunlight. It may have been a trick of the light, but Wren could have sworn her form was fainter than it was in the Hall of Whispers.

You look better, Saoirse said, the words echoing through Wren's mind. *Sorry to scare you, but I needed to speak with you alone.*

"You surprised me," Wren corrected her, crossing her arms over her chest though the water crested her shoulders. "What do you want?"

Ila and her captors will arrive at Caer Sidi soon.

"Shit." Wren glanced up at Saoirse with a wince. "I mean—shit. Alaric and I won't reach them in time. I have to fly."

Saoirse shook her curly head. *You're not ready. Your wounds need time to heal. Besides, you need Alaric.*

"What for?"

The child just smiled.

If you take the Widow's Pass, you may still reach them in time. Saoirse paused, her brow rumpling. *There is something else. Someone is with her. Their energy is—different. I don't know what they are or why they're with her, but I don't think they mean her harm.*

"What—"

"WREN!"

Saoirse evaporated like smoke in the sun. Alaric burst through the tree line, a jagged blade forged of his own power in hand. He slid to a stop at the mossy edge of the basin. His eyes were wild.

"Wren," he repeated. "Wh—"

Wren grabbed Alaric by the ankles and yanked his feet out from under him. He hit the water with a splash that arced over her head. His conjured blade dissolved when he released it, sputtering and cursing.

"What the hells was that for?!" he bellowed, shooting to his feet in the pool. The hot water lapped at his middle.

"I told you if you tried anything I'd throw you off the mountain!" Wren shouted, turning her back on him and glowering at him over her shoulder. "Consider yourself lucky."

"I heard you scream; I thought you were in danger!"

"Likely story."

Alaric shook his head, flinging droplets of water everywhere. "Gods, you're a piece of fucking work, you know that?"

"Good thing I won't be a problem in two days, then."

Silence fell, broken only by the hum of the stream. Wren peered at Alaric over her shoulder. She could not help but notice the way his soaked tunic clung to his muscular chest. Her skin heated from her brow to her collarbone, and she prayed he could not scent her arousal.

"They're beautiful," Alaric murmured.

"Excuse me?"

"Your wings."

Sunlight flickered in his dark eyes like liquid gold. He blinked, then raised them to hers. She opened her mouth to respond, but every word she harbored chose that exact moment to crumble.

Alaric looked away.

"Sorry," he said. "I'll go. I saved you half the rabbit."

Without another word, he planted his palms in the moss and heaved himself onto dry land. Steam rose from his powerful body as he entered the cold air. Wren watched him, mute and dripping wet, as he strode off into the forest. When he disappeared, she sank below the waterline to calm her flaming face.

43
Alaric

Alaric returned to the campsite in a daze as if he had just drained a bottle of whiskey in a single swig. Each time he blinked, Wren was painted on the backs of his eyelids. The strong lines of her body, her breasts dappled with tiny pearls of water, her hair swirling like ink around her.

Her wings, black and blue in the morning sun.

Gods help me.

When he arrived back at camp, he stripped off his sopping clothes. Once he dumped the water out of his boots and donned fresh clothes, he began to pack. He was rolling up their bedrolls when his instincts twitched. He checked over his shoulder and nearly jumped out of his skin.

"How long have you been standing there?"

Wren stood beside the remains of the fire, fully clothed with wet plaited hair. "We have to go," she said, bending down to collect the bag he had packed for her. "The queen is slipping through our fingers."

"What are you talking about?" Alaric asked, getting to his feet.

"Saoirse appeared to me again. She told me Queen Ila and her captors will arrive at Caer Sidi soon."

Alaric swore. "We won't make it in time."

"We might if we take the Widow's Pass."

"Just when you were starting to make sense," he said.

Wren smiled, reckless and a little wicked. The memory of her stealing his dagger flared in his mind.

He had forgotten how to breathe then, too.

"We're two of the most powerful 'mares in the Reverie," Wren reminded him. "Are you really afraid of a few vexes?"

"I never said I was afraid," Alaric replied crossly, snatching his boots off the ground. Thanks to his unexpected plunge, they were stiff with frost. He stomped them on, immediately soaking his fresh socks. "I implied it was stupid."

"You should feel right at home, then."

Alaric shouldered his pack with a grimace. Wren watched him, waiting for his response. There was a hunger in her eyes he recognized, one native to his own body. Time did not numb it, food did not satiate it, and rest merely exacerbated it. The only relief was at the end of a blade.

"You really want to do this?" he asked.

"I wanted to disappear quietly, but you roped me into this ridiculous quest. We might as well have a little fun while we're at it."

"You call walking through a ravine half a league long and crawling with cannibalistic vexes fun?"

"You don't?"

That dragged a genuine chuckle from Alaric. "Fine. We'll take the Pass on one condition." Wren folded her muscular arms. He grinned, mirroring her posture. "Tell me something I don't know about you."

"You don't know anything about me."

Alaric rolled his eyes at the lattice of tree branches. "Then tell me something no one knows about you."

"This is childish," Wren complained. He could have sworn he saw a splash of color in her cheeks. "You're just making things harder for yourself."

"How so?"

"Killing a stranger is easier than killing a friend."

Alaric felt his stomach plummet. He tried to mask it with a snide comment. "Good thing we're not friends."

Wren smiled, fleeting as a splinter. "What do you want to know?"

"Anything."

Wren sighed. Her eyes drifted to the east. Alaric waited, holding his breath as if the slightest breeze would send her running for the hills.

"Dancing."

Alaric blinked. "What?"

"I always wanted to dance," Wren told him, finally allowing her eyes to meet his again. "I never learned how."

Alaric gazed down at Wren in the pale morning light. With a blade in her hand, she was a symphony of power and grace. Now she just looked like a girl burdened with too much power. An immortal robbed of life.

Promises he could not keep welled in his mouth. The one he made her loomed larger than the rest.

How in the name of the gods will I keep my word?

"Come on," Wren prompted him, jerking her head at the path. The mountains beyond it were shrouded in bluish mist. "If we leave now, we can reach the Pass by nightrise."

Rather than tearing off as Alaric expected, she lingered, waiting for him to join her. He waved her on.

"Go. Gods know you'll just end up passing me sooner or later."

Wren flashed her sharp canines. "At least you're learning."

☽○☾

They made good time. Alaric kept pace with Wren until they broke for supper in a basin between two mountains. Cutting off the trail, they wound through a grove of chalky ashwood trees until they reached the bubbling stream Wren had smelled. They sat on a slab of stone jutting over the water, their legs dangling.

"How are your wounds?" Alaric asked, digging into his pack in search of their meal.

Wren peeled back the neck of her tunic to show him. Baby pink skin had formed over the injury above her collarbone. Opposite it, the blessing Saoirse imparted on her burned steadily.

The very sight of the handprint still made his pulse sprint.

"Fine, see?" she said, releasing her shirt.

Alaric nodded, passing her a crisp roll that fit in her palm like a large egg. She sniffed it, then broke off a piece and stuck it in her mouth.

"Do you like it?" he asked.

Wren swallowed. Hard. He could almost feel the unchewed crust scraping her throat on the way down.

"Hang on, did you make this?" she asked, stifling a cough.

"That bad, are they?"

Wren tore off another generous piece and stuck it in her mouth, speaking through her chewing. "I like it more than I like you."

Alaric grinned, glowing like a sprite.

"Bonehunter the baker," Wren mused, tossing the remainder of the roll into the air and catching it. "Para Warwick would not approve."

"I aim to live my life in a manner that ensures he would be profoundly ashamed."

"I think you do that by breathing."

Alaric took a roll in hand, examining it. "When I first arrived at Caer Bheinn, I was a mess. I have no idea what Luken thought he saw in me, but nobody else saw it, least of all me. It took me years to find joy in anything besides killing."

"And you found joy in baking?" Wren asked incredulously.

"Not exactly." Alaric took a swig from his waterskin, then offered it to her. She took it. He lay back, his arms cradling his head and his legs hanging over the edge of the rock. "I started looking for things that made me feel something other than nothing. Baking works, sometimes."

"Sometimes?"

He shrugged against the smooth stone. "Other things help, too. Drawing, hunting, reading, sex."

"And they really make you feel better?"

Alaric rolled his head to the side to observe Wren. She was still, a rabbit caught in the torchlight of his gaze. He flicked his eyes back to the silvered sky.

"Sometimes." A pause, then, "Tell me about them."

Out of the corner of his eye, he saw Wren throw a skittish glance his way. He kept his gaze fixed on the sky.

"Who?" she asked with poorly cultivated nonchalance.

"The person who helped you, the one you loved."

He heard the crust of her roll crackle as her grip on it tightened, sending a shower of crumbs raining down on her thighs. She brushed them away. "You said you wouldn't ask about my past anymore."

Alaric returned his eyes to her face, sober. "They're not your past if they're still with you."

Wren gave him a funny look, so he elaborated. "You just destroyed your entire life for the mere memory of them. I'd say they're still your present."

"I never thought about it like that."

Alaric did not answer. He felt the absurd urge to hold his breath, as if the slightest movement would send her fleeing just when she was beginning to open up.

Wren hesitated a moment, then joined him on her back, resting the remnants of the roll on her stomach. She was close enough that he could feel the heat pouring off her body.

"His name was Bram," she began. "He was a luminae. We met in Rook Wall. I'd been sent to kill some vex. Never did find out why."

"Did he try to stop you?"

"No." A fleeting smile brushed her lips. "I saw him in the market beating the shit out of a 'mare who attacked a kip."

"Sounds like someone I would get along with."

"I thought it was ridiculous at the time. I couldn't

understand why a luminae would waste so much energy on a mortal." The veil of nostalgia over her face melted to despair. "I should have never gotten involved. I should have just let him be, but I was curious."

"What did you do?"

"I killed the nightmare and asked Bram what the hells he was doing. He said he was tired of 'mares treating kips like shit." She paused. The creek ambled along beneath their dangling feet. The skeletal ashwoods creaked and groaned like the lines of a ship. "I don't think he knew who I was. Not then, anyway."

"What was it about him?" Alaric asked. "What made you fall?"

"My life was nothing but death," Wren answered. "I don't know how many people I killed. I lost count so long ago. Somehow, he saw beyond all that. Just like Luken saw beyond your past."

"What do you think he saw in you?"

Wren kept her eyes on the featureless sky. "Something that was not really there."

They fell silent. Alaric wanted to ask more, but it was clear his questions were wearing on her. Instead, he climbed to his feet, looking down on Wren pensively. She squinted up at him in the stark sunlight.

"I don't know if it matters," he said, holding out his hand. "But for the record, I see it, too."

For a long moment, Wren was still. Then, slowly, as if she was approaching a flame, she took his hand.

44
Caine

When they arrived in Black Root, Caine and Ila were both on the verge of passing out. The prince's wrists were nearly worn to the bone by the ropes binding him to Spineripper. Their captors had not allowed them food or rest for more than a day.

Tick, the woman, and the orc departed at the edge of Black Root. They were headed for a tavern, saying something about a game called echo stones. The woman gave Spineripper the tether that bound her to Ila before leaving.

"You'll have your cut this evening," Spineripper promised her, still astride Peony.

The woman only grunted, exhausted and still wearing the jacket she stole from Ila.

"Good luck dealing with the Para, boss," Tick said, aiming a final kick at Caine. The prince was too spent to dodge it. "See you later, princeling."

"You better hope not," Caine growled.

Tick merely winked. With a final lazy salute at Spineripper, he and the others departed.

"Get moving," Spineripper barked, jerking both their tethers. "We're already late."

Black Root was not wholly unlike the villages in Wolfhelm. Low buildings with thatched roofs lined the muddy roads, which were full of pedestrians and carts. The villagers themselves were a blend of human and myth. They observed Caine and Ila curiously as they shambled along but averted their eyes as soon as they saw Spineripper.

"Caine."

The prince glanced over at Ila. Her condition had deteriorated over the past few hours. Her skin was gray and clammy. The red rings around her wrists matched her knife wounds. He imagined he did not look much better.

"What is it?" he asked in a low voice.

"I need to tell you something."

Caine shuffled closer to her, narrowly avoiding stepping in a steaming pile of dung. Ila bit her lip until it blanched white. She shivered, and he knew it was not from cold.

"There is something you must know," she whispered, her blue-gray eyes glued to Spineripper some ten paces ahead. "Something about Saoirse."

A shout from the ragged crowd caused them both to jump. Caine craned his neck to see a child with a round belly and a face like a tabby cat pointing at them. An older woman swooped him off the ground and shushed him, but he still gawked at them over her shoulder.

"Caine," Ila breathed, her gaze fevered. "Listen to me. Saoirse is dying inside that box. She was never meant to stay in it for so long. Even so, I won't open it for Para Warwick. He'll have to kill me first."

"I won't let that happen."

"Para Warwick, the rebels, even Morthil, they all believe I'm the only one who can open the box." Ila inched closer still. Her next words dusted to the curve of his ear. "But there is a fail-safe in the event of my death. It is a violent, dangerous process, but when I'm gone, it will be her only chance. I need you to find Saoirse and free her."

"I—"

"Promise me, Caine."

His throat tightened as he gazed down at her. Beneath the layers of sweat and blood, she blazed with unshakable defiance.

"I promise."

The relief that washed over Ila was palpable. Strange guilt took root in Caine's stomach. The weight she had been carrying alone was unfathomable.

"Remember these words," Ila said, her voice soft as falling snow. "Sol liv hjent warren."

"Sol liv hjent warren." The Vaettirin phrase sounded clunky with his accent. "What does it mean?"

"Promise me you'll care for her as if she were your own. Tell her"—Caine watched helplessly as she struggled to regain her voice, blinking back a sheen of tears—"tell her I love her, and that I tried."

"Tell her yourself."

Even to his ears, the words sounded empty.

"I hope to," Ila said with a faint smile.

They left Black Root behind, exchanging the tired buildings for the eerie sprawl of the Tanglewood. They were close to the clearing where the portal had dumped them, Caine realized.

Fate had a strange sense of humor.

Evening dragged the counterfeit sun below the horizon, ushering in the twilight. Ila and Caine marched on in silence behind Spineripper and his stolen horse. He kept his hand on the pommel of his sword, his crossbow strapped across his back.

If I could just get my hands on that bow, Caine thought grimly.

"Caine."

Caine glanced at Ila. She stared dead ahead. All traces of color had drained from her face, save for the yellowed bruise on her cheek and the gash below her eye. He followed her line of sight.

Through the inky trees was a towering wall. Beyond it, twelve towers black as pitch spiraled toward the sky. Like the sun, it was a shade of its twin in the Wake, but Caine knew it all the same.

"Caer Sidi." His attention snapped back to Ila. "How?"

"Your home is an echopoint," she whispered. "A place that exists in both worlds."

Caine felt his pulse climb as they approached the near doppelgänger of the castle. Torches were mounted on either side of the skysteel gate. His eyes darted to the battlements. They were studded with armored guards.

Spineripper halted before the entrance. Silence reigned as the sentries gazed down at them, bored. Silver-and-blue flags stitched with the visage of a two-headed wolf fluttered in the breeze.

"Open the gate," Spineripper commanded in a booming voice. "We have the prince and the weaver."

One of the guards, who appeared human, jerked his head at a tusked creature easily twice his height. The beast grunted and lumbered out of sight. A tremor rippled through the gates. They began to slide into the hidden slits in the walls.

Just like home.

Spineripper clicked at Peony. The horse started off again, agreeable as ever. Ila and Caine were drawn forward. Snow and gravel crunched beneath their boots as they passed through the gate.

"Ila," Caine said out of the side of his mouth.

"Yes?"

"No matter what happens, I need you to trust me. Promise me."

There was no hesitation in her answer. "I promise."

The great double doors peeled apart with a shuddering moan. They were varnished black unlike their counterparts in the Wake, but the ornate engravings were the same—thorns and choking vines. Spineripper brought Peony to a halt a few paces from them and jumped down.

"Home sweet home, princeling," he said, sauntering toward them. He drew the dagger he stole from Ila with a flourish. "Hands."

Caine lifted his bound wrists to Spineripper, glowering at him. Spineripper gripped his forearm and sliced through the ropes. He winced as the raw skin was exposed for the first time in days.

"Try to run," Spineripper began, grabbing Ila by the arm

and cutting her bonds. She inhaled sharply but did not cry out. "Try to fight, and I'll break her legs. Understand?"

It took everything Caine had not to bust his already crooked nose right then and there. Instead, he and Ila both nodded.

Not yet.

"Excellent," Spineripper cooed. He slammed the dagger back into its sheath. "Now move."

☽○☾

The halls of Caer Sidi were a mocking shade of the home Caine knew in the Wake. The light was the first thing he noticed. The windows were all curtained and shuttered. The only illumination came from the torches on the walls. Their glow was oddly hollow. He wondered if they produced heat at all.

Caine and Ila were ferried through the halls by Spineripper. He knew where they were going. He would know his home if it were in ruins.

This isn't home, he reminded himself as they passed a grimacing statue of a wolf with two heads. *This isn't home.*

Still, he found himself searching for familiar faces in the dream beings they passed. Even the friendly face of a stranger would have been welcome, but here, everyone walked with their eyes downcast, parting for them like waves for a ship.

"Nearly there, princeling," Spineripper hissed in his ear.

They turned a corner, and Caine felt his mouth go dry. Stained double doors loomed at the end of the hall. The throne hall. Ila reached for his hand, but he snatched it away. Her shocked gaze scorched the side of his face. He ignored it.

The walk to the throne room felt longer than their journey through the Bone Hills. Oil paintings of horrifying creatures watched their progress from both sides of the hall.

The doors parted. Ila slowed her pace. Caine grabbed her by the forearm, just above the ring of flayed skin at her wrist, and dragged her with him across the threshold.

Stay with me.

"Caine," she breathed. "You're hurting me."

He did not respond, nor did he release her as the throne hall unfurled around them. It was nearly identical to the one Caine knew. The windows were forged of crystal rather than stained glass, but the diamond shape of the panes was the same, as was the shape of the chandeliers drooping from the vaulted ceiling. At the far end of the room, lounging in the dark mirror of the throne Caine would one day occupy, was Para Warwick.

His father.

At first glance, the King of Wolfhelm was just as Caine remembered him. The bone crown rested on his brow, and the rings containing the gemstones from kingdoms he had conquered glimmered on his fingers. A closer look revealed inconsistencies with the man Caine thought he knew.

The age lines in his face had disappeared along with the gray in his hair. He was taller, more imposing. Even more disturbing were his eyes. They were no longer blue but fully black from pupil to lid.

"The prince and the weaver as promised, Para Warwick," Spineripper announced as they arrived at the base of the steps to the throne. He dropped to one knee, gesturing to Ila and Caine as if they were on display at a circus. A tendril of sweat slithered down his spine as Caine locked eyes with the Para. It was then he realized that the bone crown did not rest upon his head, but grew from it.

"You were told not to harm the prince," the Para said coolly, regarding the wounds at his wrists and the various bruises he had collected over the course of their journey. Caine swallowed. It would have been easier if his voice was as unrecognizable as his eyes, but his father sounded like himself.

"I apologize, my Para. He proved difficult to manage."

"Is that so?" Para Warwick locked eyes with Caine again. "Leave us."

Spineripper looked up with a start. "But—"

"Now."

Caine could not resist a smirk as Spineripper rose, bent at the waist, and skulked away. Clearly, he was expecting more than a dismissal upon his triumphant return.

"You have some explaining to do, Prince Caine."

Warwick lounged on the throne in a manner Caine had never seen, one leg crossed over the other, his head propped up with his hand. He looked almost bored. In the Wake, he carried himself with stiff elegance.

"As do you," Caine replied, sounding far bolder than he felt. He still held Ila's arm in a vise. She was silent and trembling.

"I suppose so," Para Warwick said, though he pressed his lips into a bloodless line.

Caine clasped his hands behind his back and stood tall. "The night we disappeared, Queen Ila poisoned me." Ila flinched at his side as if he had struck her. It took everything he had not to reach out to her. "Fortunately, it was not a fatal dose. I woke to discover her attempting some sort of ritual in the sanctum."

"The sanctum," Para Warwick repeated. His onyx eyes flicked to Ila. "How did you know she would be there?"

He snorted. "It was hardly a challenge. She was sloppy. I thought her a witch, but I have since learned she is a weaver. What I took to be a ritual was her creating a portal to the dream realm."

"Caine—" Ila whimpered.

"I followed her through the portal," Caine continued. "I would have killed her on the spot, but I knew I needed her to get back to the Wake. I've learned more from her than I expected to while we've traveled together."

"And what did you learn, Prince Caine?"

Caine clamped down on the soft center of his soul, the one Ila spotted through the fog of his cowardice and ego, the one she told him to guard against wickedness and apathy—and shattered it.

"I've learned that she is weak and foolish, and that you are more powerful than I ever could have imagined." He dropped to one knee, bowing his head. "The Vaettir queen means nothing to me. Do what you like with her. All I ask is that you let me serve you in both worlds, my Para."

For an endless moment, Para Warwick was quiet. The words sizzled between them. Caine could feel Ila watching him, her gaze searing the side of his face. He kept his eyes trained on the floor.

"When your mother fell pregnant with you, I prayed to the gods to bless me with a son." Caine heard Para Warwick stand

and start down the steps at a languid pace. "The day you were born was the happiest of my life, but I quickly learned you were frail in spirit." The prince tensed when a pair of polished leather boots filled his vision. "It appears I was mistaken."

Caine raised his face to his father, whose eyes were gleaming with pride. Not long ago, he would have given anything for him to look at him like that. Like he was worth something.

"Rise, Prince Caine."

The prince climbed to his feet. Para Warwick clapped a gloved hand to his shoulder. His knees nearly buckled beneath the strain. His father was strong in the Wake, but not like this.

"You and I—" the Para began.

"You fucking bastard."

Caine felt his blood run cold. He turned slowly to face Ila. Angry tears streaked her cheeks, and the whites of her eyes were red.

Para Warwick released his shoulder with a soft chuckle. "I almost forgot you were here, weaver."

Ila ignored him. Her gaze never strayed from Caine. "You're worse than him; I hope you know that. You're a liar and a coward."

The Para moved in slow motion. Caine stood rooted on the spot as he cranked back his arm and struck Ila across the face, sending her sprawling over the flagstones with a fractured cry.

Caine bit the inside of his cheek to keep from screaming.

"Guards," Para Warwick called lazily. "Take her to the sanctum. Bloodreaper deserves some entertainment after his ordeal with Nightstrider."

Caine watched as two guards with the heads of rats grasped

Ila under her arms. They dragged her to her feet. Blood trickled down her chin from her split lip.

She did not scream. She did not fight. She just stared at the prince with shattered eyes as they hauled her away.

"As I was saying before that Vaettir whore interrupted, you and I are going to change the worlds, son," Para Warwick said.

Caine smiled. "When do we start?"

45
Alaric

Alaric had seen the Widow's Pass from a distance before but had never approached it—he did not go looking for trouble, no matter how much Mica insisted he did.

The Pass was a ragged scar in the land. Half a league long. Narrow, craggy, and utterly inescapable. It had swallowed dream beings of all sorts without a trace.

"How do you want to do this?" Wren asked, tucking her long braid into her jacket. She was brimming with erratic energy.

"This was your idea," he answered. "Don't put this on me."

"I would love to fly over this mess—"

"Doubtful."

"But Saoirse assures me I'm not yet healed. Not to mention my minder is vertically challenged."

Alaric snorted, looking back to the entrance to the Pass. He heard somewhere that the vexes who called it home often strung up their victims at the mouth of the ravine, but all he saw were unforgiving rocks and scrub.

"Can you see in the dark?" Wren inquired.

"Some."

"Good." She drew one of her long knives, her fingers dancing along the hilt.

"Are you sure we should go in tonight?" Alaric asked.

"Scared, baker?"

"No. Smart."

"Look, this isn't ideal, but Saoirse said this is the only way we'll have a shot at reaching Queen Ila in time," Wren argued with strained patience. "Not to mention, nobody would be stupid enough to enter the Pass in the middle of the night. They won't be expecting us. We'll have the advantage."

"We'll have *an* advantage. We'll still be outnumbered ten to one."

Wren rocked her head from side to side, the cool shadows across her face shifting like sand. "More like twenty to one. Oh, come on," she griped when Alaric balked. "I've faced worse odds alone. Surely you have, too."

"Yes, but that doesn't mean we should take unnecessary risks."

"If you want to save the queen, this is a necessary risk. Come on, what do you have to lose?"

"A lot, actually."

He had not intended it as a jab, but as soon as the words left his tongue, Alaric wished he could retract them. Wren looked away.

"Just stay close to me," she muttered, turning her back on him.

"Wren—"

But she was already running toward the canyon. Half a beat later, Alaric followed.

Approaching the Widow's Pass was like marching for the gallows. The nightmares slowed as they came upon the entrance. Alaric tilted his head back to view the dizzying heights. The moons were on the rise, following one another through the hazy twilight.

"Follow me," Wren whispered. "Stay sharp."

She darted into the ravine with feline grace and zero reserve. Alaric sent up a prayer to whoever might be listening and charged after her.

The air was thick and heavy inside the Widow's Pass, and it was dark in a way the Reverie rarely was.

Part of Alaric expected these supposed cannibal vexes to mob them the moment they set foot in their territory, but they did not. Quite the opposite, Alaric could not detect any signs of life. Wren did not seem to sense anything, either. She forged ahead with dogged determination.

The deeper they traveled into the canyon, the closer the walls squeezed together. At one point, they all but swallowed the sky, allowing only a sliver of moonlight through. Eventually, the Pass widened again, but not enough to allay his claustrophobia. All the while, his magic hummed like a wasp inside his chest.

Thud.

Alaric screamed to a halt. Wren rounded on him.

"What are you doing?" she snarled, wading back to him through the shadows. He raised a finger in response, pressing his free hand to his sternum. The magic burrowed beneath it bristled. "What is it?"

"I don't know, but—"

Alaric was slammed into the rock face. The side of his head cracked against the stone. Vicious hands ripped his bag from his back. He called an onyx blade to his hand and slashed haphazardly. Caustic blood spurted as it raked through something tough. His attacker disappeared with a wounded screech.

He slumped against the wall, panting and wiping his own blood from his eyes.

Chaos.

Wren was a blur of muscle, feather, and steel. Her eyes were black. Vexes of every sort surrounded her, nameless beasts from the bowels of haunted dreams. They tripped over themselves and one another in a desperate attempt to reach her, but each attempt proved as futile as the last.

Half a dozen bodies were already at her feet.

A creature with a gaping maw lined with teeth where its face should have been swiveled toward Alaric, its form rippling through the fog of his rattled brain. It screeched and began to lope toward him, too-long arms swinging and—

Rancid green blood sprayed Alaric as a blade exploded through its maw. The creature gurgled as its head collapsed in on itself like rotting fruit. It crumpled before Alaric, the hilt of Wren's blade sticking out the back of its skull.

"ALARIC!" Wren bellowed, turning to stab a vex with sagging papery skin through the eye. "FIGHT!"

Alaric snapped into razor-sharp focus.

His fists closed around two energy bolts. He launched himself at the nearest vex, a creature not unlike an orc with a single mottled tusk, and drove both into his barrel chest. By the time he could think to scream, Alaric had yanked them and moved on to the next enemy. And the next.

And the next.

And the next.

Somewhere in the crush of blood and bone, Wren and Alaric slammed into each other, back-to-back. He could feel her rapid pulse against his skin. Bodies were piled around them, pierced with blades of metal and magic. Just beyond the corpses, a ring of living vexes snarled at them.

"I told you this would happen!" Alaric shouted at Wren.

"And I told you this would be fun," she returned with an unhinged laugh. "Lean forward!"

Alaric did as she asked. She bent with the curve of his spine and sent a vex flying with a powerful kick.

"How many do you have?" he yelled, eyeing four who still lingered in his line of sight.

A hiss, a squelch, and a thud.

"None. Be right back."

"Wh—"

Wren peeled from Alaric. A gust of wind ruffled his hair when she spread her injured wings with a raw scream and shot into the air. He craned his neck to follow her progress. Her feathers blotted out the moons, but her grin was bright enough to scatter the dark.

This was not Wren, Alaric realized with a jolt.

This was Nightstrider.

Two blades he did not even know that she had appeared at her fingertips. She hurled them at two of their remaining adversaries. The knives struck them dead between the eyes, and they went down.

The second-to-last vex shrieked at Wren from beneath their ragged hood. The sound was so loud it seemed to make the air warp. Alaric clamped his hands over his ears, but the piercing note was cut short when Wren nailed the creature in the heart with a throwing knife.

Only one vex remained, a creature ten feet tall with the head of a bison, matted fur, and eyes like tiny marbles. He palmed a massive broadsword. For a split second, Alaric thought he was going to charge.

Then he turned tail and galloped away.

Nightstrider dropped like a dark star, landing on the vex's shoulders. He did not even have time to shout before she grabbed him by the horns and cranked his head around with a crunch.

The vex dropped his blade and collapsed to his knees.

The nightmare flipped off his shoulders with deadly grace, landing on her feet as the creature slumped.

Alaric stared.

Nightstrider was robed in gore. She tucked her wings with a wince, then used the back of her wrist to wipe the blood from her face. Her bottomless black eyes flashed to his. She smiled, lifting only one corner of her mouth.

"Not bad for a baker."

Alaric did not answer, staring around at the carnage. He had only managed to fell twenty or so vexes, but her pile included dozens, all either with blades in their heads or their throats slashed with surgical precision.

He had only known her injured and on the run, but even so, she was a force of nature.

How could he ever allow such a being to end at his hand?

"Red suits you, you know."

Alaric looked back to Wren, surprise knocking a grin onto his face. He was about to reply—something witty and sharp—when a brutal realization slammed into him. He touched his shoulder, hunting for the straps of his pack.

His bag was gone, and Saoirse with it.

"You lost the dreambreaker."

Alaric bowed his head like a scolded dog.

"Let me rephrase," Wren continued in a monotone. "You brought the dreambreaker with you, decided not to tell me, then lost her to a vex who was bleeding out in front of you."

"I was trying to help you," Alaric snapped. His tone did not match the panic and guilt churning inside him.

"I had it sorted."

"You told me to fight!"

"If I had known you were protecting—"

Wren wheeled around with a gasp. Alaric raised a hand, ready to blast another vex to the tenth hell, but there was no one there.

"Stop doing that," Wren snapped, talking at the wall of the ravine.

For a moment, Alaric wondered if she'd been clobbered over the head, then understanding rolled over him. "Is that Saoirse? Is she here?"

Wren waved him off.

"What happened?" Wren demanded, talking to an invisible Saoirse. She paused as if listening to a response, then shot a scathing look at Alaric. "Yeah, I see that. Where are you?"

Another pause.

"No, kid, wait!" Wren reached out, grasping at the air, then swore violently and kicked the body of a vex covered in boils. Alaric heard its ribs snap like twigs as its growths burst, sending droplets of green pus flying. "Fuck!"

"Does she know where she's been taken?" Alaric pressed.

"No, but she said I can find her."

"How . . . ?"

Their gazes dropped to her chest. Wren tugged aside the neck of her tunic. The once-brilliant blessing Saoirse had imparted on her in the Hall of Whispers had faded to a subtle glow.

If it were much lighter out, it would have been invisible.

"Did you see which direction he went? The vex who took her?" Wren asked. Alaric continued to stare at the handprint, mute. "Alaric." She snapped her fingers twice in front of his face. "Did you see where he went?"

"No, but I have a guess." Wren rolled her wrist impatiently. Alaric jerked his chin in the direction they had been traveling before they were ambushed. "I don't think these were the vexes who live here. They were after you and the box. They all but ignored me until I started cutting them down. One guess who sent them."

"Para Warwick," Wren muttered.

Alaric nodded grimly. "They're probably headed for Caer Sidi now."

Wren scanned the battlefield, shaking her head. "How did I not hear them coming? Or smell them?" Her keen eyes flicked to Alaric. "You sensed them. How?"

"My magic warns me when danger is near."

"I still should have been able to . . ." Wren trailed off, sniffing the air. "Do you smell that?"

Alaric inhaled through his nose. "No."

"Exactly."

Wren squatted beside the corpse of the nearest vex, a female with a bloated body covered in patchy feathers. She wore no garments, but there was a pendant around her neck.

Narrowing her eyes, Wren ripped the necklace from the body.

Alaric dropped into a crouch beside her as she held it up to the stained-glass moonlight. It appeared to be nothing more than a leather tie threaded through a black stone.

"What is that?" Alaric asked.

Wren rose. He followed suit, watching as she lashed the split ends of the cord together.

"A few years back, Para Warwick hired some mercenaries to track down a faction of kips who had overthrown their governor," she said. "Or something like that, I forget. The point is, he gave each of the mercs a shard of pier glass for the job."

"Pier glass?"

"It can absorb and reflect magic. Para Warwick started mining it a while back. He probably infused this stuff with cloaking magic and sent them after us. Fat lot of good it did them."

Alaric frowned. "Since when does Para Warwick deal in magic?"

Wren snorted. "Funny."

She stepped over the vex she stole the pier glass from, headed for the body of a vex face down in the dirt.

"What sort of magic are we talking about?" Alaric called.

"How hard did you get hit?"

"Wren."

His severe tone seemed to give Wren pause. She stopped what she was doing and turned to face him fully.

"Well, if you consider a para creating nightmares magic, he can do that. And he can cross the Boundary, though apparently that isn't too special."

"What else?" Alaric pressed.

Wren returned to her task, heaving the body of the vex over with a grunt. He flopped onto his back to reveal a squashed face and two stubby tusks. At his neck was another shard of pier glass. She snatched it from him.

"He can disappear and reappear miles away," she listed. "He can create fire, move things around without touching them."

"Is that it?"

"You can't have forgotten this much," Wren snipped.

"I didn't forget, Wren," he said, his tone grave. "Para Warwick didn't have that kind of power when I was the Hand."

Wren stared at Alaric as if he had just spoken in tongues. The pier glass necklace she stole off the vex swayed gently in her grip.

"I don't understand," she finally managed.

"That makes two of us."

Para Warwick had always possessed awesome power. His ability to create dream beings and cross the Boundary aside, he was gifted with unparalleled speed and strength. His senses were unmatched. He could hear a dog bark a league away, could see a speck of dust across a room. Coupled with his mastery of manipulation and sheer zeal for violence, his status was near that of a god.

But Alaric had never known him to be a mage.

"Tell me—what the hells are you doing?" Alaric snapped. Wren was examining a pair of brass knuckles slick with blood, her boot on the chest of a blubbery vex. "Could you focus, please?"

"I'm listening."

"I need you talking."

Wren twirled the brass knuckles around her index finger, then pocketed them. Her face was blank, dispassionate.

"What do you want me to say, Alaric? I tried to tell you Para Warwick couldn't be beaten."

"If I had known he was evolving, I would have paid more attention."

Wren shrugged. "Not my problem."

"It is your problem." Anger welled in his chest when she put her back to him again, stepping over a disemboweled vex. "We have to figure out how he's gaining these new abilities. We have to warn the rebellion."

Wren stomped on the skull of a vex, cracking it like a rotten egg.

"Let me explain something to you," she said, pronouncing each word with devastating clarity. "There is no 'we.' I won't let Warwick get his hands on Saoirse, but after that, I'm out. I'm not a rebel, I'm not a zealot, and I don't share your desire to be forgiven for my sins."

"No, you just want to die for them."

Wren whipped around. Her teeth were bared, her jaw set. Black bled into the whites of her eyes. Somehow, he could still see the fear lurking there.

"At least I'm free," she hissed. "At least I'm not a guard dog for a bunch of luminae who got rid of me the second I thought for myself. You killed a man who deserved it, and they cast you out because it was a 'mare he tried to fuck. What does that say about what they think of *you*?"

"They did not cast me out," Alaric snapped. "Reichart promised to pardon me."

"After you come back from a suicide mission with the enemy? Wake up, Alaric." She stalked over to him until they were a breath apart, her chin tilted up so they could lock eyes. The color was high in her cheeks still flecked with blood. "Mica might care about you, but the rest of them will never see you as one of them."

"Luken—"

"It isn't about him! This is about you." She jabbed a talon into his chest bone hard enough that he had to brace his knees. His lip curled, his pulse pounding in his ears. "Stop looking for absolution in the arms of people who would discard you without a second thought."

Alaric was silent. The fight bled from him as a mournful wind whistled through the canyon now slick with gore.

"They don't have to care for me," he said in a low voice. "And I stopped looking for absolution a long time ago. There isn't any to be had."

"Then what the fuck are you doing?"

He shrugged. "What feels right."

Wren shook her head again, then blinked away the dark matter in her eyes. He felt his recede as if in response. Wren craned her neck back and lifted her eyes, scanning the skies for something, but he doubted he could have looked away from her if he tried. The stars reflected in her rich brown irises, the blood of their enemies beaded on her skin like a veil of crimson pearls.

She snorted. "Gods, I was right."

"About?"

"You're a fool, Bonehunter."

She drooped her chin to look at him again. Something like longing wandered across her face. She was so close he could feel the tide of her breath, could see the fine details of her face. How someone as foul as Para Warwick had created something so beautiful was beyond him. There was such elegance in her high cheekbones, the strong bridge of her nose, her lush lashes, and her lips . . .

Wren inhaled sharply and retreated a step. "You're a fool," she repeated. "And you're without a doubt the worst monster I've ever met."

Before he could think to respond, she turned on her heel and walked away, braid swinging behind her and knives at her hips. She did not look back.

46
Wren

The road through the Bone Hills was slick with mud and melting snow, as were the great headstones between them. The monuments had always raised the hairs on the back of her neck. It only got worse when rain clouds crowded the sky, pelting Wren and Alaric with sleet as they ran.

She would have flown over the storm if she was able. The air was cold, lonely, and thin so high above the realm, but it was worth it to watch the elements thrash and blaze below.

Unfortunately, even her brief flight in the Pass was excruciating.

Saoirse was right. She was not strong enough.

Alaric appeared at her side, startling Wren more than she cared to admit. They had both donned a pier glass charm before exiting the Pass, meaning their footsteps and scent were masked. He had been running behind her for some time, quiet after their battle turned shouting match.

The way they fought, their backs flush and their bodies moving as one, was akin to the dizzying, euphoric high that came with sex. But the way he had looked at her, even as she yelled at him and called him a fool—*that* was something else.

Something she had to shut down.

"Can I see?" Alaric asked, nodding at the blessing covered by her jacket. His rain-darkened hair was plastered to his brow, his horns slick. The blood had been washed clean from his skin. She almost wished it had not.

Red really did suit him.

Gods, focus.

Wren peeled back the drenched leather of her jacket. The print was almost as bright as it was when she first received it.

"We're close," she said.

Silence grew between them again, deepened by the absence of their footfalls. Even their breaths were muted.

Wren kept her eyes on the horizon when she spoke. "I shouldn't have said what I did about the rebellion."

She saw Alaric shake his head in her peripheral vision. "No, you were right."

"I could have said it better."

"You were still right."

She slowed her pace, scuffing to a soundless halt in the shadow of a broken headstone jutting out over the road. Alaric followed suit. She flicked her gaze to his only briefly before looking away again.

"I never thanked you for what you did. Stopping him, I mean." Strangely, she could not bring herself to say his name. It stuck on her tongue like a burr.

"You did the same for Solene."

Wren shrugged. "Of course."

She looked to Alaric in time to see a somber smile pull at one corner of his mouth. "There it is."

"What?" she snapped, already exasperated. Her blessing gave a solitary pulse. Wren tugged her jacket aside again.

The handprint blazed against her skin, its glow slicing through the gloom. Alaric and Wren locked eyes. She could have sworn she heard the thunder of his pulse through the pier glass. Movement over his shoulder hooked her gaze. She squinted at the horizon. Alaric followed her line of sight.

A smokestack curled from the basin of two hills less than a mile ahead.

Wren drew the blades at her hips. Every wisp of sentimentality plaguing her mind was stamped out by bitter focus. Alaric called a single onyx bolt to his hand. Together, they took off again in a dead sprint. Their muffled footfalls splattered their legs with mud and melting snow. They slowed when the scent of a cookfire permeated the air.

Gravelly voices joined the murmur of the rain just beyond the next rise.

Wren waved at Alaric to get his attention and gestured at the far side of the hill. He nodded and moved off, gracile as a cat. Once he disappeared, she sank into a crouch and approached from her own vantage point.

Six dream beings were clustered around a fire over which some sort of rodent was roasting. Three were hooded with perfectly round, deep yellow eyes beaming from the shadowed depths of their cowls, two were grizzled male kips, and one was what could only be described as reptilian. He was roughly the size and shape of a kip, but his pupils were square, and flaky gray scales covered his body.

None of them wore visible pier glass.

Beyond them, huddled in a mass to shun the cold, were seven young kips bound together with rope, and beside them, sitting at the top of a small pile of bags, was a leather pack with a single torn strap.

Saoirse.

Wren sheathed her blades with a muted click and stepped into the open.

It took the dream beings a good five seconds to notice her. Between the pier glass, the rain, and her dark clothes, she was all but a ghost. Finally, one of the hooded creatures flicked his yellow eyes toward her. They flared impossibly rounder.

She smiled at him.

He lurched to his feet with a spitting hiss. The others followed suit, dropping their food and drawing their weapons.

"Good somnia," Wren greeted them.

"What do you want?" one of the kips barked.

"A rest and a hot meal. Perhaps some information."

The dream beings exchanged suspicious glances. Wren flicked her eyes to the captive kips. Some looked hopeful, but most were terrified.

"Dangerous for a girl to be alone in these parts," the man said, his murky eyes flicking up and down her body. "But you don't look like just any girl."

"Is that supposed to be a compliment?"

He smiled, vulturine. "Take it however you like."

"What sort of information are you after?" one of the hooded

creatures hissed. “And what do you have for us?”

“Simple.” Wren took a small step forward. The dream beings stiffened, brandishing their weapons like torches against the night. “You answer my questions, and I consider letting you live.”

The dream beings gawked at her. One of the cloaked creatures gained his voice first.

“Get out of here,” he spat.

Wren sighed. “Guess we’re doing this the hard way.”

“What—”

But her blade was already between his eyes, their yellow light snuffed like candles in a gale.

The captive kips screamed as he hit the soggy ground.

“No one else has to die,” Wren said sweetly, drawing her next knife to examine it. “As long as one of you answers my questions.”

“You bitch!” one of the kips howled.

Wren slicked her soaked hair out of her face, heart hammering and bloodlust surging. Gods, this was what she needed. “Boring.”

Before he could respond, Wren felled him with a knife to the throat. He and his mace hit the muddy ground with a *splash*.

“Enough!” The remaining man tossed his short sword to the ground and threw his hands up. “We yield!”

“All of you?” Wren inquired, her eyes flicking to the remaining dream beings. Two of the hooded creatures and the reptilian.

The cloaked creatures—vexes, based on the sour scent of the dead one’s blood—dropped their staffs.

"And you?" Wren asked politely, eyeing the vex with the scales. A rattling hiss slithered through his mouth. He tossed his curved blade to his feet, fuming. "Excellent," Wren cooed. "Now, tell me what you're doing out here."

"Gathering laborers for the Para," the kip explained curtly.

"Why?"

"We don't know. We're supposed to deliver them to Marrowrun."

"Marrowrun?" Wren repeated, her tone reflecting her confusion. "Why the hells is the Para doing business with the free city?"

"Well—"

Wren cocked a brow, a question as much as a threat.

"He said he wanted kips who would hold up under hard labor."

Wren cast a doubtful look at the huddle of kips across from her. Only two of the seven fit the criteria. The rest were too young or sickly.

"You sure there's nothing else?" Wren asked.

The vexes nodded in unison, eager and painfully earnest. The reptilian maintained his stony silence.

"Thank you for your cooperation, gentlemen." They sagged with relief. "I just have a few more questions for your friend here."

The reptilian sized up Wren, his rectangular pupils shrinking.

"He isn't with us," the man interjected quickly. "Just sharing our fire."

Wren inhaled deeply through her nose. "I smell blood."

"Plenty of blood here," the reptilian finally spoke. His voice was low and rasping, his words stilted as if his mouth were not meant to form words.

"This smells older," Wren argued smoothly. "I'll only ask you once. Where did you get that wound?"

"Fuck off."

"Wrong answer."

Wren hurled her blade at the reptilian. He dodged it with unprecedented speed and shoved the man into the path of the knife. It struck him in the shoulder, and he fell with a howl. One of the hooded vexes grabbed their staff and flew at Wren with a scream. The reptilian scuttled away on all fours, shedding his cloak to reveal a serpentine tail.

"Alaric!" Wren shouted.

Alaric burst into the open, firing a tendril of magic at the reptilian and snaring him by the leg. He went down with a noise halfway between a scream and a hiss. Alaric yanked the tether, dragging him through the muck. With his free hand, he conjured a bolt and sank it into his chest.

The reptilian let out a gurgling screech and stilled.

Wren made quick work of the remaining vexes, felling them where they stood with quick swipes to the throat.

"Wren."

She whipped her head around to find Alaric offering her a bundle of rags.

Saoirse.

Wren snatched the parcel from him. Unknotting the tattered rags, she cast them aside and took the box in hand. It no longer blazed as it did when she first saw it in the sanctum, maintaining only the faintest glow.

"Does that hurt?" Alaric asked numbly. "Touching it?"

Wren shook her head absently. She handled the box the way one might cradle an injured bird. Something stirred deep in her chest, an emotion she had never experienced and could not name.

Nightstrider.

Wren jerked around, searching for the flickering form of a child, but there was only Alaric and the kips, who gazed at her with varying degrees of confusion and trepidation.

"Saoirse, where are you?" she called.

I can't create an image anymore. I'm not strong enough.

"We're getting close to Queen Ila. Just hold on."

We're too late. She is being held at Caer Sidi. You need to set me free now.

"How?"

There is a fail-safe. It is dangerous, but you must—

The phantom voice cut off. Wren tightened her grip on the box as if she could squeeze Saoirse out of it. Her heart pounded in her ears, two beats for every weak pulse of the blessing pressed into her skin.

"What happened?" Alaric asked, inching closer to her.

"I have to open it."

"I thought only Queen Ila could—"

Wren sank to her knees in the muck and shrugged off her jacket. With careful hands, she placed the box on the fur lining. She closed her eyes and placed both hands on the lid. The handprint on her chest ignited, and beneath her palms, the box shone like a fallen star.

"Sol liv hjent warren."

★ ★ ★

One moment, Wren was in the rain with Alaric. The next, she was on a featureless plane veiled with fog. She spun in a circle. Her thoughts raced her pulse.

Am I back in the Hall of Whispers? she thought. *Did I ever leave?*

"Hello, Nightstrider."

"Saoirse." The dreambreaker stood before her. Her body was as solid as her newfound voice. Her projection had not allowed Wren to see her face in full detail. Tiny freckles dappled her pale skin, and dimples marked her round cheeks. "Where are we?"

"Inside my box." Words were jarring, coming straight from her mouth.

"How do I get you out?" Wren asked, dropping to her level. "Tell me what to do."

"I don't know," Saoirse admitted.

"You don't know."

"Ila created the fail-safe; you triggered it, but I don't know what—"

Wren snatched Saoirse by the arm and whipped her behind her back, spreading her wings to shield her further. Her wounds were not numbed like they were in the Hall of Whispers. Pain shot through the healing tissues of her wings and back.

"I know you're there!" Wren shouted into the dizzying mist. "Show yourself."

Saoirse tugged on the hem of her shirt. "Nightstrider."

Wren shushed her, squinting into the abyss. Her muscles coiled when a silhouette appeared in the distance. It wavered for a moment, uncertain, then began to advance. The winged nightmare drew two knives and sank into a fighting stance.

"Nightstrider," Saoirse squeaked.

A man appeared out of the gloom. His smile was easy, his golden eyes warmer than she deserved. He walked the fine line between confidence and cockiness. Grace was woven into every strand of his body, the kind that could not be learned.

"Good somnia, my love."

Wren dropped her knives, sending fog wafting.

"Bram," she breathed.

"Whoa!" Bram rushed forward to catch her as she teetered on the spot, easing her down to her knees and kneeling with her. Her skin bloomed with exquisite heat where he touched her.

"Am I dead?" Wren whispered. "How are you here?"

"I never left you." Bram took her face in his hands and used his calloused thumbs to wipe her tears. His blond hair drooped forward as he pressed his brow to hers. "Not for a second."

"I'm so sorry. I failed you."

"You could never fail me." Bram cupped the back of her head with his palm and ran it over her hair.

A sob tore from Wren. She collapsed forward, pressing her head into his chest. She inhaled deeply, drinking in his sweet scent. She could not seem to get close enough to the miracle of him.

"Forgive me."

"There's nothing to forgive."

"Please," Wren rasped, clinging to his shirt. It was the

evergreen one she used to wear to sleep when they were forced to be apart. "Please, forgive me."

Bram pushed her gently into an upright position, again taking her face in his hands. He pressed his brow to hers as heaven unfurled around them.

"You're forgiven," he said. "Now and always."

Wren dissolved into him, utterly drunk on his scent. Bram was here. Safe and whole in her arms. It was impossible, yet what about anything she had been through was remotely possible?

"Alaric told me I can be severed from my anchor," she told him, the words tumbling out like an avalanche. "We can be together forever. We can be free. Saoirse will help us once we..." She trailed off. Bram gave her a curious smile, his hands still cradling her face. "Where is Saoirse?"

"Who?"

"Saoirse," she repeated, freeing herself from his caress and sitting back on her heels. "The little girl. She was just here."

Bram frowned, reaching for her again. She leaned away, so he took her hands instead and brought them to his lips, kissing them.

"You have been through so much, Wren," he murmured. "Let me ease the burden."

"You're not listening to me. There was a girl here a second ago. Where did she go?"

Bram shook his head, still holding her hands. "There is no one here but you and me, you silly thing."

"Silly?"

"I just mean you're tired, my love."

"No, this is her box." Speaking the words aloud sparked panic in her chest. She had all but forgotten where she was the moment he appeared from the fog. "This is..."

Wren scanned the familiar planes of his face, her core filling with dread. Every inch of him was wrought with flawed perfection: the scar above his left eyebrow, the flush in his cheeks, the stubble across his jaw.

But her Bram would never dismiss her.

"This isn't you," she whispered.

Bram kissed her hands again and leaned his brow against them as if in prayer. "My love, you've been fighting for so long. Come with me. We can leave all this behind."

"I—" All the right words evaporated on her tongue. "I can't. This isn't real. You're not real."

Bram lifted his head, pinning her in place with his gaze. "Are you real? You're just a dream, after all."

Wren jerked her hands free and scrambled to her feet. Bram followed suit.

"You're a test," she snarled. "This is the fail-safe."

"Perhaps, but I'm still Bram. I can still make you happy."

"You're not. Bram would never have left a child to die, not for me. Not for anyone."

"I would do anything to protect you, Wren," the false Bram said. She flinched. He said her name like it was holy. "I love you."

"You're not him." She began to back away into the vast plane of fog. "I have to find Saoirse. I have to save her."

Bram curled his lips into a snarl worthy of a wolf. "Save

her? How could you ever save anyone? You couldn't even save me."

His words should have shattered her, but they did not. Instead, rage sparked at her center. Keening flooded her ears as her eyes went black, burning away the tears. She freed the blades at her hips.

"Watch me."

Wren lunged at him with a strangled cry. Two identical knives materialized in his palms, and he parried.

"You'll pay for stealing his face," she spat.

"You'll still be too late."

The false Bram lashed out with expert precision. Wren blocked, but his blade still nicked her hand. She sprang back. The imposter mirrored her. They began to prowl in steady circles, locked in a deadly dance. He struck again. She deflected and aimed a powerful kick at his neck. He stumbled.

That was all she needed.

With a savage scream, Wren sprang forward and drove her blade home. The shade of Bram sucked in a stunned breath, staring down at the knives hilt-deep in his chest. His weapons fell and were swallowed by the fog lapping at their feet.

"Wren." Blood seeped from his mouth, dribbling down his chin. "What have you done?"

"What Bram would have wanted."

His eyelids fluttered shut. His legs folded. Wren released the hilts of her knives and stepped away. When he hit the floor, the mist rushed to engulf him. His body, the body he stole, faded to dust.

"Wren." Saoirse appeared in the place the imposter stood.

Her eyelids were heavy, her skin pallid. She swayed where she stood. Wren rushed to catch her, sinking again to her knees. "Takja," the dreambreaker whispered as sleep washed over her. "Takja."

They dissolved.

47
Ila

When Ila was young, she and her brothers used to sneak out of their home to sleep outside, stuffing coals beneath their sleeping mats and furs to stave off the cold. Even in the deepest part of the night, the sky was alive, dancing with ribbons of green light and peppered with stars. She still called it darkness.

Hours ago, two guards with the faces of rats dragged her from the throne hall with a bag over her head. She had called that darkness, too.

She was wrong. That was not darkness.

This was darkness.

Oppressive, suffocating, horribly exposed darkness. No matter how her pupils strained, there was no light in the sanctum to feed them.

Ila shifted against the curved wall, flinching when a brittle bone snapped beneath her. The floor was littered with them. Her wrists were shackled above her head, so she could not even clear herself a space. She had attempted to access her weaver sight, but it quickly proved futile, unsurprisingly.

Hours trekked by, and memories began to take shape in the blackness. Ila and her brothers on horseback, cantering through a sunstruck forest. Kneeling on the altar at Llyr in her white robes, preparing to take her vows. The first kiss she shared with Nils the summer she turned sixteen. Saoirse seeing snow for the first time. In that moment, she was just a child, not a weapon.

Caine.

She played the last few days over and over in her mind, searching for signs of deceit, but nothing stood out to her. His rage, his agony as he began to digest the true identity of his father had seemed so genuine. The softness in his face when he cast his eyes on her had stirred girlish butterflies in her stomach, even when she found herself berating him.

Hoste, how had she been so naive?

Numbness swept through Ila. After the guards shackled her to the wall, she had cried until she made herself sick. Great, heaving sobs that could not have been less queenly. She cried for Caine, for Saoirse, for her people, for the Wake, for the Reverie. She cried for everything she had lost and everyone she failed and everything she would never have.

Now she was empty.

Screeeee . . .

Ila stiffened against the wall. "H-hello?"

Screeeee . . .

An involuntary noise of terror escaped her throat. She started to fight the metal at her wrists as her rational mind crumbled. Hot blood oozed down her forearms as the wounds at her wrists were reopened.

"Such a pretty plaything." The voice was high and grating, like a blade scraping across ice. It seemed to come from everywhere at once. "I haven't had such a lovely guest since Nightstrider."

Ila forced herself to be still as foul breath rolled over her. Time stopped when a papery palm was pressed to her cheek.

"The prettier they are"—Ila shuddered when it pressed its talons into the side of her face. They did not break the skin. Not yet—"the more fun they are to ruin."

"Please," she found herself begging. "Please—"

Screee . . .

Hoste, he's laughing.

"I am called Bloodreaper, Queen Ila."

Razor-sharp talons punctured her cheek. Ila opened her mouth to scream, but the sound died in her throat. Itching, burning, searing agony traveled from the wounds to her bloodstream. It circled her heart, burrowed in her stomach, her legs, the tips of her fingers.

"When I am done with you, you will no longer be Queen Ila of Galesborough. You will be nothing, and you will give me everything."

Bloodreaper retracted his claws. Blood ran from the five puncture wounds. A cool breath of air dusted her face as he moved.

"The dreambreaker is in our grasp again. The rebels failed, and so did you."

"No," Ila breathed.

"This is your doing. You sent her to this world alone."

A powerful shudder ripped through her body. Her fingers

and toes cramped, paralyzed at unnatural angles. Every beat of her heart sent poison hurtling through her veins.

"You could leave her to starve in that box," Bloodreaper coaxed her. "Or you could set her free."

"I won't open the box for your Para," Ila spat. Her mouth tasted like rust. "I would rather die."

"All in due time, child."

Ila squeezed her eyes shut against the pain, the dark, the world. Tears streamed down her cheeks as her paralyzed muscles trembled in agony.

"You will open the box for the Para," the creature told her. "Soon, you will beg to."

Through the fog of torture, a thought pricked Ila.

Para Warwick still believed she was the only one who could open the box. He had to, or she would have been dead hours ago. That meant Caine had not told him about the fail-safe.

Not yet, at least.

What is he waiting for? Unless—

The scream that had died in her throat was finally pulled from her when Bloodreaper snapped her left pointer finger like a twig. She tried to twist, to fight, but her muscles had turned to stone. She could feel the paralysis creeping up her throat. Soon, it would lock her jaw, and she would not even be able to scream.

"I will leave you to consider," Bloodreaper said silkily. Ila felt rather than saw him retreat into the blackness.

Sol liv hjent warren. Sol liv hjent warren. Sol liv hjent—

Time became fractured and warped. Her blood was on fire, her frozen muscles creaked like rotting wood, and the puncture wounds on the side of her face stung.

Slowly, she regained the ability to move. But with that came a new sort of torment. Every movement sent fresh pain singing down her nerves to her shattered finger. As her jaw unfroze, her ability to scream returned, but she bit her lip until it bled.

Sometime between a second and an eternity, Bloodreaper returned.

"I must admit, I am impressed."

Hot breath caressed her face. Ila squeezed her eyes shut against it, but of course, nothing changed.

"Generally, my poison is enough to pull an answer out of my guests. It has reduced the most powerful luminae to quivering masses. Perhaps you need a little more incentive."

Ila could not hold back a shriek of agony when he snapped two more of her fingers on her left hand. Shards of bone sliced straight through her skin. Blood oozed down her suspended arm.

"Are you prepared to open the box for the Para?"

"I c-can't," she said through her tremors.

"But you will."

"N-no. I can't. I'm left-handed."

A hysterical laugh burst from Ila when Bloodreaper did not respond at once. The laughter quickly melted into dry heaves when a wave of nausea rolled over her. It cut off when the nightmare grabbed her face with spindly fingers.

"Listen well, girl. The Para needs you alive for now, but

once you have served your purpose, you will be granted your end. You have a choice about how you want to spend your final hours."

Her head lolled forward when Bloodreaper released her. A breath of air stirred her hair as the nightmare glided away, leaving her alone again. Her lids drooped. She could feel unconsciousness lurking just out of sight and welcomed it.

Ila.

Her mouth twitched. *Saoirse.* She could hear her sweet voice. Was she coming to take her to the afterlife, to reunite with her sworn god?

Ila, this is real.

The voice echoed through her mind, cutting through the crush of pain. Ila frowned, confused.

The box was opened; I'm safe. We're coming for you.

"No!" Ila twisted in her shackles, gasping as her shattered bones flared with nauseating agony. "No! Stay away!"

Sol liv hjent warren.

"Stay away!"

Screee . . .

Bloodreaper had returned. "It appears you're losing your grip," he noted, his voice dripping with glee. "Wits are always the first to go."

Ila scarcely heard him over the thunder of her pulse. Saoirse was free, meaning the fail-safe was triggered. *How?* The only person who knew the password besides Ila and Saoirse herself was Caine, but it couldn't be him.

Saoirse was coming for her.

There was no stopping her. The link that existed between their minds only worked one way. Saoirse could contact Ila, but not the other way around. Even if it went both ways, there was no way she could convince the dreambreaker not to come for her.

As long as she was breathing, Ila was a threat to Saoirse.

The weight of the revelation nearly crushed her. She slumped, the manacles cutting even deeper into her flayed wrists. Her thoughts went dark in waves. She was sinking, sinking, sinking.

Freezing water slammed into Ila. She jerked in her chains, coughing and sputtering. Bloodreaper was inches from her again.

"I need you awake," he growled.

"Kill me. Please."

Screee . . .

"You may as well be dead." She shuddered as the nightmare dragged a single talon down the soft underside of her forearm, nearly hard enough to break the skin. "The Para told me about you, you know. Your family is gone. The weavers despise you. The prince used you. You have no one but a halfling locked in a box. You're alone."

Ila wanted to scream that he was wrong, that she was not alone, but that would be a lie. Her family was dead. Nils, Ashild, and the rest of her people were a world away. Morthil had no idea where she was.

Saoirse was all she had, and if she came to Caer Sidi, she would lose her, too.

"Perhaps I should amend my statement."

Bloodreaper pierced the skin of her arm with his poisoned talon. Ila let out a noise that was more animal than human.

"You're not alone."

Convulsions racked her again as the paralysis began to take hold, drawing fresh blood from her mangled fingers. Bloodreaper pressed his flaky lips to her ear, and when he spoke, his needle teeth scraped her skin.

"I will be with you until you have served your purpose. Then I will rip the meat from your bones. I will be with you until your skeleton turns to dust. You will be forgotten by everyone, save for me."

A whoosh of stale air and Bloodreaper was gone, swallowed by the blackness of the sanctum. Ila was left alone with the echo of her sobs until even they dissipated. Until the paralysis choked her vocal cords. Until she was nothing.

48

Caine

Caine stared dead-eyed at his food. He could not bring himself to pick up his fork. The cutlery was identical to the set he grew up using save for the fact that it was silver rather than gold. The same was true of the dishes, napkins, and table dressings. They were all shades of his memory.

"Is your meal not to your satisfaction?"

Caine and Para Warwick were seated at opposite ends of a long table laden with platters of steaming food. Three different types of meat, mountains of ripe fruit and loaves of bread baked to perfection. Mounted above the fireplace behind the king—the *Para*, Caine reminded himself—was the dual-headed doppelgänger of their crest.

Three servants waited with their backs to the wall. Even in the dim light, he could see how spent they were.

"Prince Caine?"

"The meal is excellent." Caine picked up his fork and impaled a seasoned potato, sticking it in his mouth. "I apologize, my ki—my Para. I was lost in thought."

Para Warwick smiled. Night had risen in the Reverie. After Ila was dragged away, Caine was whisked off to a bedroom by a pair of maids. They offered to bathe him, which he quickly declined. After washing himself and changing into a fresh set of clothes, the wounds at his wrists were dressed by a healer.

When Caine asked what had been done with the weaver, the healer blanched and left in a flurry of apologies, but not before Caine could ask him for a tonic to numb pain.

He had a feeling he might need it.

"Tell me," the Para began, drawing him back to the present. "What are your thoughts?"

"Regarding?"

"This." Para Warwick gestured broadly at the dining hall, a sick replica of the one Caine knew. Only days ago, the prince had sat next to Ila at a table just like this one. It seemed a lifetime ago. "The Reverie."

"It is . . . more than I ever could have imagined," Caine answered.

"Come now," Para Warwick drawled. "You can do better than that."

Caine forced a chuckle and took another bite to bridge the gap. "Things are certainly wilder here than they are in the Wake. I imagine it must be difficult to keep everyone in check."

Para Warwick made a noise of agreement and drank deeply from his goblet. He snapped his fingers. A girl with mousy hair rushed over to refill his drink. Even from the opposite end of the table, Caine could see her hands were trembling.

"Ruling in the Wake is a very different business than ruling in the Reverie," his father agreed as she retreated. "The territories in the waking world are bound by kingdom and blood. No such distinctions exist here."

Caine raised his own wine to his lips. The taste was sweet and heady. "How do you maintain control, then?"

"Foster the division between the different breeds of dreams. The kips, vexes, luminae." Para Warwick fluttered a ringed hand dismissively. Firelight collected in the facets of the bulbous jewels. "If they cannot unify, they will not rise up. Even if they could move against me, they will not."

"Why?"

Para Warwick stabbed a chunk of meat with his knife and examined it.

"Fear," he answered simply. "In the Wake, anyone with a blade and an idea can change the world. Humans all bleed the same. Here, there are only gods, monsters, and maggots."

Caine jumped in his seat when a crash rang out. The wine bearer had dropped her pitcher. Red liquid seeped from the shattered remains at her feet as she clutched her throat, eyes bulging.

Caine started to stand, but his father raised a finger at him.

"No need for heroics, Caine. She is just a kip, a fleeting phenomenon. Simpler than a child."

His brain worked slowly, bogged down by horror. By the time Caine realized his father was choking her without touching her, the girl was already blue.

"This is unnecessary," Caine said over his sprinting pulse. Her eyes rolled back into their sockets. The other servants were still. One of the boys cried silently, his knuckles white around the handles of the platter he held. "She did nothing wrong."

Para Warwick sighed. "I suppose not." He snapped his fingers. The girl crashed to her knees, gasping and wheezing. Her skin faded from blue to pink. "Get her out of here and clean up this mess."

One of the servants slung her arm over his shoulder and ferried her toward the door. The remaining girl began to pick up the shards of glass with a cloth. Para Warwick paid them no mind, watching Caine through narrowed eyes.

"Ever the hero."

"I'm no more a hero than you," Caine replied, leaning back in his chair with feigned nonchalance. "But perhaps we can make better use of our time."

"Indeed." The Para smiled again. "How do you intend to assist me in the Reverie?"

"Where would I be most useful?"

"An apt response, but I want to know what you want. The Reverie has no need of a prince, so we must find a different role for you. Where do you see yourself in this court?"

The prince hesitated. It seemed like an open-ended question, but there was a correct response and an infinity of incorrect ones. They had played this game before, but the stakes had never been so high. By now, Ila was deep beneath the castle in the sanctum. Gods know what they had done to her.

Caine shut down the thought. He could not help her if he panicked.

"At your side," he said. "Doing whatever it takes to see your vision of this world come to fruition."

The fire crackled behind the Para. The wind threw itself against the crystal windows.

Then Para Warwick chuckled.

"Well played, Prince Caine."

He tossed his napkin onto his plate and shoved back his chair. Caine followed him to his feet.

"I have matters to attend," the Para said. "One of the servants will show you to the guest suite."

"Do my chambers not exist in this realm?"

Para Warwick paused. A vein in his temple bulged as he tightened his jaw. "They do, but here they belong to Nightstrider."

"Nightstrider?" Caine inquired nonchalantly.

"A story for another time. Good somnia."

"Good night," Caine murmured, but he was already gone.

☽○☾

Caine wore a path in the plush rug as he paced before the fire. The room he was given was in the north tower, far from his chambers. Or rather, *Nightstrider's* chambers. He turned her name over and over in his mind like a featureless stone. It seemed to follow them wherever they went.

Ila.

He dragged a hand down his face.

The Para needs her alive.

At least, he believed he did. Caine paused at the edge of the rug, his eyes pinned to his reflection in the dark, rain-flecked window. How in the name of the gods was he supposed to rescue Ila and find Saoirse before the dreambreaker wasted away? Before Ila was broken beyond repair?

A wave of nausea engulfed him, forcing him to drop into one of the armchairs by the hearth.

He could still see her stricken face when he betrayed her, could still hear his father striking her.

Bloodreaper deserves some entertainment after his ordeal with Nightstrider.

Caine did not know who Bloodreaper was, but if his name was any indication, Ila was in grave danger.

He had to do it, Caine reminded himself. He had to pretend to discard her. If he had stood by her side and betrayed his father, they both would have been at the mercy of this Bloodreaper. They would have no chance of getting out of Caer Sidi alive.

Not that things were much better now.

A tentative knock at the door set his teeth on edge. Caine approached cautiously and cracked it open. He exhaled in relief when he found it was only a servant girl.

"Can I help you?" he asked, opening the door farther.

The girl looked at her feet. She carried a metal pail, brush, and dustpan. Her fingers were stained with soot.

"Could you come back later?"

"Please, my lord," she begged softly. "They will punish me."

Shit.

"Come in."

The girl squeaked out a thank-you and hurried past him, making a beeline for the hearth. Caine shut the door behind her.

"Do you have a name?" The girl started, nearly dropping her brush. "Sorry," Caine said, raising his hands. "I didn't mean to frighten you."

"N-no, my lord. My name is Alma."

"Alma," he repeated, studying her in the firelight. She had coppery hair and expressive blue eyes. "I'm Caine."

"I know, my lord." She wiped her grimy hands on her apron and rose to face him. "The Para speaks of you often."

Surprise flickered through Caine. His father rarely spoke of him at home. Strange that he would here.

"Do you mind if I ask you a few questions, Alma?"

Alma paled, palming the fabric of her skirt. "What kind of questions?"

"I won't hurt you," he assured her. "I'm not like my father."

Liar, a voice in the back of his mind whispered. The splinter swarm beneath Mount Anvil swept through his mind. The half-remembered dreams freeing him from his bonds, responding to his commands.

Only a monster—a *nightmare*—could do such a thing. But maybe a nightmare was exactly what they needed to get out of here.

"Someone I care about is in danger," Caine said. "Her name is Ila. Para Warwick is holding her captive in the sanctum. I need to get to her before it's too late."

Alma bit her lip, looking anywhere but his face.

"I know I'm asking a lot of you. If you want to leave, I understand. I only ask that you keep this between us."

The girl set down her pail and brush carefully, as if she was afraid to make any noise. Slowly, she raised her eyes to his.

"I will help you, my lord. What is it you need?"

Caine exhaled in relief. Crossing back to the armchair, he sat heavily. Alma shook her head when he gestured for her to have a seat in the other, instead standing before the hearth.

"How much do you know about this castle?"

"My lord?"

"Is the layout identical to the Caer Sidi in the Wake?"

"I—I think so." Alma tucked a silky lock behind her ear. "That is what they say."

"Thank the gods," Caine muttered. At least he would not fail Ila by getting lost in his own house. "What about the sanctum? What do you know about it?"

Alma began to chew her thumbnail, then seemed to think better of it. "Bloodreaper lives there," she said, lowering her voice to a furtive whisper. "People go down there, and they don't come back. Except Nightstrider."

That name again. "Who is Nightstrider?"

"The Hand of the Para." Alma glanced around as if someone might be lurking in the exposed corners of the room and dropped her voice to a whisper. "But she deserted a few days ago. They're hunting her now."

"Why did she leave?"

"I don't know, but I wish she hadn't. She was…kind." Her eyes fogged with tears. "I had a friend who disappeared the same day as Nightstrider. She said she was attacked in the Tanglewood, and Nightstrider *saved her.* Though I haven't seen her since."

Caine dammed his questions while Alma dried her eyes. "What happens in the sanctum?" he asked when she had collected herself.

"We…hear screams in the night." Alma shivered, hugging her arms to her chest. "But no one knows exactly what he does to them. Bloodreaper, I mean." She glanced over her shoulder at the door.

"My lord—"

"Just one more thing. Is the sanctum entrance guarded?"

"Please, sir." To his surprise, Alma reached out to clutch his hands. Hers were caked with soot and slick with sweat. "If she has been taken to the sanctum, she is lost. You must let her go."

Caine's jaw hardened. He tugged his hands back from the servant and turned away. "That will be all," he muttered. "Thank you."

Distantly, he heard Alma murmur a farewell and collect her tools. It was only when he registered the door clicking shut that he allowed himself to come undone, snatching the crystal pitcher of water that had been left on the table and hurling it at the wall. It shattered, sending a thousand droplets and shards of glass flying.

Caine stared at the mess, shoulders heaving as his breaths came in short rasps.

She is lost. She is lost. She is lost.

49
Wren

There was nothing. Just endless void and a hollow ringing in her ears. Then consciousness slammed into Wren like a hurricane. She sat bolt upright, looking around wildly. Her vision was scattered.

"You're okay, Wren. You're okay."

"Alaric?" Wren called, hating the panic in her voice as much as she hated that she had called for him first.

Two warm hands intercepted her own, anchoring her. The smell of ash tickled her nose. Her pulse slowed automatically.

"You're safe."

Wren blinked the world into view.

Alaric knelt beside her on the muddy ground. The bodies of the vexes they had slain were piled a few dozen paces away from the fire, which still crackled weakly. The captive kips were gone, the frayed remains of the ropes binding them curled on the ground.

And beside her, lying on the jacket she had set the box on, was a girl. No longer a specter, but flesh and bone.

"Saoirse," Wren breathed.

Saoirse opened her eyes, bright green and clear as a mountain spring. They went first to Wren, then to Alaric.

"Hello, Bonehunter," Saoirse said, sitting up as if waking from a nap. Alaric blinked. "Good to see you again."

"Again?" Alaric asked blankly.

"I see you often, in my dreams," Saoirse explained. Her voice was high and youthful but heavy with wisdom beyond her years. "Though not as often as I see Nightstrider."

"I—okay. What happened?" he asked, his bewildered gaze flicking from Saoirse to Wren. "How did you get out?"

Wren did not answer. Jumbled memories of the past few days rushed to fill her rattled skull, smothering all coherent thoughts. The bite of metal at her wrists, Ondine falling through the dark, the immovable weight of his body on top of hers, crushing the life from her.

You killed him.

Wren squeezed her eyes shut in vain.

"We should give her some space," she heard Saoirse tell Alaric distantly. "Do you have any food?"

"Uh, yes."

Wren heard Alaric rise and cross the campsite, his boots squelching through the muck. She focused on her breathing, on the gentle rain.

"Here you go," she heard him say after a moment.

"Takja," Saoirse said. "Go. She needs you."

There was a pause. Then wet footfalls struck up again. She felt Alaric crouch beside her and lay a hand on the space between her shoulder blades. She flinched involuntarily but did not pull away.

"What happened?" Alaric asked.

Wren lifted her head. His brow was creased with concern. More than she deserved.

The bite of metal at her wrists, Ondine falling through the dark, the immovable weight of his body—

"You got Saoirse out," Alaric told her, nodding at the dreambreaker. Wren looked around to find the child sitting on one of their packs, nibbling a piece of jerky. She watched them with attentive round eyes.

When Wren spoke, her voice was a ghost of its usual bravado. "I saw him."

"Saw who? The Para?"

"No. Bram." Speaking his name was a kick in the gut. It made her want to wilt forward again, but she forced herself to remain upright. "It was a test. The box offered me what I wanted most in exchange for Saoirse."

Wren felt his hand tense against her back. "And that was Bram."

"Not just him." Wren turned her face to the overcast skies, searching for something that was not there.

"What, then?"

Again, she did not answer. If she did, he would hear the stickiness in her throat, the tears she was holding back. Eventually, Alaric gave up with a sigh and climbed to his feet. He crossed the campsite again to sit beside Saoirse, leaving Wren alone with her haunted mind.

She must have fallen asleep at some point, because when Wren opened her eyes, she was lying on a musty cloak with her jacket folded under her head. The campfire crackled to her right.

She sat up and peered around the campsite. The rain had dissolved much of the remaining snow while she slept, revealing balding patches of grass. The foothills and their hallowed gravestones were quiet around them. The only sounds were the wind and the patter of a solitary heartbeat.

Saoirse observed her across the flames, silent and inquisitive.

"Hello, Nightstrider."

"Where's Alaric?" Wren asked.

"He went to collect firewood."

"Your voice is different here," she noted. "You sound younger."

Saoirse turned pink. "I wanted to sound bigger inside the box," she admitted. "I wanted you to take me seriously."

"I'd be an idiot not to take you seriously."

Saoirse smile vaguely, studying Wren with a tilted head. Pools of firelight shivered in her moss green irises.

"It isn't nice to stare, you know," Wren muttered.

"Oh, sorry." Saoirse ducked her head as her blush crept to the tips of her rounded ears. "I don't meet many people."

Wren winced internally. She was about as clumsy with children as she was with poetry.

"I don't meet many children."

Saoirse peeked up at her through her lashes with a bashful smile. It melted almost immediately, and her eyes flooded with tears. Wren stiffened. Gods, what had she done?

"I'm sorry," Saoirse whispered.

"What the hells for?"

The dreambreaker picked at a patch of dead grass next to her. "For what you saw in the box."

Wren leaned back with a grunt, abruptly guarded. "A warning would have been appreciated."

"I swear, I had no idea."

Saoirse locked eyes with Wren again. They glimmered with acute distress. She looked less like a weapon and more like a child, lost and alone in a strange world.

"I believe you," Wren assured her. "What I don't understand is why we spent the last two days chasing your queen across the Reverie if she was not the only one who could free you."

"The fail-safe is dangerous. Really dangerous. I think if you had gone with that man, the box would have killed you, and I would have starved in there."

"Fair enough."

Saoirse produced a piece of jerky from her pocket and began to chew on it. It was nearly the size of her hand. Wren tipped her head back, scanning the cloudy night sky for a single nick of light and finding none.

"Why me?"

Saoirse stopped chewing. "What?"

"Why did you give me this?" Wren tugged her shirt aside to reveal the blessing. It burned brighter than ever. "There are thousands of better candidates, dream beings who would save you without a second thought with nothing in it for them."

"Like Alaric and his friend."

"Right. So why did you bless me?"

Saoirse balanced the remainder of her snack on her knee.

"I have dreamed of the future my whole life," she said. "Or, possible futures, I guess. Sometimes, I see little things, like what I'll have for breakfast tomorrow. Other times, I see big things. Scary things. When I dream of those things, there's always one person at the center of it all."

"Who?" Wren asked, dreading the answer.

"You."

The nightmare scoffed. "Please don't tell me this is some sort of prophecy."

Saoirse surprised Wren by shaking her curly head. "There's no such thing as prophecy, not really. We can change the future just by knowing it."

"How old are you again?"

"Eleven," Saoirse answered, pushing her shoulders back. "Well, in two moons, I'll be eleven."

Great, Wren thought bleakly.

"What have you seen of my future, then?" she asked, surrendering to the bizarreness of the conversation.

"Well, things are blurry." Saoirse pulled her knees to her chest and wrapped her skinny arms around her legs. "I just know something is coming; a clam"—she tripped over the word, her brow rumpling—"a calam—"

"A calamity?" Wren deadpanned.

"Yes." Saoirse bobbed her head eagerly. "A calamity."

"And I, what, cause this *calamity*?" Wren probed, unable to dam the frustration spilling into her tone. "Sounds about right."

"No, no. You don't cause it. At least, I don't think you do. I think you stop it."

"Have you seen a future where I die tomorrow? Because Alaric has a promise to keep."

Saoirse pursed her lips. Wren looked out into the darkening

foothills, inhaling deeply through her nose.

"When did Alaric leave?" She looked back at Saoirse to find fat tears pouring down her cheeks. "Oh gods, what now? What did I do?"

"I saw it," Saoirse breathed. Her voice was so soft Wren could barely hear it.

"Saw what?"

"The night Bram died. I saw what they did to you, what they made you do."

The world withered around Wren. Her next words were monotonal, almost mechanical.

"Don't tell Alaric."

"But—"

"Saoirse, please. Don't tell him."

"I won't," the dreambreaker promised. "But you should."

Wren got to her feet, snatching her crumpled jacket from the ground. She shook it out and donned it, ignoring the ache of her healing wounds.

"Get some rest; I'll have Alaric take you back to Caer Bheinn tomorrow. You'll be safe there."

"No."

Wren froze, poised to latch the top clasp of her jacket. "Excuse me?"

"We're not going back to Caer Bheinn. We're going to Caer Sidi to rescue Ila."

"Are you fucking kidding me?"

"No." Saoirse rose, standing as tall as she could.

Wren pinched the bridge of her nose with her thumb and forefinger. A headache was building here.

"Saoirse, I'm sorry, but if Para Warwick has her, she won't last much longer. She may already be dead."

"Ila is alive." Saoirse tapped her pointer finger to her temple. "I can feel her. As long as the Para believes she is the only one who can open the box and I'm still inside, he'll keep her alive. We can still save her."

Wren took a steadying breath, willing her expression to remain calm. She was not keen to scare the child, but her nerves were becoming increasingly frayed.

"I did not spend my final hours tracking you across the Reverie and keeping you away from Para Warwick to deliver you to him on a platter!" she shouted.

"Everything all right?"

Saoirse and Wren looked around. Alaric had appeared with a pitiful bundle of twigs in hand. He dropped them by the fire, raising an inquiring brow at Wren. She just shook her head.

"The Para has taken Ila," Saoirse explained. "We're going to get her back."

☽○☾

Wren expected a fight. A tantrum, perhaps. That was what children did, was it not? But when Alaric calmly informed her that returning to Caer Sidi was too dangerous, she simply smiled a vague and mildly unnerving smile and asked for more food.

Now she slept soundly, burrowed beneath one of the less-bloody cloaks they had pulled off the dead vexes. Her face was a small white moon peeking through the gray clouds.

"Well?"

Wren glanced at Alaric, who was warming his hands over the fire she had been staring into for far too long. She blinked away the smoky sting in her eyes.

"Well what?" she asked, knowing damn well what he meant.

"How are we doing this?"

"I knew it," Wren groaned. "You spineless piece of—"

"I've been thinking it over, all right?" Alaric cut her off. "Everyone wants to use Saoirse for their own purposes. Everyone except Queen Ila. She is the only one who wants the best for her, not to mention she can watch over her in the Wake *and* the Reverie."

"I thought the rebellion wanted Saoirse," Wren said, resting her elbows on her knees and leaning toward the fire.

"They do." He glanced at her, then away before she could unravel his expression. "Maybe I don't care."

Wren raised her brows. "Defecting again, Bonehunter?"

"Not exactly." He offered her some of his meal, which she declined with a shake of her head. "I've been thinking—"

"When have you had time to do all this thinking?"

"We're a good team, Wren."

Wren went still, staring at him in the rippling firelight as that damned hope he kept choking on eclipsed his face. She knew what he was going to say before he said it.

"Fighting together, it felt good. I know you felt it, too. I want to keep fighting with you." He hesitated, then reached toward her and took her hand. His was warm, either from the fire or his elevated heart rate. "The two of us can do more damage to Warwick together than everyone in the rebellion combined, and we can start by getting Queen Ila out of Caer Sidi and getting Saoirse home."

"You really are terrible at this."

"At what?"

"Being a monster."

Alaric smiled cautiously, his hand still enveloping hers. She let him.

"Say we did this," she began begrudgingly. "How would it work?"

"I'm glad you asked."

Wren wrenched away from Alaric at the same time he did, as if they had been caught in the act. Through the column of smoke and heat, Saoirse was sitting up in her nest of cloaks and observing them with her inquisitive round eyes. Wren got the sense she had been watching them for a while.

"*You* are not going to Caer Sidi," she said flatly.

"Even if I can get you inside like this?" Saoirse snapped her fingers demonstratively.

"You can, can't you?" Alaric muttered. "That was how you and Wren ended up in the Tanglewood."

"It was hard to do from inside my box," Saoirse said, sitting crisscross and wrapping one of her cloaks around her. "It will be much easier now."

"We can be in and out before anyone raises the alarm," Alaric went on, nodding to himself. "You get us in, we grab Ila, then you two go to the Wake."

Saoirse bobbed her curly head eagerly.

"What about my anchor?" Wren broke in. "Warwick still has it. We won't get very far if he incinerates it."

"You can free her, can't you?" Alaric pressed, looking to the dreambreaker.

"Oh..." Saoirse tucked a curl behind her ear. "I don't know."

Alaric blinked. Wren felt her vision slide from focus and the voices of her companions recede. "What do you mean you don't know? You're a dreambreaker."

The child stared at him blankly. "Why would that mean I could cut her from her anchor?"

"My friend Luken. He was a dreambreaker. He freed me from mine."

Wren could hear panic edging into his voice, but she could not feel it herself. Her body was a distant, wrecked shell she had crawled from.

"Why would that mean I could do the same? Can you do the same things Nightstrider can?" Saoirse shook her head. "I can't free her."

"You have to," Alaric snapped. Vaguely, Wren registered Saoirse recoiling and the horned nightmare dragging a hand down his face. "I'm sorry, kid. I just don't understand."

"I do."

Wren rose slowly, her hands on her knees as if she were an aged kip, and drew herself to full height.

"I'm going alone."

Alaric stood and closed the space between them in a heartbeat. She stared up at him, searching the taut planes of his face. His pupils were pinpricks, the blood leached from his face. She had seen such desperation before and knew what it meant.

"You're not going to keep your promise, are you?" Wren asked quietly. "You can't."

"I thought things were changing."

"You don't want me, Alaric. Everyone I get close to dies." She threw a glance at Saoirse, who watched them with her makeshift blanket tucked around her. The tip of her nose was pink. "No," Wren gritted out, returning her eyes to Alaric. "I'll get Ila out, she'll get Saoirse to safety, he'll destroy my anchor. It'll be over."

The end had never scared her before, but now she felt a chill scale her spine, rustling her feathers. Or maybe it was the way Alaric was looking at her, like she had just pried apart his ribs and plunged her talons into his chest.

"We can still save you," he rasped. "We can steal your anchor."

"He conjures it at will. I don't even know if it exists in this world."

"We'll find it. We'll—"

"Alaric." She had intended to shout, but his name came out a whisper too soft for a nightmare. "I'm already gone."

She started to back away, but before her foot even graced the soggy ground again, he had snatched her hand, anchoring her in place. His grip was a vise, his eyes wild, but she was not afraid.

"You were meant for better things," she told him. "Better than me."

"Bullshit," he growled. "We're both nightmares."

"Some nightmares are worse than others, and they all come to an end." She covered his hand with her free one and felt it soften as she leaned in and pressed her lips to his cheek. She breathed in his scent, winter and embers, and tucked it away like a trinket. A memento of what almost was. Her lips brushed the slant of his ear and felt a shiver run through him. "Good somnia, Alaric."

She twisted his wrist in a violent motion, shoved him backward with all her strength, then whipped around and sprinted into the hills. He shouted in pain and tore after her, but she was faster. She snapped her wings out with a gust that stirred the earth and launched into sky.

She did not look back.

PART FOUR
RUIN AND WRATH

50

Caine

Caine could not bring himself to lie down. He spent a sleepless night roaming his room like a restless spirit. Three times he stood frozen before the door, fighting the urge to burst through it and race to Ila, but he knew how that would end.

Eventually, the cold sun slunk into the sky. Caine splashed some water on his face and neck and dressed in the fine clothes the servants brought him. The black velvet jacket was embroidered with the sigil of the two-headed wolf. He did up the clasps, stomped on his boots, and exited the guest quarters with his head high.

You're the son of the Para, he reminded himself as he started down the corridor. *Act like it.*

This was easier said than done. The skeleton of the castle was familiar. Its occupants were not. The Guard was predominately made up of vexes. At least, he assumed the uniformed creatures were vexes. The servants all appeared human. Less homogenous were the nobles. There were dream beings with horns, pearly scales, cat eyes, fur, and fangs.

Caine was trying not to stare at a woman with the beak of a shrike when he slammed into a servant carrying a wicker basket of laundry. She gasped and dropped it, the basket rolling onto its side and dumping soiled clothing onto the flagstones. Laughter rustled through the passersby.

"Sorry," he said, dropping to help her collect the clothes and simultaneously realizing this was the last thing the son of a Para would be doing. Their eyes locked. "Alma?" He might not have recognized the kip were it not for her coppery hair. Her face was a patchwork of bruises. "Gods, what happened?"

"Nothing."

"But—"

"Tonight," she whispered. "Half past twelve. *Go.*"

"Alma—"

But she was already gone, the basket on her hip and her head tucked low.

"Princeling."

Caine rounded on the familiar voice.

"Spineripper," he drawled. "You're looking undecorated. Is the reward for our capture metaphorical?"

Bathed and dressed in fresh clothes, he had to admit Spineripper looked like he belonged in court. Even his blond hair, once stiff with grease, was washed and tied into a respectable knot. He still oozed a slimy sort of disdain.

"Enjoying sleeping alone?" the nightmare asked.

Caine glanced at a group of curious kips clustered farther down the hall. They scattered like dust blown off a tabletop when they noticed him looking.

"What do you want?" he asked Spineripper.

"Not here."

"I'm not going anywhere with you."

Spineripper took him by the shoulder and steered him to a statue of a rearing centaur. Caine allowed it to avoid another scene. "Don't think I don't know what you're doing," the nightmare growled in his ear.

The prince shrugged off his grip. "You will have to be more specific."

Spineripper glared at him like something stuck to the sole of his shoe. "You may have fooled the Para, but you have not fooled me."

"It appears I already did. Queen Ila is an enemy of the Para. I gained her trust in order to learn her secrets. Any affection you saw us exchange was an act." He was surprised by how easily the lies rolled off his tongue. "Now, if you will excuse me, I have more important matters to attend."

He started to retreat, but Spineripper grabbed him by the arm.

"Take your hands off me, or I will ensure you lose them," Caine said softly.

His grip tightened.

"You know what he will do to her?" Spineripper snarled. "Those pretty little cuts I gave her are a mercy she will beg for. I've only seen one bitch come out of there alive, but her screams?" He blew a low, warbling whistle through his teeth. "Made even my blood run cold."

Caine shoved the nightmare off him. Spineripper stumbled, surprise flickering across his face before he could snuff it.

"I heard you scream, too," Caine said in a low voice. "In

the cave." He took a step toward him, and though Spineripper did not retreat, he did flick his eyes up and down Caine as if in search of a weapon. "I can make that happen again."

"The Para will see through you," Spineripper snarled. "You and that weaver bitch will—"

Caine slammed his fist into his nose. Shouts of surprise from passersby flew up like startled birds. The nightmare swore, staggering as blood gushed from his nostrils, then lunged at Caine. The prince held up a hand.

"You have three seconds to get out of here before I have you gutted."

Spineripper's face was bone white against the blood drizzling down his lips and chin. His eyes, their pupils pinpoints, darted to their audience. His lips curled into a true snarl as he returned his gaze to Caine, then he spun on his heel and stalked away.

The world churned on after a tense moment.

Caine collected himself beneath the watchful gaze of a portrait of an eyeless woman with snakes coiling from her scalp, arranging his face into an emotionless mask, and hoping against hope no one could hear his heart hammering against his ribs.

Tonight. Half past twelve. Go.

☽○☾

Everything was too loud. His footfalls on the flagstones, the push and pull of his breath. The halls of Caer Sidi were deserted at the late hour, but Caine still found himself tensing with every corner he rounded.

I'm allowed to be here, he reminded himself as he passed the statue of the two-headed wolf. *I'm the son of the Para.*

Even in his head, it sounded unconvincing.

The walls seemed to contract like behemoth lungs when he entered the east wing of the castle. His own were paralyzed when he spied the narrow archway between a pair of torches. Oil paintings of past paras were mounted on either side of the fixtures, a red-eyed devil and a woman with a scythe.

There was nothing but a plain wooden door sealing the entrance to the catacombs, no guards or deadbolts to stop him from entering. He swallowed on a dry mouth as he approached to lay a hand on the handle.

A blade was pressed to his throat.

"Don't scream."

"I'm the son of the Para," Caine said, keeping his voice low so it did not shake. "Kill me, and you're dead."

"I already am."

A hand gripped his shoulder and spun him around. Dark eyes framed with darker lashes scowled at him from under a heavy cowl. She was dressed in black fighting leathers, and multiple knives were strapped to her hips and thighs.

"Nightstrider."

Instinct brought the name to his lips. Her blade jumped to his throat again, compressing his windpipe.

"The famous Prince Caine." He could hear the sneer in her voice. "Your father speaks of you often."

"Funny, he never said a word about you."

Nightstrider studied him from the depths of her hood. "What are you doing here?"

"I could ask you the same thing."

"You could," she admitted. She pressed the knife deeper into the skin of his throat. "But I think you'll find answering more beneficial."

She's not with my father. She deserted.

"Saoirse," Caine began carefully. "Is she safe?"

Slowly, Nightstrider took her blade from his neck, though she did not sheath it. The prince resisted the urge to massage his stinging neck.

"Yes," she answered after a weighty pause. "She is." There was a protectiveness in her voice Caine did not anticipate.

"Are you with the rebellion?"

"No. You haven't answered my question."

Caine weighed his options, battering down panic. He knew he could not trust Nightstrider, but what choice did he have? Someone was bound to discover them if they kept loitering outside the entrance to the catacombs, and there would be no explaining a chat with an outlaw.

"Warwick has my—my friend in the sanctum," Caine told her.

Nightstrider cursed and sheathed her blade. She swiped her cowl from her head. She was strikingly beautiful.

"You and I are here for the same person," she explained snappishly. "We're also walking into a trap."

"What?"

She flicked her heavy braid over her shoulder. "Did you really think you could just walk into the catacombs in the middle of the night? There should be at least two guards here, and a patrol should have passed two minutes ago."

"Then what the hells are you doing here?"

"Walking into a trap." Nightstrider drew her blade again. Her nails were soot dark and pointed. They were closer to talons, really. "There's a storm drain beneath the catacombs. Do you know it?"

"I think so."

He and Theodosia once discovered it on one of their excursions into the subterranean tunnels. Assuming this Caer Sidi truly was a replica of their home, he should be able to find it again.

"Yes or no?" Nightstrider snapped.

"Yes."

"Good. We free your queen, and the two of you escape through there."

"What about you?"

"Once you're out, head for the rebellion," Nightstrider continued as if he had not spoken. "Tell Ila that Alaric has Saoirse and will keep her safe until she gets to her, and tell Alaric . . ." She trailed off. Her eyes clouded like frosted windowpanes. "Never mind."

Nightstrider shouldered past him and wrenched open the door. Cold, dank air rushed to greet them. She stared into the void like she saw something there, something he was unable to discern.

"Sol liv hjent warren," she muttered under her breath.

Caine inhaled sharply. He started to speak, but Nightstrider had already taken off down the steps, her blade held out before her. The blackness swallowed her almost at once. The echo of her footsteps was the only indication that she had not winked out of existence.

"You coming?"

Caine grabbed one of the torches off its bracket and followed her into the abyss.

51

Wren

Caine stayed on her heels all the way down the staircase. His torch nearly singed her hair. Twice. Wren was not sure what to expect of the blood child of Para Warwick, but *human* and *fucking sentimental* were not on her list.

They halted when they reached the first leg of the catacombs. The torchlight gleamed on the slimy walls and revealed their warped reflections in the puddles on the floor. Wren turned right and moved off down the tunnel. Caine followed. Every one of her senses was on high alert, searching for a wick of life, but there was nothing. Not even the snuffling of a rat.

Then . . .

"Nightstrider," Caine muttered.

"I see it."

Patches of firelight had flickered to life ahead, apparently of their own volition. Wren motioned at Caine to douse his torch. He set it in a stinking puddle. The flames hissed as they died, their smoke trails wriggling like earthworms. Wren blinked, forcing her eyes to adjust. Caine looked even paler without the torchlight to shade his skin.

She drew one of the shorter blades at her thigh and pressed it into his hand. His fingers were slick with sweat.

"Can you fight?" she asked.

He tossed the knife into the air, catching it easily though his sights were trained ahead.

"What do you think?"

Wren smiled like striking a match.

With each step toward the sanctum, she felt her end creeping closer. Her anchor burn throbbed with renewed vengeance. Just as bad, her flight to Caer Sidi had reopened the injuries she sustained from the rebels' grappling hooks. Her tunic was drenched with blood beneath her jacket.

The hair on her arms stood on end when she detected the murmur of a third heartbeat ahead.

"H-hello?" a raspy female voice rang out. Caine inhaled sharply. Before Wren could suggest caution, he hurtled off toward it.

Idiot.

She jogged after him.

The sanctum was even more fearful in the torchlight. Half a dozen flames cast vicious shadows on the walls caked with decades of gore and rot. Piles of bones picked clean pressed in from all sides. The stone dais that once supported Saoirse's box was gone.

Directly opposite the entrance was a girl in chains.

Her wrists were shackled above her head, the fingers of her left hand splintered. Her shirt, arms, and ivory hair were all caked with blood, some fresh and some dried. She blinked at them with lusterless eyes.

Her scent, aside from her blood, was different than any Wren had encountered, like sweet morning fog.

So *this* was a weaver.

"Ila."

Caine sank to his knees in front of her. Ila shrank into the wall, bones crunching beneath her.

"Ila, gods, I am so sorry. I had to make him believe I was on his side. Gods, I—" He reached out to touch her face. She flinched, and he retracted his hand.

"Is this real?" she croaked. Her voice was laced with a coarse accent, one Wren had never heard before.

"Yes, this is real. Saoirse is safe. We're going to get you out of here."

Clarity sparked in Ila's eyes, then panic. "No, she's coming here."

"No, she isn't."

Both Caine and Ila looked up at Wren in unison, shocked. She could hear their pulses racing, racked with adrenaline.

"She wanted to come, but I wouldn't let her," she explained. "Alaric is watching her."

The ache of speaking his name was dulled only by the adrenaline thrumming through her.

"Alaric," Ila murmured. "Why do I know that name?"

"He's with the rebellion."

Caine rose to face Wren. "We don't have time for this. Where are the keys?"

Rather than answering, the nightmare crouched before

Ila. She looked even worse close-up. Tiny puncture wounds crawled up the side of her face and dappled her raised arms. *Bloodreaper.*

"This will hurt," Wren warned, scanning the mess he had made of her wrists and hand.

Instead of crying as she expected, Ila simply closed her eyes.

"Wait!"

Wren paused as Caine dug into his pocket and produced a vial of cloudy liquid. He uncorked it and offered it to Ila.

"Here," he said. "It should help with the pain. Drink it, quickly."

Ila nodded, allowing him to bring the vial to her cracked lips and pour it down her throat. She swallowed it in two gulps. Almost instantly, her pupils began to dilate. She blinked rapidly as if to disperse a film over her gaze.

Caine pocketed the empty vial and nodded at Wren.

She grasped the root of the chain nailed to the wall. Iron, not skysteel. Easy.

"One," Wren counted aloud. "Two—"

The nightmare snapped the shackles from their base. Escaped links ricocheted off the floor. Ila went from white to green as her arms dropped. She raised her mangled hand, which trembled uncontrollably.

Caine brushed past Wren, reaching down to help Ila to her feet. The girl swayed on the spot. He slipped an arm around her waist while she cradled her hand to her chest, not quite letting her fingers touch her body.

"What now?" the prince asked Wren.

"You get out of here."

"Wait," Ila spoke up weakly. "Why are you doing this?"

Wren undid the top clasp of her jacket and tugged her tunic aside. Her skin was smeared with her own blood, but it did nothing to douse the blessing blazing over her heart.

"Saoirse." Ila reached out to touch the mark with her good hand. Wren let her, turning her head to the side awkwardly. "I don't understand. How—"

"Go." Wren looked to Caine for reinforcement. He nodded, fingering the blade she gave him. "Get out of here."

"What about you?" Ila asked.

Wren's lips twitched. It was a wonder the human heart did not beat out of its cage. Of course, it was not just humans with luminous hearts.

I want to keep fighting with you.

"I have some unfinished business to attend to."

"Indeed."

The voice was ice cracking beneath a boot. Caine pulled Ila closer, raising his blade. Wren drew both of the knives at her hips.

"Get out of here," she growled at them.

They did not argue, skirting the curved wall and fleeing for the exit. Out of the corner of her eye, she saw Caine snatch another torch off the wall.

Time slowed as she turned on her heel.

The Para had materialized in the center of the sanctum in a simple black jacket ornamented with silver. He had not even bothered to wear armor, but there was a broadsword sheathed at his side, one she did not recognize. He smiled, slow and poisonous.

"Nightstrider. What a relief to have you home safely."

52
Alaric

Saoirse sat with her chin in her hand while Alaric paced circles around their dying fire, the strained tendons of his wrist still throbbing. It was a wonder he had not worn a trench in the mud by now. He kept sneaking glances at the overcast skies, waiting for Wren to drop from the clouds.

Her eyes were seared into his memory, gleaming with bittersweet resolve. His aching hand wandered to the spot her lips had graced his cheek. The skin there prickled with her absence.

"I have to go after her," he muttered for what might have been the second or twelfth time. He came to a halt in front of Saoirse. "I can take you to Morthil; he'll keep you safe."

"We've been through this. I can get you to Caer Sidi in an instant."

"I know, but I don't think I can protect you alone. There are too many of them."

"So what, you're going to *run*?"

"If I have to," he snapped.

Saoirse flinched at the bite in his voice. He swore under

his breath and put his back to her when he felt his eyes begin to turn black. He squeezed them shut. Footfalls approached, then he felt a cold hand on his elbow.

"I am a dreambreaker, Alaric."

He looked down to find her peering up at him with huge green eyes.

"I was born to help people. Please," she implored him. "Let me help."

"No."

Faster than he could track, her eyes flared white, her small face contorting with rage and her voice echoing tenfold through the hills.

"I am the most powerful being on either side of the Boundary," she snarled. "Do not treat me as if I am anything less."

Saoirse returned to her usual state in a blink, tucking a dark curl behind her ear. Alaric had not realized he had taken a step back from her until she reached for him again.

"If we wait, we will both lose someone we care about."

Alaric mastered himself with a deep breath.

"Fine," he said. "One condition."

The dreambreaker bobbed her head in acceptance.

"You get us into Caer Sidi, but once we're inside, you do exactly what I tell you. I know you're strong, but you're not trained. If I tell you to run, you run. If I tell you to hide, you hide. Understand?"

Saoirse nodded again, grave as a monk, and wiggled her outstretched fingers.

Alaric sent up a prayer to any gods who might be listening and took her tiny hand.

"Now what?" he asked.

Saoirse offered her other hand. He took it. "Be quiet. I need to focus, or I might cut you in half."

"Ah."

Saoirse shut her eyes. Tranquility swept across her features. There was a certain stillness about her that Alaric had never seen in a child. The air around them began to shimmer, sending ripples through the drab colors of the Bone Hills, the dying embers of their fire.

His skin began to tingle. Distant at first, but rapidly becoming unbearable.

"Hold still," Saoirse warned, anticipating his urge to rip his hands from hers. "Close your eyes."

Alaric did as she commanded. He started to ask what was going to happen. Then sound was sucked from the world. The air was wrenched from his lungs. His threads unraveled before he could shout.

He was falling, flying, spinning, drowning. For the briefest infinity, he was nothing at all.

"Alaric."

Alaric opened his eyes to a snare of shadows. Moisture and mildew hung heavy in the air. Even in his disoriented state, he knew exactly where they were. He had spent days, weeks in this tomb pulling screams and secrets from countless dream beings.

"The catacombs," he said aloud.

"Are you all right?" Saoirse asked out of the darkness.

"I just never thought I'd be back here."

At least not with his head still attached to his body.

"We should be near the sanctum," she whispered.

"Should be?"

"I did the best I could, okay?" She paused. "Can you see in the dark?"

"Not as well as Wren," Alaric admitted, squinting into the dense shadows. There was little to see. Just curved ceilings and walls coated in centuries of groundwater and gods knew what else. "If I knew where we were in relation to the sanctum, I might be able to get us there, but I have no idea where you dropped us."

Saoirse took his hand again, or rather, two of his fingers. "I can feel Ila. I will guide us there; just stop me before I walk into any walls, okay?"

The dreambreaker started forward, but Alaric stayed rooted on the spot. She paused, looking back at him inquisitively.

"What did you see?" Alaric asked.

"What?"

"I overheard you talking to Wren yesterday. You said you saw her in the future, at the center of a calamity. What did that mean?"

Her silence echoed through the tunnels, a visceral presence. "I wish I knew," Saoirse finally said. "All I know for sure is a feeling. Like the worlds want to spin out, and she is holding them together."

"She has to survive then, right?"

Saoirse did not respond. That was answer enough. She tugged on his hand again, guiding him forward. This time, he let her.

They walked in silence, guided by her intuition and his

eyes. He had forgotten how massive the catacombs were. When he was the Hand of the Para, he had never stopped to wonder what their original purpose was.

Now the thought chafed him for reasons he could not pinpoint.

All the while, his magic thrashed and shuddered in his chest, warning him of the danger all around them.

"Can I ask you something?" Saoirse asked after a time.

Alaric glanced down at her. He could not make out her expression, but her tone was tinged with embarrassment.

"Sure."

"Are you in love with Nightstrider?"

Alaric slowed his pace, blindsided. "Why would you ask that?"

"Because"—Saoirse hesitated—"I see the way you look at her. I was wondering if that was love."

"We barely know each other," Alaric replied. "Love takes time."

The words were a flimsy shield against the brunt of the truth. That looking at Wren, be she smirking or grinning or drenched in blood, was like the first spear of sunlight through a violent storm. That in only days she had worked her way under his skin, lodging herself firmly, infuriatingly, in the fabric of his soul.

"I see," Saoirse murmured. "I've spent most of my life either hiding or locked up. I've only really known a few people. I've never seen love—*that* kind of love—up close before. I want to know what it feels like."

"You will, someday, if that is what you want."

He could almost hear the melancholy in her voice when she responded. "That sounds nice."

Alaric scuffed to an abrupt stop, halting Saoirse. She tightened her grip on his fingers.

"What is it?" she whispered.

"Get behind me," he growled. "Someone's coming."

53
Ila

Ila was suspended somewhere between reality and oblivion. Whatever potion Caine had given her was a godsend. The pain had been dulled significantly, but with it, she had lost most of the sensation in her limbs. Her movements were sloppy, unsteady.

Caine half led, half carried her through the winding catacombs. His torch strained heroically against the encroaching darkness, but still, Ila could barely see three paces ahead.

She stumbled, doubling over with her mangled hand curled to her chest. She retched, vomiting nothing but acid.

"We have to keep moving," Caine whispered urgently. "We're close."

Ila could hear the lie in his words.

"Caine," she said in a hoarse voice. "You have to leave me."

"Never." Before she could protest, he switched the torch to his other hand and drew her good arm around his shoulders. As he heaved her upright, his words in the throne room burst to the front of her mind.

The Vaettir queen means nothing to me.

"I thought you betrayed me," she whispered as they started off again. "You were so . . ."

"Vile?" Caine smiled bitterly. Sweat had beaded on his brow. "I had a good teacher." When she did not respond, he continued. "I couldn't tell you what I was planning. It had to be believable."

"It was."

Caine was quiet. The silence let the pain rear its head, and so she kept talking as they rounded a corner.

"What about Saoirse?" Shredded cobwebs drooped from the ceiling, glinting like fresh snow in the torchlight. "What do you know?"

"Not much. I met Nightstrider just before I found you. She was here to save you, too."

I'm safe, Saoirse had said. *We're coming for you.*

She said *we*. Not *I*. In the midst of her torment, Ila had not picked up that detail. How long had Saoirse been with this 'mare? Why had Nightstrider come in her stead? Each question ignited ten more, but another wave of dizziness enveloped Ila, and all she could think of was not falling. Her vision slid from focus and her knees buckled.

"Whoa," Caine said, easing her to the floor and crouching beside her. "We have to keep moving."

"Rakk, just give me a minute," Ila wheezed.

Caine fell quiet, resting a hand on her back as her heaving breaths slowed. He glanced behind them periodically.

"The mark Nightstrider had on her chest, what does it mean?" Caine asked.

"It is a blessing. Different blessings have different purposes. I would have to examine it to know what it is for."

"You!"

Ila and Caine twisted in place. A torch bobbed in the distance, illuminating three armored figures coming straight at them. Swearing, the prince cast their own torch aside and shot to his feet, drawing the knife he had tucked into his belt.

One of the soldiers let out a thunderous battle cry. The ground rumbled and dust shook from the ceiling, but Caine held his ground. The faces of the soldiers drew into focus. They were almost human, but their skin was gray and appeared wet to the touch like some sort of salamander. Their expressions were twisted with sick glee.

"Ila!"

Time slowed to a crawl as the familiar voice punctured the gloam from the other direction. Ila turned in slow motion.

A name was called to her lips laced with terror and joy.

"Saoirse!"

"Get down!" a deep male voice bellowed.

Ila ducked on instinct. Caine threw his body over hers, shielding her from whatever was coming. A faint whistling skimmed over their heads followed by the unmistakable sounds of flesh ripping and bones crunching.

Then silence.

The queen raised her head cautiously.

All three soldiers were crumpled on the floor. Bolts of what appeared to be black diamond were lodged in their chests. As she watched, the shards began to disintegrate, leaving gaping holes behind. Caine got to his feet, one hand on her shoulder and the other palming the knife.

A pale blur shot out of the darkness, headed straight for her.

"Ila!"

Ila raised her injured hand above her head just before the child slammed into her. Dizzying pain roiled through her, but she scarcely felt it.

"Saoirse," she breathed. "Saoirse."

The child clung to Ila for dear life, her arms around her neck, her legs wrapped around her torso. Ila used her good hand to stroke her hair, rocking her back and forth on the floor.

Both trembled with quiet sobs.

"I thought I lost you," Ila said, pulling back to look Saoirse in the face. "I never should have sent you away."

Saoirse shook her head furtively, her curls shivering. The skin around her eyes and nose was pink from crying.

"It was the only way," the dreambreaker replied through sniffles. "You saved me; now I get to save you."

Movement out of the corner of her eye caused Ila to look up. She pulled Saoirse closer, still holding her broken hand aloft.

A man had appeared out of the darkness. He was a few inches taller than Caine with wild black hair and a lean, muscular build. Most notably, a set of notched black horns curled from his head.

Something told Ila that if she viewed him with her weaver sight, she would see a 'mare, but she was not afraid.

"You're Alaric," she said, less of a question and more of an observation.

"You two know each other?" Caine asked, glancing back and forth between them.

"Where is she?" the nightmare asked in a low voice.

The prince and the weaver locked eyes briefly.

"Who?" Caine inquired.

"Nightstrider. Where is she?"

Guilt flickered through Ila. Saoirse nestled closer to her, pressing her face into the space between her neck and shoulder.

"She freed me and helped us escape," Ila answered. "Para Warwick is there."

Alaric was off before she got out the last syllable, leaping over the bodies of the soldiers he felled and flickering out of sight.

"Ila," Saoirse said urgently, peeling back again to look her guardian in the face. Her eyes were wide and somber. "She is the one."

"What?"

"Nightstrider is the one I've seen in my dreams. The one at the center of everything."

Ila went still.

"Caine," Ila began, her voice distant to her own ears. "We have to go back."

The prince blinked. "Sorry?"

"We have to help Nightstrider."

"Absolutely not." His voice was as tense as his muscles, which strained visibly against his anger. "Look at yourself, Ila."

Ila motioned for Saoirse to get up. The girl scrambled to her feet and reached down to assist her. Holding her ruined hand out of the way, the queen rose haltingly and straightened.

The simple act nearly drained her.

"Do you remember what I told you the night I arrived in Wolfhelm?" she asked Caine.

"You said lots of things."

"I told you passivity was a deadly weapon. If we're passive now, if we let Nightstrider die, we're sealing the fate of the worlds." Ila glanced down at the dreambreaker, who bobbed her head encouragingly. "Saoirse sees a great cataclysm coming, and at the center of that event is—"

"Nightstrider," Saoirse finished.

"The future isn't written," Ila forged on. "If we allow her to die, the Wake and the Reverie may unravel."

"Para Warwick has her anchor," Saoirse said, turning to face Caine fully. The prince shifted in the face of her gaze, which Ila knew was often uncomfortably severe. "If we get it from him, we can save her."

"Gods help me," Caine muttered, looking up at the ceiling as if a god would reach down and pluck them from this snare. "Fine, I'll go back and help Nightstrider and her...whoever the hells that was."

"Alaric," Saoirse piped up helpfully.

"Sure. I'll go help them. You two get out of here."

"But—" Ila started to protest.

"You can barely stand."

"I'm not leaving."

Caine crossed to the queen and took her bloodied face in his hands. His eyes pinned her in place.

"I'm sorry, Ila," he said, his voice a mere whisper. "I would have taken your place a thousand times."

"Caine—"

"Your duty lies with Saoirse. Get out while you still can."

Before Ila knew what she was doing, she crushed her parched lips to his. He kissed her back, his hands falling to the small of her back to draw her closer. They broke apart, staring at each other.

"Caine," Ila began again. "I— Where is Saoirse?"

They sprung apart, spinning in useless circles in the withering light of the torches on the ground. Nothing but the dead vexes and their quivering shadows.

Saoirse was gone.

54
Wren

"I thought I had broken you. Yet, here you are."

Wren adjusted her grip on her knives, her only reply, as Para Warwick observed her from the center of the sanctum. His shadow flickered on the wall behind him, the spikes of the bone crown standing up like broken antlers.

"Nothing to say for yourself, Nightstrider?"

"Why?" she ground out.

The Para smiled insidiously. "You will have to be more specific."

"Why did you send me after the rebels if you already had the dreambreaker?" Her voice was steady though her insides writhed like maggots.

"You know why."

He was right, she realized. She did.

"To keep me away from her; to keep me in the dark. You knew I might try to steal her from you."

Para Warwick chuckled, resting a loving hand on the hilt of his broadsword. "Do you honestly think I would trust you with something as precious as the dreambreaker after your betrayal?"

"No, thank the gods." Wren spat at the floor. "I was sick of doing the things you were too much of a coward to do yourself."

The smirk sloughed off his face. Satisfaction knifed through Wren.

"Such a shame that luminae infected your mind," Para Warwick said flatly. "You were my most treasured creation. And now, sadly, my greatest disappointment."

Para Warwick thrust out a hand.

An invisible force slammed into Wren, throwing her into the far wall. Her vision went white when her head struck the stone, and her blades flew from her fingers. She landed in a garden of bones next to the place Queen Ila had been restrained. She tried to rise, but an omnipresent force pinned her down.

"Where is the dreambreaker?" the Para hissed, abruptly an inch from her. "Where is it?" A scream of raw agony tore from Wren when he snapped her forearm like a twig. "Are you really going to make me do this, Nightstrider?"

Wren looked up, her eyes as black and searing as his. A manic laugh bubbled from her mouth.

"You think you can torture this out of me?" She spat out a wad of blood. A glob of it landed on his nose, dripping down his lips. "You lost. There is nothing you can take from me that has not already been taken."

Para Warwick gritted his teeth. The force holding her down lifted temporarily.

"Perhaps," he said, wiping his mouth with the back of his arm. "But what if I were to take it again?"

The Para stepped aside. Wren felt her stomach bottom out.

Ondine was dressed in a black silk gown, her red hair wound into a severe knot. Spidery bruises crept up her neck. Her features were taut with pain. She stared down at Wren with passionless black eyes.

"How?" Wren breathed. "How are you here?"

"My uilebheistan found me," Ondine answered in a monotone. "And you—" She squatted to look Wren in the face, balancing on the balls of her feet. "You betrayed me. Again."

"Ondine, please."

A gleam welled in Ondine's void eyes. Wren's heart seized. She almost reached for her once lover. To apologize, to plead, she did not know.

But in the end, she was still.

"Souldrinker," the Para said lazily. "Begin."

Ondine pressed a hand to Wren's cheek. She squeezed her eyes shut. She could still feel Para Warwick leering down at her. A whimper escaped her as Ondine drew her soul to the surface of her body, pulling, tugging, teasing the fragile threads that bound it.

"Get away from her."

Wren snapped her eyes open. Ondine lurched to her feet and spun around. Para Warwick, too, turned to face the source of the new voice.

"*Bonehunter*," he breathed.

Wren rose haltingly. Neither Ondine nor Para Warwick moved to stop her, transfixed by the arrival of the revenant.

She skirted around them, her back against the wall as bones splintered beneath her boots.

Alaric stood at the entrance to the sanctum, dwarfed by the grand archway. His eyes were fully black from pupil to lid. Somehow, they were still warm when they met hers. Blades of his own making flashed in his hands.

"How?" the Para growled.

"Care to guess?"

"I destroyed your anchor. I burned it to ash." Para Warwick spat each word out like a broken tooth.

"Did you?" Alaric sneered. "I was wondering how you would finish the job."

Para Warwick laughed, but Wren heard the strain beneath it. "You always did know how to make an entrance, Bonehunter." He considered his traitorous creation. "Are you mortal, then?"

"Not in the slightest. I'm unanchored."

"A rare blessing, indeed. Unfortunately, Nightstrider is not so lucky."

Para Warwick struck Wren with another invisible wave of energy, this one pressing down on her from above. She crashed to her knees, swallowing a grimace.

Alaric raised one of his onyx blades, but Para Warwick clucked his tongue in a chastising manner. Wren kept her eyes locked straight ahead as the Para returned to her side and placed a hand on the top of her head as if he were about to crush her skull.

"Don't touch her," Alaric snarled.

The Para laughed like an out-of-tune violin. "You've done it again, Nightstrider. Wrapped another poor soul around your finger. Should we show him what happens to the people who get close to you?"

"Don't hurt him," Wren whispered.

"Begging again?" He bent down to press his lips to the curve of her ear. "I won't hurt him, not yet. This isn't about him."

Para Warwick stepped away from her. Wren opened her eyes to find Alaric staring at her, his entire body quivering with rage. She could smell the dark magic brewing just beneath his skin.

Run, she begged him silently. *Go.*

"Souldrinker has been working on a new trick," Para Warwick announced, his voice booming through the cavernous space. "She's going to show us what happened here a year ago."

Ondine approached Wren again. She rested a hand on her shoulder. Her expression was void, but a solitary tear rolled down her cheek.

"Ondine." Wren and Ondine both looked at Alaric. He had dissolved his blades and now held up his hands, a surrender and a plea. "Whatever you're about to do, you don't have to."

"You know I do," she said quietly.

Ondine tightened her grip on Wren.

The world was swallowed, and all of them with it.

They took her from her bed on the coattails of dawn.

It took six vexes to keep her pinned and two more to wrestle the skysteel cuffs onto her wrists. She pelted them with threats and obscenities as they dragged her through the vacant halls of Caer Sidi. Her nightshift was ripped from her back. The cold nipped her skin as they descended into the catacombs.

Somewhere between an eternity and an instant, they arrived in the sanctum. The vexes threw her to the floor unceremoniously. They departed as she got to her knees, naked and shivering.

By the light of a single torch, she glimpsed a figure tethered to the wall.

"Bram!"

Her voice roused him. His golden eyes flashed open.

"Wren! No!"

Bones scattered beneath him as he strained to reach her. She started to crawl toward him, but a kick to her spine sent her sprawling. A scream ripped from her throat when the boot came down on her knee, crushing it.

"You bastard!" Bram roared as the Para flipped Wren onto her back with the tip of his boot.

"Quiet," Para Warwick barked. Wren whimpered as he straddled her. "It seems a shame to mar such a divine creation. Perhaps we could have a bit of fun before—"

"Don't fucking touch her!"

"Should we make him jealous?" Para Warwick purred. "Or should we make you bleed? Or both, perhaps?"

Wren stiffened as he reached behind his back, expecting a blade. Instead, he produced a journal with crisp white pages.

"No!" Bram bellowed. "Please! Kill me!"

Para Warwick ignored him, letting the journal fall open in his hands. "Can you tell me what this says?" He turned the book over, holding it up for Wren to see. There was only one word on the page.

Nightstrider

"My name," Wren whispered.

"Say it for me."

"Nightstrider."

"Very good." He snapped the journal shut. She flinched beneath him. "Do you know what happens if I destroy this?"

"I—I die."

Para Warwick chuckled, shaking his head.

"Heartless creatures cannot die. You will be unmade. Unless . . ." His eyes drifted up to the luminae anchored to the wall.

"No," Wren breathed.

Para Warwick rose, straightening his velvet jacket. He drew a serrated blade from his belt and tossed it to the floor. Wren gasped when it clattered next to her head.

"Go to him," he ordered. Her muscles hardened like drying clay. "Now."

Shuddering, Wren rolled onto her stomach and picked up the knife. She no longer felt her shattered knee. She felt nothing. Not the cold, damp floor beneath her belly. Not the eyes of the Para on her back as she inched toward Bram.

Nothing.

When she reached him, he caught her with hands like the sun. His eyes held her, liquid gold or fields of wheat. Aching kindness. He smiled, pressing his hand to her chest. Warmth blossomed beneath his palm, spreading through her like a slow breath.

"You will live," he whispered.

"No."

"Yes." He guided the blade she held to his heart. The taut skin bowed beneath the sharp point.

"No!" Wren twisted in his grip, but he held her steady. The tip of the blade still hovered over his heart. "We go together."

"Wren, please." He pressed his brow to hers. "Please."

"No."

A match struck in the dim. Wren went still, eyes round with terror. The exposed skin of her abdomen began to itch and burn as if molting. She looked down to find a swath of skin erupting in blisters, smoking like a warpath, creeping up her chest.

Her mouth opened in a silent scream.

"I love you."

Bram jerked her forward, plunging the blade deep into his heart. Blood welled beneath the steel, bathing her numb hands. His fingers relaxed around her wrist. His eyes flickered shut, an eternal sunset. Wren crumpled, but a hand gripped her by the hair, forcing her to look up.

"Look what you've done. You've killed him."

55
Alaric

Souldrinker released them from the vision. The past dissolved like swiftly melting snow, and the sanctum slid back into view. Wren was folded forward, her forehead pressed to the floor and her hands over her ears. Ondine was rigid at her side, her expression stricken.

Para Warwick stood nearby, gloating.

"Do you understand now, Bonehunter?" Para Warwick taunted. "Why she despises herself so?"

"What I understand," Alaric replied, "is that irony is a bitch." Wren raised her head. Tears streaked her dirty cheeks. Despite the ache they caused him, he could not help but bark a grim laugh. "You don't know, do you?"

"Know what?" Para Warwick snapped.

"That you had a dreambreaker in your grasp a year ago. His name was Luken Bram Ehrenreich, and you killed him."

Satisfaction lanced through Alaric as the color drained from the Para's face. It was immediately snuffed when Wren let out a noise like a wounded animal.

Ondine shuffled away from her, guilt gnawing at her bruised face.

"Is that so?" Para Warwick murmured.

Had Alaric not spent a quarter of a century at his side, he would not have noticed the tightness at the corner of his mouth, the bulge of the vein at his temple. Even after all this time, his tells remained.

"That is a shame," the Para continued with forced indifference. "How fortunate that I have found a suitable alternate, then. I know she's here somewhere. I can feel her. Which brings me to my proposition."

The Para snapped his fingers, and a blue flame ignited in his palm. With his free hand, he pulled a journal from thin air. Alaric recognized it immediately from Ondine's illusion.

Wren shrank from her anchor.

"Ondine isn't the only one with new tricks," Alaric noted dryly.

Para Warwick moved the anchor closer to the hungry flame in his hand. "Tell me where the dreambreaker is, or I'll unmake her."

Alaric looked at Wren again. She stared up at him, pleading silently, but not for her life.

"Get on with it, then," Alaric said brusquely.

A hush settled over the sanctum. Wren was petrified save for the tears streaming down her face.

"She murdered my brother," Alaric pressed on, spitting out the words like chunks of glass. "She can die with him."

Para Warwick stared. So did Ondine, her pale arms loose against the dark flowing fabric of her gown. Wren was as still as the bones heaped around her.

Then the Para laughed, the unhinged sound ricocheting off the walls of the circular room.

"And here I thought you had lost your taste for blood." He heaved a disenchanted sigh. "So be it."

The Para opened the journal with an almost tender hand. The fire in his palm slithered down to it, coiling around the anchor.

Wren maintained eye contact with Alaric. There was no fear in her gaze, not anymore, only acceptance. A thousand unspoken words passed between them. Her anchor burst into flames.

Nightstrider closed her eyes.

The pages of her anchor were devoured, and still, she knelt.

The leather crisped and curled, and still, she knelt.

The wilted corpse of the journal tumbled to the floor. Para Warwick took a half step back, his mouth agape.

Wren opened her eyes.

She jerked the neckline of her tunic aside with her uninjured hand. Ondine gasped. Para Warwick snarled. Alaric smiled.

There, on the plane of skin over her heart, was the radiant handprint of a dreambreaker. This one did not belong to a child, nor did it blaze white. It was much larger and spilled golden light.

"Bram," Wren whispered.

"Luken," Alaric corrected patiently. "He was never a luminae. He was a dreambreaker. You may have held the knife, but you did not kill him." *Neither did I.* "It was Warwick. It was always Warwick."

Wren wavered for a split second, balancing on the edge of the truth and what she thought she knew. Then her teeth gnashed together. Dark matter flooded her bloodshot eyes.

Cradling her broken arm to her breast, she rose, unsheathing her last knife.

"Enough of this," Para Warwick barked. "Guards!"

Alaric conjured twin onyx blades. The thunder of militant footsteps rattled the cavernous room.

He darted to the center of the sanctum. Wren smashed into him, and they were back-to-back once more. Two streams of vex soldiers poured inside, skirting the walls to form a thick ring around Alaric and Wren and blocking the only exit. They were tougher than the average vex; he could tell by the thick smog of dark energy that billowed from them. They would not be as easy to kill as the lowlifes in the Widow's Pass.

Para Warwick and Ondine slipped behind the soldiers like snakes through tall grass.

"Any ideas?" Wren asked Alaric over her shoulder.

"Try not to die."

"Guards," Para Warwick bellowed, his deep voice arching to fill the subterranean space. "On my mark!"

Swords scraped from scabbards. Arrows were nocked. Axes were raised.

Wren and Alaric were flush against each other, pulses sprinting and breathing shallow.

It would not be so bad, he thought. To meet his end with her pressed against him.

"It was an honor," Wren said. "To fight by your side."

"I wish I could have taught you to dance."

Alaric could not help but smile when a bewildered laugh thrummed through her body. "Maybe in another life."

"Three," Para Warwick called. "Two—"

Alaric tightened his grip on his weapons, sizing up the vex directly opposite him. Wren shifted against his back, feathers rustling with restless energy. He would not go down without a fight, and neither would she.

"STOP."

Wren and Alaric stiffened as a high youthful voice pierced the silence.

"Saoirse," Wren breathed.

56

Caine

The crossbow Caine had lifted off one of the dead soldiers was slick with sweat, and he struggled to keep a grip on it as he and Ila raced back through the catacombs in search of Saoirse.

Ila's footsteps and breathing were irregular. He knew the only things keeping her moving were the tonic and the adrenaline, and both would give out soon. Still, she managed to keep pace with him and hold their torch aloft with her working hand.

A distant rumbling shook dust from the ceiling. Footsteps, dozens of them, accompanied by the unmistakable clang of armor.

Caine and Ila slid to a stop in the middle of the tunnel. The weaver tossed their light into a puddle of murky water, drowning them in shadow. The babel dissolved into stony silence.

Then a voice came out of the blackness.

"Guards! On my mark!"

Shit.

Ila and Caine took off again before the echo of the Para's voice faded. Their boots splashed through foul water and gods knew what else. They rounded a sharp corner. Orange light cracked the darkness ahead.

The sanctum.

Caine pushed himself harder, faster. Ila trailed behind him, wheezing.

"Three."

The arched entrance to the sanctum expanded ahead, studded with the silhouettes of armed guards.

"Two."

Caine nocked an arrow into the chamber of his crossbow, still running flat out. Ila was fading behind him, her steps stumbling.

The prince slid to a stop fifty paces from the entrance to the sanctum and raised his weapon, staring down the flight shaft at one of the soldiers silhouetted in the archway. He exhaled, willing his hands to be steady. His finger curled around the trigger.

Ila limped into view beside him.

"STOP."

Caine released the trigger and looked over at Ila. He could just make out the profile of her bloody face in the light creeping from the sanctum ahead. It was not the queen who had spoken but someone with a childlike voice and a distinct singsong accent.

"I wondered when you would arrive, dreambreaker," Para Warwick said from inside the sanctum. His form was hidden by the wall of guards.

"Let them go," Saoirse ordered, her voice as smooth as the tide. "Take me instead."

"No!" someone shouted. *Nightstrider.* "Get out of here, kid!"

"Someone shut her up," Para Warwick commanded. Caine could almost hear him rolling his eyes. There was a scuffle from inside the room, and Nightstrider was silenced with a muffled *mmfph*. Another shout of anger, then a second voice was silenced. *The other nightmare, Alaric.* "The dreambreaker and I have much to discuss."

"Let them go, and I'll give you what you want," Saoirse bargained.

Ila flinched.

"Such bravery." The Para chuckled, condescension dripping from his tone. "If only courage could save you."

Ila started to march forward, but Caine caught her by the elbow and hauled her back.

"Not yet," he muttered in her ear.

"Do you know what this is?" Chills erupted on his skin when the unmistakable sound of a sword being drawn rang out. Ila gripped him by the arm, her fingernails digging into his skin. When Saoirse failed to respond, Para Warwick continued. "This is Oathflayer. Can you guess what it is forged of?"

"I don't need to," Saoirse replied tersely.

"Then you understand what it does and what I want from you."

"You have to let my friends go first."

"Friends?" Para Warwick clucked his tongue. "These two disgraceful nightmares? Such company you keep, little one."

"They're more than they seem," Saoirse replied. "Just like you. Isn't that right, *dreambreaker*?"

Silence erupted in the wake of her words. Caine looked to Ila, perplexed. Shock warped her features. Her grip loosened on his arm.

The prince reeled back to his conversation with Morthil at the inn when he had asked about crossing the Boundary.

Has there ever been a para who could leave the Reverie?

None that we knew of before Para Warwick.

"What is this?" Para Warwick demanded.

"I see you, Warwick Fallon," Saoirse continued in a voice that seemed to rattle the very foundation of Caer Sidi. "I see your soul. Your weaver heart—your *human* heart. Your luminae blood."

"Enough of this! Seize her!"

"You're mortal!" Saoirse shrieked over the shuffle of footsteps and the clank of metal. "You're just pretending to be a para, stealing magic to make yourself more powerful, but you will never have what you want most! You'll never be *immortal*!"

A shout of fear, small and broken.

Ila bolted, streaking toward the sanctum like the north wind, seemingly oblivious to her condition, to the wall of soldiers blocking the sanctum entrance.

She won't make it.

Cold focus claimed Caine as the revelation took root in him. He let his crossbow clatter to the floor. Closing his eyes, he tipped back his head and raised his palms to the ceiling.

It was not something he had been taught to do.

It was what instinct demanded.

Come.

A noise like the howl of a war horn knifed through the catacombs. Pressure mounted from all sides, but it was no longer painful. It clung to Caine like armor.

Splinters slithered around him, whispering, watching, waiting.

Second . . . born . . .

Shadow . . . spinner . . .

"Go," he commanded.

The splinters exploded forward, snaking around Ila harmlessly and shooting into the sanctum. Screams of terror flew up as the torches on the walls were extinguished. The guards standing at the mouth of the chamber scattered, crashing into one another in their mad scramble to escape.

Fever and bloodlust like he had never felt ripped through Caine. He grabbed his crossbow off the floor and raced after the splinters.

57
Wren

The splinters descended on the sanctum with a bone-chilling moan. The torches died in waves. Wren felt her mind snap into brutal focus. She ripped her mouth from the gloved hand of the huge vex who had been trying valiantly to keep her subdued.

"Saoirse!" she shouted.

Wren drove the elbow of her good arm into the nose of the vex. He stumbled back as the ravenous splinters dove to devour him. She turned in a frantic circle, scanning desperately for Alaric and Saoirse, both of whom she had lost track of in the chaos.

Even with her keen vision, she could barely see through the curtain of half-remembered dreams. The air was growing thin, but for whatever reason, the splinters did not seem to have any interest in her. They wove between her legs and looped around her waist in search of other meals.

"Wren!"

Alaric slammed into her, gripping her by the shoulders.

Blinding pain tore through her broken arm as the winds rose around them.

"We have to find Saoirse!" she bellowed.

Shards of white light sliced through the gloom.

Wren broke away from Alaric and hurtled through the hurricane of splinters, a desperate hand stretched out before her.

"Saoirse!"

Wren skidded to a halt, shielding her eyes with her forearm.

Saoirse hovered at the heart of the sanctum, her toes six inches off the floor. Her eyes were fully white. Her hands were cupped before her as if to cradle a bird, but in her palms was a sphere of pulsing energy that matched her gaze.

"Kid!" Wren shouted, inching toward her. It was like walking headlong into a gale. "What are you doing?"

"Saoirse!"

Ila had arrived beside Wren. She was white as ash.

"Min sterjn!" she screamed.

"Ila." Saoirse turned her face to her guardian in midair, bobbing up and down as if suspended by a gentle tide. A melancholic smile curled her lips. "I'm glad you are here."

"Let it go, Saoirse," Ila implored her, offering her good hand to the child. "Whatever you're making, let it go!"

Making, Wren thought wildly.

"This is the only way." Her blank eyes fell to the globe in her palms. Tracks of tears raced down her round cheeks. They were faintly luminous against her skin. "I wish there was another."

"Saoirse," Wren tried. "We have to go."

"Nightstrider." Saoirse turned her boundless gaze on Wren. Foreboding cut through the winged 'mare. "Luken sacrificed his life to save yours. Don't waste it. All of this will make sense someday, I swear."

Confusion and anger surged in Wren. She snatched Saoirse by the elbow and yanked her down from the air. Ila shouted in fear. A shock wave ripped through Wren, through the room, as Saoirse lost her grip on the knot of energy.

Wren drew the dreambreaker into an embrace and crashed to her knees, shielding the child as the splinters scattered with a blistering screech.

Silence.

Wren lifted her head, still holding Saoirse, peering around the sanctum as, one by one, the torches reignited.

Shells of vexes littered the floor, their souls snatched, their skin sapped of moisture. Their mouths were locked in eternal screams. A stone-faced Prince Caine stood in the entrance, a crossbow on his shoulder, as he watched the splinters phase through the walls.

Alaric approached Wren and Ila—battered but very much alive. It appeared the splinters had somehow missed the lot of them. Even better, Para Warwick was nowhere to be seen. Relief flowed through Wren, guttering briefly when she realized Ondine was gone, too.

"Nightstrider," Saoirse mumbled, stirring against her.

"Saoirse." Wren took her small face in her hands though her broken arm screamed in protest. "You're okay."

Alaric stepped in front of Wren, who still knelt on the sanctum floor. The black matter had receded from his eyes, revealing warm brown. She knew it had bled from her eyes, too. He stretched down a hand for her to take.

Wren reached for it, but a weight on her shoulder pulled her back to the floor. A cold wind caressed her back. Hot breath traced the curve of her ear.

"Good night, Nightstrider."

Crunch.

Saoirse went rigid, still clinging to Wren like a life raft.

Alaric froze, horror morphing his features.

Wren looked down.

A blade cut straight through her middle and disappeared somewhere in Saoirse's stomach. Wren's lips parted in a soundless cry.

The child looked up at her with achingly human eyes, a tiny smile quivering on her mouth.

"Don't worry," Saoirse said softly. "I always knew."

The blade was drawn from them, sliding through the caverns of their bodies. Blood welled from their twin wounds. Somewhere far away, someone was screaming.

Wren slumped to the side, dragging Saoirse with her.

The last thing she saw before the darkness claimed her were the eyes of a child already clouded with oblivion.

58
Alaric

The world narrowed until there was nothing but her. Wren collapsed on the floor, her blood finding the cracks in the flagstone. Her eyelids closed over flickering black voids and she went still. Painfully still. Why was she so still?

Saoirse was curled beside her. Her eyes were partially closed, revealing only a sliver of lusterless green.

A terrible scream broke Alaric from his stupor. Ila cascaded to the floor, dragging Saoirse into her lap. Her head lolled to the side, her lips parting to reveal a missing front tooth.

Slowly, as if his muscles were steeped in tar, Alaric raised his head.

Para Warwick stood over their bodies. His black sword, Oathflayer, dripped with their blood. He smiled, waiting, and Alaric understood.

Oathflayer was forged of pier glass.

"You bastard."

The words came from Alaric's mouth, but they sounded

nothing like him. They were raw with grief and rage, almost animalistic.

The Para—the *dreambreaker*—chuckled. He gave Oathflayer a careless flick, speckling Wren and Saoirse with their own blood. Ila hunched over the body of the child, rocking her back and forth and murmuring in Vaettirin.

"In my youth, I found it strange no one questioned my ability to pass between realms." Para Warwick sheathed his blade without cleaning it. "As time passed, I began to understand that people see what they want to see. No one wants to believe a dreambreaker could be brutal, just as no one wants to believe a 'mare could be sentimental. They crave consistency, simplicity, and order."

"Is this what you call order?" Alaric ground out.

Warwick laid a hand on the hilt of his sword. "You're in no place to judge me, Bonehunter."

"Why do you think I left?"

"Ah yes. The kip child. What was her name?" Para Warwick shook his head almost pityingly. "Did you really think I would let her live, just because you were too weak to finish the job?"

Alaric did not have time to respond or even to let horror snare him. Burgeoning light drew his attention to the floor. Queen Ila sat up, hope shining through the dried blood on her round features.

Saoirse was still, but something stirred deep inside her body, a radiant coil of power.

"Yes," Para Warwick breathed, greed swelling in his black gaze. "Come to me."

The radiance grew within Saoirse, blotting out the dark stain on her sweater. Ila, realizing what was happening, unraveled into hiccupping sobs. Alaric felt his eyes go black. He switched them to Wren. She had not moved, though blood still ran from her wound.

Fight, he wanted to scream.

This could not be what took her. Not when she had survived so much. Not when she was finally free.

Not when they were only just beginning.

Something whistled past his ear.

Alaric looked up in time to see the arrow lodge itself in the chest of the false para. The boy from the catacombs stepped up to stand beside Alaric, his crossbow raised and his eyes pinned to his target. The line of his jaw and the shape of his nose were familiar.

Prince Caine.

"You're mortal," the prince said, nocking another arrow. "That means I can kill you."

Warwick smiled. The air around him rippled with power.

"Would you care to try, son?" he asked, breaking the arrow off in his chest and tossing it aside. It clattered against the floor and rolled into a nearby heap of bones.

"My whole life, I've stood by and watched while you killed and conquered." Caine was pallid, but his hands were steady. "No more."

He squeezed the trigger and fired another arrow. This one, the dreambreaker caught between his thumb and forefinger.

"Your resolve is admirable." Warwick let the arrow fall. "But I'm afraid I have no time for your antics."

Caine nocked another arrow, stubborn and bitterly determined.

"Saoirse—"

All eyes fell to Ila, who still knelt with the child in her lap. The white light trapped in Saoirse had left her body, curling into the air like lazy tendrils of smoke. Para Warwick laughed, unhinged.

"You wanted to bear witness to my true power, Caine. Now you have the chance."

"No," Ila whispered. "Look."

Time was suspended as the ribbons of magic pouring from Saoirse swooped to envelope Wren. The nightmare's skin began to glow. Subtle at first, but steadily brighter. Brighter.

Alaric shielded his eyes with his hand. The sanctum began to shudder, rattling the garden of bones and the chains on the walls. Screams erupted as they were drowned in blinding light.

All at once, the radiance contracted, condensing to an impossibly small point deep in the hollows of Wren's broken body.

Her eyes flew open.

They blazed white.

Wren sprang to her feet and snapped her wings out, launching herself into the air. Power crackled her fingertips. Para Warwick let out a roar that should have cracked the sanctum in half.

When Wren spoke, her voice echoed threefold.

"True power cannot be stolen," she said, gathering a knot of snapping energy in the palm of her hand. "Only earned."

Wren raised her arm and brought it down in a swift arc.

A bolt of blistering energy erupted from her palm, streaking toward her creator. There was a deafening bang as another shock wave swept through the room. Alaric grabbed Caine by the elbow and jerked him back as chunks of the ceiling began to rain down on them.

Then stillness claimed the sanctum.

"Ila!" Caine shouted, tearing free of his grasp in the haze of dust and debris. His entire body was bathed in white powder. "Ila, where are you?"

The prince plunged into the roiling dust. Alaric stayed rooted on the spot, gazing around the destroyed room.

A massive, blackened crater marked the place Para Warwick once stood. His body was nowhere to be seen. There was no blood.

He's still alive, Alaric thought grimly.

He craned his neck backward.

Wren still floated at the peak of the sanctum, her wings sending little stirs of air sizzling with chaotic energy through the room. The aftermath of whatever she had done. The blazing light in her eyes flickered out. Her lids drooped shut.

She dropped like an anchor to the bottom of the sea.

59

Caine

Caine spun in time to see Alaric catch Nightstrider before she hit the floor. Her body was limp in his arms, her eyes closed. The prince whipped back around, still searching for Ila in the field of rubble.

His father was nowhere to be seen.

Relief surged in Caine when he spotted Ila kneeling among the chunks of fractured stone, her head bowed. Leaping over the body of a splinter-drained soldier, Caine raced over to her and crouched beside her.

Ila stared dead ahead with blank eyes. She, like everything, was robed in dust. In her arms was Saoirse. Her skin was gray, her tiny face unbearably still.

"Ila." Caine pressed the flat of his hand to her back. She did not react.

"Caine."

Caine looked over his shoulder to find Alaric standing behind him, a still-unconscious Nightstrider in his arms. Dust crowned his dark hair. Her blood stained his hands and shirt.

"We have to go."

"Ila," Caine murmured.

"No!" she yelped, hunching over the body of the child. "No, we can't leave her!"

"Ila—"

"We have to bury her!"

"If we stay here, we die," Caine said. "Saoirse would have wanted you to live."

Silent sobs rippled through her body as Ila clutched the body closer. She pressed her cheek to her pallid brow, rocking her and singing in a near whisper. It was the same sort of song she had woven in the sanctum in Wolfhelm—wordless, yet full of meaning. This one was wrought of grief, and it cut Caine deeper than any blade ever could.

He could feel Alaric staring, could feel time slipping through their fingers. Swallowing, he reached for Ila again.

She kissed Saoirse on the forehead and released her, laying her down in a bed of dust. Slowly, arduously, Ila rose. Caine offered his hand, but she limped past him.

He took one last look at Saoirse. Her eyes were still partly open. He bent down to close them.

"I'm sorry," he told her.

The glint of metal from inside her fist caught his eye. Caine took her hand in his and uncurled her small fingers. A silver necklace with a round pendent the size of a coin was nestled in her palm. He lifted it by its long chain. The metal links were warm, as if they were just forged, and tiny silver ornaments dangled from the spherical pendent.

"Caine," Alaric barked from across the sanctum.

"Sol liv hjent warren," he whispered to Saoirse, arranging her hands so that they covered the mortal wound at her center and brushing the hair from her face. He pocketed the necklace and followed his companions.

☽○☾

The journey through the catacombs was a blur. Alaric barreled ahead with unfettered determination. Despite carrying Nightstrider, who Caine could not imagine was especially light, he constantly urged him and Ila to go faster.

The queen did not speak. When Caine moved to assist her, she sidestepped away, refusing to meet his eyes. After a time, Caine stopped trying.

They did not meet any soldiers, despite occasionally hearing shouts from deep within the labyrinth. They were probably searching for the Para, though Caine supposed the title no longer suited him.

King. Father. Para. Dreambreaker. Monster. His title did not matter if he was dead, though Caine had not seen a body in the crater Nightstrider made in the sanctum floor. Perhaps he had been incinerated.

The writhing in Caine's gut suggested otherwise.

It was snowing when they exited the catacombs through the storm drain that dumped into the Tanglewood. Large clumps of flakes drifted to the ground with mocking tranquility.

Everything was bathed in the bluish predawn light.

They walked until the triplet moons dipped below the horizon and the sun started to show its face. Until all Caine knew was the sound of their boots crunching snow and the exhaustion that ate at him.

When they finally arrived at the base of a hill, he was on the verge of passing out. Caine lifted his head, squinting in the pale dawn. A disbelieving smile cracked the frozen muscles of his face.

They had arrived back at Morthil's inn.

"Keep moving," Alaric said, adjusting his grip on Nightstrider with a grunt. She was wrapped in his jacket, leaving him with nothing but his tunic.

They trudged up the snowbound hill. This time, Ila allowed Caine to assist her, ensuring she did not fall on her shattered hand. Caine approached the front door of the inn, but Alaric shook his head and led them around back. Firewood was stacked high against the side of the building.

Alaric jerked his chin at the back door varnished with peeling red paint. Caine stepped up to the threshold and knocked with chapped knuckles.

A pause. Then it opened.

"Caine." Morthil was dressed in a loose sleep shirt and drawstring pants, his feet bare. "Alaric, Ila." His white eyes widened as he took in their party. "Gods, what happened?"

"We'll explain later," Alaric promised in a strained voice. He heaved Nightstrider higher. "Please."

Morthil ushered them inside. Caine took Ila by the hand and pulled her across the threshold, making way for Alaric and Nightstrider. Morthil led them through the tidy kitchen to a cellar door that blended perfectly with the stone floor.

He opened it with a creak of old hinges and started down the steps.

Alaric trailed after him with Nightstrider. The wooden stairs groaned with each step they descended. A match flared below. Caine motioned for Ila to go first, then followed her underground.

The cellar was surprisingly spacious. A large woven rug covered most of the dirt floor. Two cots heaped in quilts squatted on the right. Opposite them was a chest, a small table topped with a pair of lanterns, and a threadbare armchair.

Morthil lit a second lantern as Alaric lay Nightstrider on one of the beds, smoothing her hair from her face. Caine guided Ila to the chair. She had gone from quiet to vacant. Morthil leaned over her, swearing when he saw the state of her hand.

"Gods," he breathed. "Who did this?"

"Can you fix it?" Caine asked urgently.

"Yes," Morthil answered, but he could not miss the hesitation in his voice. "I'll get her something for the pain."

Morthil disappeared back up the stairs. Caine looked on in silence as Alaric undid the clasps on Nightstrider's jacket and lifted her blood-drenched tunic. A white scar ran across her abdomen, and her skin was smeared with blood, but the stab wound from the pier glass sword had disappeared without a trace.

"How?" Alaric skimmed the place the gash had been only hours ago with his fingertips.

Morthil reappeared with a wooden box in hand. He set

it on the table and opened it to reveal a surgical kit, bandages, and dozens of tiny glass bottles filled with herbs and tonics.

"This will take time," he said, aiming his words at Ila. "It will be painful."

"Don't worry," Ila replied, letting her head fall back against the cushioned armchair. "You can't hurt me."

60

Ila

Morthil spent hours on her hand alone. He gave her a sedative in a cup of tea that rendered her half conscious and partially numb. In truth, that was not far from her natural state. Ila watched through a veil of fog as the luminae meticulously set the delicate bones of her fingers. Every now and then, a shard of agony would pierce her. In those moments, Caine was there to hold her steady until she melted into oblivion again.

When Morthil finally braced her last finger and cleaned the puncture wounds on her arms, face, and chest, Caine helped her from the chair and led her to the unoccupied cot.

She closed her eyes.

Next thing she knew, Ila was on her back with several quilts tucked around her. Her hair and skin were sticky with cold sweat. Her hand throbbed through the layers of bandages. The murmur of low voices drew her mind into focus.

"...had a dreambreaker on the throne all these years," Morthil was saying. "I never thought such a being could be so cruel."

"Mica says the lines we draw between dream beings are rarely as stark as they seem." Ila matched the baritone with Alaric.

"Warwick isn't some sniveling vex with a sentimental side. He's a monster. You know that better than anyone."

"I know." There was a pause racked with tension. "All these years, he's been mortal. I could have killed him countless times. Now we might be too late. He's stealing magic from other dreambreakers, and gods know who else."

"He didn't get *her* magic, though."

Morthil did not have to say her name to put a spear through Ila's heart.

"No, he didn't," Alaric agreed.

"But someone else did," Ila said.

She heaved herself into a sitting position with her good hand, ignoring the groan of her muscles.

Morthil and the nightmare, Alaric, looked up at her from across the dim cellar. The luminae sat on the rug with his back against the wall. Alaric occupied the chair. Besides a few cuts and bruises, he did not appear to be seriously injured. Lying on the other cot was Nightstrider, her eyes closed and her body still as death.

"Ila," Morthil said, getting to his feet. "How are you feeling?"

Ila ignored him, focusing on the infamous winged nightmare. Morthil and Alaric protested as she shoved back her covers and scooted to the edge of the mattress, leaning over Nightstrider across the narrow aisle between their cots. She peeled back the blankets and lifted her tunic.

An old scar was sprawled across her muscled abdomen, but there was no sign of the stab wound.

Just as Ila thought.

"Why is she like this?" Alaric asked in a strained voice.

"She's going through a metamorphosis." Ila spoke in a lifeless monotone she did not recognize. "When Warwick stabbed"—she choked on the name—"when Warwick stabbed them, Nightstrider absorbed the power he intended to steal. The power of a dreambreaker."

"But how?" Morthil pressed.

Ila grasped her bedsheets with her working fingers, squeezing until they started to hurt.

"Saoirse blessed Nightstrider. She knew. She knew she was going to die, and she needed a vessel for her power."

All at once, the air was too thin, her body too heavy. Ila raised a trembling hand to her lips as bile pooled in her mouth. Distantly, she heard Alaric say something to Morthil. Moments later, someone sat down beside her.

"Ila."

Caine.

The truth came in an avalanche.

"I lost her," she breathed. "Hoste, I lost her. I promised her I w-would protect her. I s-sent her here. I left her alone. This is my fault. This is all my fault."

"Shhh..."

"We never should have left Galesborough; we should have stayed. She could have been safe."

Caine eased her head onto his thighs, smoothing her tangled hair from her eyes.

"You are not to blame," he told her. "You are not to blame."

Her tear ducts were empty, but her body still wanted to cry. Dry sobs racked her, sending shudders through her and Caine. He rocked her until her tremors subsided, until she knew nothing but the gentle motion. Until there was nothing left in her but a voice, sweet and sure.

Sol liv hjent warren, Ila.

61
Wren

Wren knew she was dreaming.

Her bare feet did not leave impressions in the snow as she walked. She could not see the sun, but she could feel it watching her as she crossed the tundra. She did not know where she was headed, only that she could not stop. Something drew her forward, tugging at her soul with gentle insistence.

A city bled into view on the horizon. Gleaming, churning, pulsing with indomitable life. Wren picked up the pace, but the faster she went, the more it receded. Dismay washed over her as the city was lost over the horizon. Finally, she came to a halt.

That was when the sky cracked in half.

Wren was thrown onto her back by the shock wave that followed, skidding across the faultless ground.

Half the sky was swallowed by the silver sun, the day bringer she could never hide from. Cold, distant, unyielding. The other half was scorched with the heavenly fire of the Wake. The giants began to drift toward one another, steel and liquid gold.

Their rays embraced like lovers, and they ignited.

Wren was ash before she could scream.

☽○☾

Wren jolted awake. The world weighed heavily on her eyelids. The air was warm, almost too warm, and smelled of earth and embers. Someone had tucked a quilt up to her chin. A faint murmur became a familiar voice.

"She did not ask for this," Alaric said.

"Neither did Saoirse," a female voice returned.

"None of us asked for this," another male voice cut in. "But whatever happens, I'm going."

"Going where?"

Alaric, Caine, and Ila looked around at Wren as she sat up with a groan. She glanced around suspiciously.

They appeared to be in some sort of cellar. The walls, floor, and ceiling were all made of smooth earth. Ila sat in an armchair, her shattered hand now set and wrapped in clean bandages. Caine leaned up against one of the walls with his arms folded. Alaric perched on the edge of a table.

All three had bathed and wore fresh clothes.

"Nightstrider," Ila greeted her in a stiff voice. She had a row of stitches under one of her eyes. The loathing in her expression was undercut by her palpable grief, a fraction of which squeezed Wren's own chest at the thought of Saoirse.

"She prefers—" Alaric started to tell the weaver.

"Call me what you want," Wren said, cutting him off.

Silence in the little room. Wren felt three sets of eyes on her as she took stock of her body. She had been dressed in a clean white tunic and drawstring pants several sizes too big. Her broken arm had been set and did not pain her. She pressed her hand to the flat of her stomach but did not need to see it to know there was no wound there. It was as if it had all been a dream.

A nightmare.

"How long was I out?" Wren asked no one in particular.

"Three days," Alaric answered. He rose and moved to sit beside her on the cot, leaving a finger length of space between them. It might as well have been a league.

"What happened?"

"Warwick stabbed Saoirse through you with a pier glass sword," Ila answered in a toneless voice. "Her power went into you instead because of the blessing she imparted."

Wren brought her hand to her heart. The blessing was gone. So was the one Bram gave her. Her eyes flooded. Her throat constricted. She swallowed thickly, fighting encroaching panic at the prospect of crying in front of Alaric again.

"Could you two give us a moment, please?" the horned nightmare asked quietly.

Caine and Ila shared a glance, then migrated up the wooden steps, the prince supporting her on her good arm. A squeak of hinges ushered in silvered daylight, but it was quickly blocked by the thud of the cellar door.

"Wren—"

"I'm so sorry," Wren whispered. Fat tears bloomed in her vision as she stared at her thighs, unable to look him in the eye. "Bram—*Luken*—he was your best friend, your brother, and I killed him. I'm so sorry."

"No, Wren, I am." Her watery gaze snapped to Alaric.

He still did not touch her, but his eyes were full of a softness she had only seen once before. "For everything you endured because of my choices."

"You could not have known he would create me."

"Perhaps." He reached out with a knuckle and wiped a tear from her cheekbone. "But selfishly, I'm glad to know you, and I'm glad you're here."

"You—you don't hate me?"

"Never."

Wren made a sound between a laugh and a sob. Alaric smiled. A brief hesitation, then he slipped an arm around her waist. She let him pull her closer, let her head sag onto his shoulder as she had that first night of their journey. His heartbeat hummed against her skin, his now-familiar scent itself a balm.

"What happens now?" she asked after a time.

"Assuming the worst—"

"Obviously."

"Warwick survived whatever the fuck you did to him."

"He survived," Wren said, surprised by the certainty in her own voice. "I can feel it."

"He'll be looking for us, for you. Morthil suggests we head for Marrowrun."

Wren pulled away from Alaric, her brow furrowed. "Marrowrun." The image of the shining city beneath the colliding suns flared in her mind. Not quite a memory, not quite a dream. Was it Marrowrun? She had never seen the city before, not even from a distance. "Why?"

Alaric arched a brow. "They call it the free city for a reason."

"We should go farther. Past the Known Regions." When Alaric did not respond, she narrowed her eyes. "There's something else, isn't there?"

"Apparently, Ila has a friend in Marrowrun, an exiled weaver with more experience than her. She thinks she can help you hone your gifts."

"My gifts," Wren repeated blankly. She pressed her hand to her stomach again, feeling for a wound that was not there. The image of Saoirse slumped on the sanctum floor, lifeless, flickered in her memory. "I don't want them."

"I know." Alaric pulled her close again as if to shield her from her own thoughts. For reasons she had yet to unravel, she let him. It felt inexplicably natural. "But Saoirse chose you for a reason."

"Do you think she made a mistake?"

"No." It was hard not to be swayed by the confidence in his voice.

"And if I told you I wanted to run away and never look back, would you come with me?"

"Yes."

Wren shifted to look Alaric full in the face again. His eyes were home to the sort of warmth that could only exist in darkness, like soft flames against the night. "And if I told you I wanted to fight, to destroy Warwick and take back what was stolen from us, would you stay by my side?"

"Does this mean I don't have to kill you?"

A tiny smile unfurled on her mouth. Wren's heart bloomed with wrath.

"Not today."

EPILOGUE

Wren

They rose before dawn. Most of the snow had melted during the five days they spent in the cellar, revealing ugly brown grass. The sky was powdered blue and violet, and the clouds had pooled in the valley below.

Wren's borrowed horse shifted beneath her and whickered, restless. She scratched behind his ears. She kept her sights on the smudged horizon as Alaric arrived at her side astride his own mount.

"How are you?" he asked.

"Next person who asks me that gets a broken nose."

Alaric chuckled. She tossed him a look. He wore a heavy dark cowl, the hood thrown back to reveal his horns and wild hair.

"Hate to break it to you, but this is what happens when somebody gives a shit about you."

Wren scoffed but couldn't deny the inexplicable lightness that filled her chest. The feeling did not last long because her companion spoke again.

"At the risk of a broken nose—"

"I'm fine, baker."

It was not wholly a lie, but it was far from the truth.

Her fractured arm and other injuries had healed, but the power Saoirse blessed—or cursed—her with was a storm at her center. It rattled and squalled, scarcely contained by the bars of her rib cage.

It felt like the seed of a wildfire, her body a forest in a drought.

Movement to her left hooked her gaze. Caine and Ila brought their horses to a halt beside her.

The prince looked well enough, but the weaver was another story. Morthil, who Wren had quickly grown to like over the course of their stay in his cellar, had done a fine job tending her injuries, but he could not mend the hollowness behind her eyes. Wren had seen it before, mostly in soldiers haunted by war.

"How far is Marrowrun?" Caine asked no one in particular. He had a crossbow slung across his back.

"A fortnight, if we're lucky," Alaric responded. "And assuming we're not murdered along the way."

Caine sighed. "Fantastic."

Wren brought her eyes to the horizon again. The wind lifted, stirring her hair and feathers. Dawn was breaking. Soon, it would scatter the fog pooled in the valley below. Her fingers tightened around the reins as the image of the silver and gold suns colliding eclipsed her thoughts.

"Are you ready, Nightstrider?"

She looked around to find Alaric watching her. There was a

certain stillness in his expression, but there was also a hunger. The same hunger that stirred within her, deeper even than the new coil of volatile power. For revenge, yes, but something more. Something ancient and arcane. She did not have a name for it yet, but it did not matter.

She was unanchored, and she would chase it across the worlds.

The story continues in . . .

Veilweaver

Book TWO of Nightstrider

ACKNOWLEDGMENTS

Adam—you are golden, my love. Absolutely, incorruptibly good to the core. I keep waiting for the honeymoon stage to wear off, but it never does. You light up every room of my heart. You make the bad days better and the good days brilliant. I could not write a better partner if I tried. Ráhkistan du eambo go ovttage eará.

Mom—how many people can say that they had a parent who supported their artistic dreams with such fervor? You are my biggest cheerleader, my most honest critic, and an outstanding first editor. I never would have made it this far without you.

Dad—you are my rock. My safe place to land. Thank you for introducing me to music and art so young. Thank you for reading every single one of my books even though they could not be further from your taste.

Stephanie—I cannot even begin to explain how grateful I am for your warmth, patience, and exhaustive efforts as my editor. I am so lucky our paths collided and cannot wait to keep working together.

Bethany—you are a rock star. Reaching out to you for representation was one of the best decisions I ever made as an author, and I am beyond grateful to have you in my corner. Thank you for championing my work, for guiding me, and for calming me down when I need it, and we both know I need it.

The Orbit team—you are all lovely, talented humans, and I am so deeply grateful for your efforts in bringing this book to life.

Lili—thank you for your efforts ensuring my BIPOC characters did not stumble into any harmful tropes or stereotypes. I deeply appreciate both your candor and your warmth.

My friends—Allie, Belle, the Lovely Fantastic Amis, the Skeleton Clique (did you catch the references?), Isa, Mac, Aparna, Jodi, Ava, Bri, Maddie, Nisreen, Sydney, Koren, the 2024 Publishing Children Discord (which I barely belong in, but thanks for grandfathering me in), Alex, Angela, and Andrea, Anna, our D&D group (see you Thursday, theoretically), my publishing mutuals, and so many others—your friendship means the world to me. Thank you for cheering me on, for letting me vent, and for always being a text or call away.

And lastly, of course, to my readers—it is because of you that this story lives. Every review, every video, every post, every message, every hard-earned dollar you gave to the Nightstrider Kickstarter long before Orbit was even on my radar has nudged me closer to where I am now. My gratitude is boundless.

Thank you. Giitu. Takja. And of course, good somnia.

Love,
Sophia

meet the author

Julie Hanson

SOPHIA SLADE has been writing since she was still losing her baby teeth. She independently published seven books ranging from dark fantasy to poetry before signing with Orbit. Sophia is a graduate of New York University and now lives in the Midwest with her lovely husband and their two cats, Mothman and Matcha. She loves antiquing, twenty one pilots, and frogs.

Find out more about Sophia and other Orbit authors by registering for the free monthly newsletter at orbitbooks.net.

Made in the USA
Las Vegas, NV
12 September 2024

95183599R00316